ITALIAN MYS

Gothic Classics

Italian Mysteries
Or,
More Secrets Than One

by

Francis Lathom

Edited by James D. Jenkins

Valancourt Books
Chicago

Italian Mysteries, or, More Secrets Than One
First published 1820
First Valancourt Books edition, August 2005

ISBN 0-9766048-6-8
Library of Congress Control Number: 2005929372

Cover design © 2005 Ryan Cagle and Valancourt Books
Introduction, Note on the Text, and Notes © 2005 James D. Jenkins
All rights reserved.

"Valancourt Books", "Gothic Classics", the Gothic Classics logo, and
the dancing skeleton logo are trademarks of Valancourt Books.

Published by Valancourt Books, Chicago, Illinois
Printed in the United States of America

CONTENTS

INTRODUCTION

Were it not for a sequence of unlikely events worthy of one of his Gothic novels, the name and works of Francis Lathom, one of the most popular and prolific authors of the late eighteenth and early nineteenth centuries, would long ago have been consigned to literary oblivion. That Lathom is remembered today, if indeed he is at all, is owing to no less a writer than Jane Austen. In *Northanger Abbey* (1818), Austen's satire on the contemporary fashion for Gothic novels, she has Isabella Thorpe recommend several such "horrid" novels to her friend Catherine Morland:

> '[A]nd when you have finished Udolpho, we will read the Italian together; and I have made out a list of ten or twelve more of the same kind for you.'
> 'Have you, indeed! How glad I am! – What are they all?'
> 'I will read you their names directly; here they are, in my pocket-book. Castle of Wolfenbach, Clermont, Mysterious Warnings, Necromancer of the Black Forest, Midnight Bell, Orphan of the Rhine, and Horrid Mysteries. Those will last us some time.'
> 'Yes, pretty well; but are they all horrid? are you sure they are all horrid?'
> 'Yes, quite sure […]'

For a century after the publication of *Northanger Abbey*, critics divided on whether the so-called "horrid novels" really existed, or whether their titles were invented by Austen to satirize similarly-titled works which filled the shelves of every circulating library. The Victorian critic George Saintsbury held that the *Northanger* novels did not exist, and furthermore, that such works as Austen mocks were "unprofitable" and "undelightful" to modern readers.

Fortunately, neither Saintsbury's erroneous view on the existence of the *Northanger* canon nor his critical estimation of the value of Gothic fiction prevailed for long. Montague Summers soon tracked down a copy of *Horrid Mysteries*, and inferred that the other titles, too, had undoubtedly once existed. The indefatigable researches of bibliophile and critic Michael Sadleir soon turned up the remaining novels, and in an article published in 1927, 109 years after the publication of *Northanger Abbey*, Sadleir could declare the *Northanger* novels found.

In his article, Sadleir predicted that "so long as Jane Austen is read – which will be for at least as long as there are readers at all – the titles at least of *The Castle of Wolfenbach, Clermont, The Mysterious Warning, The Necromancer [...], The Midnight Bell, The Orphan of the Rhine,* and *Horrid Mysteries* will survive as tiny stitches in the immense tapestry of English literature."[1]

Although the other novels in the *Northanger* canon and their authors perhaps merit no greater place in the "tapestry of English literature" than Sadleir allows them, it is unfortunate that Francis Lathom, author of *The Midnight Bell* (1798), has not fared better in literary history. However, despite his long and prolific writing career, which was both popularly and critically successful, only one of his novels was reprinted during the twentieth century; the rest of his works and indeed, the author himself, remain almost entirely forgotten to this day.

Lathom began writing in his late teenaged years, with some plays which were acted with modest success on the Norwich stage, although it does not appear that they were presented in the larger London theatres. He turned to writing novels with *The Castle of Ollada* (1795), a youthful effort heavily influenced by Horace Walpole's *The Castle of Otranto* (1764) and the novels of Ann Radcliffe. The novel brought him immediate success and ran into a second edition in 1831.

---

[1] Sadleir, Michael. "The Northanger Novels: A Footnote to Jane Austen," The English Association Pamphlet No. 68. Oxford: Oxford University Press, 1927.

He followed *The Castle of Ollada* with his most famous work, *The Midnight Bell* (1798), and over the next three decades, he published a number of other Gothic novels, all with extremely intriguing titles: *Mystery* (1800), *Astonishment!!!* (1802), *The Impenetrable Secret* (1805), *The Fatal Vow* (1806), *The Unknown* (1808), *Italian Mysteries* (1820), and *Mystic Events* (1830).

But although Lathom is remembered today chiefly for his Gothic romances, he was actually a writer of many talents and considerable depth. He was adept not only at writing works of terror, but also novels of contemporary manners, satires, and historical fiction. Montague Summers called Lathom's *Men and Manners* (1799) his masterpiece and worthy of Dickens. His *Very Strange, But Very True!* (1802) is a rollicking farce which still retains much of its humour even after two centuries. *Live and Learn* (1823) is a coming-of-age novel with well-drawn characters, and with its portrayal of the relationships between the two young heroes, which Summers described as "clearly uranian," it may be one of the earliest gay novels in the English language.

Very little is known for certain about Francis Lathom's life, beyond the bibliographical details of the books he wrote. One of the few scraps of biographical information which has survived is found in *Notes and Queries* in 1857, in which a reader seeking information on Lathom wrote:

> Can any of your readers give me an account of Francis Lathom, who was well known as the author of a number of novels and romances, published in the beginning of the present century? I have not been able to discover the date of his death, but he published a romance in 4 vols. in 1830. Probably this was his last work. He resided, I think, in Norwich.

The response was as follows:

Francis Lathom. – A gentleman, who was generally called Mr. Francis, lived for many years with a farmer in the parish of Fyvie in Aberdeenshire. While residing there, he published several of the works of the class referred to, *Young John Bull, The Mysterious Freebooter, Puzzled and Pleased*, and others. [...] He died in 1832 or 1833, and is buried in the churchyard of Fyvie. He was believed to be the illegitimate son of an English peer, and from his income, &c., was looked on as a great man in the district. There was certainly something mysterious in his history.

Just what this "something mysterious" was, the editor of *Notes and Queries* provides no clue. Montague Summers, however, in his *The Gothic Quest* (1938), provides a possible explanation:

> The secret is that Lathom was of a homosexual temperament, and it is supposed that there had come into his life some person – in Shakespeare's phrase – 'Lord of my love, to whom in vassalage' he gave 'all the all of me.' That his affection was reciprocated, and that he found happiness may reasonably be supposed."

Summers follows this startling (and unsupported) statement with a number of other details. Lathom, he writes, moved to Scotland with his lover after the success of his first few books. There, he took up residence on a farmer's land, where he enjoyed the two things that meant the most to him: his writing and the love of his friend. He enjoyed sitting around the fire at the local inn, telling stories to the townspeople, who revered him for his fame and wealth, and partaking of a bit too much whisky.

Of course, since Summers is unable to provide a single source to support any of these assertions, he may well have invented it all, surmising it from various details in the plots of Lathom's books. What emerges is less a real person than a sort of mythic character. However, although we cannot ultimately prove the accuracy of Summers' assertions, neither can we disprove them, and his biographical account is the only one we have.

At some point between 1800 and 1802, Lathom moved to Scotland, where he spent some of his most productive years. He churned out at least one, and sometimes two, novels per year until 1809, when he stopped publishing altogether for eleven years.

During these eleven years, Lathom apparently travelled extensively before making his triumphant return to the literary world with *Italian Mysteries*, which was published in 1820. The prefatory letter to the publisher which accompanies the work is addressed from New York, indicating that Lathom must have penned the novel during his travels in America. Lathom apparently spent a considerable time in the young republic, for in 1823, he addresses another letter from Philadelphia.

Italian Mysteries is somewhat of a strangely anachronistic work. When it was published in 1820, the popularity of the Gothic novel was on the wane, and the genre itself was in its decadent phase. Reviewers had gone from panning Gothic works to ignoring them completely, devoting space in the reviews to the new works of Byron, Scott, or Hogg. The Gothics that were still being published were mostly outright plagiarisms of earlier works, or at least recapitulations of old plots. The occasional spark of brilliance could still be seen, as in Catherine Smith's *Barozzi* (1815) and Charles Robert Maturin's *Melmoth the Wanderer* (1820), but these books were not, like the earlier romances of Walpole and Radcliffe, intended to elevate the reader's soul by the use of sublime terror, but rather to shock the reader with an accumulation of blasphemy and horror. It is strange, then, to find a novel like *Italian Mysteries*, which clearly looks back to the style of Radcliffe for its model, being published as late as 1820.

However, Lathom must have found success with his novel, at least among those readers who still fondly remembered reading Ann Radcliffe's romances in the 1790s. The novel was sufficiently popular to be translated into French in 1823, and must have been successful enough to induce Lathom to continue writing novels throughout the rest of the decade.

Lathom's Gothic novels have been frequently condemned by modern critics, with Sadleir characterizing *The Midnight Bell* as clumsy and humourless, and Frederick Frank largely dismissing *The Castle of Ollada* as dull and formulaic. In these earlier works, Lathom tends to take his subject matter overly seriously, perhaps fearing to dissipate the terror he is striving to achieve with an infusion of too much humour; the result, as has been justly remarked, often was a novel that was fairly plodding and not always enjoyable. In *Italian Mysteries*, however, Lathom changes tack: he takes himself and his novel less seriously and allows his unusual sense of humour to shine through.

At one point, Valeria has read some autobiographical pages her beloved Julio has given her, in which he reveals that he has a long-lost sister, whose identity is unknown to him. He begs her to come visit him and hear a secret from his own lips. By this time, the jaded Gothic reader must have expected Julio's secret to be that Valeria is, in fact, his sister, and this is precisely what Lathom writes:

> "Oh, Valeria! Heaven grant that thou mayest receive the disclosure which I am about to make to thee with fortitude of mind; for thou, Valeria, thou art intimately connected with the sequel of my melancholy tale!"
> The agitation of Valeria's mind beamed through her eyes, and she almost trembled at the solemnity of the tones in which Julio had addressed to her his last words.
> "Oh, my Valeria!" he proceeded by saying; "my adored, my idolized sister!"

But Lathom follows this immediately with:

> "Sister!" repeated Valeria, falteringly.
> "Not by the ties of blood," replied Julio; "but in love, in friendship, and in soul."

It is evident from passages like this one that Lathom is toying with the conventions of the Gothic novel, and he satirizes another Gothic standby, the distressed heroine, later in the book, when Paulina learns she has been kidnapped by a marquis who is in love with her:

> "What!" exclaimed Paulina, starting frantically from her seat; "am I then brought hither to be made the victim of a villain's passion? Sooner shall my forfeit life——"

Similar statements might be found in the works of any of a number of Radcliffe's imitators, but would always be uttered by the heroine, and received by the reader, with the utmost earnestness. But here, the servant attending her responds "Pshaw! nonsense! abate your ecstasies," thus quite humorously undercutting the apparent urgency of the scene.

Humour is also amply supplied throughout the novel by the constant bantering of the servants Terence and Francisca, who are perpetually insulting one another using Shakespearean quotations and old proverbs, and the occasional use of ironic foreshadowing, as when the long-lost love of Francisca's life, whom she remembers as having legs so elegant they appeared to be made of wood, reappears as a double amputee with two actual wooden legs.

On a base level, *Italian Mysteries* does not appear to be a terribly significant or original novel. The principal event of the book, the kidnapping of the young heroine by a lascivious marquis, and her subsequent immurement in a castle, is essentially the same plot as Radcliffe's *Romance of the Forest*, T. J. Horsley Curties's *Ethelwina, or the House of Fitz-Auburne* (1799), and any number of other novels. As in those novels, the principal terror in this novel is psychological, the heroine's fear of being raped by her persecutor. But unlike those novels, neither the reader of *Italian Mysteries* nor the characters in the book seem much concerned that anything too terrible will take place. In fact, for a work of terror, *Italian Mysteries* is decidedly unterrifying. Even the heroine Paulina, after receiving a letter from the marquis declaring his intention to confine her in his castle until she should marry him, "read his resolve, if not with indifference, at least without terror."

Italian Mysteries, with its light-hearted style and frequent flashes of humour, is certainly among the most enjoyable of the later Gothic novels. Although never particularly terrifying, the plot never flags either, unfolding at a brisk speed with sufficient mysteries along the way to keep a reader interested. Ultimately, in fact, the sheer number of mysteries provides one of the most humorous (perhaps unintentionally so) aspects of the book, as the plot gets so hopelessly convoluted by the end of the second volume that Lathom is forced to devote almost the entire third volume to simply unravelling it, often through the most absurd and contrived coincidences. By the end, when the novel's improbable events are explained by even more improbable causes, and we find that every character in the book (and there are many!) is related to one or more of the other characters, we come to realize that while the novel is facetious at times throughout the story, it is also so on a larger scale. *Italian Mysteries* is, at the same time, a fine example of a Gothic romance, and also of a very subtle Gothic satire.

Valancourt Books is pleased to present this undeservedly long-forgotten Gothic classic to a reading public we hope will enjoy it just as much as an earlier group of readers did 185 years ago.

James D. Jenkins,
Chicago, June 2005

FURTHER READING

Frank, Frederick S. *The First Gothics*. New York: Garland Publishing, 1987.

Jenkins, Lucien. "Introduction" to *The Midnight Bell*. London: Skoob Books, 1989.

MacConochie, Arthur Alastair. *Francis Lathom: Forgotten Goth*. [Charlottesville, Va.], 1949 (unpublished doctoral dissertation).

Nause, John. *The Eclipsed Orb: a study of Francis Lathom, his life and Gothic romances, plays and experiments in forms of fiction*. Ottawa: National Library of Canada, 1989.

Summers, Montague. *The Gothic Quest: A History of the Gothic Novel*. London: The Fortune Press, [1938].

Drama

All in a Bustle (1795)
Orlando and Seraphina; or, The Funeral Pile (1800)
The Dash of the Day (1800)
Holiday Time; or, The Schoolboy's Frolic (1800)
Curiosity (1801)
The Wife of a Million (1803)

Novels

The Castle of Ollada. 2 vols. London: Lane, 1795.
 Second edition, London: A.K. Newman, 1831.
 Modern reprint, Seattle: Valancourt Books, 2005 (ed. James D. Jenkins)

The Midnight Bell. 3 vols. London: H.D. Symonds, 1798.
 Modern editions: London: Folio Press, 1968 (ed. Devendra P.
 Varma); London: Skoob Books, 1989 (ed. Lucien Jenkins).

Men and Manners. 4 vols. London: Wright and Symonds, 1799.

Mystery. 2 vols. London: H.D. Symonds, 1800.

Astonishment!!! 2 vols. London: T.N. Longman, 1802.
 Second edition, London: A.K. Newman, 1821.

Very Strange, But Very True! 4 vols. London: T.N. Longman, 1803.
 Second edition, London: A.K. Newman, 1821.

The Impenetrable Secret, Find it Out! 2 vols. London: Lane &
 Newman, 1805. Second edition, London: A.K. Newman, 1831.

The Mysterious Freebooter. 4 vols. London: Lane, 1806.
 Reprinted, London: Jaques & Wright, 1829 and London: W.J. White, 1844

Human Beings. 3 vols. London: Crosby, 1807.

The Fatal Vow; or, St. Michael's Monastery. 2 vols. London: Crosby, 1807.

The Unknown; or, The Northern Gallery. 2 vols. London: A.K. Newman, 1808.
 Second edition, London: A.K. Newman, 1826.

London, or Truth Without Treason. 4 vols. London: Lane & Newman, 1809.

The Romance of the Hebrides. 3 vols. London: A.K. Newman, 1809.

Italian Mysteries, or, More Secrets Than One. 3 vols. London: A.K. Newman, 1820.
Modern edition, Chicago: Valancourt Books, 2005.

The One-Pound Note and Other Tales, 2 vols. London: A.K. Newman, 1820.

Puzzled and Pleased, or The Two Old Soldiers and other Tales, 3 vols. London: A.K. Newman, 1821.

Live and Learn, 4 vols. London: A. K. Newman, 1823.

The Polish Bandit; or, Who is my Bride? and Other Tales, 3 vols. London: Newman, 1824.

Young John Bull; or, Born Abroad and Bred at Home. London: Newman, 1828.

Fashionable Mysteries; or The Rival Duchesses (and Other Tales). 3 vols. London: Newman, 1829.

Mystic Events; or The Vision of the Tapestry. 4 vols. London: Newman, 1830.

Translations

The Castle of the Tuileries. 2 vols. London: Longman and Rees, 1803. (translation of *Le Château des Tuileries* by Pierre Joseph Alexis Roussel).

Erestina. Norwich: Payne, 1803. (translation of *Ernestine* by Marie-Jeanne Riccoboni).

NOTE ON THE TEXT

The text of the Valancourt Books edition of *Italian Mysteries* is taken from the first edition, published in 1820 at the Minerva Press for A. K. Newman. The book was never reprinted in English, although it was translated into French as *Les Mystères Italiens, ou le Château della Torrida* in 1823. This is the second English-language edition of the novel.

The text of the first edition presents few problems for the modern editor, thus I have been able to reproduce it nearly exactly as originally published. No effort has been made to modernize or standardize spelling. Three obvious (and very minor) errors have been corrected, the details of which are as follows. In Volume I, Chapter 1, the sentence beginning "Nothing worthy relating," has been corrected to read "Nothing worth relating." In one instance in the third chapter, Lathom omits the "Di" from the name of Sancho Di Borges. In the second chapter of the third volume, Lathom mistakenly refers to Di Borges as Di Cavetti. A few other errors, mostly factual, have been maintained, but are noted in the explanatory notes at the end of this book.

In order not to disrupt the reader's attention unnecessarily throughout the course of his reading by numerous footnotes, I have instead included notes at the end of the book. Literary and historical allusions are explained, and particularly difficult words are defined. I have not used superscripted numerals to indicate which words and phrases are defined in the back of the book, as these are frequently distracting to readers; instead, readers who discover an unfamiliar word or phrase that they wish to have explained, may refer to the notes as needed.

Thanks are due to Paul Scott for helping me edit an earlier paper on Francis Lathom, a significant part of which I employed in the introduction to this book.

ITALIAN MYSTERIES;

OR,

More Secrets than One.

A ROMANCE.

IN THREE VOLUMES.

BY

FRANCIS LATHOM,

AUTHOR OF

THE MYSTERIOUS FREEBOOTER; LONDON; THE UNKNOWN; MEN AND MANNERS;
ROMANCE OF THE HEBRIDES; HUMAN BEINGS; FATAL VOW; MIDNIGHT
BELL; IMPENETRABLE SECRET; MYSTERY; &c. &c.

For I will tell you now
What never yet was heard in tale or song,
From old or modern bard, in hall or bower.
MILTON.

VOL. I.

London:
Printed at the Minerva Press for
A. K. NEWMAN AND CO. LEADENHALL-STREET.
1820.

NEW YORK,
October 24, 1819.

SIR,

    IN consequence of the communication made to me by our mutual friend, J. B. on his return from England last summer, respecting the liberal terms which you were prepared to offer me for a Romance, I have transmitted to you the three volumes which accompany this. A very handsome offer had already been made me for the manuscript, by a publisher in this country; but, in consequence of your application, I found myself not less bound, than inclined, to continue to move under the auspices of an old friend, to whose liberal and gentlemanly conduct I with pleasure embrace this opportunity of confessing myself to have owed many advantages.

    I am,

        SIR,

            With every respect,

            Your obedient humble servant,
            THE AUTHOR.

To Mr. A. K. NEWMAN,
    Minerva Press,
        Leadenhall-Street,
            London.

Address
TO THE READER

FOR his fable the author is indebted to a friend, who permitted him to avail himself of a small manuscript, containing the heads of the subsequent Tale, which had been taken down, in the form of notes, by a lady of his acquaintance, during a temporary residence in Italy, about twenty years ago, and which had been communicated to her by a person intimately connected with some of the most prominent characters included in the narrative.

CHAPTER I

What means that ghastly look?
Hast thou the furies seen? Why stand'st thou speechless?
What means that deep-fetch'd groan?
Why does Despair stare through thy haggard eyes?

DENHAM.

"HARK! the clock strikes two!" ejaculated the half-weeping Valeria, "and still my dear father does not return. What can detain him? Blessed Virgin, shield him from injury!"

"I should think so excellent a man as he is," rejoined Paulina, "can have no danger to apprehend; for the good qualities of his heart are his safeguard against enemies."

"True," answered Valeria; "and I have heard some of my father's most intimate friends affirm that, even in his youth, he was never addicted either to gallantry or play, those too common provocatives in this city to the stiletto of the less-favoured lover or unfortunate gamester; and in proportion as I feel myself unable to propose any cause for his absence, my alarm is heightened."

"Is it not probable," said Paulina, "that the increasing illness of the patient whom he went out to visit this evening, and of whose life he told us he despaired, may have detained him?"

"No, no, no," replied Valeria; "you know he is never absent beyond the time at which he teaches us to expect him, without conveying to us a note or message explanatory of the cause."

A silence of a few moments ensued; the tear again started into the eye of Valeria—"Something has befallen him, I am certain," she said; and, pressing the hand of her companion in hers, she added—"You know not, my dear Paulina, what it is to feel anxiety respecting a father's fate."

"Oh, Valeria," replied Paulina, "is he not *my* father as well as yours? Is he not the only being from whom I have ever known a parent's tenderness—a parent's love? And is it not the most elevated joy of my heart to extend towards him the obedience of a daughter, the gratitude of a friendless orphan? Oh! should we be deprived of him——" The throb of sensibility choked her utterance, and she fell upon the neck of her friend.

"What would become of us indeed," ejaculated Valeria, "without a friend, without a protector!" and their tears were mingled together.

"Without a friend or a protector you never can be, Heaven bless your angelic souls!" exclaimed the voice of one, of whose entrance into the apartment during the last few moments they were unconscious, "whilst Terence O'Donnovan can raise voice or arm in your *sarvice*. Pardon the freedom of one whose first wish is your happiness; but I know the feelings of both your hearts at the present moment. I can in patience wait no longer myself for my dear master's return, and I am come to consult *wid* you what is to be done for the best; for,

> ' 'Tis now the very witching time of night,
> When churchyards yawn, and hell itself breathes out
> Contagion to this world;'

and therefore he must not be left unsought after any longer in this town of laurel-juice and stilettoes."

"Kind, faithful creature!" ejaculated Valeria. "But where can he be sought with any prospect of success?"

"That will best be seen, lady, when every possible quarter has been tried for him; and that myself is going to set about this moment," answered Terence.

Valeria and her cousin warmly applauded his intention— "But do not, pray do not go out alone, at this unsafe hour in the morning," added the former.

"I have called up Riccardo, the gardener, to be my companion, lady," answered Terence; "his is the stoutest heart in the house, next to my own, I *belave;* and the reason of my stepping into your presence uncalled, was to make you at acquainted *wid*

4

my absence, and to beg you'd lock the door after me: 'Fast bind, fast find—a proverb never stale in thrifty mind,' lady."

"Heaven crown your efforts with success!" said Paulina.

"I'll call first at the house of the signor in the *faver*, that he went out to visit last night," said Terence.

"And if he is not there," Valeria interrupted him by saying, "do not relax in your endeavours—use every expedient to discover him; believe me, your exertions shall meet their merited reward."

"Reward, lady!" echoed Terence, feelingly, but half-indignantly—"What is it keeps me out of dear little Ireland, living in this Italian country, but that the load of gratitude would burst my heart, if I had not occasional opportunities of relieving it, by *sarving* the best of masters and of men. He saved my life; I carry my reward about *wid* me in my existence, and live to be prouder every day of the hand I received benefit from."

"Indeed, good Terence," replied Valeria, "I should have known you too well to——Excuse me—are all the servants in bed, except yourself and Riccardo?"

"Sure and they are, my lady," answered Terence. "Was yourself wishing any attendance during my absence?"

"No, not attendance," rejoined Valeria; "but, at this dreary hour, combined with dreary thoughts, a companion. Call up my father's medical assistant, old Jeronymo, before you go; he shall sit with us till your return."

"I'll do that thing immediately," replied Terence; and leaving the apartment, and beginning to ascend the stairs leading to the chamber of Jeronymo, he proceeded, repeating—

"I do remember an apothecary,
And hereabouts he dwells," &c.

Descending again in a few moments, and announcing that Jeronymo would speedily attend their summons, Terence and Riccardo departed, followed by the prayers of Valeria and Paulina for their success; and we shall avail ourselves of the interval occupied by Jeronymo in rising from his bed, to make our readers better acquainted with the persons just introduced to their knowledge.

Signor Urbino di Cavetti, the parent of Valeria, was a man of independent fortune, and a physician of the first eminence in the city of Venice. From his father signor Urbino had inherited his possessions and his profession. Early in life the signor had entered into the marriage state with a lady nobly connected, but, as is, in all countries, not uncommon with those who boast the longest line of ancestry, slenderly portioned; she however contributed to the happiness of his existence during the period nature had assigned to her for her sublunary pilgrimage, which was only protracted till she had given birth to a son and a daughter, whose innocent smiles were the only alleviation of their widowed father's grief.

About a year after the death of his wife, signor Urbino introduced into his family Paulina, at that period a new-born infant, stating that she was the child of a near relation, who had disobliged her parents by an unbecoming marriage, and who had entrusted her offspring to his care; and the children of Urbino were taught to name her their cousin.

Nothing worth relating, materially connected with the family Di Cavetti, occurred till about eighteen months before the opening of our tale, except that the three children grew in fascinating qualities and accomplishments, both of mind and person, and that their hearts were stored with the most liberal instructions, which the superintendence of their education by a father, who was himself a mild assemblage equally of the Christian virtues and of those sciences which alike embellish and enrich life, could bestow. At this period the felicity of Urbino received a wound, from which it was doomed never perfectly to recover. His son, the pride of his existence, the successor to his reputation and his name, the only male relative he possessed, fell in a duel; the hand which gave the deadly blow was never known, and the son of Urbino died unrevenged. Bending to the will of a first Power, Urbino endeavoured rather to impel his mind to bless the hand of Providence for what it had spared to him, than to repine at the loss which it had inflicted; but stifled grief sinks deepest into the heart, and the forced smile and furrowed cheek too evidently betrayed the destroying traces of anxiety.

The once gay and hilarious family of Di Cavetti, the animation of society and the zest of every polite resort, now became the melancholy tenants of a solitary home, where serious conversation, or the slow notes of the harp, were the only relief of the mild but gloomy scene.

We have already learned from the words of his daughter, that the habits of Urbino had ever been virtuous and regular; since the unhappy death of his son, seven, or, at the latest, eight o'clock in the evening, had been the undeviating hour of his return from his professional cares to his family; and hence arose the anxiety with which we have seen those interested in his welfare affected at the mystery of his absence on the present morning.

Of signor Urbino di Cavetti and his relatives we have said enough for our present occasion; relative to the introduction of Terence O'Donnovan into his family we have a few words to impart. About six years had now elapsed since signor Urbino had been one day sent for to attend a foreigner in a dangerous state of illness: he found his patient to be an English gentleman, of manners remarkable for their manliness and conciliating grace; to every individual the humanity as well as skill of our physician was open—to a stranger he conceived them to be doubly due, and his conduct appeared to the invalid a challenge to intimacy. His patient informed him that he had for several years of his life been a star in the theatrical hemisphere in Great Britain; but that, having amassed a comfortable independence, he was indulging himself by appropriating the fruits of his past labours to the visiting of foreign countries.

In the course of a few days, symptoms of an alarming nature taking place in his patient, signor Urbino, perceiving the natural fortitude of his mind, ventured to impart to him the perilous state in which he believed him to stand. The Englishman received his information with thanks for his candour; and having caused a will, which he immediately sent off to his own country, to be drawn up, he informed the good physician that there was now only one point relative to which he felt any anxiety, which was the safe return of his servant to his native land. He proceeded to say that his domestic, whose name was Terence O'Donnovan, and whom Urbino had perceived to be an athletic young fellow, of about thirty, or three-and-thirty years of age, had first fallen under his notice as a performer in a strolling company in the west of England; that, having been a poor scholar in his native country, Ireland, he had received a tolerably liberal education; and that the drama assimilating more to his taste than any other study, he had learned by rote innumerable passages from Shakespeare, with which only recommendation for becoming an actor he had enlisted in the train of Thespis. The gentleman concluded by saying, that, having found him to be of a most worthy and faithful disposition, he had dissuaded him from the pursuit of the stage, and taken him into his own service; in which capacity he had fully answered his expectations; but that he had found it impossible, though he had redeemed him from acting, to break him of the constant use of dramatic quotations.

Urbino smiled at the account Terence's master gave of him, and promised that his wishes in his behalf should be faithfully executed.

In the course of a few days the English gentleman died. Terence was extravagant in his grief for the loss of his fosterer, and the good Urbino proved himself his affectionate consoler;

as one point of which consolation he adduced the trite but impressive observation of Nature's undeviating law with regard to all her children.

"Oh, I know it, your honour—I know it," said Terence—

> 'All who live must die,
> Passing through nature to eternity.'

Pardon my tears! they will flow—and no sin either, I hope; my poor mother used to say they were the cream of feeling, and all lamentations *widout* them only skim-milk. I'll dry them as soon as I can. I know what your honour would say—

> 'Dispute it like a man. I shall do so;
> But I must also feel it as a man."

The day appointed for the funeral being arrived, the coffin which contained the body of the deceased was placed in a gondola, for the purpose of conveying it to the spot appointed for its interment; Urbino, and some friends whom he had selected as mourners, accompanied by a priest, entered after; and Terence was allowed to attend them, and be a witness of the last earthly rites paid to the remains of his valued master. The gondoliers threw out their oars, and having gained the centre of the stream, the priest, at the head of the coffin, began a solemn chant for the repose of the dead. Till this moment the sighs and lamentations of Terence had been confined to the undertones of his voice, but, encouraged to freer accents by the elevated notes of the priest, he threw himself upon the lid of the coffin, and in unrestrained exclamations poured forth the true Irish howl.

The priest conceiving his lament a mockery, commanded him to be silent; but Terence, as unacquainted with the language of those about him as they were with his, heeded not what was addressed to him, but, as his feelings warmed, redoubled his cries and his groans.

The priest became enraged, and declared he would proceed no further with a heretic; and two of his attendants, in compliance with the will of their superior, pulled Terence off the coffin and endeavoured to stop his mouth. Signor Urbino and his friends, who were perfectly conversant with the English language, endeavoured to adjust the misunderstanding, and to explain that Terence was fulfilling a natural duty, as he believed it to be, to the remains of his master; but whilst this explanation was going on, a false step, made by Terence in his struggle with the priest's attendants, plunged him into the water.

In a few seconds Urbino perceived that Terence was ignorant of the art of swimming; he immediately offered a sum to any one of the gondoliers who would venture in to his rescue; but, awed by the gravity of the priest, they declared they would not risk their own lives for the sake of a heretic.

"What can be done to save the poor fellow?" said one of the physician's friends. "I believe there is not a swimmer amongst us."

"Except myself," replied Urbino, and accompanying his words by throwing off his hat and cloak, he dashed into the stream, caught Terence by his hair, and placed him safely in a boat, the rowers of which having been witnesses of the occurrence, had plied to their assistance.—Urbino having called to his friends, requesting them to attend to the interment of the deceased, as his present state precluded him from taking any share in the ceremony, he directed the boatmen to take them to a spot near his dwelling, from which he immediately proceeded homewards, accompanied by Terence.

To say that Terence was grateful for the preservation of his life, bestowed on him by signor Urbino, would be saying nothing—no words can give an adequate idea of his feelings and gratitude, or his attempts to evince it: he wept, he knelt, he begged, he entreated to be allowed to serve the physician without wages as long as he lived; and the worthy Urbino, delighted with the warmth of his sensibility, gave him his hand as a pledge of his welcome beneath his roof.

Terence acted religiously up to all he had professed; he was the friend as well as servant of the family; he would willingly have been its slave, but that Urbino and his children were too great respecters of the order of beings of which they themselves formed a part, to allow the momentary degradation of a link in the chain of humanity; and whilst he faithfully served his fosterers, the sallies of his humour not unfrequently contributed to their amusement. Intimately acquainted with the language of the divine bard of Avon, and not less enamoured of his works than capable of estimating their excellence, Terence frequently recalled some of their most favourite passages to their memory, and equally excited their risibility by the national twang and consequential air of proud theatrical strut with which they were delivered.

A sentence or two respecting Jeronymo, and our introductions are, for the present, at an end. Jeronymo di Zubica, a man now in the vale of life, had for half a century past held considerable repute as an apothecary in the city of Venice. He had for many years been the sole preparer of the medicines administered by the father of signor Urbino, and at his decease had fallen into the employment of his son. Jeronymo was a character of by no means an uncommon nature; he had deeply studied books, but he was utterly ignorant of mankind, too wise to be serviceable to himself, and too learned to possess the true use of his faculties; and though devoid of every passion (most of all, the miser's lust), except a desire of gaining knowledge, sleepless nights, and even weeks, innumerable, had been toiled through by him in the fruitless study of alchymy.

In stature he was remarkably tall, and in figure the exact prototype of the "lean and slipper'd pantaloon;" but the curve with which old age had stooped his shoulders, and the projection with which it had bent forward his knees and contracted his elbows, had greatly diminished his height, and converted his shape from a straight perpendicular into a complete form of acute angles. His never-varying habit was of a dark-grey stuff; so compactly fitted to his limbs as glaringly to display the scantiness of the flesh with which they were covered. His aquiline nose, which the loss of his teeth had nearly brought in contact with his chin, formed the constant saddle of his ebon-mounted spectacles; and a nightcap of green network surmounted the lank grey hairs that hung sparingly about his temples.

Nor were his manners less extraordinary than his person; roots were his diet and water his beverage: but the greatest peculiarity by which his character was marked, was, that he was scarcely ever heard to speak. Yet was not his temper harsh, nor his manners repellent; on the contrary, the former was mild in the extreme, and the latter conciliating. But his taciturnity was so admirably supplied by his expressive features and the gestures of his limbs, that those who had for a short time been in his acquaintance always felt themselves in conversation with him whilst in his presence. But those who had taken little pains to investigate his character, turned his peculiarities into jest, and for many a lustre he had been known by no other name throughout the city than that of *Il Speziale muto*—The dumb Apothecary.

The old man had been the father of two sons, who, more attentive to the pleasures of life than the welfare of their parent, had involved him in debts and entanglements, in the midst of which they had fled and left him, till accumulating misfortunes, added to his ignorance of the concerns of life, had nearly reduced him to a state of beggary. At this crisis the humane Urbino, respecting him as an old servant both of his own and his father's, offered him an apartment in his mansion, restricting him in future to prepare only the drugs for which he had himself occasion. Jeronymo was betrayed into a speech of thanks, and took possession of his new abode.

When Jeronymo entered the apartment where Valeria and her cousin sat awaiting him, he greeted them with a courteous smile, intended to display his readiness to serve them.

"Oh! my father! my dear father!" cried Valeria.

Jeronymo raised his countenance with a look of mingled surprise and inquiry.

"He has been out ever since five o'clock last evening," said Paulina, "and is not yet returned."

Jeronymo clasped his hands in agony together, and mournfully shook his head.

"What can be become of him?" exclaimed Valeria

Jeronymo repeated his shake of the head, but with more solemnity.

"The agony of our minds is insupportable," rejoined Valeria.

"And I am sure you participate in our sorrow," added Paulina.

Jeronymo sunk upon a chair—*"Lasso! lasso!"* escaped in scarcely-articulate accents from his lips; his head sunk upon his breast, and he wrung his hands.

A few moments of mournful silence ensued; it was broken by a sudden start on the part of Valeria; she heard the lock of the outer door of the mansion creak in its wards, and, aware that no individual of the family but Urbino himself possessed a key which could open it, she darted forward into the vestibule with the precipitancy of joy, and caught her parent in her arms.—"Oh! my dear father!" she exclaimed, as she held him in her strict embrace—"The Virgin be blessed for your return! you know not how your absence has alarmed us. But are you safe? are you well?"

"Thank Heaven! I am both," replied Urbino, in a tremulous tone of voice, in which his daughter and Paulina were unaccustomed to hear him speak.

Gazing upon his pale and ruffled countenance with tenderness and anxiety—"But where have you been, dear father? what has so long detained you?" rejoined Valeria.

"Question me not, urge me not," emphatically replied Urbino, "for it is impossible that I should reply satisfactorily to your inquiries; but prepare yourselves, my children, to quit Venice immediately."

"To quit Venice!" echoed his daughter and Paulina.

"To quit Venice!" solemnly pronounced Urbino; "after the expiration of another hour we shall probably never behold its walls again."

"And whither is our course to be bent?" asked Valeria.

"You must be satisfied to remain in ignorance of the spot of our destination till we arrive at it," said Urbino. "Once more," he added, in a hastier tone of voice, "I adjure you to go and prepare yourselves for your departure from hence: your packages must be small; and in your choice of what you carry hence with you, select rather the useful than the valuable or ornamental; for the latter you will in future have no occasion. Lose no time, I again enjoin you; and whilst you are thus employed, the faithful Terence, who is alone to accompany us, will assist me in the few preparations which I have to make."

"Terence," replied Valeria, "is——"

"In my study, awaiting my coming," her father interrupted her by saying; "I met him at the gate—now then be speedy;" and in mute astonishment Valeria and her friend began to ascend the stairs which led to their chamber.

At their departure Di Cavetti was proceeding to his study, when he felt his hand suddenly grasped; and on turning round his head, perceived, on his knees by his side, the old Jeronymo, with the tears streaming down his cheeks, and the palsy of agitation shaking his limbs. Never was his silence so eloquent as at the present moment; the most florid rhetoric could not have uttered—"What will become of me when you are gone?" with so irresistible an appeal to the feelings.

The physician eyed him for a few seconds with sympathy, but uncertainty; at length, after a momentary pause of thought—"Thou shalt not leave me," he exclaimed; "collect together a few useful medicines, and meet me here in five minutes;" and with these words he hastened to his study. Jeronymo did not try to speak, but endeavoured to sing for joy, and ended his attempt with bursting into a fresh flood of tears.

"Have you sent Riccardo to bed, as I directed you?" inquired Urbino of Terence, as he entered the study.

"I have done that thing, according to your honour's bidding," answered Terence.

"We are going to travel, Terence," rejoined Urbino; "provide yourself with a change of linen; we are going to set out immediately."

"*Wid* all my heart, your honour," replied Terence; "so long as Terence is by the side of yourself, he does not care the snuff of a potato for the name of the ground his foot stands on.

'Master, go on, and I will follow thee
To the last gasp, with truth and loyalty;' "

and with these words he hastened to fulfil his master's directions.

On the return of Terence to the vestibule with his slender equipment, he was met at the door of Urbino's study by Valeria and Paulina with theirs, which, together with a package that had been made by Urbino, were collected in a cloakbag, and placed under the guardianship of O'Donnovan. They perceived that Urbino had girt his rapier to his side, and wore a brace of pistols in his girdle; with a pair of similar weapons he furnished Terence; and taking up a small casket, which he refused to commit to the charge of any one but himself, he cast a hasty look of farewell, during which the stifled emotions of a labouring heart were sensibly depicted on his countenance, upon those walls which had been the scenes of all his studies, his labours, and his hours of recompensing reflection and composure from the toils of life, and darted out into the vestibule.

Against the outer door stood old Jeronymo, with a small medicine-chest clasped under his arm, and guarding, as it appeared by the situation which he held, against the possibility of being left behind.

Urbino opened the door, and waved his hand to his companions to pass on. Terence was the first to obey; Jeronymo followed him with all the speed he was able to make. The females, half weeping, half confounded, moved on, scarcely conscious of action; and at last came forth Urbino, compelled to close upon himself, perhaps for ever, that portal which had so long opened to him as its respected master.

CHAPTER II

Sure never day of grief was known like this.
——————Are we not,
Like wretches in a storm, whom every moment
The greedy deep is gaping to devour?

N. ROWE.

THE season was that of the infancy of spring, and the first tints of dawn were just beginning to streak the sky. Objects were scarcely discernible, and the paths along which they passed were obscured by the surrounding buildings.

Urbino placed an arm of his daughter and Paulina under each of his; the poor Jeronymo, little accustomed to venture abroad, even by day, stumbled at almost every step, and held for support and security by the pocket of Terence, whose arms were both engaged with the baggage that had been committed to his charge.

Moving along cautiously, and in silence, somewhat more than a quarter of an hour brought them to one of the houses of resort for the gondoliers, whose avocation it was to ply in the gulf. A few minutes conversation between Urbino and one of these men gained them the accommodation of a vessel; and in ten minutes more they were gliding swiftly down the stream.

The mystery of their situation held every tongue silent; and the current of the tide favouring the exertions of the gondoliers, their progress was so rapid, that when the sun rose to view from behind the mountains, his golden beams glittered on the distant spires of Venice.

Valeria continued to gaze upon them without any defined emotion, but that of their appearing to stand to her in the relation of old friends, whom she had been warned that she was never again to behold; and as the city of her birth at last faded in the obscurity of the grey distance, a heavy sigh escaped her lips. At the same moment she encountered the eye of her father; it beamed with a mingled command and entreaty to repel the weakness in which she appeared to be indulging; and too much accustomed to derive pleasure from unvarying obedience to the best of parents, she gathered something like a momentary comfort, from believing it in her power to grant his evidently-sorrowing soul the slightest shadow of alleviation for its woes. She accordingly compelled herself to appear composed, and even resigned.

The profession of Urbino had confined him closely to the limits of the city in which he had resided; and as he had disapproved of any protector but himself for his daughter and his *protégée* upon excursions of pleasure, Valeria and Paulina had never been more than three leagues from Venice. Under any other situation of mind, the beauties of the favoured country by which they were surrounded would have arrested their attention, and excited their admiration; but under the influence of their present feelings, it passed unobserved, or at least left no impression behind.

About an hour before noon the gondoliers drew in their oars, and laid their vessel to the banks of the shore. Urbino gave the signal for stepping upon the land, and a walk of a few minutes brought our travellers to a rural *albergo*, situated in the centre of a little garden, perfumed by the musk-rose, the heliotrope, the jonquil, and every flower which cast its odour into the opening lap of spring.

Refreshments were procured, which consisted principally of the delicacies of the dairy. With the exception of Terence, every one appeared faint and harassed, but still negligent of supplying the necessities of life. After nearly an hour had been expended—"If you think you are all able to proceed half a league, or perhaps somewhat more, on foot, the sooner we set off the better," said Urbino.

A ready assent having been given to his proposal, for all present were too well acquainted that he alone knew in what manner their proceedings were best regulated, as he alone was master of the spring by which their actions had been put into motion, Urbino engaged a lad from the *albergo* to point out to him a path which lay across the hills; and an easy hour's walking brought them to a posthouse, where Urbino ordered beds for the night.

When they had retired to a separate apartment, Urbino said—"As we had none of us any repose last night, and have a long journey for young travellers," he added, attempting to smile as he spoke, "to perform to-morrow, I recommend that we should all retire as soon as possible to rest; we shall be the better able to rise with the dawn, at which time it is my wish that we should set out."

This arrangement having been made, Urbino continued thus—"You will perhaps expect—*desire,* I am persuaded you all do, that I should render you some explanation of the mystery by which my present conduct is regulated. That I shall ever give you a solution of the past you must not hope—it cannot be; my plans for the future I shall detail to you at the close of to-morrow's journey."

He was listened to in silence and in wonder; and shortly after pressing a hand of each of his companions in his, with a kind "good-night" accompanying the action, he retired to his private apartment, into which he was heard to direct implements for writing to be brought to him.

Jeronymo and Terence enjoyed tolerable repose, for change of place had not deprived them of the comfort they most valued, which was the presence of their friend and master. Valeria and her cousin wept and wondered alternately; and when they resolved on silence, and endeavoured to induce the approach of sleep, regretted visions of the past, and anticipated disappointments in the future, drove repose from their pillow.

The rising dawn had scarcely eclipsed the morning star, ere the bustle which prevailed throughout the posthouse informed Valeria and her friend that preparations were making for their departure; and shortly after hearing Terence inquiring for his master's apartment, and the long-drawn step of Jeronymo passing their chamber-door in his way to the staircase, they rose, and decided likewise.

The foot of the staircase was immediately opposite to the door of the house, and at the instant they arrived within view of it, the combined influence of a lanthorn, suspended in the passage, and the emanating beams of day without, served indistinctly to show them a horseman, who stopped before the open door. He was muffled in a long black cloak; the deep verge of his hat was drawn down over his face, and the steed on which he was mounted panted loudly with fatigue.—"I would speak with signor Urbino di Cavetti," he said, in a rough voice, addressing himself to two or three persons who were crossing the passage.

It chanced that one of these was Urbino himself; he started at the sound of his name, and involuntarily raised his head towards the speaker.

The horseman recognized him, and added—"Signor Urbino, I have a letter for you."

Urbino advanced a few steps towards the door; the horseman extended his hand towards him with the letter. Urbino received it in his, and the horseman set off at full speed.

Urbino darted towards the lanthorn, and tearing open the paper, hastily perused its contents.

Valeria, who had closely watched her father during the transactions of the last few moments, saw a smile of serenity steal over his features. An instant served for the perusal of the paper; and placing it carefully in his pocket, he advanced, with a faint smile, to meet her, and led her to the breakfast apartment.

Their meal being concluded, Valeria, her father, Paulina, and Jeronymo, took their seats in a post-carriage; and Terence, mounted on a sturdy mule, jogged by their side.

The day appeared long and tedious; the country through which they travelled was for the most part rugged and uncultivated; the forest had not yet acquired its verdure, nor the mountain-plants their bloom. Stopping occasionally, more for the convenience of the drivers and their cattle, than for their own refreshment, and moving painfully slow when they did proceed, at about seven in the evening they reached a post-house, situated at the foot of the chain of hills which the day had been employed in crossing.

Valeria and Paulina were not only greatly fatigued, but unwell. The want of repose which they had for the two last nights experienced—the anxiety of mind which they had endured—the confinement of travelling, to which they were unaccustomed, had all conspired to subdue both their strength and spirits. The silently-watchful Jeronymo perceived their feelings; and no sooner had they entered an apartment than, unlocking his medicine-chest, he advanced towards them with a phial of hartshorn drops.

"No, no," said Valeria, "they will be of no service to me—I need repose."

"Throw physic to the dogs," cried Terence, waving his hand to Jeronymo to withdraw his medicine; then turning to Valeria, he added—"Lady, your medicine must be sleep—

'Sleep, that knits up the ravelled sheave of care,
The death of each day's life, sore labour's bath,
Balm of hurt minds.'"

Urbino, who had been detained in discharging the drivers, at this moment entered, and overhearing O'Donnovan's last words, he said—"Indeed, my dear children, Terence is very much in the right; you do both of you greatly require the refreshment of sleep; let me therefore prevail on you to retire to rest, and defer receiving from my lips that explanation of my future plans which I promised to give you this evening, till to-morrow morning, when you will be better able to attend to my words, and to digest my intentions."

Jeronymo gave an immediate nod of assent, and drew his nightcap from his pocket. Exhausted nature had scarcely left the females the power of dissenting from Urbino's proposition, and they were accordingly conducted to a chamber.

On the following morning, after their repast was concluded, Urbino, calling Terence into the apartment where he was assembled with his family, thus addressed him.—"Terence, as from your proved fidelity to me and mine, it is my choice to make you the chief agent of some important concerns which I am about to transact, it is highly necessary that you should be present at the relation I am now going to make."

A gentle bow of humility, with a look of strict attention to his master's words, were Terence's reply.

"Before I speak of my future intentions," continued Urbino, "I think it right once more to state to you, that with the cause of my sudden departure, probably for ever, from Venice, you never must expect to be made acquainted; it is a point upon which your curiosity never can be satisfied; and I most earnestly request that you, who love or respect me, will never attempt to urge me to a disclosure which I cannot make."

This injunction was received with another gentle inclination of the head on the part of Terence, and a similar acknowledgment from Jeronymo. The countenance of Valeria fell, and Paulina heaved a smothered sigh.

"You are well acquainted, my child," continued Urbino, addressing himself to Valeria, "and the circumstance is well known to all of you, with the exception of Terence, that a few months before the great Disposer of events called your excellent mother to her reward in heaven, that she had unexpectedly bequeathed to her, by a distant relative, an estate and mansion."

22

"I think I have heard you name it—the Castello della Torvida" said Valeria.

"The same," returned Urbino. "As it did not at that time suit my plans to quit Venice, I immediately exposed the estate for sale, and was surprised to find that no purchasers offered themselves; but, upon further inquiry than I had yet made concerning my new property, I found that the land was unfertile, and in a state of meagre cultivation, and that the Castello was very ancient, and considerably out of repair; that it had been for some years uninhabited, and that its gloomy and unalluring situation was unlikely to procure it a tenant. However, after some time, the lands were hired of me by a farmer in the neighbourhood, who was tempted to the engagement on account of their lying contiguous to his own, and he has ever since continued to rent them; but the Castello still remains uninhabited. And," continued Urbino, after a few moments pause, "as it is necessary that I should, for some time at least, live in absolute seclusion from the world, it is my intention to retire to the residence of which I have been speaking." Again he paused, then added—"I hope it does not afflict my children that their father's fate compels him to devote them to an exclusion from society?"

"Whatever constitutes your happiness," replied Valeria, "the duty which I owe you as a parent commands me to behold in the same point of view in which you perceive it; any life is preferable to that of being torn from you."

"And for myself," said Paulina, "I can only aver, that the being whom your kindness has reared and fostered, can know no will but that of her protector."

Urbino embraced them both, and then turned aside to wipe the dew of sensibility from his overflowing eyes. He proceeded to say, that he was unacquainted at what exact distance they now were from the Castello della Torvida, but that he would immediately question their host where the village of Malina lay, one league to the north of which he was acquainted that the Castello was situated; and with these words he left the room to prosecute his inquiries.

"How different a life shall we pass at the Castello to what we were accustomed to lead in Venice!" remarked Paulina.

"We have tasted few of the pleasures of society," replied Valeria, "since the death of my poor brother; ourselves and our home have of late been our chief enjoyments and those comforts we shall still possess."

"True," answered Paulina; "but for all that, I am afraid it will be very melancholy to live in such a solitude as your father describes our future residence to be."

At the word solitude a smile of pleasure stole over Jeronymo's face, and he clapped his hand upon the medicine-chest, with an air which implied that he foresaw how serviceable, in such a solitude, its contents might prove.

In a short time Urbino returned to the apartment; he said that the host had told him, that it was necessary they should proceed to another posthouse, seven leagues and a half off, at a short distance from which lay the village of Malina, and at which they would not fail to gain every information they required. Accordingly instant orders were given to prepare for their departure; and with all the expedition which they could persuade their entertainers to use in befitting their horses and servants for the journey, they set out.

Their cattle were on this day worse than on the former, and the hills they had to ascend more steep; thus, notwithstanding Urbino contrived to suffer as little delay as possible upon the road, it was dim twilight when they reached the posthouse.

On attempting to alight, they were saluted by an exclamation from the landlady, that every bed in her house was occupied. She however mollified her unpleasant tidings by saying, that if the signors chose to take a refreshment by the kitchen-fire, they should have the best her house could afford, and might sleep in the carriage, as the drivers could not return till the morning.

The evening was cold, and the promise of a good fire readily tempted them into the kitchen, where Urbino, by the promise of extraordinary payment, endeavoured to prevail upon his hostess to relinquish her own bed for the night to his daughter and Paulina; and her reply was, that it should have been at their service, but that she had already granted it to another party.

"For myself and my male companions," said Urbino, "it matters not where we take our nap; but my poor girls are far from well, and much fatigued into the bargain. Could no expedient be contrived for accommodating them?"

The hostess looked at Valeria and Paulina, and saw Urbino's assertion respecting them to be true. She appeared affected by their interesting appearance and turning again to Urbino, she said—"I know but one chance. Our only neighbour is a rich old farmer, whose house is but a stone's throw off. He has sometimes granted us the use of a bed upon such an occasion as this, and I can but ask him the favour."

"And little fear of your being denied," said a voice, which was that of the host, at that moment entering the kitchen; "Sancho di Borges is a good old fellow, and I never knew him refuse to do a good turn."

Sancho di Borges was the name of Urbino's tenant for the estate of Della Torvida.

"Sancho di Borges!" echoed Di Cavetti. "If you will have the goodness to let me see him, I have no doubt of procuring my suit."

"Do you know him then, signor?" asked the host.

"Not personally," replied Urbino; "but I believe a few words spoken together will prove us old acquaintance."

"Well, signor," said the host, "I am at your service to show you the way to his house;" and Urbino having, in a whisper, communicated to his daughter who Sancho di Borges was, he signaled to his host to proceed, and followed his steps.

On arriving at the house, which Urbino perceived to bear the marks both of opulence and comfort, he requested a few moments private conversation with its owner; and being shown into an apartment, was almost immediately followed into it by a highly-respectable-looking man, who had counted at least sixty-five summers, and who, in a tone of blunt but honest civility, requested to know his business with him?

"You are, I believe, my friend, acquainted with the name of Di Cavetti?" said Urbino.

"If you mean signor Urbino di Cavetti, who resides in Venice, and who, I understand, is a physician, I have been his tenant for these nineteen years past," answered Sancho.

"The same," replied Urbino; "he is at this moment travelling through this country on business of importance, and having this evening arrived at the posthouse at the foot of your garden, he has found it impossible to procure a bed for his daughter and niece who accompany him, and if you could indulge them with a bed beneath your roof, I need not say how great a favour you would confer on him."

"Most willingly, signor," answered Sancho, "and with another for himself. He has been a good landlord to me; never pressed me for my rent, nor ever raised it upon me, though I must confess the land has turned out much better than I expected it would. We have been known to each other by letter for a long while past, and I shall be glad of an opportunity of becoming better acquainted with him by word of mouth."

"Di Cavetti thanks you heartily, and begs leave to shake your hand," replied Urbino.

The farmer grasped the extended hand, and, as he pressed it in his, he said—"I thought you were he, signor, the moment you mentioned the name; I am glad to see you—I am indeed.

Go and fetch your daughter and niece hither, and all shall be ready to make them comfortable in five minutes."

Urbino returned to the posthouse, and having made the best arrangements in his power for Jeronymo and Terence, conducted his daughter and Paulina to the farmhouse. They were met at the door, with a hearty welcome, by Sancho, and conducted by him into an apartment, where he introduced them to his wife, a venerable-looking woman, who was sitting in the chimney corner, and for whose not rising to receive them he apologized, by saying that she had for many years been blind.

A flask of excellent wine was produced, in a bumper of which Urbino and the farmer pledged each other as old friends; and shortly after, an inviting supper was placed upon the table. During their meal they were waited on by a servant-girl of, at most, twelve years of age, and a female who appeared, at least, forty, with all the flippancy of seventeen, and who, by the familiar and sometimes even impertinent manner in which she addressed and by turns contradicted Sancho and his wife, seemed to rank in the family above a common domestic. Perceiving the weary state of our female travellers, when the cloth was withdrawn, the good farmer begged that they would discard all ceremony, and retire to bed whenever it suited their inclination to do so. They thanked him for his kindness, and begged leave to avail themselves of his offer without delay.

"Surely, surely," answered Sancho; "to do as you please, signoras, under my roof, is the best way to please me. Here, Francisca," he cried, addressing himself to the elder female, "take a light, and show the signoras to their chamber, and see that every thing is to their mind."

"I believe I know very well what to do without your bidding," replied Francisca, tartly; "there's not a girl in Italy has waited on more real ladies than I have done, and 'practice makes perfect,' as the proverb says." With an affected courtesy to Valeria and her cousin, she then intimated that she was ready to show them the way.

On entering the chamber, which was neat, and the bed inviting—"Now, signoras," asked Francisca, "is there any thing I can do to assist you? I have undressed some of the first ladies in Italy, I assure you."

"We will not give you any farther trouble," said Valeria.

"Trouble, signora!" echoed Francisca; "it cannot be trouble to wait on ladies of elegant appearance like yourselves; no, no, I could be up day and night to serve people of fashion and gentility, and think it no trouble; but such homebred creatures as my uncle and aunt below stairs put me out of all temper. All I can say or do, they wont try to polish; but 'you can't make a silk purse of a sow's ear,' as the proverb says," and with this elegant apostrophe and a sliding courtesy, she left the chamber.

"Thank Heaven," said Valeria, "my dear father's mind seems relieved by the kind reception he has met with from the farmer. Pray the saints, that those evils, which are perhaps magnified to us by being wrapt up in mystery, may gradually evaporate, and restore to our protector his wonted equanimity of mind!"

"Let us entreat the blessed Virgin that it may be so," answered Paulina.

Valeria drew her missal from her pocket, and having passed some time in prayer, they entered their bed, and sunk to sleep.

CHAPTER III

————————For something still there lies
In Heaven's dark volume, which I read through mists.
WALPOLE

AFTER every other member of the household had retired to rest, Sancho di Borges and Urbino continued for a considerable time in conversation together. The unaffected openness of heart, so conspicuous in the good farmer, challenged for him the esteem and confidence of the discerning physician, and he felt happy in the acquaintance of so valuable a man, in the solitude to which he was about to retire. Accordingly, Urbino, without reserve, unfolded to him that he had resolved to pass the remainder of his days in retirement, and that he intended to make the Castello della Torvida his abode.

"I am truly happy, and proud too, signor," replied Di Borges, "to find that I shall possess a neighbour like yourself in the evening of my days, and I shall not regret bartering part of my farm for your society."

"I don't understand you!" said Urbino—"what do you mean?"

"That, as you are bent upon a country life," was the reply, "you will, of course, take your land into your own hands."

"Indeed not," replied Urbino; "I am utterly unacquainted with the art of agriculture, and it is too late in life for me to become a scholar to any science."

"I am glad to hear you say so," replied Di Borges. "I am attached to the land, on account of the thrift which it has made under my culture; but you must increase your rent; it is worth nearly twice as much as it was when I first took it."

"Which improvement is owing to your skill, and therefore, in my opinion, you have the best right to the benefit produced," rejoined Urbino; "however, time enough to talk of that. But tell me, how far is the Castello from hence, and what kind of a dwelling do you think it will make for me and my family?"

"The distance from hence is about a league and a half," answered the farmer.

"The road to it lies through the village named Malina, does it not?" inquired Urbino.

"The nearer road is to leave the village to the left," said Sancho; "but there is no positively direct road to it; the high road, along which you have hitherto travelled from Venice, turns off to Mantua at the bottom of the hill, a stone's throw beyond my orchard; it is a by-road to the Castello, over fields, and partly through a small wood. As to the state of the house itself, I can say but little about it; for it is a long while indeed since I have even passed through the gate which leads into the sycamore walk, through which lies the main approach to the building. I was, I believe, in every room of it once, about two years before you came into possession, with a stranger who inspected the premises, but declined the purchase. It is a gloomy and an old-fashioned place, but I think capable of being made comfortable to its inhabitants."

"I should like to see it as soon as possible," replied Urbino, "that I may fix my determination."

"I will walk with you to it to-morrow morning after breakfast," said the farmer. "I suppose you have a set of keys to the premises yourself?"

Urbino's reply was in the affirmative.

"And I have another," said Sancho; "so we can't be at a loss to gain admittance. But, mark me," added the farmer, "as I am sure repairs must be required in a place which has been so long uninhabited, not an hour shall you or your family reside there, till I pronounce it fit to receive you: you have a home at your command; you have nothing to do but to excuse the inconveniences of a farmhouse, and to use it as your own."

Urbino received this kind invitation with a silent smile of gratitude, aware that elaborate thanks must have been unacceptable to a mind formed in the mould of Sancho's.

When they at length retired to rest, no two individuals ever parted with a stronger impression in favour of each other; and Urbino's heart overflowed to Heaven in gratitude for the valuable friend to which it had introduced him, at the most trying crisis of his life

On descending from his chamber on the following morning, Urbino found that Jeronymo and Terence had been invited from the posthouse by Di Borges, and added to his establishment. Urbino remonstrated by saying—"That he entreated accommodation might be procured for them elsewhere, as the addition of five persons was too great a burthen upon Sancho's family." To which argument Sancho replied, that if there were any thing amiss in the case, he felt the quarrel his, that any member of Urbino's travelling-companions, from a sense of false delicacy, had been excluded from his roof on the preceding evening.

"Politeness is a virtue," said Di Borges; "it has saved many a man's throat from being cut, many a woman's reputation from being defamed, and many an individual's purse from being pilfered; but false ceremony produces only the evil consequence of proving a bar to the conference and acceptance of benefits. Excuse my philosophizing," he added, with a smile to Urbino; "I have had no instructor in these matters but experience, a keen, but a true monitor. You'll know me better by-and-by, signor, and put up with me and my logic."

Their meal being concluded, Sancho and his new friend prepared for their walk. In passing through the little garden which lay in front of the house, they were met by Francisca— "Now remember, my girl," said Sancho, stopping to address her, "let us have the dinner in the best order you can, and not ready sooner than three o'clock; for the signor and I have a long walk to take before our return—not sooner than three—do you hear?"

"Do you think I am deaf?" returned Francisca: "you've said it twice already; 'twice done is ill done,' says the proverb, and I am sure twice said is quite as bad; but some people never know when they have said enough."

"Ah, ah!" cried Sancho, shaking his head, "that girl's tongue is unaccountable and ungovernable. For my part, I care not how much she frets and scolds; but I am sorry for my poor old wife, whose dark state obliges her to receive every little service at her hands, and not appear to heed her temper. She is my niece, signor; her mother, my elder sister, ran away with a soldier when she was quite young, and followed him on his campaigns. When the Spanish wars were ended, they returned to Italy, and kept a lemonade shop in Mantua, placing out their only child, this Francisca, as waiting-maid in some family of distinction. Her parents are now both dead; and when my wife lost her eyesight, thinking that a relative to attend upon her would be preferable to a stranger, I sent and invited her hither. She has now been with us three years; and although I believe her heart at bottom is good, signor, it is a long way to it through the fencework of airs and nonsense in which she keeps it enclosed."

"Had you never any children of your own?" asked Urbino.

"Only one, signor, only one," replied Sancho, with a faltering voice, "as pretty a little girl as ever——but we'll not speak upon that subject just now, signor; if we dwelt upon it, I should be very bad company for the rest of the day." He blew his nose, wiped his eyes, and immediately talked of the roads and the weather.

A tolerable path, corresponding with the description given of it by Di Borges, brought them to a spot from whence the grey summits of the Castello della Torvida were seen towering above a dusky knot of waving trees, whose branches the early spring had yet but meagerly clothed. As they proceeded, Urbino perceived that gloom was the characteristic of the universal scene; craggy rocks, upon whose rugged bosoms grew only partial clumps of scanty vegetation, closed in the view on every side, and the distance beyond the Castello presented an amphitheatre of deep and mazy forests, broken at intervals by the conic tops of mountains mingling with the clouds.

As they drew nearer, Urbino observed that the wall, which had once encircled the square of ground in the centre of which stood the Castello, was in many parts levelled with the ground, and the gates leading into the sycamore walk, of which Sancho had spoken, fallen from their hinges.

"The hand of Time appears to have been very busy here," he remarked.

"It is always most bold where it is unchecked by observers," rejoined Di Borges; "but recollect," he added, "that this walk has been exposed to the weather, and that the inside of the Castello has been protected by the substantiality of the building."

As they continued to advance, they encountered an aged and ragged female, who was gathering fuel.—"Ah! dear signor," she cried, addressing Sancho, "*un soldo, un soldo, per l'amor di Dio!*—My poor boy has scarcely been an hour without a fit for this month past."

"Here, here, Bianca," said Di Borges, throwing her two or three pieces of coin; then turning to Urbino, he added—"She is indeed an unfortunate creature, and the mother of a most unfortunate son, who is both a victim to the fits of which she has been speaking, and an idiot into the bargain."

Urbino added his mite to Sancho's, and they moved on, attended by her prayers and blessings.

As they were on the point of passing through the gateway into the sycamore walk, they heard a shrill shriek behind them; and on turning round their heads, saw old Bianca hobbling towards them as fast as she was able, and beckoning to them to stop.

"Now, what is the matter?" asked Sancho, when she approached within hearing.

"Oh, worthy signors," returned Bianca, "you have bestowed your charity on me, and would I suffer you to run into danger in return! To be sure you are not going to be so rash as to venture within that gate?"

"Rash! why so?" inquired Di Borges.

"Oh, signor Sancho," returned the old woman, "you that live in these parts cannot but have heard the report there was about five months ago, that real, natural smoke was seen coming out of one of the chimneys of the Castello, though not a human inhabitant has it had these seven-and-twenty years."

"Nonsense, nonsense!" ejaculated the farmer; "old women's tales, fit only to impose on the ignorant and superstitious!"

"But it is proved now not to be an old woman's tale, signor," replied Bianca; "it is confirmed; my poor boy Calvino saw a light in one of the windows of the Castello only about three weeks ago; and because the poor creature is not quite right in his brain, some may call him a fibber for saying so; but I aver he knows a light when he sees it; and see it, he swears, he did, poor boy; the boy's not blind, signor."

Urbino and the farmer both smiled, but pretended to thank Bianca for her caution, and proceeded on their way, apparently to the no small discomfiture of the old woman, whom they for some time heard exclaiming—"Ay, ay, you can't say but I warned you; you'll find poor Calvino not such a fool as some folks think; but self-willed people must take their own way. Blessed saints preserve you! Holy Virgin look down upon you!"

As they continued to advance, Urbino found the Castello to be a building of extensive dimensions, surrounded by a heavy colonnade, and with a flight of steps leading to the principal entrance. Having ascended them, they produced their keys, and with little difficulty gained admittance within the walls. The wards of the lock, and the hinges of the door, had become rusted with disuse; but a trifling exertion of skill and strength easily overcame these impediments.

Having examined all the apartments on the ground-floor, they ascended a staircase at the extremity of the vestibule, which, at the elevation of twelve steps, branched off by a second ascension to the right and to the left, conducting to the opposite extremities of a gallery, which ran round the upper story of the building, and upon which opened the doors of various chambers. Almost every door stood open, and thus they found their keys of less use than they had expected to find them. From the chambers situated in the angles of the building, short passages led to confined apartments, which appeared to have been intended for the use of domestics; and a door, which terminated one of these short passages, was the only one which they found fastened. They applied to their keys, and quickly discovered one which without difficulty moved in the wards of the lock; but the lock being turned, the door still refused to open. Sancho placed his shoulder against it, and endeavoured to overcome the difficulty, but in vain.

"No matter," said Urbino; "we have seen sufficient of the other apartments to conceive the nature of this."

"Most probably," returned Sancho, "some of the stones from the balustrades (for you must have observed without, that it has fallen in several places) have forced their way through the roof and blocked it up."

"Most probably indeed," rejoined Urbino; "however, that will all be seen and remedied when the workmen arrive."

They now descended, and having locked the portal, and taken a short survey of the desolate garden by which the Castello was encircled, they began to retrace their steps towards the farmer's house.

"Well, signor," said Di Borges, "what do you think of the Castello for a residence? I am half afraid to hear your opinion, for, to speak the truth, I should not like to have been only tantalized with the expectation of having my landlord for a neighbour."

"My resolution is by no means shaken," replied Di Cavetti; "the situation is certainly very gloomy, and the mansion very much out of repair; but the latter defect is easily rectified, and hearts blessed with cheerfulness and content will, I trust, prove a powerful antidote to the influence of the former. My chief objection is the size of the Castello; for, according to my idea of comfort, the inconveniences which a large family suffer from a small dwelling, are infinitely preferable to the nakedness which chills the eye, and almost the heart, where two or three scattered individuals occupy a large extent of building."

"But if that is your only objection," rejoined Sancho, "I should think a part of the Castello might be selected for the residence of your family, and the doors of communication with the rest of the mansion entirely blocked up; by which means you may make a small house out of a large one."

"I will consider of it," answered Urbino. "My pillow is a friend which upon almost every concern of any importance I am in the habit of consulting; and after I have done so to-night, I will return to the Castello to-morrow, and digest my plans on the spot."

"To-morrow," replied Sancho, "I cannot be your companion, for I am compelled to go to Mantua on business which I must not neglect."

"If I were at any time a momentary restraint upon your actions," rejoined Urbino, "I should no longer derive pleasure from your society. Now I am acquainted with the way thither, I need no companion at all; but I shall take my servant Terence with me, because I doubt not that he has a better knowledge of many conveniences necessary to be observed in preparing for the accommodation of a family, than I myself have."

"Good, good," replied Sancho. "I shall be at home to-morrow evening, time enough to hear how your second inspection of the old Castello pleases you."

On entering the house, they found Valeria engaged in reading from a religious book to Sancho's wife. Upon their arrival she closed the volume, and the blind Averilla, recognizing Sancho's step (for the loss of one faculty invariably renders the perception of those which remain more acute), said—"Ah, my dear husband, I have not experienced so great a pleasure for this many a day as I have done this morning; I seldom hear a passage from those good books now, which it was once my greatest satisfaction to dwell upon; and this amiable young signora has been reading to me from one of them like an angel."

The observation passed unnoticed, except by a silent smile of thanks from Urbino to his daughter, for having endeavoured to render herself engaging to those whose friendship he coveted.

When dinner was over, Urbino, addressing himself to Averilla, said—"As my daughter has been so happy as to gain your approbation, it is but fair that her cousin should have a chance of insinuating herself into your good graces too; she is an excellent singer, and one of her songs may amuse you."

Paulina cheerfully accepted the general invitation given her, and sung the following

BALLAD.

Within a convent's dreary shade,
    The hapless Julia liv'd serene,
Like the fair lily in the glade,
    That dies neglected and unseen.
No father's smile her childhood blest;
    Denied a mother's kiss to prove,
Her breast each sorrow had confest,
    Except the pangs of hopeless love.

But though the gifts of fortune ne'er
    Deign'd on this abject maid to shine,
Amidst the gloom she grew more fair,
    As gems gleam brighter in the mine.
But cares more wayward doom'd to bear,
    A lot more hapless still to prove,
A lover whispered in her ear
    The luring tale of artful love.

The lover press'd—his suit he won;
    Julia agreed with him to wed;
And at the solemn hour of one,
    To Jerome's holy shrine they sped.
But when he found her friendless, poor,
    He fled; no pray'rs his heart could move,
And to the pangs she'd known before,
    Were added those of perjur'd love.

Paulina possessed a voice of exquisite sweetness, and Sancho and his wife were enraptured with her melody.

"It is like a new world to me to be thus entertained with your superior accomplishments," said Averilla, "and every one of you make so strong an impression on my senses, that I begin to know you all already—signor Urbino, his daughter, and her cousin; but there is yet one signor, whom I am acquainted is here, and yet I think I have not once heard his voice."

All present smiled, except poor Jeronymo himself, who half blushed.

"Come, signor," said Di Borges, addressing him, "you shall take my seat, next to my wife, and let us see whether you can manage to get acquainted together."

Jeronymo obediently moved towards the seat resigned to him; and Sancho having put his wife's hand into the apothecary's, a cordial shake ensued.

"You have a cold hand, signor," said Averilla, "which they say is the sign of a warm heart; and I have no doubt we shall grow better acquainted."

Jeronymo gave the hand he held in his a second shake, as an affirmative to Averilla's prediction, and silently took the chair by her side.

The evening passed off pleasantly, and even cheerfully, signor Urbino, if not forgetting, at least partially subduing the painful recollection of a past occurrence, with which his mind was, in spite of his exertions to control his feelings, perpetually haunted.

CHAPTER IV

O! day and night, but this is wondrous strange!

HAMLET

WHEN the morning arrived, Valeria and her cousin were desirous of accompanying Urbino to the Castello, eager to behold their future residence; but as the walk to Della Torvida was a long one for novices in the practice, Urbino persuaded them to defer gratifying their curiosity till they were perfectly recovered from their late fatigue; and accordingly Terence and his master set out together.

Terence was a man whom those of his own rank denominated an universal genius, that is to say, he had seen so many changes, and lived in so many various situations of life, that he knew a little of every thing, and was at all times happy in turning his knowledge to the advantage of others. Thus, before they had proceeded half their way, Terence had projected a thousand plans for promoting the comfort of his master and his family, and seemed to regard it as a matter of little importance, that he had never seen the spot where his schemes were to be brought to maturity.

When they had reached the fallen gates and crumbling wall, Terence paused in his pace, and clapping his hand emphatically to his heart, pronounced—

> "The cloud-capt towers, the gorgeous palaces,
> The solemn temples, the great globe itself,
> Yea, all which it inherits, shall dissolve,
> And, like this insubstantial pageant faded,
> Leave not a wreck behind."

"I made the same observation, your honour, at the downfall of my uncle's mud cabin at Ballyporeen; and the priest of the parish, *ould* father O'Murgathride, was so delighted *wid* my illustration, that he wrote it down in the blank *lafe* of his *sar-*

40

mon case; he was only acquainted *wid* one of the two books the world contains, that it is worth a scholar and a Christian's while to look into."

"And what is the other work you so highly estimate, Terence?" asked Urbino; "I know Shakespeare to be one."

"The Holy Bible is the other," answered Terence, touching his hat as he spoke, in reverence to the subject; "no man has any business to *bodder* his brains *wid* fiction, till he's master of the truth."

Urbino could not refrain shaking him by the hand, and applauding his meritorious sentiment.

"I wonder there are no stories of apparitions abroad about this Castello, your honour," said Terence; "I never knew an *ould* place of the kind yet, in any country, but what was reported to have its ghosts."

Urbino recollected Bianca's words, and desirous of ascertaining Terence's opinion on the subject of "the shadowy world," before he repeated them to him, he said—"Amongst your numerous good qualities, I shall be very much surprised if I find your mind infected with the weakness of a belief in spirits."

"What! Terence O'Donnovan afraid of an apparition, your honour! Many's the good thirteen stone of solid flesh this pair of hands has sent to kiss the ground at Donnybrook; and it would be strange to tell, and stranger to see, if a bit of a shadow could make that same Terence O'Donnovan wink an eye."

Urbino now related the cautions given to himself and Di Borges by old Bianca, and also the cause from which she averred that they had sprung.

"Unreal mockery, hence!" exclaimed Terence; and being now admitted into the Castello, he bustled about from apartment to apartment, pointing out his ideas of the future regulations to be observed, listening to those proposed by Urbino; sometimes confirming, sometimes amending them, and finally bringing the whole within an easy compass of alteration, which not only surprised, but highly gratified his master.

Urbino dropped a few words to this effect, and in reply Terence said—"My dear master, pardon me, but I am truly happy just now, and that is the *rason* why I prosper so well in my inventions. An Irishman is never at his ease when the brambles are pricking his shins—you don't understand me; why then the *rason* why I am so over and above satisfied, is because I am pretty sure that here I shall be your only *man-sarvant*, if ever you have any *oders* at all at all; and devil's the *casion* Terence sees for them. But that's as you please about the women-creatures; but if I am your only *man-sarvant*, you never was so waited on before."

Urbino said a few words in the affirmative to his hope.—"But I must confess," added our physician, "that every new trait of your character astonishes me more and more. All the servants that have ever fallen under my observation, would wish to have as many sharers of their labour as their employer would allow them."

"Och, your honour," answered Terence, "the hand's turn of such spalpeans is not worth the filings of a *harper*. Give me *lave* to tell you, your honour, since our present circumstances have brought these matters upon the carpet, what for I discharged the only master I ever did that thing by in my life."

"Discharge your master!" echoed Urbino.

"I left him of my own accord, *widout* his bidding; that's what I call discharging my master, your honour," answered Terence. "You see, your honour, I lived *wid* a great marquis, who kept seven of us to do one man's work; so one morning, when he was short of cash, he ordered me to take his curricle-horses, and get them sold at the riding school in Dublin; so says I—'My lord, if you want to raise a little money, I'll make bold to tell you a shorter way of it,' says I; 'send away all your men-*sarvants* but me, and I'll engage to do the work of them every

one.'—'What,' cried he, 'would you have me lessen my consequence by reducing my establishment? you are an impertinent
rascal!'

"Now, your honour, though the family of O'Donnovan, at
least the O'Donnovans I came of, is a poor family, they were
always proud enough not to take an unhandsome word from
richer folks, so I civilly turned my back upon him, and bid him
keep the wages he owed me for a little bit of a lift out of the
scrape his consequence had brought him into. So, your honour,
if you will but let me do all the work, I shall have the easiest
place in the world. There will be nobody to cry out, 'this is not
my place,' and 'that is not my place,' and 'I was not hired for
this,' and 'I was not hired for that;' I'll be hired for it all, and
there's an end of the whole *hipothic* at once."

"Your offers are so kind, and at the same time so honest,"
Urbino was beginning to say——

Terence interrupted him.—"Excuse me, my dear master;
pray don't be angry *wid de* freedom of one that don't know
what to say to you, to say it properly. Once more excuse me;
but if there is any drawback upon your circumstances, as well as
your *pace* of mind, from this late kind of *mystarious*—I don't
know what to call it—my wages are paid for seven years to
come, that's all."

With thanks adequate to the grateful feelings of
O'Donnovan, Urbino replied to his generous denunciation of
himself in the cause of his benefactor, but assured him, for his
satisfaction, that whatever weight recent circumstances had
imposed on his mind, the obscure event which had led him to
quit Venice had left his fortune unimpaired.

As they were ascending the stairs to the upper range of
apartments—"It appears, by what you have just been telling
me," said Urbino, "that you have served other masters besides
the gentleman at whose death you became a part of my family.

I thought that, till you had entered his service, you had only been an actor."

"Indeed, your honour," replied Terence, "there are very few situations in life but what I have filled at one time or another, and that's the very thing that will make me doubly useful to you just now; but let the progress of time *spake* for me, and prove *whider* Terence O'Donnovan does not know a thing or two."

Saying that he should leave to Valeria and Paulina the choice of their own apartments, Urbino selected two rooms, opening into each another, for his own bedchamber and study.

"And now," said Terence, "if your honour would fix upon a lodging for me, the first part of our business would be done."

"Oh, please yourself," replied Urbino; "take any room you choose; there is no scarcity of apartments here."

"I should like a bit of a place as near you as possible," answered Terence; "*becase* it would be handy to be *widin* call, if you should want attendance in the night."

The apartments which Urbino had selected for his own use were situate in one of the angles of the Castello; and in reply to Terence's last proposition, he said—"There is a small room at the back of my apartments, but I cannot say what state it may be in, for we found the door locked up yesterday."

Following the direction of his master's extended finger, Terence moved towards the door of which Urbino had spoken; but quickly returning, Di Cavetti perceived an unusual degree of emotion depicted on his countenance; and, before he had time to inquire the cause—"Pray, your honour," said Terence, "did you see any thing particular about that same door yesterday, except that it could not be opened?"

"No, nothing," answered Di Cavetti; "why do you ask?"

"Walk this way a moment, your honour; pray walk this way," replied Terence; and Urbino, not a little surprised at the agitation in which he perceived him, followed his steps.

As they advanced—"Look at that, your honour!" ejaculated Terence, pointing to the fastened door; "what can the meaning of that be?"

Urbino raised his eyes, and beheld, marked upon the door, the following sentence:—

"AVOID THESE WALLS!"

For some moments they fixed their eyes on each other in astonishment and silence; it was broken by Urbino.—"What can I think of this extraordinary warning?" he exclaimed.

"To my thinking," answered Terence, "there are some inhabitants here before us that don't want to be turned out of their lodgings; but if there are fifty iron bolts at the back of the door, by the Powers! I'll see *wheder* there is any living creature within to keep them company!" and with these words he was proceeding to use force for executing his purpose.

"Stay one moment," said Urbino; "let me find the key, and let us first ascertain, when the lock is turned, whether the door still resists our efforts."

The key was found, and placed in the lock, which turned easily to the hand, and the door was opened without difficulty. The inside presented to their view a small apartment, utterly devoid of every appearance of having sheltered inhabitants; but, what was still more extraordinary, without any means being visible by which the door had, on the preceding day, been so strongly secured.

"I think I never met with any thing so unaccountable in my life," remarked Urbino.

"It *bates* cockfighting, your honour," replied Terence. He paused, and after a few moments thought—"I beg your pardon, your honour," he said, "but do you think this warning is in any way connected with the cause of your sudden departure from Venice?"

"I am very certain it bears no reference whatever to that circumstance," answered Urbino.

"It is written with chalk," said Terence, passing one of his hands over the letters.

"Whatever the cause of these words being placed here," rejoined Urbino, "what most surprises me is how the writer can have gained access into the building."

"*Divil* of a person can be hid about the house!" replied Terence; "there is not a nook in the premises that I have not had my nose into."

"It is strange indeed," said Urbino. He paused a moment, then added—"Let us return home, and agree to mention this occurrence to no one but our landlord; in his advice and opinion I place great faith."

It was resolved that they should do so: and after once more investigating every corner of the Castello, in order to be convinced that no person was hid within its walls, they locked the portal, and proceeded on their way home.

They moved on, sometimes in reflective silence, sometimes in repeating those remarks which they had already made in the Castello, on the unaccountable admonition they had received, and the still more unaccountable means by which the writer had gained admittance to the spot where they had found it; nor did they omit to reflect, though without deriving any satisfaction from their surmises, on the extraordinary circumstance of the fastened door.

Di Borges did not return home till late in the evening; and when he did so, the conversation was general, till the females and old Jeronymo had retired to their chambers, when Urbino related to Sancho the extraordinary occurrence which had that morning befallen him at the Castello di Torvida.

The worthy farmer expressed the greatest astonishment at what he heard; he was as free from a belief in supernatural agency as any man of an unprejudiced and clearly-discerning mind could be; and thus impressed, convinced that mortal means had produced the effect witnessed by Urbino and his servant Terence, he declared himself utterly at a loss even to guess at the performer of so mysterious an action.—"There is not an individual in this neighbourhood," he said, "above the rank of peasantry, consisting chiefly of labourers in the field and vine-dressers; there are none hereabouts who could have any motive for desiring your absence, if even your intention of residing at the Castello were known; and the report cannot have circulated, for I have not yet spoken of your design to any one but my wife. Indeed I am convinced, from the general regret which I have often heard the poor round about express at the Castello remaining so long uninhabited, that they would universally rejoice at looking forward to its being occupied by a man from whose affluent circumstances they would consider that they had a claim upon his charity in their hours of affliction."

"You recollect what old Bianca told us about the smoke and the light at the Castello?" said Urbino.

"And you must recollect," answered Di Borges, "that I told her they were old women's tales."

"True," rejoined Di Cavetti; "and had it been possible for old Bianca to have been the person who had discovered the writing upon the door, and to have informed us of it, we should have treated her information upon that point with the same contempt."

"Why, undoubtedly," returned the farmer, "corroborating points form the strength of evidence; but I am very unwilling to believe any thing for which I cannot reasonably account."

"And yet you are compelled to give credit to my having this day beheld the handwriting on the door, which I am sure is as dark an occurrence as ever bade defiance to the skill of man to unravel," said Urbino.

Di Borges turned himself in his chair with a gesture which confessed an affirmative to Urbino's assertion. A pause in the conversation ensued; Urbino broke it.—"What course, think you, were it best to pursue, in the hope of penetrating this mystery?"

"Pardon me for replying to your question with another," rejoined Sancho; "has the circumstance which to-day occurred at the Castello della Torvida deterred you from the idea of making it your future residence?"

"By no means," answered Di Cavetti; "my curiosity is doubt-less strongly excited, but my feelings are not disturbed; and for two reasons; the first, that I am conscious of not deserving an enemy; the next, that, if I do possess one, he displays himself convinced of his own inferiority, by venturing to attack me only in the dark."

"Well said! well said!" ejaculated Sancho. "Now then," he continued, "I'll tell you my plan for proceeding. This is Friday evening; on Monday I will ride to Mantua, and engage the same carpenter and mason who last year built an additional story to my house, to make such repairs as are required at the Castello. Whilst at work for me, they lodged at the posthouse here hard by; but I will tell them, that as it is a very considerable distance between the Castello and either the posthouse or the village of Malina, that they shall be accommodated by me with beds in the Castello. The necessary repairs will take up at least a month or six weeks; and if the time passes tranquilly with them, I think you may rest satisfied that it will do the same with you and your family."

"The expedient is a very good one, and at all events worth making experiment of," replied Urbino.

"And in the meantime," continued Sancho, "before the arrival of the workmen from Mantua, if you should be com-pelled by the entreaties of your daughter and her cousin to take them to visit the Castello (as we know not what may happen), contrive to loiter on the road, and send either myself or your servant forward with the keys, to investigate the state of things, that nothing may occur to terrify or to disgust them at the first sight of the place."

These arrangements being satisfactorily made—"The first opportunity which occurs," said Di Borges, "I will have a little conversation with Bianca and her son Calvino. I never heard any other person speak of the Castello as she did the morning we met her, and that appears extraordinary, when all hereabouts are, like herself, unenlightened, and consequently superstitious. Her son is doubtless afflicted with the fits of which I told you; in them there is no hypocrisy; but I have at times had my doubts whether he is quite so deficient in natural sense as he endeavours to display himself, and his mother professes him to be. I have heard that Captain is a very good travelling name in England; the like is Signor Hidalgo here in the south; and idiotism is a very good apology for begging all the world over. I have my suspicions, and I am determined to search deeper into this youth's heart than I have done yet."

The subject before them affording an infinite field for surmise and conjecture, their conversation was protracted till the midnight hour admonished them to defer their consultations to another day.

CHAPTER V

On the light fantastic toe,
  At pleasure's call we fly,
Hark! they laugh, they dance, they sing,
  In merry, merry revelry;
Hark! the tabor's lively beat,
Hark! the flute in numbers sweet,
    Fill the night
    With delight,
  At the masquerade.

P. HOARE.

DURING the next day no occurrence of moment took place. On the following one, which was Sunday, it was agreed that Urbino and his family should accompany Sancho di Borges to the chapel of San Lorenzo, to which the inhabitants of the village of Malina and its neighbourhood regularly resorted every Sunday and holiday.

On this morning accordingly, for the first time since their departure from Venice, Valeria and Paulina unpacked their slender wardrobe in order to provide themselves with a change of habiliments. As Valeria was opening the package in which the few articles of apparel which she had collected together were contained, a small bunch of artificial daisies, tastefully bound with a green ribband, fell from it upon the ground.

Paulina darted forward, and hastily snatching it up, exclaimed—"Ah! notwithstanding the confusion of our departure, this relic has not been forgotten, I see, Valeria."

"You know I promised never to part from it," answered the half-blushing Valeria; "and our memories are remarkably good when the heart assists in keeping the register," replied Paulina.

"I can now never expect to see him again from whose hand I received it," rejoined Valeria, with a sigh.

"There is no saying," returned Paulina; "true love works miracles; and if he is as constant as you have——"

Their conversation was here interrupted by the assiduous Francisca, who came to offer her assistance at their toilet, and not renewed again that day. But as the bunch of daisies and their donor are of no little importance in these pages, we must pause a while in the progress of our narrative to introduce them in due form.

Two years had now elapsed since the carnival at Venice had been more numerously attended than it had been for several years before; strangers from all parts of Italy, and likewise from every adjoining country, had flocked to it, and the scene of hilarity was scarcely ever remembered to have reached the acme to which it at this period arose.

The signor Urbino di Cavetti was a father who, having bestowed on his children an education calculated to defend them against the idle temptations and weak follies of life, after having fortified their minds with the double shield of admonition and example, did not refuse their mingling in the pleasures of the world, and reaping their share of the scanty harvest of sublunary joy; but still he had limits to which he circumscribed the bounds of indulgence; and although, during this season of universal festivity, females of the first rank, shaded by their masks, were seen joining in the conversaziones held in the streets, he confined the range of his children's participation in the "golden dream of the hour" to the theatres, and private entertainments given by their friends and acquaintance.

In the first week of the joyous month, Valeria and her cousin were invited to be present at a splendid masked ball given by the marchesa della Padriva.

Valeria was at this time in her nineteenth, and Paulina in her eighteenth year. Their order of beauty was in direct opposition to each other, but the coldest heart must have confessed that they were two of the most lovely examples of nature's excellence.

The characteristic of Valeria's charms was delicately majestic, that of Paulina's playfully fascinating. In stature, Valeria was rather above the middle height of women, but her limbs were so exquisitely turned, and so admirably proportioned to each other, as to add a peculiar grace to her well-modelled form. Her hair, of the darkest sable, hung in playful ringlets around a countenance of ineffable sweetness, which her eyes, of the deepest jet, would alone have rendered eloquent, without the auxiliary rhetoric contained in the smile which adorned her ruby lips. Her manners were easy without levity, her conversation was gay without frivolity, and her deportment graceful without affectation.

Although far from being tall, Paulina displayed a form of elegance and attractive symmetry. In complexion she was truly "the fairest of the fair," and her light auburn tresses, which fell in luxuriant wantonness on her neck and shoulders, were not more in accordance with the dazzling delicacy of her skin, than the mild beams which emanated from her blue celestial eye were expressive of the sweetness of her soul. Her cheeks appeared twin roses of the maiden-blush, and her lips a bed of coral, within which reposed a double row of pearls.

On the evening of the masquerade the characters assumed by the two friends were those of Flora and Hebe. In a light robe of the palest green, strung with garlands, her head bound with the violet and primrose, and with an osier basket in her hand, containing the mingled sweets of every season, Paulina, scattering odours as she moved along, appeared the very goddess of the sylvan groves; whilst Valeria, gracefully attired in a flowing robe of the whitest silk, which a zone of amethyst confined around her waist, and with fluttering wings of azure quivering on her shoulders, darted through the admiring crowd, more like an actual member of the celestial world than the mere representative of its airy inhabitants.

When the dancing commenced, a young shepherd sought the hand of Valeria, and continued her constant attendant throughout the whole of the evening. His conversation was of the most agreeable kind; he appeared to Valeria a young man doubly gifted with a strong natural understanding, and an extensive range of acquired information. His figure was equally graceful and commanding; his language and deportment were those of the finished gentleman; and from the accidental sliding of his mask she discovered enough of his features to be convinced that they were not unworthy of the rest of his person.

From the first hour of their introduction to each other, the attentions of the young shepherd to Valeria were of a marked nature. He was by no means the first from whom she had received homage of a similar nature, but he was the first from whose lips the compliments of love had carried with them any charm to her heart.

The carnival was now drawing towards a close; scarcely an evening had elapsed on which Valeria and her cousin had not joined in the pleasures of the festival; and constant as the planet to its orb had the young shepherd devoted his attentions to his fascinating Hebe.

Still, although every sentiment he had uttered might have been construed into a mark of the tenderest passion, he had not directly spoken of love. His every breath, his every gesture, had implied admiration, but still he had not declared his passion.

Anxious to learn who that being was who had stolen into those recesses of her heart which had not yet been penetrated, Valeria endeavoured to learn from various friends the name of her attendant swain; but her attempts were in vain: one alone informed her that she had heard a mask address him by the name of Julio, and that as his acquaintance appeared to be principally students from St. Peter's at Rome, of which there were a considerable number present at the carnival, he was probably one himself.

Three evenings were now only remaining to the close of the festival, when the young shepherd and his Hebe, having mingled as usual in the soul-exhilarating dance, retired to a saloon where various happy pairs were either tasting refreshments, or reposing after their fatigues on the velvet sofas by which it was surrounded. They approached a sideboard, and while Julio by turns offered to her acceptance every delicacy which the table afforded, she in return placed before him a glass of aucharde.

"Whatever your hand presents must be acceptable, divine Hebe," he replied; "but it would be infinitely more compassionate in you to grant me a draught from your celestial vase, in order to restore to me the blessing of health, of which you have deprived me."

"You charge me with an accusation of which I feel myself entirely innocent," answered Valeria.

"When the heart sorrows, can the body be in health?" ejaculated Julio.

"If I have caused you that sorrow, would we had never met!" said Valeria.

"Would to Heaven we never had, unless you promise me that we shall meet again!" exclaimed Julio.

"If you desire it, I will do nothing to prevent our meeting again," said Valeria.

"Oh! thou angelic arbitress of my fate," he pronounced, pressing her hand as he spoke for the first time tenderly in his, "I revive beneath the promise; health is restored to me in those words."

He led her to a sofa, and having placed himself beside her, he gently drew a knot of ribband from her shoulder, and said—"Pardon, oh pardon a man whose happiness betrays him perhaps into unwarrantable freedom, but suffer this to be the pledge of your promise;" and without waiting for Valeria's reply, he placed it in his breast; "and this," he added, taking a bunch of daisies from the head of his crook, and placing it in the zone of the unresisting, half-trembling Valeria, "be this the surety of my eternal truth."

Again he pressed her hand in his, and from the fingers which he held entwined within his own received a gentle affirmative to his suit, which her tongue could not have uttered.

"In what terms can I express the overflowings of my grateful soul?" exclaimed Julio; "and yet so supremely blessed already, I seek to kill myself with joy. At the expiration of this week, thou most adored of human beings! I am doomed to a short exile from thy fascination and conversation; does not then the happy event of the few last moments authorize me to request that thy image may accompany me, in the eye of recollection, during that unwilling period of separation, and cheer me with the charm of memory?" And as he spoke, having raised his own mask from his face, an urgent but silent entreaty procured him a transient glance of the features of Valeria.

It was evident that the momentary action of unmasking did not give dissatisfaction of their choice to either party. In a paroxysm of rapture, almost amounting to phrenzy, Julio cast himself at the feet of his mistress, and as he bent forward to pour into her ear his transports and his thanks, a miniature picture, richly set in diamonds, and which was suspended round his neck by a slender chain of gold, started from his vest. The portrait represented a female, nearly in the prime of life, and of dazzling beauty. An immediate start on the part of Valeria conveyed to the sensitive mind of Julio a silent, but eloquent inquiry, to which he instantly replied—"That is the image of one whom I once adored, and still most tenderly love and pity; her story——"

At this moment loud shrieks, accompanied by the cries of "fire," which issued from the ball-room, cast the whole scene into a chaos of alarm and confusion.

In a few seconds the flames were seen playing upon the walls, and spreading devastation on all around, whilst the dancers were effecting their escape, with all the precipitancy which the peril of their situation impelled them to use. In the universal struggle for gaining the door, Valeria was separated from Julio; but shortly encountering a friend of her father's, to whom her attire was known, he led her in safety through the crowd, and lodged her in security in her father's house; and from him she learnt that the accident had arisen from one of the window-curtains in the apartment having been undrawn for air, and thrown carelessly back upon a chandelier, from which one of the lights casually falling, had communicated fire to the drapery.

No sooner was Valeria herself in safety, than her anxiety was awakened for her father and Paulina; in a few minutes, however, they appeared to relieve her alarm, but Paulina was borne in the arms of a domestic, her ancle having been strained by a false step which she had made in quitting the house. Every alleviation of her pain which medicine could bestow having been afforded her by the tender Urbino, she was placed in her bed, and a gentle opiate, which the physician had administered to her, quickly taking effect, her chamber was quitted by all but Valeria, who casting herself into a chair by her side, indulged in reflection.

Who could the interesting stranger be to whom she too sensibly felt her heart a captive? Why had he not declared to her his name, his rank, his place of abode? Why had he been explicit in no one circumstance, but the declaration of his passion? What too could she think of the portrait suspended round his neck, which he had confessed to be the image of one "whom he had once adored, and still most tenderly loved and pitied?" How strange a declaration to make at the very moment when he was professing to lay his heart at her feet! It was an enigma beyond her powers of solution, and feeling that she really loved, she only prayed that the progress of time might unravel the mystery to her satisfaction.

Paulina's accident preventing her from joining in the festivities of the two days which now alone remained of the carnival, Valeria could not be prevailed upon to quit her cousin, and thus she despaired of seeing Julio, or of even hearing of him, till that period of separation, whatever it might be, which he had told her must necessarily take place between them, had expired.

Between the cousins there were no secrets, and in the bosom of Paulina, Valeria reposed her tale of love. Paulina, who had witnessed the growing intimacy of the lovers, applauded her choice, and agreed with her in supposing him a student from St Peter's at Rome; and when Valeria would, half-despondingly, dwell upon the only-apparent drawback on her happiness, which was the circumstance of the miniature, Paulina would laughingly reply—"May not the case of your Julio be similar to that of the hero of that admirable drama of Terence's favourite English bard, of which the scene is placed in our own country, Romeo?—may not your Julio, like him, have loved one who 'had forsworn to love?'"

"It may be so," replied Valeria; but her words were followed with a sigh, which seemed to say, that she should prefer to reign in a heart where there never had been a competitor.

The time crept on, days growing into weeks, and weeks into months, but still she heard not of Julio, nor could she discover that he had been seen in Venice or its neighbourhood since the day which had terminated the carnival.

One evening, about the time that Paulina was become sufficiently recovered from her accident to venture abroad, a party was formed for the opera, in which herself and Valeria were included; and it was agreed that they were to assemble at the house of a friend, and proceed from thence to the place of amusement.

As they were adjusting their veils to set out, the ever-buoyant spirits of Paulina, tingling with joy at being once more able to quit the confinement to which the weakness of her ancle had lately subjected her, was singing, acting, and even attempting to dance in congratulation to herself, as it appeared, upon her restoration to liberty.

"Upon my word," said Valeria, smiling, "I will not undertake to be your *donna attempata* into public, if you are not a little more sedate."

"Indeed, now I recollect myself," replied Paulina, "I really think I ought to be yours; there must be something very matronly in my appearance, I am sure, for the only marked attention which I received during the whole of the carnival was from a venerable old signor, three times my own age, I am certain. Did you never observe him dangling after me?" she continued; "he was in the dress of a pilgrim, with dark hair, and very tall?"

Urbino, who was reading in the apartment, closed his book, and listened attentively to the conversation.

"Come," said Valeria, "pin on your bouquet, and let us be gone; we shall be too late."

"Ah! now you are envious of me because I have had an admirer, and I dare say you have not," replied Paulina; "I assure you I am quite proud of my conquest; the old signor must have been over head and ears in love, for he asked me such questions as he could never have dreamt of, if he had not entertained thoughts of making me his wife. He wanted to know my name, and how old I was, and whether Urbino were my father, and I know not what. I expected to have received formal proposals from him the moment the carnival was over; but I suppose the dread of a young family has put him out of tune with matrimony, and he has repented of his overtures; and, clear of this scrape, has made a vow to himself to be a good boy, and do so no more." And Paulina's equipment being completed, they proceeded to their engagement.

Urbino sat wrapt in reflection on the words which he had heard Paulina utter. The tall pilgrim with the dark hair, of whom she had spoken, had twice accosted him during the carnival, and had advanced to him some questions of an extraordinary nature, which he had felt himself rather at a loss how to reply to, yet unwilling to refuse answering. On the first evening of their meeting, he had introduced himself to Urbino by a compliment to the graceful figure and elegant dancing of Valeria, whom, he said, he had been informed was his daughter; for Urbino, taking only a graver share in the amusements of the hour, had simply thrown a domino across his shoulders, and carried his mask in his hand.

At their second encounter, the commencement of a conversation was rendered easy by their having spoken together before.—"You have two daughters, I think, signor," remarked the stranger.

"No," replied Urbino; "only one."

"The other is then, I suppose, a distant relation?" was the rejoinder.

"My niece, signor," answered Urbino.

"Indeed, your niece!" echoed the pilgrim; "though I have never had the pleasure of your personal acquaintance till within the few last days, I have known your family long, and I believed that you had never had but one sister, who had taken the veil at an early age, and died in the convent to which she had retired."

"I certainly had such a sister as you describe," said Urbino.

"But you have also had another sister, of whom I had never heard," rejoined the pilgrim.

"All whom I ever possessed are now in the grave," answered Urbino; "I am the sole remnant of my father's stock." And as he spoke, he mingled with the crowd, desirous of evading the farther inquiries of the stranger.

59

Urbino and the pilgrim met no more. Actuated by causes which cannot at this moment be explained, Urbino dwelt for a considerable period with unpleasant feelings on the minute inquiries of the stranger after the origin of Paulina; but as time moved on unmarked by any event connected with the conversation which had passed between them, he began to believe that his fears had perhaps led him to imagine more than his questioner had intended to convey; but the relation just given by Paulina strengthened his apprehensions, and revived a subject for reflection in his mind. He could read no longer; he took up his hat and cane, and proceeded to the solitude of his garden.

The hours moved upon leaden wings to the doubting Valeria; four months had elapsed since the conclusion of the carnival, and still Julio neither came nor wrote. She concealed her anxiety, but she could not relieve her heart from a weight of despondency almost approaching to wretchedness. At this juncture she was awakened from her slumber of love, from contemplating the image of a supposed misfortune, to behold the substance of grief in its most soul-harrowing form: the body of her brother, deprived of life by the sword of an antagonist, was borne by the hands of strangers to the house of his agonized father.

Every feeling mind will form for itself a just estimate of the sufferings of Urbino and his family at this moment of trial, and let us draw a veil over the rashness and immorality of the self-immolating victim, who, for "a rush, a straw," flies unsummoned into the presence of his offended Maker, and leaves his memory a curse to those from whom affection draws a tear that sterner virtue frowns upon.

From the period of this awful event, unchequered was the scene of life to Urbino and his little circle. For a while their hours were passed in endeavouring to communicate to each other that peace to which their own breasts were strangers; but gradually, for the balm of every woe lies in the womb of time, their feelings began to resume their usual tone, and even cheerfulness had again claimed a place in their society, when the sudden and mysterious event occurred which drove Urbino to quit Venice.

Once more then we return to the hospitable roof of Sancho di Borges, and prepare ourselves to accompany the worthy farmer, his household, and friends, to the chapel of San Lorenzo.

CHAPTER VI

Beneath a mountain's brow, the most remote
And inaccessible by shepherds trod,
In a deep cave, dug by no mortal hand,
A hermit liv'd; a melancholy man,
Who was the wonder of our wand'ring swains.
Austere and lonely, cruel to himself,
Did they report him; the cold earth his bed,
Water his drink, his food the shepherds' alms.

HOME.

THE devout and regular behaviour of the peasantry assembled in the chapel of San Lorenzo, communicated considerable pleasure to the feelings of Urbino, as he reflected on the tranquillity, and even respect, of which so satisfactory an appearance in his inferior neighbours seemed to promise him the enjoyment.

On their return home, Valeria passed a considerable portion of the afternoon in reading to the grateful Averilla; and Urbino and the farmer digested the various transactions which the visit of the latter on the subsequent morning to Mantua was to comprise.

The morning being arrived, Di Borges did not wait the family hour of breakfast, but departed on his mission, ere his guests were arisen. The day being remarkably fine, Valeria and Paulina again urged their request to visit the Castello, and Urbino readily consented to their petition, contriving to delay their setting out till he had sent Terence forward with the keys, upon the plan which had been agreed on between Di Borges and himself.

Every unexplained circumstance leaves the mind open to expect an increase of mystery; it was therefore not without some degree of anxiety that Urbino approached the entrance to the Castello; his feelings, however, were infinitely relieved by being met about the middle of the sycamore walk by Terence, whose countenance implied that he had beheld nothing amiss within the walls.

The observations made by Valeria and her cousin on their future residence were such as Urbino had expected to hear from their lips, "that it was certainly a very melancholy situation, but that they doubted not that the influence of custom would soon reconcile them to a solitude to which they had hitherto been strangers;" and having, at the request of Di Cavetti, selected their own apartments, and strolled for some time in the garden, which presented only a bed of weeds and unpruned trees, and formed a plan upon which they wished it to be laid out at its recultivation, they bent their steps towards the farmhouse.

In the course of a few days the workmen had begun their operations, and at the expiration of a month the Castello and its garden wore a new and almost-inviting appearance. During this period the good farmer had purchased for Urbino at Mantua the furniture necessary to his new establishment, which he caused to be packed ready for transporting to the spot of its destination, the moment a command to that effect was conveyed to the persons from whom he had bought it; and had also visited Venice, and arranged those affairs which Di Cavetti's abrupt departure from that city had caused him to leave in confusion.

Terence meanwhile never entered the Castello to inspect the proceedings of the workmen, without casting an anxious glance at the door upon which he had, at his first visit to its walls, discovered the mysterious warning which had long since been defaced by the command of his master; but no circumstance, either of a similar, or of a mysterious or alarming nature, presented itself to his observation, or to that of any one who visited the place. Amongst his other qualifications, Terence proclaimed himself useful in the tillage of the earth, and accordingly became head-gardener and director in chief of the newly-planned garden.

One day, after it had been restored to tolerable order, and its borders were even beginning to bloom with the flowerets of the spring, Terence, while proudly displaying the increasing beauties of the place to Urbino and his family, suddenly stopped, and pointing to a spot of newly-raked earth, exclaimed—"These will be as fine a bed of fruit as ever was seen, or my name's not Terence O'Donnovan."

"What will the product be?" inquired Paulina—"strawberries, or——"

Terence interrupted her—"Bless your heart, no, my lady," he said; "a far better thing than that—*potatoes.*"

"Your servant, sir," answered Paulina, laughingly; "I see you have not forgotten your own private taste."

"Your pardon, my lady," replied Terence; "there's a participator, as I may say, in the business, and I planted a little more of the fruit than I should have done, when I recollected that my old friend there," pointing to Jeronymo as he spoke, "lived upon such kind of vegetables."

The party laughed, and Jeronymo, with a smile of satisfaction lighting his countenance, laid one hand upon his stomach, and with the other clapped Terence upon the shoulder for his consideration.

"I think, as the summer advances, Valeria," said Paulina, "we must turn gardeners, or at least florists, ourselves; it will assist us in passing away our time."

"And perhaps afford us as much real pleasure," returned Valeria, "as the theatre or the ball-room."

"No doubt of it at all at all, my dear lady," observed Terence—

> "Are not these woods
> More free from peril than the envious court?
> And this our life, exempt from public haunt,
> Finds tongues in trees, books in the running brooks,
> Sermons in stones, and good in every thing."

"But to make things complete," continued Terence, "we must have a cow. I am not a bad hand at a churn myself and then we can have butter of our own."

"And buttermilk too, eh, Terence?" said Paulina, pointedly.

Terence smiled, and added—"By St. Patrick, it will be almost as good as living in Ireland! only the *devil* a drop of usquebaugh shall we come at."

"What is that usquebaugh to which I have heard your nation is so strongly attached?" asked Paulina.

"Why, my lady," answered Terence, "it is argument to the head, courage to the heart, and strength to the fist of an Irishman. It is what champagne is to an Italian, burgundy to a Spaniard, claret to a Frenchman, whisky to a Scotchman, ale to an Englishman, brandy to a Swede, or gin to a Dutch boor."

"Oh, I understand," rejoined Paulina; "a liquor in favour with your countrymen?"

"Yes, my lady," answered Terence, "it is a liquor; but many of my countrymen contrive to make both meat and drink of it. It is too often *wid* them as was the case *wid* our friend Shakespeare's friend, sir John. 'Sack, two gallons, five shillings and eightpence; bread a halfpenny. Oh, monstrous! but one half-pennyworth of bread to this intolerable deal of sack!'" And taking up his spade, he returned to his employment.

In the course of another fortnight the repairs at the Castello were in so great a degree of forwardness, that the furniture was sent for from Mantua, and a day appointed for Di Cavetti and his family taking possession of their new abode.

About this time a rural festival took place at the farm of Sancho di Borges. It had for several years past been his undeviating custom to give a treat to his neighbours and dependants on the anniversary of his wedding-day: the senior members of the party were regaled with an excellent repast; the young were provided with music for a dance on the lawn in front of the house, and the poor received alms at the gate, in proportion to their necessities and their deserving qualities.

The hilarity of the day was in its zenith, when old Bianca and her son Calvino appeared to claim their share of Sancho's bounty, and Di Borges, as he stepped forward to bestow on them his offering, speaking aside to Urbino, said—"Walk this way a few steps with me, and I will take this opportunity of proposing a question or two to this boy, as I told you some time ago it was my intention to do, but he has never since fallen in my way."

Urbino gave an assenting nod, and moved on by the farmer's side.

When Di Borges had put his gratuity into the hand of the old woman—"Well," he said, "has your son seen any more wonders of late? any more lights in uninhabited houses?"

"Oh no, signor, the Virgin be praised!" replied Bianca; "he has not been terrified by any evil appearance lately; he has trouble enough of his own, Heaven help him! to vex him, without seeing unnatural sights."

"And so you really pretend to affirm," rejoined Sancho, addressing the lad, "that you once saw a light in the Castello della Torrida?"

"*Si, signor—si, si,*" replied Calvino.

"And was this in the daytime or in the night?" asked Di Borges.

"After it was dark in the evening, certainly," answered Calvino; "people don't want candles in the daytime; to be sure you must know that."

"But as there have been for years past no inhabitants in the Castello, there could be no people there to require a light," said Di Borges.

"But candles can't move about," returned Calvino, "without people to carry them; silly as I am, I know that;" and he ended his observation with a vacant laugh.

"What do you mean by their moving about?" asked Sancho.

"Why," answered the boy, "did I not see the light in the Castello go past as many windows as——" and holding up the fingers of one hand, and touching them successively with the thumb of the other, "as all them," he added.

"And you saw a smoke proceed from the chimney too, did not you?" inquired Sancho.

"No, no, no," ejaculated Calvino, again laughing vacantly. "How foolish you must be to think that the smoke of a candle could reach to the top of a chimney!"

"No, it was somebody else that saw the smoke, not Calvino," said Bianca: "I forget now who it was."

"I dare say you do," answered Sancho, "and I shall think better of you in future, if you forbear to circulate stories in regard to matters in which you have no right to interfere;" and with this reproof he turned away from the mother and her son, motioning to Urbino to do the same.

"It is as I said at first," exclaimed Di Borges, "an old woman's tale; the smoke, you see, has already vanished, and I doubt not," he added, smiling at his own joke, "but the light will be found to end in smoke too."

"But," said Urbino, "the handwriting on the door still remains a stubborn fact."

Sancho was at this moment addressed by one of his guests, and a period thus put to their conversation.

To a mind pleased with nature in her plain and simple garb, the group this day collected on the lawn before Sancho's house presented a most interesting picture; every countenance was dressed in smiles of innocent pleasure. The airy movements of the young through the mazes of the dance discovered the lightness of their hearts, and the serene satisfaction which beamed in the eyes of the elder members of the feast, bespoke the honest pride with which they beheld their offspring reflecting credit on the parents from whom they sprung.

The gay Paulina entered cordially into the amusements of the day, and candidly acknowledged to Urbino that she had discovered there was happiness to be found at a distance from crowded ball-rooms and circles of fashion.

Valeria endeavoured to compel herself to reap enjoyment from the reflection of all being happy around her; but retiring from the gayest part of the throng, her time was principally passed in leading about the blind Averilla, who had become so much attached to her new friend, as almost to feel disgust when now compelled to receive the ruder services of her niece.

Francisca, on her part, cared not who administered to the wants of her aunt, so she was spared the trouble of attendance, and the truly amiable and grateful disposition which Valeria discovered in the resigned and patient sufferer, "shut out from the light of day," perceived it a duty to which she was called to grant her that alleviation of her misfortune which it was evident that her society so eminently afforded her.

Towards the decline of the afternoon, Averilla, requesting Valeria to lead her into the house, said—"I expect a poor woman here presently, as a sharer of my husband's alms, who is a widow with several children, and to whom I always add my mite in addition to his bounty. I have prepared a bundle of linen and other necessaries, which I know will be serviceable to her, and I have told one of the servants to inform me when she arrives at the gate. This is about the time of her coming, and as I wish to give her my present myself, I shall feel infinitely obliged to you, dear signora, if you will lend me your arm thither."

"It is my greatest pleasure," replied Valeria, "to receive your commands;" and they sat down in an apartment, awaiting the servant's notice of the poor woman's appearance at the gate.

Whilst Averilla and Valeria were thus engaged, a personage of a no less interesting than extraordinary appearance was exciting the attention of the party on the lawn. A venerable hermit, bowed down by years, and supporting his trembling form on a rude staff; upon which both his hands were rested, with his cowl drawn down upon his face, entered the gate, and with a lowly inclination of his body, and his hands upraised by turns in supplication, presented himself before the guests of Sancho di Borges.

Attracted by the singularity of his appearance, all present who were not at that time mingling in the dance, crowded round him, and beheld suspended from his neck a label of paper, on which were inscribed these words—"PITY A DUMB RECLUSE."

The hand of Di Borges was immediately extended towards him with the offering of his charity—"Poor wretch!" he at the same time remarked, "he must be unacquainted with this country, for I never met him in any of my rides, which are not very circumscribed; and it is very hard, in his melancholy situation, to be reduced to beg of strangers."

"I have seen him once before," said an old peasant. "Near to the spot where I cut wood, is a cell dug in the side of the mountain, which, neighbours, you must all recollect, was once inhabited by a solitary man, named father Anselmo."

"Oh, yes; we remember father Anselmo," was replied by several voices.

"Well," returned the peasant, "by the side of the little brook which runs within a stone's throw of the hut in which father Anselmo dwelt, I saw this very man sitting about a fortnight, or three weeks it may be, ago."

"It is but likely," rejoined another, "that he may now occupy the same dwelling."

"Whatever he is," said Urbino, "he strongly merits our compassion and charity." He accompanied his words by putting some pieces into the old man's hand, and his example was followed by several of Sancho's guests.

Jeronymo, who had been a silent spectator of what had passed, now approached the hermit; and having shaken him by the hand, in token of intended friendship, proceeded, by various signs which he made to him, to endeavour to persuade him to suffer his tongue to undergo an anatomical inspection, in the hope of the defect by which it was tied being discovered.

The hermit gently disengaged himself from his grasp; and shaking his head as a negative to his proposal, he turned to view the other side of the label, which he wore upon his breast and discovered these words—"THE POWER OF MAN CANNOT GRANT ME RELIEF."

"I dare say," remarked a female present, "that he has been made a prisoner of war by the Algerine pirates, who have cut out his tongue."

Jeronymo's countenance implied his instant adoption of the idea, and he again advanced his fingers towards the lips of the hermit, as desirous of inspecting his oracular organs.

The recluse again waved his hand to him to forbear; and having pointed his finger upwards, and followed the action by an humiliating inclination of his body, he implied that the privation under which he was suffering was the ordinance of Heaven, to which he submitted with resignation; and having bestowed his tacit thanks on his benefactors, he began to recede slowly from the spot where his necessities had been relieved.

As he approached the gate, he was met by Valeria and Averilla, who were returning from a short interview with the poor widow, who, it has already been mentioned, was the favourite object of Averilla's beneficence.

The side of the label which was now turned outwards on the hermit's breast, contained the sentence of—"PITY A DUMB RECLUSE;" and Valeria observing it, communicated what she beheld to Averilla; and their sympathy in his misfortune produced him instantly a small gift from each, which the moment Valeria had extended to him, hastily extracting from his sleeve a small substance, he pressed it into her hand, and continued his progress towards the gate.

Surprised by his action, Valeria immediately tore open the envelope, which was of paper, and, to her unutterable astonishment beheld the very knot of ribband which Julio had taken from her shoulder on the last evening that she had beheld him at the masquerade; and within the envelope were traced, with a pencil, the words, "CONSTANCY AND SECRECY."

Utterly at a loss what to conclude from so extraordinary an occurrence, and so mysterious an admonition, Valeria hastily concealed the paper and its contents in her bosom, thankful that Averilla had been her only companion during the transaction of the last few moments, and that it had thus passed unobserved by every individual.

With her mind upon the rack, she durst not allow herself for the present to indulge in either surmises on the future, or reflections on the past, lest the absorption of thought into which she might fall, might betray that she had received some cause to diminish that gaiety which she had throughout the day professed herself to feel; she accordingly conducted Averilla to the green, where they found the assembly amused by the exertions of Terence, who was entertaining them with an Irish lilt, to which he was obliged to be his own musician, as all his instructions had not been able to succeed in producing him any notes to his satisfaction from the instruments of the band upon the green.

When he had concluded, and the novelty of his performance was obtaining him the plaudits of all present, not even excepting Jeronymo, whose slapping of palm against palm did not infringe on his practice of taciturnity, "So then," exclaimed Francisca, "in Ireland, I perceive, it is the fashion for the men to dance by themselves, and leave the ladies to look on—well, 'live and learn,' as the proverb says."

"Upon my soul and you are quite in the wrong, my jewel," returned Terence. "Ireland is the place of all the world for politeness to the ladies; there is not a set of fellows under the sun that show more respect to the petticoat than the sons of St. Patrick!"

"If those at home are so pre-eminent, they send very bad specimens abroad, I think," answered Francisca.

"You are wrong there again," replied O'Donnovan; "there is not a better specimen in the world, though I say it myself, than Terence; for now I have had my bachelor's lilt, as I may call it, by my lone self; I'll dance my legs off but I'll pair for a jig with every girl on the lawn between seventeen and twenty-seven; so sit you down there by the side of them *oder* two *ould* ladies, and see if I don't keep my word."

"Oh the vulgar fellow! oh the outlandish brute! but 'what is bred in the bone,'" muttered Francisca between her teeth, and pretending to trip along to a tune of her own humming, she entered the house with affected gaiety, but with an inward vow of eternal hatred to the sons of St. Patrick, who, according to Terence, appeared to fix twenty-seven as *finitum* of the dancing age.

At length the setting sun gave the signal for putting a period to the dance; and the guests having departed, no apology was required after the fatigues of the day for retiring early to rest. Paulina, exhausted with her exertions, was no sooner in bed, than she became locked in the arms of sleep; and Valeria was thus, according to her wish, left to silence and reflection.

"Could it have been Julio," she inquired of herself, "who had put into her hand the paper and its contents, or an emissary deputed by him to that end? And whichever was the case, what could so long have detained him from her sight, and by what means could he have gained a knowledge of her present residence, which she believed to be known only to the peasantry in the neighbourhood?" It was an enigma which grew in intricacy at every fresh attempt which she made to solve it.

She drew the mysterious packet from her bosom; and having minutely examined the ribband which it contained, felt convinced that it was the same which Julio had begged of her as a pledge of her truth. She next examined the envelope; the only words inscribed within it were, "CONSTANCY AND SECRECY." The former must apply equally to himself as to her: he could not desire her to be true without being himself the same; but the latter seemed to refer only to herself, and to require silence on her part respecting their correspondence.

Tenderly loving, as we have already perceived Valeria to have done, and at this moment soothed into a degree of happiness by the acknowledged constancy of him on whom her heart was bestowed, the mystery in which his actions had hitherto been wrapped appeared a faint consideration, when opposed to the knowledge that his affections had never wandered; and, bending at the shrine of sensitive love, she resolved that her secrecy should be inviolable to every human being.

CHAPTER VII

We wish remov'd what standeth in our light,
And nature blame for limiting our sight,
Where you stand wisely winking, that the view
Of the fair prospect may be ever new.

WALLER.

WHEN the time appointed for Di Cavetti and his family to take possession of their new abode arrived, it was with the sincerest regret that Averilla parted from Valeria, and not without exacting from her a promise that she would frequently visit her. Di Borges likewise was not much better pleased to be separated from the only friend and companion whom for years past he had met with who possessed congeniality of feelings to his own; but as the distance at which Urbino and himself were going to reside from each other was but trifling, they agreed that very few days should pass on which they did not meet.

The hours of Urbino were spent in exercise, in reading, and in social intercourse with his family; those of Paulina were occupied with her music, to which she was greatly attached, and in gardening, for which amusement novelty had given her a zest; whilst Valeria, who constrained herself to wear a smile upon her lips in the presence of her father, experienced no relief for her agitated mind but that of retiring to the solitude of her chamber, and indulging in reflection.

In most minds cheerfulness increases with the growth of summer; the smiles of nature animate the heart of sensibility, and create in it a sentiment of gratitude towards the liberal Power which clothes the forest, embroiders the flowery garden, and swells with nutriment the blushing fruit and golden harvest; and blessed with minds which nature and education had combined to render sensitive, Urbino and his children reaped a hitherto-untasted luxury, from their unrestrained wanderings through the mazes of uncultivated nature, which the surrounding scenery afforded them.

One day, when Paulina was displaying to them her flower-garden, and expatiating on the beauties of some of her favourite plants, Terence, approaching his master, said—"The poor soul returns your honour his humble thanks." Urbino smiled, and Terence added—"that is, to be sure he did not *spake* a word, but he made a great many grateful signs, your honour, and all that, when I gave him the bit of money and the bread."

Terence moved to another part of the garden, and Urbino said—"Terence was speaking of the poor dumb recluse, whom you saw at our friend Sancho's festival. I have discovered that he lives in the hut at the side of the brook, in which the peasant mentioned that a father Anselmo had once resided; and as I think there cannot be a greater object of charity than himself, I include him in the number of those whom I occasionally relieve."

Valeria felt her colour change, and stooped down to examine Paulina's flowers, with an earnestness that was highly gratifying to their cultivator.

About a week after this conversation relative to the dumb recluse, an event took place which threatened to interrupt the peace of the inhabitants at the Castello della Torvida. But before we proceed to state what this occurrence was, it is necessary to rectify an omission which we have made, in not acquainting our reader, that Sancho's niece, Francisca, was become one of Di Cavetti's family.

Urbino, considering it necessary that his daughter and Paulina should have at least one female attendant, had mentioned his idea to Di Borges, and the farmer, with a request from whom it was not very easy for him to refuse compliance, had urged him to make experiment of his niece, saying that his wife infinitely preferred the services of the little girl whom he saw in their house to those of her relative; and that he doubted not, although Francisca was both disobedient and impertinent to them, with whom she placed herself upon an equality, on account of their connexion in blood, that she would prove serviceable and willing to others, whom she considered her superiors. The bargain was accordingly concluded, and Francisca declared herself both proud and happy to be once more in the service of signoras, who, as she said, possessed elegant manners, combined with a knowledge of both life and fashion.

To return to the event of which we were beginning to speak, when we were interrupted by stopping to relate the transplantation of Francisca into the family of Di Cavetti:—The day had been passed by Urbino, his daughter and niece, at the farmhouse; and on their return to the Castello in the evening, as they entered the sycamore walk, they beheld Francisca sitting on the steps leading to the portal, and no sooner did she perceive them than she came running forward to meet them, in a hurried manner that excited their surprise, which feeling was not a little increased by the emotion, which, on her nearer approach, they observed depicted on her countenance. Half out of breath, and scarcely waiting till she was sufficiently near to be heard by those whom she was addressing—"Oh, my dear signoras, I beg your pardon, and yours too, signor Urbino!" she exclaimed; "but I must quit you directly; not that I have any objection to my place—oh no, indeed! such polite ladies must win the esteem of every discerning person like me, who have seen the world; but I would not enter the Castello again for millions—I could not—dare not do it!"

"What is your reason?" asked Valeria.

"Oh signora," ejaculated Francisca, "the Castello is haunted, awfully and diabolically haunted."

"Haunted!" echoed Paulina.

The countenance of Urbino became serious; that of Valeria impatient.

"Haunted, signora! haunted!" repeated Francisca, half-weeping at the recollection, as it appeared, of some alarm which she had received; "oh Blessed Mother! accept my thanks that I am safe out of its walls!" She crossed herself, and added—"Yes, signor, I say again, haunted! it is as positively true as I am a living soul and a virgin. These eyes have seen the ghost, seen and beheld it as it sat writing a letter at the table in the closet next the signora Valeria's bedchamber."

"A ghost writing a letter!" cried Paulina, laughing aloud; "I never heard of a ghost that possessed a quality of that nature before."

"Ay, it is something new, and wonderful too;" replied Francisca: "but you would not have laughed if you had been in my place, signora."

"Compose yourself," said Urbino, "and come with me into the house, and explain with less incoherence what it is you mean."

"Into the house! into *that* house!" rejoined Francisca; "I would not set foot into it again to be made a *duchessa!* oh no, signor, 'a burnt child dreads the fire,' as the proverb says, and I shall never, never have that horrid spectre from before my eyes as long as I live."

"What was it like?" inquired Paulina.

"A young cavalier, signora! a young cavalier!" answered Francisca.

"There is nothing so very horrid in that, I think," remarked Paulina.

"No, signora, not if it had been a real, live man; but an apparition, signora! only think of an apparition!"

"But how did you know it was an apparition?" asked Paulina.

"Because it vanished, signora," answered Francisca, "and you know nothing but ghosts can vanish. Praised be the saints that I have not lost my senses with the fright! Terence and signor Jeronymo know all about it."

At this juncture Terence approached them.

"What is the fright which Francisca has had," said Urbino, addressing O'Donnovan, "and of which she appears herself unable to give any distinct account?"

"Fright!" repeated Terence, affecting to laugh as he spoke, though the expression of his eyes conveyed to his master that he did not absolutely consider it a laughing matter; "I believe, your honour, it is all *blarney.*"

"That may be your Irish name for a thing of the kind," ejaculated Francisca, "but every one must call things by the names they understand, and in plain Italian I do say, swear, and maintain, that it was a ghost I saw."

Urbino requesting that one only would speak at a time, Terence took upon himself the office of elucidator, and proceeded to say, that in the afternoon, whilst employed in hoeing his favourite bed of potatoes, he had been startled by the shrieks of Francisca, who running up to him in the most violent trepidation, informed him that having accidentally gone into signora Valeria's bedchamber, from which the door of communication with a closet, in which her library and various articles of amusement were placed, standing open, she had beheld the ghost of a cavalier, as she had expressed herself, sitting writing at the table which stood in the centre of the apartment, and that she had immediately fled in terror from the spot, and had communicated what she had witnessed to him.

Terence added, that Jeronymo and himself had directly repaired to the spot where she had received her alarm, but had found nothing to corroborate her account; that they had minutely searched Valeria's bedchamber and the closet adjoining, and from thence proceeded to investigate every room in the Castello, but without discovering the slightest mark of any person having been within the walls; and moreover, that in the closet adjoining to Valeria's bedchamber, the implements for writing were not upon the table, but on one of the shelves which supported her books.

"I recollect that I placed them there myself this morning," said Valeria.

"I care not," ejaculated Francisca; "I am positive that when I saw the ghost, he had paper before him, the inkstand by his side, and a pen in his hand."

"It has been a waking dream of yours, I am after fancying," returned Terence.

"A dream!" exclaimed Francisca, "oh Heavens! oh the saints! would you call my eyesight and my word of honour in question? A dream! oh blessed saint Ursula! Well, dear signoras, fare you well! I know it is very ungrateful in me to leave you at such short notice, but you know my reason; I am safe out of the ghost's clutches this time, but there is no saying what might happen if I was to fall in his way again; and indeed, if I might advise, you had all better go back to my uncle's; after such a sight as I have seen within those walls, it is almost tempting Providence to live within them: well, if you do continue here, Heaven send you have no cause to repent your rashness! I'll not say good-bye, for I hope I shall often have the pleasure of seeing you at the farm. And, dear signora Valeria, if you do sleep, as usual, in your own chamber, next to that haunted closet, pray burn a light in your room, that you may be upon your guard what comes near you; and if you should see that dreadful spectre, be sure and speak to it, if you can; for a priest, who you know must understand those kind of things, told me, if a person had the courage to speak to a ghost, it could do them no harm afterwards."

Valeria received the admonition with a smile, and Francisca added—"Ah, signora, 'a little experience is worth a deal of wit,' as the proverb says; but if I don't make haste, it will be dark before I get home, and I am sure, as it is, I shall think that I see the awful spectre every step I set." And with these words she hurried out of the gate.

Urbino and his family entered the Castello in silence, and Valeria, anxious, from various almost-inexplicable causes, to visit the spot where the late mystery was said to have passed, and to investigate whether any traces of the enigma were left for her discovery, began to ascend the stairs which led to her apartments. Paulina came running after her.—"I never was afraid of a ghost in my life," she said, "and I am determined to be the first to venture into the haunted closet, as the silly Francisca called it." And darting forward into Valeria's bed-chamber, she proceeded towards the door of communication with the closet, when suddenly stopping, her countenance underwent a visible change, and as Valeria approached her, in a faint voice she said—"Listen, I am sure I hear somebody breathe within the closet; don't you?"

"I do, I do," replied Valeria, and stepping forward, with an eagerness for which Paulina was at a loss to account, she discovered old Jeronymo sleeping in a chair.

The laugh excited by his appearance awoke Jeronymo, and in the longest sentence which he had uttered for many a year, the old man informed them, that having sat down where they found him, to watch whether any circumstance would occur to corroborate Francisca's tale of the ghost, wearying of solitude, he had fallen asleep on his post.

Terence and his master being meanwhile left together, it will be readily imagined that their conversation was on a subject to which their ideas had long recurred, namely, the writing which they had formerly seen on the door, and their surmises whether the alarm received by Francisca bore any relation to that miraculous occurrence, to which they had themselves been witness, and upon the authenticity of which they were alone tempted to give any degree of credit to the assertions of Francisca; and although they resolved to hide their feelings from their companions, their minds were not a little agitated by the succession of events for which they were utterly unable to account.

"Whoever they may be that play us these pranks, or whatever may be their reason for so doing, I wish with all my heart they had confined their tricks to my apartment, where they first began them, and not shifted their ground to that of my dear young lady," said Terence.

"As I know that a surprise is frequently as fatal to a delicate mind as any real cause for alarm could be," said Urbino, "I will change apartments with my daughter to-night; the impression which must be made on her senses by Francisca's prattle may cause her sleepless hours if she remains in her own chamber, though pride may withhold her from making the confession."

"And if she lies in your chamber, your honour," replied Terence, "she'll be close by mine, and I shall be at hand, if she requires protection or consolation."

The females now entered the apartment, and Urbino informed his daughter of his resolution.

Valeria remonstrated against his purpose, by declaring herself entirely free from apprehension; but Urbino remained fixed to his point; and Valeria was compelled, however reluctantly, to abide by his decision.

Whilst at supper, Urbino, addressing Terence, who was attending in the apartment, said—"Take down the two pair of pistols suspended over the chimneypiece in my study, and load them; one pair I will keep in my chamber, and the other you shall take with you into yours. We will at least use the precaution of preparing ourselves against a surprise in the night."

"You are a gentleman of good conceit," replied Terence; "it shall be done."

"Oh, surely there can be no occasion for such a precaution," said Valeria.

81

"I hope not," replied Urbino, "but too great security can never be observed in any case of ambiguity."

Valeria turned sick and faint; it was possible, she believed, that Julio might be the supposed spectre, and should he, by any means, have secretly gained access into the Castello, in the hope of procuring an interview with her, be discovered by her father or Terence, and fall a victim to their false suspicions—she could scarcely support herself on her chair. Explain or discover her anxiety she durst not; in a few seconds she assumed courage to say—"I would not, for the wealth of worlds, that my dear father should stain his hand with the blood of a fellow-being; my peace of mind would at that moment vanish for ever."

"Surely not, my child," replied Urbino, "if the action were committed in self-defence: in such a case mercy would be un-justifiable in me, as I should commit myself a sacrifice to my enemy, and expose you to the loss of a father and a protector."

"Great Heaven, avert the dreadful contingency!" ejaculated Valeria.

In a short time Terence returned to the apartment, and informed his master that the pistols were all loaded, and lying upon the table in his study.

Eager to conceal the agitation under which she was labouring, Valeria arose, and saying, that as her father was to occupy her chamber, she would require a few minutes to remove some articles of which she stood in need from her own apartment into his, she rose to retire.

Paulina followed her example, and half-smiling at the idea of her uncle being alarmed at the folly of Francisca, as she called it, and declaring herself utterly devoid of apprehension, she bade her cousin good-night, and proceeded to her own chamber.

Valeria closely examined her closet, in order, if possible, to discover if any traces of the supposed spectre were left on the spot; but her researches were fruitless; and retiring to the apartment that night allotted her, she shortly after heard her father and Terence ascend to their respective chambers, and universal silence then prevailed through the Castello.

The night passed undisturbed. In the morning Urbino was scarcely risen when Di Borges appeared at the Castello, anxious to inquire into the truth of the report which Francisca had borne to the farm; for although the fear of losing his respected neighbour had caused him to treat with the greatest apparent indifference every tale which had been circulated to the prejudice of the Castello, he had often, in the privacy of his own mind, reflected with a sensation approaching to wonder, on the circumstances of the smoke, the light, and, above all, the writing on the door.

Di Borges passed the day at the Castello, but the conversation of Urbino and himself, which was principally confined to one subject, served to throw no light on the matter discussed. Di Borges approved of the precaution which Urbino had taken to prevent a surprise from a concealed enemy, if such a one he had, and promised to pass as much of his time with him as his avocations would permit.

A considerable period elapsed, during which the tranquillity of the Castello remained undisturbed; Di Borges proving constant in his visits to Di Cavetti, and Urbino and his family in returning them at the farmhouse. One day, when they had agreed to dine with Sancho, whilst the farmer and Urbino were engaged in a ramble over the lands of the former, and Valeria occupied in reading to Averilla, Francisca, contriving to draw apart Paulina, said—"Oh, dear signora, I have such a piece of news to tell you! you have got an *amante*, one of the sweetest young signors I ever set my eyes on in my life."

"And pray who is the signor that does me so much honour?" asked Paulina, laughing.

"That is more than I can tell you, signora," answered Francisca; "but to my thinking, he's not a cavalier of these parts, for I never saw him before in my life. You must know that the evening before last, when you had been here to pass the afternoon, you had not been gone ten minutes before this very signor, whom I had observed for a considerable part of the day at the posthouse, introduced himself to me, as I was standing by the little gate at the foot of the lawn, and paying me a handsome compliment, by saying that he saw by my manner I was a girl of discernment and knowledge of the world, that might be trusted with a secret, he asked me to tell him who the beautiful young lady was that he had just seen leave the farmhouse. 'There were two of them, signor,' said I. 'That I know,' returned he, 'but I mean her with the light hair, the dimpled cheeks, and the smile of an angel. You must have observed me,' he continued, 'gazing upon her from the road, when she was gathering flowers in the garden by its side; and I gazed so ardently,' he added, 'for the charm conveyed to my heart was so irresistible, that I almost fear I may have offended her.' — 'Oh no, I hope not, signor,' said I; "a cat may look at a king," as the proverb says; not that I mean to compare you, signor, to a creature of that kind, only for the sake of the similarity in conversation."

Francisca paused, and Paulina increasing her laugh, said— "And is that all the wonderful secret you have to tell me?"

"Ah, signora," replied Francisca, "but the best of it is yet to come.—'What is the name of the divine creature?' said he.— 'Paulina, signor; the signora Paulina.'—'Where does she reside?'—'With her uncle, the signor di Cavetti, at the Castello della Torvida.'—'One more question, and my heart will be at ease; I hope she is single?'—'I believe I may answer for that,' said I. Oh! how his eyes glistened with joy when I told him that! He put two pieces of gold into my hand, and said—'Have the great kindness to convey to my adored Paulina, for I will call her mine, that it is my resolution instantly to lay my suit for her hand before her uncle, and that my life or death depends upon the favour with which my proposals are received."

"This is love at first sight, indeed!" replied Paulina.

"'Love must have a beginning,' as the proverb says," returned Francisca.

They continued to discourse for some time on the same subject, but their farther conversation only served to inform Paulina, that, whoever her sudden admirer was, he was tall and handsome; a gentleman in dress and conversation, well mounted, well attended, and that he wished to resign his liberty at the shrine of her charms.

The heart of Paulina had hitherto escaped unwounded by the darts of the blind god, and she had latterly often reflected that it was not unlikely that her uncle's plan of seclusion from the world might condemn her to become a leader of apes. She therefore considered, that if the unknown cavalier were really the man in person and address which Francisca had described him to be, and that his professions with regard to herself were fulfilled, she might stand as great a chance of happiness in her connexion with a man who had been captivated by a glance of her person from the road-side, as with one enthralled by a similar glance from a box in the theatre. Marriage, she was aware, is at best but a lottery-ticket, to which a blind chance of felicity is attached; for those persons between whom the union of wedlock is once decided to take place, so carefully conceal from each other their defects or unpleasant qualities, till the gordian knot is tied between them, that the act of their inseparability can alone, with any degree of certainty, prove to them whether they have drawn a blank or a prize from the wheel of life.

Whilst Urbino and his family were absent from the Castello, Terence, leaving Jeronymo employed in gathering simples from the surrounding woods, proceeded to the village of Malina. He had requested the wife of the miller, of whom he was in the practice of purchasing flour for his master's household, to procure him a servant in the place of Francisca, and his purpose in going thither was to ascertain whether she had succeeded in her attempts.

The woman's reply was, that she had made his proposal to a young female, whom she could safely recommend as a useful and honest servant, but that the girl was partly under an engagement to the major-domo of the marchese di Valdetti; "but," added the miller's wife, "I recommended her to serve your master in preference to the marchese; every body knows the signor Urbino di Cavetti to be a kind and a good man, and not many know any thing of the marchese at all, and still fewer any thing of him that is to his credit."

"Who is this same marchese that you are speaking about?" replied Terence; "I never heard of him before, I am after thinking."

"I dare say not," answered the miller's wife, "for it is about twenty years since he has been seen in these parts. His palazzo stands about a league from hence to the south; but for the period of time I was mentioning to you, it has been inhabited only by servants and his sulky old major-domo, who, they say, pilfers the marchese as greedily as the marchese preys upon others. It is not long since he had like to have been amenable to the laws of his country, as report says, for peculating the state; but he got clear of that, as men with interest and money generally contrive to make their way out of every scrape; and the latter end of last week, without an hour's warning of his coming, he appeared at the palazzo, and I fancy not so great, or at least so rich a man as he left it. The world says he has had a vast loss at the gaming-table, and that the reduction of his property has driven him into retirement.

Whilst they continued chatting together, the miller entered, accompanied by a young man in livery, and producing a flask of wine, invited Terence to take a cup with them.

After drinking to Terence, the miller, turning to the stranger, said—"Well, Paulo, better luck to you, my lad; it may be your good fortune, one of these days, to fall in with a master such as my friend here," pointing to Terence as he spoke, "serves."

"Indeed!" replied the young man, "pray, who may the good signor be?"

"Nobody that you know; a stranger here," replied the miller; "his name is signor Urbino di Cavetti; but for my part, I call him the butcher, baker, brewer, clothier, and comforter of the whole neighbourhood; for I truly believe he studies nothing but the doing of good."

"I serve a very different kind of man indeed," answered the stranger.

"Paulo is an old friend of mine," rejoined the miller, addressing Terence, "whom I have not seen for some time, and I am sorry that the chance of service has led him into such bad company as I find he is returned with into our country, which is the place of his nativity."

Paulo said that he had been but a short time in the service of the marchese, and therefore knew but little of his private history; but he had heard his fellow-servants mention several circumstances connected with his former life, similar to what the miller's wife had been recounting to Terence: he said that the domestics in his employment were treated in the most tyrannical and humiliating manner; that their pay was small and uncertain; their fare hard; and that they expected a curtailment of even the few privileges which they did enjoy, as it was confidently reported that the marchese had retired to the country in order to repair his broken fortunes by economy.

"The oppressor's wrong, the proud man's contumely," muttered Terence between his teeth.

Without comprehending or attending to what he said, the miller rejoined—"Yes truly, I never knew so worthy a man as your master, and though I say it to your face, I have observed that you possess qualities yourself that leave you little behind him in the scale of goodness."

"He saved my life," replied Terence, "and it is a duty I owe his humanity to prove to him that he did not preserve a being unworthy of existence."

"Has the marchese any family, Paulo?" asked the miller.

"Only a nephew," answered Paulo, "signor Vincentio, who is as amiable and as much beloved as his uncle is disliked. Signor Vincentio is every one's friend whom he has it in his power to serve." And the flask being concluded, the miller returned to his labour, and Terence and Paulo retraced their steps towards their respective homes.

In the evening Terence informed his master of the arrival of a nobleman, named the marchese di Valdetti, in the neighbourhood, and Urbino declared himself utterly unacquainted with either the man or the title.

CHAPTER VIII

Art thou any thing?
Art thou some god, some angel, or some devil,
That mak'st my blood cold and my hair to stand?
Speak to me—What art thou?

Julius Cæsar.

NOTWITHSTANDING the light manner in which Paulina had treated the information conveyed to her by Francisca whilst in her presence, she considered it with some degree of seriousness when left to her own reflections. She felt a wish to know whether the unknown were really as handsome and engaging as he had been reported to her, what his name was, where he resided, and whether he really intended to lay the proposals of which he had spoken before her uncle.

Not less occupied were the thoughts of Valeria, and her despondency of mind increased with every hour which rolled on, and still brought her no explanation from Julio of his ambiguous conduct; her days were passed in affected serenity, and her nights in sleepless anxiety, whilst her health was suffering under a nervous languor, produced by the constant restraint which she was compelled to impose on her feelings.

Upon this evening, on retiring to her bedchamber, unusually reluctant to enter that bed where repose so seldom visited her, she threw herself into a chair; and having passed no inconsiderable portion of time in a state of inactivity consonant to the apathy of her mind, during which period she heard the other members of the house, as usual, retire to their chambers, she took from the table before her a volume, which contained a collection of tales of mingled fancy and superstition. As she cast her eyes over the leaves, they glanced upon a romantic fable, which she recollected that her father had pointed out to her as an eligible subject for a little poem, and had requested her to turn it into verse—an art which she had from her youth cultivated with a fondness equal to the ardour with which Paulina had devoted herself to the science of music; and, conscious that occupancy is the most effectual shield against the tortures of an anxious mind, she resolved to attempt complying with her father's request, and sketched the following lines:—

THE WARRIOR AND THE WITCH.

A ROMANCE

O'er Ravia's wild and rugged plains
A warrior, flush'd with victory, rode;
His courser champ'd the frothy reins,
Proud of his sanguinary load.

Daring and fearful was his mien;
Bred in the battle's fierce alarms,
Carnage his ruthless nurse had been,
And rear'd him in her sinewy arms.

Caio from youth had dauntless led
His legions to th'embattled field,
Where 'midst the dying and the dead,
Sword clash'd with sword, and shield met shield.

Whilst arrows, thick as driving sleet,
From thousands snatch'd the quiv'ring breath,
Some spirit, 'midst the battle's heat,
Blunted for him the dart of death.

Round Vida's towers, in gay parade,
The blood-stain'd banners wav'd on high,
Whilst the vain pageantry display'd
The dear-bought meed of victory.

But soon his heart, with impious pride,
Scoff'd at the powers of earth and sky;
Both heaven and hell he would deride,
    And each indignantly defy.

But fate, to damp his daring mind,
Drugg'd deep for him a cup of woe,
And, with the art of hate refin'd,
    Blasted the laurels on his brow.

For, as he cross'd a barren heath,
A dingy figure met his eye,
And sulph'rous was her tainted breath,
    Whilst muttering spells of sorcery.

And, when she saw his horse draw nigh,
She lifted up her straggling hair,
Full on him fix'd her rheumy eye,
    Then murmured on the murky air—

"Stay, Caio, stay, and hear me read
The page that holds thy destiny;
Why make unprofitable speed?
Halt! halt! such haste there needs not be."

"Begone!" he cried, "unholy hag!
Nor dare to cross me on my way;
Hence thy foul, loathsome body drag,
    Meet carrion for the birds of prey!"

Cursing, on him she loudly rail'd,
Invoking Heaven, and earth, and sea;
Then cried, as through the air she sail'd,
"Proud knight, thou shalt remember me."

Unmov'd, the dauntless warrior heard
The curse she mutter'd on her tongue;
His snorting courser straight he spurr'd,
And loud his rattling armour rung.

O'er plains and wastes the warrior speeds,
Till plains and wastes are seen no more,
And Vida's mountains rear their heads,
Like friends upon his native shore.

For, as the soldier homeward hies,
And blood and carnage leaves behind,
Visions of peace benignly rise,
To tranquillize his rugged mind.

Now mists drove furious o'er the plain,
And night the gathering gloom renew'd,
Whilst shivering sleet and driving rain
The weary traveller pursu'd.

Loud from the vale the deep-ton'd bell
Fell fearful on his list'ning ear;
The warrior heard the solemn knell,
And sudden stopp'd, appall'd with fear.

Borne on the blast, responses rise,
Then, soft and softer, faintly die.
"The monks a requiem chant," he cries,
"For one who's gain'd eternity."

But, as near Vida's towers he drew,
A blasting object met his eye;
For, as the bleak winds wildly blew,
Wav'd the black flag of Death on high.

The warrior spurr'd his foaming steed,
Eager his hastier steps to urge;
A hollow voice cried—"Onward speed!
They chant Mabella's funeral dirge."

The knight turn'd pale—"Mabella's cold—
In Death's cold arms Mabella lies:
It was for her the death-bell toll'd—
Vain are your tears, and vain your sighs."

Now here, now there, he turn'd his eye,
Eager the phantom to pursue;
Nought but the bat flew swiftly by;
Yet Caio shudder'd as it flew.

Torn with predicted fatal woes,
His spur still gor'd his courser's side,
Till Vida's towers majestic rose,
And frown'd upon the glossy tide.

The silver wave, as in dismay,
Trembling receiv'd the massy pile;
The pile, more beauteous from decay,
Trembled at Time's rude touch the while.

As near his castle Caio drew,
With glittering lights the casements gleam'd;
An awful splendour round they threw,
And with a solemn stillness beam'd.

"What may this mean?" he frantic cried;
"Ye saints, in charity declare."
A voice inscrutable replied—
"Mabella's freed from mortal care."

Again he turn'd with wild affright,
And quick his glittering falchion drew,
To scare this spirit of the night,
That mutter'd murder as it flew.

But nought his ruthless rage avail'd—
He cleav'd alone the yielding air;
The voice mysteriously prevail'd,
And fill'd his heart with wild despair.

At length he gain'd the ivy'd tower,
And the shrill horn blew sharp and loud;
The vassals, conscious of its power,
Around their pallid master crowd.

"Is my prediction true?" he cried;
"Instant, ye dastard crew! declare.
Those glimm'ring lights from far I spied:
Hold me no more 'twixt hope and fear."

Mute as the grave the vassals stood,
Nor dar'd the dreadful truth reveal;
Their silence froze his curdling blood,
And riv'd his brain like bolts of steel.

Swift as he pac'd the dismal halls,
Loud plaints of woe assail'd his ears;
Funereal trappings from the walls,
Mingled with casques and glitt'ring spears;

And sable figures cross'd his view,
Augmenting more the gen'ral gloom;
And sudden gusts unseemly blew
The crested helmet's towering plume.

"Spirit of vengeance!" Caio cried,
"The truth now bursts upon my brain;
The imprecation I despis'd
Strikes me with agonizing pain.

"Why did I mock that fiend of hell,
And for myself this woe prepare?
Ambiguous was th'accursed spell
She mutter'd on the murky air."

His footsteps echo'd through the dome,
Till he Mabella's chamber spied,
Where, in the vestments of the tomb,
Repos'd his once-bewitching bride.

She, the mild solace of his hours,
Breathless in pallid beauty lay;
Her cold hands clasping wreaths of flowers,
Chill'd their frail beauties to decay.

Yet still a look divinely mild,
Soft o'er her tranquil features play'd;
As if in sleep she sweetly smil'd,
Or with clos'd eyes devoutly pray'd.

And oft the requiem through the air
Stole swelling on the ear of Heaven,
Whilst angels leant the strain to hear,
And seem'd to whisper sins forgiv'n.

The sable plumes, with sombre pride,
Droop'd graceful o'er the silent bier,
Whilst friends, by mutual woe allied,
Profusely shed th'unbidden tear.

Next morn, with solemn steps and slow,
Assembled round the mournful throng,
In all the pageantry of woe
The dark procession mov'd along.

But who can Caio's anguish tell,
When the cold earth was lightly turn'd,
And on the coffin's lid it fell,
And dust to dust again return'd!

The sacred dust to earth resign'd,
Homeward the slow procession mov'd;
And oft the warrior look'd behind,
On the cold grave of her he lov'd:

When suddenly a whirlwind loud
Rouses the spirit of the storm,
And dim along the shadowy cloud
Glides the loath'd witch's hideous form.

And as she sails the heavy air,
And drives the whirlwind o'er the sea,
These words her vengeful spleen declare—
"Proud knight, thou *hast* remember'd me."

When Valeria laid down her pen, she felt pleased that she had obeyed her father's wish, and also that the night was so far spent; for, on consulting her watch, she found that it was some minutes past three o'clock; but, on reviewing her little production, she, with a sigh, confessed that it was greatly inferior to many others which she had composed in a happier tone of mind.

Having folded up the paper on which it was contained, she opened a little drawer at the bottom of her inkstand, for the purpose of depositing her performance in it till she had an opportunity of showing it to her father, when, what was her astonishment at discovering a note directed to herself, and securely wafered! She tore it hastily open, and found these words— *"Let not my adored Valeria be surprised at the unexpected sight of her Julio, at whatever hour, or on whatever spot, she may chance to behold him."* Again and again she read the mysterious warning, and, with eyes fixed in anxiety, was almost endeavouring to search into the paper on which the words of admonition were inscribed, when suddenly the report of a pistol from the chamber in which her father lay struck her senses; at the sound she sunk breathless into a chair. Almost instantly the first report was followed by a second, and immediately the few inhabitants which the Castello contained were heard in motion.

Assuming a strength which nature appeared to deny her, she thrust the paper into her bosom, and darting out into the gallery upon which her chamber-door opened, proceeded as quickly as she was able to that of her father.

The smoke emitted from the tubes of the pistols, with which the apartment was filled, for a while prevented her from discovering objects; as it died away, she beheld her father in his nightgown, with a lamp in his hand, eagerly examining the walls of the closet which communicated with the bedchamber, and Terence and Paulina proposing to him inquiries, to which they could for a while produce no reply.

After a time, Urbino proceeded to state that, ever since he had lain in Valeria's chamber, in order to be prepared against any sudden alarm, he had always made it his practice to throw himself upon his bed in his nightgown, after having placed his lamp and pistols on a table by his side: that he had hitherto slept uninterrupted, but on this morning he had been awakened by a rustling noise, and on raising his head had perceived the figure of a man standing in the doorway of the closet. He had twice called to him, demanding who he was, and what his business? and upon receiving no answer, had discharged at him both his pistols, enveloped in the smoke of which the figure had disappeared; and, what was quite as extraordinary, he was not able to discover in the pannels of the wainscot which formed the walls of the closet, any spot where the bullets had entered.

All around him stood wrapt in silent astonishment; to account for so miraculous a circumstance, without admitting the interference of supernatural agency, appeared impossible, even to a mind of the strongest sense.

> "Can such things be,
> And overcome us, like a summer's cloud,
> Without our special wonder?"

at length exclaimed Terence. Jeronymo fell on his knees, and raising his hands towards heaven, pronounced a silent invocation for their preservation. The countenance of Urbino displayed a mind distracted with doubts, but unwilling to confess the sense of apprehension with which it was evidently affected. The features of Valeria bespoke terror mingled with resignation; whilst Paulina appeared almost incredulous of the facts, to a detail of which she had listened.

Again and again did Terence and Di Cavetti examine the walls of the closet; but fruitless was their investigation—no possible means could be discovered by which any human being could have entered the place; and it was also fully ascertained that the bullets had not penetrated the wainscot.

Tremblingly Valeria inquired of her father a description of the figure which he had beheld; and Urbino replied, that it had appeared to him a man of the middling height, wrapped in a dark cloak, which was all he had seen, as the light had not been favourably placed for his gaining a view of his countenance.

A considerable time having been passed in vain researches for an elucidation of the impending mystery, and in surmises and reflections on the only subject which could at the present moment be supposed to engross their thoughts, the morning was already advancing, and Urbino proposed that they should take an early breakfast, and walk to the farm, as he had particular reasons for wishing to see Di Borges that day, and was apprehensive that, if they did not visit him early, he might be gone to Mantua before their arrival.

Valeria and Paulina accordingly quitted Urbino, in order to prepare themselves for attending him on his walk; and Urbino, on being left alone with Terence, said—"I recollect that, when we first observed the writing on the fastened door, you inquired of me whether the circumstance might not bear any relation to the cause of my abrupt departure from Venice?"

"I remember very well I asked that thing, your honour," replied Terence.

"And I remember that I answered you that I felt certain it did not," rejoined Urbino.

"The very words your honour spoke," said Terence.

"But reflection with my own mind," replied Di Cavetti, "has latterly tended considerably to change my opinion; and I intend immediately to take certain steps which I hope may, in some degree, relieve my mind at this disagreeable crisis."

"Disagreeable it is, sure enough, your honour," answered Terence; "but I need not tell you that the man who has done nothing amiss has nothing to be afraid of. To be sure, as *fader* O'Wolloghan at Ballyporeen used to say, the best have their trials; but, if they do fall into the darkness of trouble, a good conscience makes them shine the brighter when they once get out of their misfortunes. It is only keeping up a good heart, your honour, and the long day makes all right *wid* the righteous; as *ould* Willy said—

'Come what, come may,
Time and the hour runs through the roughest day.'

But I'll be after getting the breakfast ready, your honour;" and with these words he departed, though he could willingly have prolonged the conversation in which Di Cavetti and himself had been engaged, as he considered it an unpardonable error when the negligence of the servant delayed the execution of a master's purpose.

The face of nature is one of the most effectual cheerers of a desponding mind; the beauty and regularity of her laws, discernible in every feature, calm the senses, and communicate peace to the heart. The morning was of uncommon loveliness; the golden orb of day was majestically ascending towards its zenith, through a firmament of glowing azure, unspotted by a single cloud; the mild gale which fanned the air was scented with the perfume of the wild flowerets which bloomed around, and the ear was recreated with the grateful melody of the choristers of the grove. The scene was too lovely not to excite admiration; and, soothed by the contemplation of its beauties, Urbino and his party arrived in tolerable cheerfulness at the farmhouse.

The principal part of the day was passed by Di Cavetti and the farmer in the private apartment of the latter. Valeria, as was her regular custom at every visit which she made to the farmhouse, devoted her attentions to Averilla; and the act of administering to the comfort of the placid sufferer, in the present state of her feelings, appeared to communicate unhoped-for placidity to her own mind; whilst Paulina, who having no concealed thoughts or surmises relative to the supposed apparition coupled with its recollection, and who was accordingly, of all the inhabitants of the Castello, the least affected by the occurrence of the' morning, having exhausted her sources of amusement within the house, strolled into a little wood which led from the orchard to a range of corn-fields at its extremity.

The sun was now at its meridian, the air oppressively warm, and Paulina seated herself, for a few minutes' repose, upon a verdant bank which skirted the grove. Whilst she was thus reposing, she beheld passing along the road, which lay at only a very short distance from her resting-place, two persons on horseback; they were both males, and the one who was nearest to her appeared, by his dress and manner, to be the superior of his companion; though the distinction of rank between them did not appear so positive as that of master and domestic, as they rode by each other's side, and were conversing familiarly together. Paulina viewed them cursorily as they passed, and would have thought of them no more, had she not perceived the more distinguished of the two to turn his head again and again to observe her; and when the intervening hedge shut her from his sight, she saw him raise himself in his stirrups and continue to look back upon her, till a turn of the road placed a screen to his observation. Still Paulina would have considered the conduct of the stranger as the effect of an idle curiosity rather impertinently gratified, had she not believed that she had seen his person before, although she could not form the slightest recollection when she had beheld him, if even her conjecture that she had done so were correct. In age he appeared about fifty-five, in stature tall and thin, and his dress was not in any point remarkable.

Her walk being concluded, as she was returning slowly towards the house, Francisca ran out to meet her.—"Oh, signora! where have you been?" she exclaimed—"You have lost such an opportunity! I have been to every place I could think of to look for you."

"What was the occasion of your search?" asked Paulina.

"Why you must know, signora," returned Francisca, "that I went about an hour ago on an errand for my uncle to the post-house, and as I came back again, who should ride by me but the charming cavalier I told you of, that asked me all the questions about you the other day, and sent that polite message to you that I had the two pieces of gold for delivering. The moment I saw him, I dropt him my very best curtsey (for I am never deficient in politeness to people of real elegance and gentility, of which I am sure he is one); so he drew in his horse's rein and I stepped up to his side, and he leant down his head and asked me if I could inform him whether she on whom his existence rested were well?—'Indeed she is, signor,' returned I—"as healthy as hysop," as the proverb says. It is lucky you rode this way to-day: she is on a visit hard by, and if you will loiter about here a little while, I have no doubt but I can procure you an interview."

"How incautious!" exclaimed Paulina. "Do you think I should have been mad enough to have acceded, if even the request had been made to me?'

"Well, I beg your pardon," rejoined Francisca; "I only did for the best. I know that many young ladies of high fashion prefer stolen interviews."

"I hope I shall never be so fashionable as to lose sight of common prudence," replied Paulina.

"That seemed to be exactly the cavalier's opinion, signora," returned Francisca; "for he answered me—'I must decline your offer; I do not wish to see her clandestinely whom I desire to espouse honourably. Have the goodness to inform my adored Paulina that I am now on my way to Mantua, and that I have business there which will detain me for three or four days; at the expiration of that time I shall pay my respects to her and her uncle at the Castello;' and so saying, off he rode, putting one piece of gold into my hand at parting; and somehow I think he was only half as engaging this time as the last."

Paulina easily perceived that Francisca's opinion was ruled by the value of the bribe which she had received; for herself, she felt happy that the conduct and professions of the stranger appeared to be such as bespoke his character to be estimable.

In a few seconds their conversation was interrupted by Francisca being called into the house; and a period was very shortly after put to the reflections of Paulina by a summons to the dinner-table.

CHAPTER IX

Some six or seven, who did hide their faces
Even from darkness.

SHAKESPEARE

THE cloth being removed, Urbino and the farmer, who had spoken but little during the meal, again retired to the private apartment of the latter. Their conversation during the morning had consisted of a recapitulation of such unexplained circumstances as had taken place at the Castello; and Di Cavetti at length said—"Conscious as I am that I never deserved an enemy, and firmly believing, as I do, that, six hours before my abrupt departure from Venice, there was not a being in existence who ever nourished displeasure against me, I can only, upon mature reflection, suppose that my refusing to perpetrate an action which I considered to be criminal, and to the performance of which I preferred to quit my native city, and the friends and acquaintance of my youth, as you are already aware that I have done, has drawn upon me the unceasing enmity of one whom my denial has offended, and who ungenerously tortures me in revenge for his disappointed views."

"I can be no judge of the truth of your surmises," replied Di Borges, "without I were acquainted with the circumstances out of which they arise; and as you have hitherto so carefully concealed from me the secret, I suppose you are withheld by a vow from disclosing it?"

"I am not indeed," rejoined Urbino; "I have only been solemnly warned that its promulgation may involve me in trouble, from which a strict secrecy may preserve me. This admonition, more for the sake of their peace of mind with whom I am connected than for my own safety, has hitherto closed my lips; but as I begin to be doubtful whether the terms proposed by my adversary are adhered to on his part, and as I can also no longer deny myself the gratification of a wish which I have long felt to admit a tried friend like yourself to my confidence, I am resolved this day to reveal to you the cause which brought me into your neighbourhood."

"I need not, I believe, assure you that your confidence shall not be abused," said Sancho.

"And I need hardly add," rejoined Di Cavetti, "that I wish that confidence to be confined to your own breast; for I believe it is truly said, that a secret loses its existence if reposed in more than two hearts: the vanity of showing that we are entrusted with matters unknown to others, the pleasure of displaying ourselves possessed of superior information to our neighbours, and a thousand little causes which proceed in most hearts more from carelessness than evil intention, have too often propagated facts which have led to the ruin of those whom they concerned."

"I am neither a boy nor a woman," returned Di Borges; "that hand," he added, shaking Di Cavetti's as he spoke, "is the pledge of my heart; and indeed, signor, I am truly glad that you are come to the resolution of imparting your secret to me—not for the idle gratification of my own curiosity, which, I confess, has been considerably excited by many hints which you have occasionally dropped relative to the cause of your having quitted Venice so abruptly, but because, though I am not so great an admirer of proverbs as my niece Francisca, I believe there is considerable truth in that which affirms, that two heads are better than one; and though mine is certainly not the best in the present instance, it may be able to discern some bypath to lead you out of your dilemma, which, whilst wandering on the high road, has escaped your observation."

"Without farther preface then," said Urbino, "I will begin my relation."

Sancho placed himself in an attitude of attention, and Urbino spoke thus:—"It was one evening about the hour of five that I quitted my house in Venice, for the purpose of visiting a patient who lay in a dangerous state. As the invalid was an intimate acquaintance, I remained some time with his family, conversing with and consoling them by turns. On my return homewards, passing by the opera-house, and perceiving that *La Clemenza di Tito* was the performance of the evening, to some of the airs contained in which piece I have always been extremely attached, and looking at my watch, and finding it to be within a few minutes of the hour of commencement, I went into the house and took my seat.

"Some time before the conclusion of the performance I quitted the theatre, and on stepping into the street I was accosted by a man wrapped in a dark cloak, who addressed me by saying—'Signor di Cavetti, there is a person at the end of the next street who wishes to see you immediately.' As he was acquainted with my name, I concluded that he knew my profession, and that the person to whom I was called was ill, and required my advice; I accordingly followed him, and on approaching the water's edge by which the street was terminated, I felt myself suddenly seized by several hands, and my head muffled in a cloak, which stifled my power of utterance, or at least prevented my cries from being heard. I was hurried into a gondola, which was immediately put into rapid motion; and when it had gained the middle of the stream, the cloth was removed from my head, and a bandage placed over my eyes, which I was prevented from removing, by one of my hands being held in those of two persons who sat on each side of me.

"On recovering the power of making myself heard—'Who are ye, and why am I thus abused?' was my first demand.—'Fear nothing, signor,' pronounced the voice of one who appeared to be standing opposite to me, and whom I conjectured to be the same person who had addressed me in the street—'no evil is intended you; on the contrary, you are invited to accept a rich reward for the temporary inconvenience under which you are suffering.'—'But to what purpose am I detained your prisoner?' I replied.—'We are forbidden to explain,' answered the same voice; 'the motive will be in a very short time unfolded to you: but, I repeat, be assured that it is the reverse of evil to which you are conducting.'—'Every unlawful restraint which is inflicted on one who is not criminal must be evil,' I rejoined.—'A very short time, I repeat again, will unravel what I am withheld from explaining,' answered the same voice; and every question which I afterwards advanced was only received with silence by my companions.

"After a time, the oars were pulled in, and the motion of the vessel ceased. I was then led on shore, and having ascended a flight of steps, I heard a door closed behind me; from which sound and the echoes of the footsteps by which I was surrounded, I concluded that I had entered the vestibule of some palazzo situated on the banks of the gulf. I considered it in vain to expostulate, and therefore awaited in silence the development of this extraordinary occurrence.

"My conductors continued to lead me forward through various turnings and windings, sometimes moving along a level ground, sometimes ascending and sometimes descending, but more frequently the former, till, entering an apartment which appeared to me to be situate at the extremity of a long gallery, my hands were released, and the bandage removed from before my eyes.

"I perceived myself to be in a handsome room, and my companions to be four or five men, wrapped in dark cloaks and closely masked. Of these, all immediately retired but one, who, pointing to a sofa, requested me to repose myself after my fatigue, adding, that I would be detained only a few minutes till the person who sought my services appeared before me; and with these words he departed likewise.

"You may easily conceive, my friend, how extraordinary was my situation at this moment; long past the age of gallantry, and believing it impossible that my medical skill should be sought under the ambiguous veil which had attended my entrance into the mansion where I now was, I felt utterly at a loss to divine the sequel of my adventure.

"At the expiration of about five minutes, a door, opposite to that by which I had entered, was opened, and another man, also wrapped in a dark cloak, and as closely masked as those whom I had already seen, appeared before me. He advanced towards the spot where I was standing, and bowing to me with an elegance of manner which bespoke superior rank, he said—'I know not, signor Urbino, in what words to attempt apologizing to you for that most unwarrantable liberty which I must have appeared to have taken with your person, by conducting you hither in the mysterious manner in which you have been treated.'—I replied, that I felt it impossible to deny that a liberty which required some explanation had been used towards me.—'For that liberty,' replied the stranger, 'I do most sincerely entreat your pardon, and will immediately proceed to the explanation which you so justly require.' He then requested me to be seated, and begged me to taste some wine and fruit, which were placed on a table near the sofa, upon which, following the example of my extraordinary entertainer, I had taken my seat.

"After a short pause he said—'The very high opinion, signor di Cavetti, which I entertain of your skill as a physician, and your honour as a man, has prompted me to use the freedom with you of which I have this night been guilty. I have at this moment, signor, a female within these walls in a dying state, and to whom the relief of medicine must be administered with the secrecy of the grave.'—'Signor,' I returned, 'I am too well acquainted with what the duty of a medical man is, to have required such precautions as you have taken to ensure my secrecy upon any point connected with my profession.'—'Have I not already told you my opinion of your honour?' said the stranger, pressing my hand in his as he spoke. 'Unknown as I am to you, signor, and beheld by you only beneath a veil, it is but just that I should disclose to you some part of myself which may be seen without disguise—the liberality of my heart is all which I can at this moment display to you. These two purses,' he said, placing them upon the table before me as he spoke, 'contain each a thousand pieces of gold; I hope you will deign to accept them, as a slight mark of my regret at the inconvenience which you have this evening suffered on my account: and should you be fortunate in granting positive relief to the female of whom I have spoken, five thousand others shall be your immediate reward.'—'Signor,' I replied, 'you offer terms more liberal than I can feel myself justified in accepting. I hold it right that every professional man should be rewarded for his skill and attention, but I deem it equally wrong that, presuming upon his success, he should become an encroacher on the liberality of a heart which overflows to him with gratitude for the beneficial effects of his knowledge.'—'Signor Urbino,' he returned, 'you speak with a most commendable moderation, commensurate with the other great and good qualities of your head and heart; but if a grateful soul which can afford richly wishes to reward liberally, your hesitation to accept such an offer is but a voluntary undervaluing of your own talents;' and as he spoke he pressed towards me the purses containing the two thousand pieces of gold. But there appeared a something so altogether incomprehensible and extraordinary in the transaction in which I had blindly and involuntarily become a party, that I declined all remuneration till I had seen my patient, and proved whether my skill were effective in producing the desired relief.

"Finding me resolute, he rose, and requested me to follow him. He opened the door from which he had first appeared to me, and we entered a chamber dimly lighted by two wax tapers, which burned on a table at the foot of a richly-ornamented bed.

"He drew aside the curtains, and I could perceive a human form reposing in the bed, whose features were concealed by a thin veil spread over the countenance.—'This is your patient,' he said; 'we may speak aloud, for I have already administered to her a sleeping draught, which precludes all apprehension of her waking;' and as he spoke he drew from beneath the clothes with which the bed was covered a female arm of exquisite delicacy, which was uncovered nearly to the shoulder.

"I was advancing to take her hand, when the stranger withdrew it from me, and said—'Permit me a few words. I have in this case been myself the physician, and decreed for my patient a prescription, which I only require of you to administer; a single touch of your lancet upon any one of these,' he added, pointing as he spoke to the veins of her arm, is all I require of you.'—'But I must first make myself acquainted,' I answered, 'whether the malady under which she is labouring requires the loss of blood.'—'Did I not tell you,' he said, pressing my hand significantly as he spoke, 'that I wished her to obtain positive relief? and what relief,' he whispered, after a moment's pause, 'can be so positive as that of the grave, especially when we pass to the change through the oblivion of sleep?'

"His views were no longer hidden to me; I saw the horrid motive for which I had been trepanned into his society—the cruel object for which he had offered to prostitute his gold; my eyes swam, my tongue faltered, my limbs trembled—'Murder! commit murder!' I pronounced in scarcely-articulate accents, and sunk half-fainting upon a chair, near to which I had been standing.

CHAPTER X

Expectation stood in horror.
MILTON.

"AFTER a few minutes," continued Urbino, "I recovered sufficiently from the horror and astonishment with which the stranger's disclosure of his criminal purpose had affected me, to be able to pronounce—'Signor, your words and intentions bear a strange contradiction to each other; the breath is scarcely cold with which you were pleased to extol the honour which, you said, you were acquainted was the inhabitant of my heart, and you now endeavour to tempt me to the performance of an act from which a hired bravo would recoil. Your praise was therefore either mockery, or from a false habit of judging; from having accustomed yourself to consider the servility with which those whom you select as the instruments of your inclinations obey your desires to be honour, you have dared to abuse my feelings, by ranking me in a class of beings alike unworthy of existence and the name of humanity.'—'I entreat you,' replied the stranger, 'to be calm and hear me.'—'To be calm,' I echoed, 'and listen to your request that I should become a murderer! I know not what you are, signor, nor do I care who you are—I feel myself at least the superior man. I am within your mansion, surrounded by your minions; I scorn yourself and your offer. Disappointment of your views may perhaps render the extinction of one life as grateful to your feelings as that of another; if so, the eye of Providence watches over me, as it appears that it has hitherto done over the unhappy victim of your displeasure contained in that bed, by having led you to make choice of me as the agent of your sinful purpose.'—'Hear me! I entreat you, hear me, signor di Cavetti!' exclaimed the stranger. 'Can you possibly imagine that I would commit an injury against you, when I have already so powerfully displayed to you my inclination to serve you?'—'That was when you hoped to gain my consent to the execution of your nefarious desires,' I answered. 'But let me solemnly assure you that I would think lightly of perishing myself, to becoming the instrument of a fellow-being's annihilation.'—'You are warm beyond discretion, signor Urbino,' rejoined the stranger, a degree of mingled irritation and displeasure becoming, for the first time, apparent in his accents; 'you know not the necessity, the justice, which may exist for the act at which I have hinted.'—'If she is criminal, expose her to the retribution of the law,' I answered.—'Impossible! impossible!' he exclaimed; 'such an exposure would carry in its train a series of misery and disgrace attaching equally to the innocent and the guilty. Had not inviolable silence been required in the disposal of her fate, where had been the necessity of conducting you hither with the secrecy which has marked this night's transaction? whence the unbounded offer of reward by which your services were sought to be repaid? The case is unparalleled, unequalled; it must not—cannot be divulged.'

"He paused, apparently in the greatest agony of mind, and I availed myself of his silence to say—'Signor, there is only one condition upon which I can listen to you for a moment longer—that of my perceiving any probability of my persuasions and counsel being able to convert you from your guilty purpose; but if you declare that your heart is steeled against all interposition between yourself and your crime, I demand immediate enlargement from my present captivity.'

"After a moment's hesitation, he requested me to retire with him to the apartment which we had just quitted. I complied; and having entered it, he locked the door of the chamber which contained the unhappy female. He took out the key. I expected him now to speak, but he began to traverse the apartment with hasty strides, as it appeared, wrapped in reflective silence.

"In a tone of greater decision than I had yet spoken, I repeated my demand of enlargement; and as I spoke I advanced towards the door by which I had been admitted. My companion crossed upon me, and endeavoured to take my hand in his; I indignantly withdrew it, and hastily placing himself between me and the door towards which I was advancing, in accents of the wildest agitation he offered to double the five thousand pieces of gold which he had before offered me.—'You add insult to crime,' I exclaimed, 'and, whatever your rank in life may be, display yourself equally unworthy the name of gentleman as that of man, when you would thus rudely and unwarrantably force an innocent person into becoming a sharer of your atrocities.'—'You know not,' he ejaculated, 'the misery of my mind;' and accompanying his words by casting himself upon his knees before me, that meanness which is ever a concomitant principle in the heart of a villain, now displayed itself in the incoherent ravings and entreaties which he uttered, in the hope of ultimately gaining me over to his suit.—I firmly replied, that I was resolved not to speak again till my enlargement was granted me.

"Finding me unshaken by his words, and resolute in my own determination, wildly exclaiming a request that I would consider of his proposals for one hour, and at the expiration of that time my freedom should be no longer denied me, he darted out of the apartment, and locked upon me the door.

"Conscious that I could gain egress from the house only by his commands to that effect, I endeavoured to compose my mind for meeting any event which might arise out of the night's mysterious occurrence.

"The minutes crept on, and an uninterrupted silence prevailed. I examined the apartment I was in, in order to ascertain whether I had any recollection of having seen it before, as my profession had led me to most of the principal houses in Venice; but I felt convinced that I beheld it for the first time. The room was handsomely, but plainly, furnished, and there were in it neither paintings, busts, nor any ornaments by which it could at a future period have been identified.

"At the expiration of a precise hour, as my watch informed me, the stranger returned. Few words served to convince him that my opinion had undergone no change; and with the certain overthrow of his hopes, at least as far as my adjunction in his plan was intended to have forwarded them, he poured forth the torrent of his displeasure in the bitterest threats and upbraidings. The exact words of which he made use I cannot, I believe, just now repeat, but the sum of what he uttered was to this effect:—That I was ignorant of his high rank and consequence, more especially of his influence in the state of Venice, arising from a public authority with which he was vested: that what I had seen of him must have convinced me that he was capable of any action which promoted his advantage or favoured his inclinations: that having been admitted to his confidence, as I had been that night, and having refused to pursue the measures which would for ever have bound him my friend, he did not attempt to conceal the hatred which my refusal had excited for me in his heart: that the feelings to which my obstinacy, as he termed it, had given rise, had once nearly determined him to prevent the possibility of my repeating the facts of which I had been witness; but that, on one condition, he had resolved that we should part as we had met. 'In the course of a few minutes,' he proceeded to say, 'those who conveyed you hither shall reconduct you to the spot from whence you were brought; and, if you value the safety of yourself and your family, ere the sun be three hours high, quit Venice for ever; retire to any residence you please, at the distance of not less than fifty leagues from this city, and your days shall pass uninterrupted by myself or my agents; but if you persist in still remaining in Venice, where accident or design, slender as is the possibility, may lead you to a knowledge of the rank or name of him before whom you are standing, I swear by every power capable of showering good on man, or hurling down upon him condemnation, that your hardiness will draw the poniard of revenge either against your own breast, or that of one whom you perhaps more value than yourself. Signor Urbino, a native as you are of this country, you must be well acquainted with the tempers and usages of its inhabitants; I need not explain to you how quick their sense of vengeance, nor how readily the assassin flies to execute the purpose which is rewarded by the gold of his employer.'

"With an oath of the most dreadful nature, and in a tone of voice the most horrid and emphatic, he repeated his determination; and believing, doubtless from my silence, that he had impressed upon my mind his denunciation and his resolution not to waver from his point, he introduced his agents into the apartment. My hands were again seized, the bandage was placed before my eyes, and I was led back to the gondola in the same manner in which I had been conducted from it. At the head of the last flight of steps leading from the mansion to the water's edge, a momentary interruption to the rapid pace at which they had before been moving was made by my guides, and the voice of the stranger, close by my side, solemnly pronounced—'Remember my terms—your fate is in your own hands; remember my oath.' The voice ceased, and I was hurried on board."

For the first time since the commencement of his narrative, Di Borges now interrupted Di Cavetti—"The sequel of your tale is evident," he said; "and truly happy am I, my friend," he added, "that you were sufficiently temperate in your proceedings to pursue the advice which was given you, although it came from the lips of one whom circumstances had made your enemy. I have lived nearly the whole of my life in the country, where atrocities of every description are rarer than in crowded cities; but I am no stranger to the spirit of vengeance which some of my countrymen possess, or the ready means which are to be found for its gratification, where the purse is able to lend assistance to the inclinations of the heart: and though the compulsion under which you have suffered is doubtless in the highest degree an infringement on the rules of justice, still, having been involved in the strange circumstances, into a knowledge of which you were blindly led, I think that, upon the whole, you may congratulate yourself that no consequence of a more serious nature was the result of the mysterious occurrence."

"You are well acquainted," replied Urbino, "that without the assistance of my profession, my fortune is sufficient to procure me not only the comforts, but the luxuries of life; and thus circumstanced, I considered that it would be madness in me wantonly to expose the safety of my child and myself to the threats of an exasperated and disappointed villain."

"What appears to me the most extraordinary circumstance in the whole affair," returned Di Borges, "is, that a man of diabolical principles, such as your unknown tempter evidently must have been, should have sought you as an assistant in his plan—that he should have hesitated to have executed the deed of death with his own hand, or at least by that of one of his agents. Why admit a stranger thus obscurely to his confidence, in a point where there appears no material cause for his requiring an additional participator in his actions?"

"I have often dwelt on the same consideration," returned Urbino, "but without having been able to produce any elucidation or satisfaction from my own reflections."

"You can have no idea who the stranger was, I imagine," said Sancho.

"I cannot form the most remote conjecture," answered Di Cavetti, "and consequently his motive for desiring the death of the female whom I beheld must be equally a secret to me."

"You have fulfilled his terms," said Di Borges; "your residence is situate at the distance of two leagues more than the number to which you were restricted from the city of Venice."

He paused a few moments, then added—"No, signor, I cannot suppose that the events which have recently occurred at the Castello della Torvida have any relation with either the persons or facts contained in the recital which you have just given me."

"Your opinion upon this point will gain strength, then, from a circumstance with which I have still to acquaint you," resumed Di Cavetti. "On the first morning after that on which I quitted Venice, at the moment I was descending from my chamber in the posthouse where we had lodged, I heard myself asked for by name, by a voice on the outside of the door which opened upon the road, and on stepping forward to answer the inquiry, received from a horseman, who was muffled in a cloak, and the verge of his hat drawn down upon his face, a letter, which the instant he had put into my hand, he rode off at full speed. You may guess my impatience to read the contents. The words were these—*'Proceed as you have done, and you have nothing to fear. I am not the enemy of those who forbear to injure me.'* The intelligence was certainly satisfactory to my mind; but it proved that my proceedings had been watched, and prompted me to use every precaution in my future conduct, as spies, of whom I was unconscious, might at any hour be observers of my actions and my words."

"The character which your unknown villain gives of his principles, if so they may be called, is not an uncommon one, as the biographers of many dazzling heroes have shewn us," returned Di Borges; "but what is his real nature, is of little importance to you, so that you escape suffering from the evil propensities of his heart." Again he paused, then resumed—"Yes truly, as you say, the letter which you mention adds great force to my argument, that he is not the interrupter of the tranquillity of the Castello."

"But to what cause then can be attributed the extraordinary events which I have witnessed within its walls?" exclaimed

Urbino; "for to mortal means I think it scarcely possible to impute them."

"And you will find it very difficult, I assure you, to gain me a convert to a belief in supernatural agency," replied Sancho di Borges; "nothing but experience can convince the mind how strongly certain events in life, which the book of time can alone develop, have strength to impress us with an opinion of the intervention of powers more than mortal."

"But," asked Urbino, "how are we to proceed in regard to the Castello? for it is not my wish to take my children back to it for the present, though I am resolved to leave no experiment untried myself for developing the mystery in which it is involved."

"I had already resolved in my own mind," rejoined Di Borges, "that your daughter and Paulina should not return thither, till it can be done with more satisfaction to all parties. My proposition is, that a constant watch be kept in the Castello by day and by night, and if those on duty vigilantly perform their task, the progress of time must either produce us some elucidation, or success in driving our troublesome assailant from his haunt; and in order to guard against all neglect, either you or myself, or both of us, will constantly pass the night there, as shall Terence and two of my stoutest servants; and when the ghost, whoever he is, finds that we are well armed into the bargain, depend upon it that we shall have little to fear from his attacks. What do you think of my plan?"

"It is not only a rational one," replied Di Cavetti, "but the only one which I think can be adopted in the present case."

Their conversation was now changed for action, and they proceeded to make preparations for both passing that night at the Castello.

When Valeria and Paulina were informed of their arrangements, the latter, as usual, declared herself quite a heroine in the cause, and averred that she had not the slightest fear of returning to her old apartments; whilst Valeria pressed a request to the same effect with so much earnestness, as in some degree to excite the surprise of her father, till, with a stifled tear, she declared that she could not bear the idea of his being in danger whilst she was at a distance from him.

The worthy farmer applauded her filial affection, but at the same time pointed out to her the propriety of her remaining at his house; and her father earnestly expressing his own wishes to the same effect, her entreaties were at length overruled. Accordingly, about the hour of sunset, Urbino, accompanied by his friend Sancho and two of his men-servants, proceeded to the Castello, on arriving at which they found that the hours had passed undisturbed by Terence and Jeronymo.

During the day, Valeria had believed that she had perceived in a lad, who was one of the servants of Sancho's farm, an anxiety to attract her attention, and, as it appeared, to address her; and in the present disturbed state of her mind, catching eagerly at every spark of hope which seemed to promise any elucidation of those undefinable circumstances by which she was surrounded, her father and the farmer were no sooner departed, than she contrived to throw herself in the way of the youth who had excited her suspicion.

Looking eagerly around to assure himself that they were unobserved, he darted hastily towards her, and pulling a paper from his breast as he spoke, said—"There is a letter, signora, which a young signor gave me a couple of ducats to deliver to you, and he charged me, with the strictest injunctions, not to make any individual acquainted with the circumstance, and I have obeyed his commands."

"Where did you see him?" impatiently asked Valeria.

"On the road, signora, at the distance of about a quarter of a league from this house," replied the lad, and immediately vanished at the sound of an approaching footstep.

The superscription was, "To the signora Valeria di Cavetti," and the handwriting was the same as that of the note which she had discovered in the drawer of her inkstand.

Retiring to the privacy of her chamber, she found her epistle to contain the following words:—

"MY ADORED VALERIA,

"Too long have I been to you an enigma; but the time is come for me to unveil the mystery in which I have been clouded, and to unfold to you myself as I really am; but this explanation can proceed only from my lips; it can neither be communicated by the pen, nor entrusted to the confidential ear of an intervening friend; I therefore entreat my beloved Valeria to grant me an interview, the last which we shall perhaps ever be fated to enjoy on earth; yet without which the heart of Valeria must continue to sicken in doubt—the soul of Julio to linger on a rack of torture. Guide then your conduct by the following instructions:—On the first opportunity which occurs to you of wandering abroad unattended, visit the hut of the dumb recluse by the side of the brook; he will bring you to Julio: meanwhile guard, with the utmost secrecy, the avowal which this paper contains; its promulgation were perdition to one, if not to both of us: above all, arm your heart for a disclosure, which it may require extraordinary fortitude in you to bear, of which it will be agony to me to impart to you the knowledge. Once more, observe my warning long since conveyed to you—*constancy and secrecy*—farewell! with every fervent wish that love and adoration can devise, I implore you to seize the first happy moment for appearing before your devoted

"JULIO."

What conclusion was it possible that she could draw from what she had read? Every line contained an intricacy inscrutable. From what cause could he portend that the interview which he solicited might probably be their last?—What could be the confession which he had directed her to fortify her mind to hear? She recollected the miniature portrait—a portrait which he had acknowledged represented one whom he had once adored, nay tenderly loved and pitied. "Her story" were the words which he had been uttering, when their conversation was interrupted by the confusion which had taken place in the ball-room. Might it not be possible that the story of this female was the important communication which he was now desirous of making to her, to receive which he warned her to prepare her strength of mind; and, still more dreadful possibility, might not that portrait represent his wife—her beloved Julio prove a married man? The bare supposition was agonizing beyond endurance, and (for we always endeavour to persuade ourselves that our real opinions accord with our wishes) she struggled to believe that the portrait which Julio had worn had rather been, as Paulina had surmised, the image of one who had repulsed his advances towards her heart, than the counterfeit resemblance of one who had interchanged her vows with his.

The subject which occupied her thoughts drove off the attacks of sleep; her night was restless, and her anxiety to visit the cell of the recluse became so uncontrollable, that she resolved at all hazards to repair to the hut by the side of the brook, though infinitely perplexed what apology to adduce for absenting herself for so long a period of time from the society of her friends.

The night passed away undisturbed at the Castello della Torvida; and the arrangements making at the breakfast-table by her companions, conveyed an expectation to the heart of Valeria, that an opportunity would be given her for visiting the cell of the dumb recluse. Urbino, it was agreed, was to ride with Di

Borges to inspect a vineyard which he rented at some distance from his farm, and Paulina, attended by Francisca, who was not afraid to approach the Castello by day, so she were not compelled to enter within its walls, had resolved to visit her flower-garden.

Our readers may perhaps imagine that she had a concealed reason for selecting Francisca as her companion; we shall not however be so uncharitable to her feelings as positively to satisfy them on this head, but merely to state, that the two parties having set out on their respective expeditions, Valeria easily formed an excuse for leaving Averilla, and began to trace her steps towards the spot which she longed, yet dreaded to approach.

The hut of the dumb recluse was situate at a short distance from the high road communicating with the posthouse and the village of Malina; at its foot ran a gliding brook, which supplied the inhabitant of the solitary abode with water, and upon a declivity at its back rose a clustering grove, which afforded shelter equally from the wintry gale, and the scorching rays of a summer sun.

Arrived within a short distance of the rustic dwelling, Valeria cast her eyes around, and perceiving no observers, she continued courageously to advance. The wicket door of the hut was closed; with a palpitating heart she tapped upon it with her knuckles; in a few seconds it was opened, and the dumb recluse appearing within, waved to her to enter. She complied with the signal; the door was again instantly closed, and the recluse throwing back the cowl which had hitherto concealed his countenance, presented to her the person of Julio!

Although half prepared for the elucidation which she had received, a smothered ejaculation of surprise burst from her lips.

Julio caught her hand in his—"In what words, in what language," he exclaimed, "shall I attempt to apologize for a conduct which cannot but appear to you to be ruled by the incoherency of madness? Can you, will you, forgive me?"

The countenance of Valeria plainly bespoke that astonishment at that moment superseded every other feeling in her heart.

"Let me endeavour to compose myself," he continued, "and to observe towards the mistress of my soul that respect and humility which are due from me to her."

He rose, and leading Valeria to a seat, placed himself by her side.—"I need not inquire," he resumed, "whether you received my letter; your presence is my answer. Oh, Valeria! have you not blamed, condemned, almost resolved to renounce all future intercourse with a being who appeared to neglect the treasure he had won, as I have done?"

"It is not my nature to condemn unheard," replied Valeria; "but I must confess that your conduct has strongly excited my surprise; the silence which you observed towards me, after our last meeting, whilst I remained in Venice, and the extraordinary notices which I have received from your own hand, of your being near me, during my residence in this neighbourhood——" She paused; the expression of her features distinctly revealing the anxiety of mind with which these circumstances had affected her.

"Oh, Valeria, beloved mistress of my soul!" exclaimed Julio, "I am a wretch, fated to involve in misery the transcendent being whom I best love. Pardon me," he added, after a momentary pause; "this is an hour at which our inmost thoughts must be revealed to each other without disguise."

"Would they had been so sooner," answered Valeria, "since the necessity of their becoming so now, seems to labour in a cloud which you appear apprehensive of bursting."

"Valeria," emphatically pronounced Julio, "the last time we met, an hour you cannot have forgotten, at the moment I declared to you my devotion, my idolatry to the fascination of your image and your mind, I pledged a vow to Heaven, that no one but yourself ever should possess my heart; I have maintained, and ever will preserve my oath!" He gazed upon her for some moments in silence, with an expression of countenance which conveyed to Valeria a sense of the tenderest affection, embittered by some goading reflection. She did not reply, and he spoke thus—"Arbitress of my fate, too lovely and too excellent Valeria, I am now about to propose to you a question, your resolution of which will either gild with the happy beams of contentment and serenity my future days, or plunge me, abandoned, lost, and hopeless, into a gulf of misery and despair."

"Oh, be explicit, I beseech you," answered Valeria; "your looks and words alarm me. If there is any service, as you seem to hint there is, that I can render you, I think you need not apprehend I should deny it to you."

"I think, when I behold you here," returned Julio, "that my doubts are replied to you as I could wish they should be; but the ardency of love proves itself in the disbelief of its own happiness, and upon this axiom I can alone excuse myself to you for those fears which almost preponderate against the happiness I still believe myself possessed of. Speak then, beloved Valeria! let your lips seal your Julio's doom! dare I hope that you still think of me, as, at our last interview, you blessed me by confessing that you did?"

A few words on the part of Valeria, confirmed to him his expectation that he was still sensibly alive in her affections. He received the avowal with a joy, which although extravagant in expressing his felicity, still appeared to be tinctured with regret.

After a few minutes of silent admiration on the part of Julio, and, as Valeria believed and almost feared, with a tear, against which his soul appeared to struggle, starting into his eye, he said—"My letter informed you that I had a disclosure to make to you, for which I begged you to fortify your mind; but from the moment I had conveyed to you the information that such a necessity existed, I have felt myself unequal to the task. Take, therefore, these papers," he added, placing a small manuscript volume in the hand of Valeria as he spoke; "they contain a narrative of the events of my life down to a certain period." He paused. "When you have perused what is here contained, my lips shall reveal to you the sequel. These papers were originally written with the intention of their evidence vindicating my memory, after my death, from—— but no matter; it is better to be vindicated in heaven than extolled on earth. On earth, it is too frequently an accident that makes or mars the name and fortune of a man; in heaven, the even balance of his actions sways his judge."

There was a solemnity in his air and voice, as he pronounced these words, which astonished Valeria. He perceived what was passing in her mind, and said—"What now appears a mystery in my words, will be explained to you at our next meeting, and I entreat you to let that be as quickly as possible, as it will end all our cares, all our inquietudes, and, I trust, consummate our loves in heavenly pureness."

Before Valeria had time to remark upon the extraordinary tenour of the last sentence which he had uttered, he again besought her to use every expedition in perusing the manuscript, and to return to his hut the moment she had done so.

The interest which she took in his fate, the pitch of anxiety to which his enigmatical conduct had wound her feelings, all rendered her willing to pursue the clue which he had given her for unravelling the mystery, and she promised to comply with his request.

A considerable time elapsed ere they parted; incoherent expressions of affection burst from the breast of Julio, and faltering accents of surprise fell from the lips of Valeria. Every look, every sentence, breathed love and adoration; but they appeared tempered in Julio by a chill of forbearance, which, by the power of sympathy, irresistibly communicated itself to the breast of Valeria.

That Valeria should return soon, was the promise upon which they parted; and Julio, at his separation from her, appeared to regard her rather as a beatified spirit, than as the enchanting mortal whom he had idolized at the carnival of Venice.

"He professes himself the same as when we last met," reflected Valeria; "but his manner is evidently changed; he professes to fear the loss of my affections, and yet he speaks as if he could not long hope to possess them. Is he already a husband, compelled to return to that circle of claims upon his heart, from which truancy of disposition has for a while exiled them? or has a second love annihilated the vows by which he bound himself to me?"

Finally she resolved to form no opinion, till she had perused the manuscript which he had placed in her hands.

With a distracted mind she retraced her steps towards the farmhouse, and was so fortunate as to reach it before the return of either her father and Sancho, or Paulina and her humble attendant.

END OF VOLUME ONE

CHAPTER I

Then, oh, you blessed ministers above!
Keep me in patience; and, in ripened time,
Unfold the evil which is here wrapt up
In countenance.

SHAKESPEARE.

IN the afternoon, excusing herself for retiring to her apartment upon the plea of a headache and slight indisposition, Valeria hastened to peruse the manuscript which she had received from Julio, and found the contents to be as follows:—

"The first circumstance of my life of which I have any recollection, is that of having been constantly attended by an aged female, of the middle rank of life, from whose side it was with the greatest difficulty that any other person could for a moment tempt me.

"We lived in a neat little dwelling, in the front of which lay a garden, where most of my infantine hours not devoted to sleep were passed, and where my female friend constantly exerted herself, with the assiduity of a parent, to entertain and to delight me.

"Oh, thrice-happy days of childhood! how unconscious are we whilst in their enjoyment, that every step by which we advance towards maturity, weakens the charm of life, and that in our progress towards the perspective of existence, new features are momentarily arising to our view to disfigure the scene of joy!

"The person who appeared most anxious to share my attention with my nurse Rinalda, was a man about the midway of life, of a pleasing and benignant countenance, in the habit of a friar; his garb was for a considerable time an obstacle to my giving myself willingly into his arms, but gradually his caresses and his presents dissipated my fears, and I would even express regret when he quitted our abode, at which he was the only frequent visitor whom I observed Rinalda to possess.

"In reading, and other minor rudiments of learning, my nurse instructed me, and the padre Antonio, which was the name of the monk of whom I have already spoken, occasionally questioned me upon my knowledge, and investigated my progress.

"When I had nearly attained my seventh year, I experienced the first anxiety of mind under which I had yet laboured, in being taken from Rinalda, and placed in a seminary, at the distance of many leagues from the only habitation in which I was conscious of ever having existed. I parted from her with tears; and the novel scenes to which I was now introduced, though they supplied new ideas to my imagination, did not obliterate the affection I bore my nurse.

"My residence among my fellow-beings opened my mind, young as I was, to a train of reflections, by which I had never before been affected. As my schoolfellows spoke of their relations, especially of their parents, I began to wonder who were mine, and why I had never beheld them; and this idea having entered my breast, I awaited with incredible impatience the arrival of Antonio, who occasionally made a journey to visit me, that I might propose to him those questions to which my own mind could furnish me with no reply.

"In answer to my inquiries, the padre said—'My dear Julio, you are as yet too young to be entrusted with your own story; meanwhile rely upon this, that in me you possess a friend, a protector, and a parent united; and should it be the will of Heaven to snatch me from you, let it be your satisfaction that you are amply provided with the means of procuring yourself a safe and happy passage through life.' More he at that period refused to communicate.

"Time passed on unchequered, except by a change of studies, and enlivened by youthful pastimes and exercises, till I had completed my fifteenth year, when I received a letter from my friend Antonio, informing me that I might expect to see him in the course of a few days, as it was his intention to remove me from my present abode to a situation nearer his own person. I received the information with pleasure, for the inexperienced mind is always eager for change; and at the appointed time Antonio arrived.

"After bidding farewell to my companions, and casting a last look at the scene of my boyish labours and delights, I entered a carriage, in which the padre had already taken his seat. We had not been many minutes on our journey, ere my companion addressed me, by saying—'We are proceeding, Julio, towards the city of Padua, in which I reside. You have seen that city, though you have doubtless forgotten that you ever did so. It was within half a league of its walls that your infant years were passed with your nurse Rinalda.'

"At the memory of Rinalda a tear started into my eye, for that amiable female had long since paid the debt of nature.

'The time is come,' Antonio, after a pause, proceeded to say, 'at which I am prepared to give you that information respecting yourself; which I at a past period refused you. But before I unfold to you your own little history, it is necessary that I should communicate a few words to you concerning myself.

'An only brother and myself were the sole descendants from a respectable line of ancestors, from whom we each inherited an ample fortune. My inclinations from early youth led to the service of the church; I accordingly entered the holy profession, and became the private priest and confessor of a family of distinction.

'My brother was considerably younger than myself; and about the time that he arrived at the age of manhood, the head of the family in which I had placed myself expiring, and the establishment in which I had lived breaking up, I fixed my residence in a monastery in the city of Padua where I could

enjoy religious solitude at my pleasure, without being compelled to pronounce a vow of seclusion from the world.

'My brother, whose passions were of the most fervid nature,
had been wounded, past all cure, by the fascinating smiles of a
rustic maid, greatly his inferior in rank and birth; but love, that
greatest leveller of distinctions, rendered him regardless of
every feeling but that of calling her his own; they were consequently married; and as affection, carried to the pitch of idolatry, is never so perfectly blest as in retirement from the world,
they fixed their residence in the romantic little dwelling where
your days of childhood were passed, under the inspecting eye of
the worthy Rinalda.

'In the due course of time the wife of my brother became
pregnant; but such is the uncertainty of human affairs, that the
very cause from which he flattered himself with an amplification of his joys, proved a source of misery fatal to his peace and
his existence. The hour which made him a father bereaved him
of his adored wife; and the infant pledge of her affection, which
she had bestowed on him, and in which, as his only solace for
her loss, he had hoped to behold her image revived, quickly
followed its parent to an untimely grave. To describe the state
of my brother's mind is impossible; it can only be estimated by
those who are capable of entering into the feelings which such
a privation is calculated to produce in the heart of love and
sensibility.

'At this melancholy juncture you were first introduced to
my knowledge. One morning about this time, as I was descending the stairs leading from my cell in the monastery in which I
had fixed my abode, to the lower parts of the building, I was
met by an inferior member of the community, who informed
me that the abbate requested to see me immediately in his own
apartment. With this superior I had, for a considerable time,
been upon terms of the greatest intimacy, and had frequently

been called upon by him for my advice in matters where he did not feel confident of his own opinion.

'On entering his presence, I found him steadfastly regarding an infant, which lay upon a table before him, nestled in various folds of linen, within a small wicker pannier, which, he informed me, had that morning been found in the porch of the monastery, with a direction attached to it, bearing his name. The infant was yourself.

'Within the basket was a letter likewise, superscribed to the superior of the house. He tore it open, and read aloud these words:—

"Holy father, the motive by which the wretched parent who now addresses to you these lines is actuated, in beseeching your protection for that child of whom he is himself compelled to abandon the charge, arises not so much out of the knowledge that your exalted situation enables you to bestow active compassion on those who seek your benevolence, as from a conviction that the nobler qualities of the heart are in yours pre-eminent. Bestow, therefore, oh holy father! a portion of your humanity on an unfortunate being, who will never know the blessing of a parent's hand to guide his faltering steps through the labyrinths of vice and misery, in which his unfriended wanderings through life could not fail to entangle him. He is neither the outcast of shame, nor the offspring of beggary, though waywardly born to a life of sorrow and mystery. Trusting then the fate of my boy to Heaven, and to you, prime agent of its will on earth, I have only one admonition to give, and one other petition to urge. The first, that, should he reach the age of manhood, he may be cautioned not to enter the state of wedlock without a thorough knowledge of her with whom he may be desirous of forming that bond of union, as he has a sister in existence, whom it is more than probable that he will never know by that name. The second, that the brooch, which will be found in the folds of the linen in which he is now wrapped, may, on his attaining the years of adolescence, be constantly worn in his bosom.

"I have done. May the angels of heaven shower down blessings on you and on him, commensurate with the prayers offered up for your happiness by the heartbroken sufferer who now bids you farewell forever!"

'Before I proceed in my narrative,' said Antonio, 'let us obey the request made of us relative to the brooch.'

"He took a small case out of his pocket as he spoke, and drew from it the trinket in question. It was a remarkably beautiful cameo; in shape an octagon; upon which was represented the catastrophe of the fatal dart, from the fable of Cephalus and Procris, in the Metamorphoses of Ovid. It was set in a rim of gold, of exquisite and remarkable workmanship; and at each angle of the cameo was introduced a ruby.

"Having granted me permission to examine it, and having placed it in the neck of my shirt, Antonio was resuming his relation—'Pardon me,' I cried, 'for interrupting you, but I cannot forbear to impart to you a circumstance of which I never thought with any degree of interest till this moment.

'About eight or nine months ago, a company of pilgrims, on their way to Loretto, attended by their minstrels, requested a night's lodging at the seminary from which you have this day brought me. It was granted; and after they had partaken of a repast provided for them, they came out upon the lawn, where my fellow-students and myself were engaged in various exercises, in which we usually closed the day.

'One of these pilgrims, who was a man tall of stature, with a profusion of black hair, and eyes of a most penetrating expression, I observed to stand several different times gazing upon me, as if my features brought to his mind some recollection which gave him pleasure; and when the hour for retiring to rest came, and we were all entering the house together, the same pilgrim, moving along by my side, said—'Are you not cold with your neck thus exposed to the evening air?'—'Not in the least,' I replied.—'But you should protect yourself against the damps of night,' he returned; and as he did so, he closed the neck of my shirt with his hand.

'The circumstance then passed by me without reflection; but it now appears to me, from the earnestness with which I observed him to fix his eyes on my countenance, that he believed himself to have some acquaintance with my person, and that he closed the neck of my shirt as a pretext for investigating whether the trinket which you have just put into my possession were worn by me.'

"Antonio coincided with me in my supposition, but he was not more able than myself to decide how far our opinion might be erroneous or correct.

"The padre continued his narrative thus—'The superior of the monastery was a man to whose feelings an appeal was seldom made in vain. Having perused the letter, he said—"Whoever the parents of this child, or whatever may be their reasons for abandoning their offspring to the mercy of strangers, the innocent babe becomes, from the very desertion of its natural protectors, a greater object of compassion." I applauded his benevolent sentiments, which were congenial with my own, and inquired of him in what manner he judged it best to dispose of you?

"I am considerably at a loss how to act for the best," he replied, "and wish your advice to that effect."

'At this instant you uttered a faint cry.—"Our decision," I said, "must be speedily formed, for the unfortunate object of our compassion, whose extreme youth must unqualify it to endure a long privation of its little comforts, may perish from being unattended by a female acquainted how to administer to its necessities."—"But where is such an one to be found?" returned the abbate.—"Let some person be sought in the neighbourhood, who will take charge of it for a couple of hours," I replied, "and

I will go immediately to my brother's villa, and in the course of the time I have mentioned, will return with the nurse who was provided to take the care of his deceased infant, and who is still residing in his house."

'The superior highly approved my plan, and I set out in quest of Rinalda. On arriving at my brother's house, and communicating to him the occasion of my visit, Rinalda was immediately admitted to our confidence, and requested to undertake the charge. She readily complied with my wish, and I directed her to proceed to the monastery without delay, whither I promised, in a short time, to follow her.

'On being left alone with my brother, I recounted to him the particulars of your extraordinary fate, and concluded by advising him to suffer you to be brought home to his own house—"This child," I said, "may, in the progress of time, grow up to repair to you the loss of him whom you so severely lament."—"Alas!" he replied, "can I ever believe a stranger's infant to be my own Julio, the offspring of her on whom alone my soul doted?"—"You cannot," I returned, "indeed be supposed to believe him your own in birth, but you may render him your own in affection. If you extend tenderness towards his forlorn state, your kindness will naturally engender for you gratitude in his heart; and his presence may keep alive in you feelings, to which a silent absorption in grief would but deaden your capacities. The mind of man must have something to rest upon, something to draw forth its sympathy, its energies; if not a human being, an animal, a plant, a book, there must be some object to which it can turn from the inward contemplation of itself. Be guided by the advice of a brother who tenderly loves you, and earnestly desires your happiness; make the experiment of devoting your cares to the little foundling of whom I have spoken, and prove whether your exertions will not be rewarded by the eventual restoration of tranquillity to your mind."

'My brother listened to me attentively; and when I had concluded, he assented to my proposal; but it was an affirmative which appeared rather a sufferance of what it acquiesced in, than a warm accordance from the heart. You consequently became a member of his family; Rinalda was retained to attend upon you; and as we were unacquainted what your real name was, if one had yet been given to you, you were baptized by that of Julio, which had been the one borne by the deceased infant of my brother.

'As time moved on, I perceived with pleasure that my brother's attentions were insensibly drawn towards you; and I am of opinion that you would gradually have succeeded in replacing to him the loss of his infant, could he have forgotten the mother who had given that infant birth; but a settled melancholy had taken possession of his features and his mind; his existence withered under its influence; and you had for little more than one year enjoyed his protection, when he sunk to the tomb, the victim of his feelings.

'As my brother and myself were without relatives, at his decease I anticipated to find that he had placed you above dependence on the world; but my expectations were most agreeably exceeded, when, on examining his papers, which were indivisibly consigned to my care and execution, I found that, with the exception of a handsome legacy to myself, and an annuity for life to Rinalda, on condition that she should never quit you while you desired her to remain with you, he had constituted you his sole heir.

'From that period little more concerning yourself remains to be said, but that no elucidation of your history had taken place; and, for myself, I have nothing to add, but that I shall fix a higher value upon your society, as my esteemed friend, the abbate, to whose care you were originally consigned, has paid the debt of nature; and the formation of new friendships is not congenial to my mind, since I have passed the meridian of life.'

"I must have been deficient in every feeling which marks the distinction between the phlegmatic and the grateful mind, could I have forborne to declare my veneration of that benefactor of my early days, whom I was fated never again to behold, or to express my obligations to him who was at this moment fulfilling to me the promise which he had long since made, of proving himself my friend, my protector, and my parent united.

"On arriving at Padua, I was taken by the padre to the house of an acquaintance, where, after I had passed a few days, I was placed in an academy, conducted by a set of ecclesiastics of superior talents, under whose auspices the sons of the nobility, and of families of public distinction, were completing their education, previously to their entrance upon the busy stage of life.

"During my residence in this seminary, I formed many acquaintance, but few intimacies, and still fewer friends. The enlightened conversation of Antonio had a greater charm for me than that of any of my younger associates; and most of my leisure time was spent in walking with him to the villa, at a short distance from the city, of which I have already spoken, and which had formed a part of his deceased brother's bequest to me.

"Not to dwell upon immaterial circumstances, but to confine myself to those events of moment, for the purpose of detailing which I have committed the narrative of my life to writing—on my quitting the academy in Padua, at which time I was entering into my twenty-first year, my abode was fixed at my favourite villa, for so it was, from a combination of reflections, truly become to me. A moderate establishment, more adapted to the comforts than the splendour of life, was provided for me, and the padre was my daily visitor.

"This was a season of happiness; but the charm was quickly dissolved by that intrusive power which neither obeys the call of mortals, nor withholds his fatal dart in compliance with their prayers. I had been scarcely six months a resident at the villa, when the unrelenting hand of death snatched from me my friend, my protector, my parent.

"The most impressive of his lessons had taught me to consider resignation to the will of a First Cause, as one of the noblest exertions of the human mind. I acknowledged the virtue of his lesson, but felt it insufficient to the task of enabling me to support his loss without displaying my regret at the privation which I had sustained; still his precepts tended to fortify my mind against the indulgence of a grief which I could not utterly vanquish; and I endeavoured to restore peace to my own mind, by reflecting on the beatification with which his immortal being was crowned.

CHAPTER II

The time for tender thoughts and soft endearments
Is fled away and gone; joy has forsaken us,
Our hearts have now another part to play;
They must be steel'd with some uncommon fortitude,
That, fearless, we may tread the paths of horror.

N. ROWE.

"MY amusements were now chiefly concentrated in my library and in my garden; sometimes relieved and varied by the conversation of a few individuals whom Antonio had ranked amongst the number of his friends, and by the exchanging of occasional visits with some young men who had been my fellow-students in the college at Padua.

"One evening, a few months after the death of Antonio, as I was returning homeward from the city, I was accosted by the voice of a female, with the address of—'Happily met, signor Julio!'

"The beams of day were rapidly declining, and the faint crescent of an infant moon, which shone with silvery lustre in the firmament, added but slenderly to the illumination of the scene; I could, however, perceive that the person who had accosted me was in the dress of a woman, and closely veiled; and as I did not immediately reply, she repeated her salute—'Happily met, signor Julio!' and as she spoke for the second time, I remarked that her tones were those of mumbling old age.

'As I have not the pleasure of your acquaintance,' I replied, 'you must inform me wherein that happiness consists.'—'First,' was her answer, 'in my having obtained this encounter with you, signor; and next in what *you* may obtain if you accept an invitation with which I am charged to you.'—'From whom?' I asked.—'Ah,' replied the old woman, 'that is a secret, which only time and perseverance can disclose to you. For the present, let this content you; though I am old myself, my employer is not so; and moreover, she has beauty and wealth for your acceptance, if you choose to become the possessor.'—'Have I ever beheld your mistress?' I asked.—'No, that I can vouch you never have,' returned the old woman; 'but she has seen you, or I had not been here upon the errand which introduces us to each other.'—'Where does she reside, and how am I to know the lady who thus honours me?' I inquired.—'There are a great many words to that bargain, signor,' was the reply; 'access to the lady is not so easy as you may imagine. All that is required of you just now is to say, whether at a future time you will accept her invitation to visit her?'

"I did not immediately reply, for being a novice in the practice of gallantry, I felt at a loss how it became me to answer this enigmatical ambassadress; and as I did not speak, she continued—'What, hesitate to visit a lady who condescends to ask your presence as a favour? A young cavalier, and a handsome cavalier, and a single cavalier, and not grasp at an offered courtesy like this? Well-a-day! well-a-day, signor! it is high time your maiden blushes were put to flight. Excuse my laughing, signor; I'm a merry old woman, and can't help it. Well, then,' she added, laying her hand with a significant pressure on my arm as she spoke, 'I'll say you'll come.'—'But if my conduct should prove you mistaken,' I rejoined.—'I should not be the loser,' she answered. 'Mistaken indeed!' and she twice or thrice repeated the word; 'what is the man afraid of? The lady in question neither inhabits an enchanted castle, nor is protected by a fiery dragon; you'll neither be swallowed up alive by the one, nor be conjured into a marble statue to ornament the other. Only satisfy yourself that I have not deceived you; you'll still be the master of your inclinations; we have no charms about us to force you into love or marriage.'—'But you refuse to tell me where it is that I am expected,' I said.—'Peremptorily,' she answered; 'but that does not prevent my either pointing out the way to you myself, or deputing another person to do so for me. In a few words, signor, you know the knot of cypress-trees, a little to the left of the high road, on this side of the city gates?'—I replied in the affirmative.—'Very well,' rejoined the old woman; 'be there to-morrow evening, about an hour after this time. When a person addresses to you the word "*secrecy*," answer, "*and silence*," and you will be known to be the signor Julio. Do you comprehend me, signor?'—'I do,' was my answer.—'Well then,' returned the old woman, 'all preliminaries are settled; and so, signor, good evening till I have the happiness of seeing you again, and against that time let me advise you to dispel your maiden blushes, and pluck up the heart of a hero for your adventure; though truly it needs little courage to encounter; for I repeat to you, that my mistress has no magical coadjutors but a pair of enchanting eyes. Excuse my laughing, signor; I am a merry old woman, and can't help it. A good-night and pleasant dreams to you, signor!' and with these words she turned her steps towards the city.

"I have already hinted that an adventure of this kind was to me a novelty, and it consequently occupied a deeper share of my reflections than it would have done of those of a man more conversant with the code of gallantry. The old woman had spoken of marriage, and from this I concluded that the affair wore more the appearance of romantic love, than of premeditated intrigue. She had asserted that her mistress was young, handsome, and rich; if, in addition to these qualifications, she proved alike amiable, I considered that a happy chance might be providing for me in the impression which I had made on her heart. Her ambassadress had also implied, that I could but behold her, and still make my inclinations the rule of my conduct. I reflected again and again, and ultimately resolved to accept the invitation which had been given me.

"A few minutes before the appointed hour I was on the spot of assignation. I had not wandered long under the shelter of the thick foliage with which the trees were clothed, when I saw a dusky figure advancing towards me, which, on its nearer approach, I perceived to be a friar, and was turning away from the path in which he was moving, when he quickened his steps; and closely encountering me, he articulately whispered—'*Secrecy.*' Thus called upon, although by far a different object to the one I had expected to meet, notwithstanding the old woman had hinted that she might depute another person to be my guide to my unknown admirer, I instantly replied—'*And silence.*'

"The monk stopped, and said—'You are known to me, signor Julio. It was only in order to grant you proof that I was the person whom you was taught to expect, that I addressed to you the word by which I accosted you.' He paused a moment, then added—'I judge, signor, by finding you here, that you are prepared to visit the lady who has already conveyed to you her wish for your acquaintance?'—I replied—'That I could not but entertain a reciprocal wish to gain a knowledge of one by whom I was so highly flattered, and that I was prepared to attend him.'—'There is one restraint, then, signor,' said the monk, 'to which you must submit in your progress to her abode: you must consent to wear a monastic habit like my own, and to suffer the cowl to be so placed as to prevent your observing whither it is that I conduct you.'—'What should you fear,' I inquired, 'from my becoming acquainted with the spot to which you take me?'—'Pardon me, signor,' replied the friar; 'you cannot be permitted a knowledge of it at present; from me, at all events, you must not obtain that knowledge. I can only obey the commission which is placed in my hands; it then rests with her who requests your presence to make to you any disclosure which she believes that she may with safety repose in your confidence.'—'What can she apprehend from my acquaintance with the spot of her residence?' I asked.—'Can it require to be pointed out to you, signor,' rejoined the monk, 'what danger the reputation of a female incurs from becoming herself the inviter of a stranger's conversation? Lovely as she is, you may not judge her so; engaging as I know her to be, she may strike you in an opposite point of view. If your expectations are disappointed, and your heart remains untouched at your introduction to her, you may vaunt of your conquest, and of your nicer taste, and render her, who has submitted herself to your judgment, from the purity of her affection, a mark of reproach to her own sex, and an object for the ridicule of yours.—No, signor, such a contingency must not be suffered to exist; you must know neither her abode nor her name, unless your heart meets hers upon the mutual terms of love and friendship.'

"I inwardly acknowledged the propriety of his arguments; my character was unknown to him, and therefore I considered him justified in acting upon the secure plan which he was pursuing. 'I approve your cautions,' I answered, 'but with me I assure you they are useless.'—'Excuse me, signor,' he answered, 'but I have only your own words to vouch for their being so.'

"I must, I perceived, either altogether decline the adventure, or prosecute it according to the rules prescribed by my conductor; I accordingly expressed myself willing to be guided by him. He drew me into the thickest shade which the grove afforded, and loosing the band with which his vestments were confined round his waist, and from which his rosary depended, a few moments displayed to me that he was provided with a monastic robe, similar to his own, for my disguise, which he had hitherto worn above the one which formed his own dress.

"Having equipped me in my novel attire, he proceeded to bind down the cowl over my eyes, as he had promised to me that he should do; and whilst thus engaged, he said—'You must not repine, signor, at being for a short time deprived of the use of your eyesight, when you consider that the god of love, whose votary you are at this moment, is condemned to perpetual darkness.'

"The adjustment being made, he placed one of my arms through his, and said—'Now then, come on, signor; a quarter of an hour will bring us to the spot of your destination; walk fearlessly, and depend upon it that I am not your enemy, nor is any evil intended you.'

"My companion having requested me to maintain silence, we moved along at an even pace; and in a short time, from the pavement over which we were passing, I discovered that we had entered the city. At length we stopped. The friar drew forth a key, and unlocked a door; he led me within it; and having done so, he again closed and locked it.

'Whatever sounds you may chance to hear, speak not at present, I conjure you,' said my conductor.

"But we proceeded in silence, till having ascended a considerable flight of steps, the floating notes of music struck my ear; and these appeared mingled with a distant but tumultuous laugh. In a few seconds unbroken silence again prevailed; and having ascended a second staircase, I heard behind me the loud clap of a closing door. The friar disengaged my arm from his, and finally removed the cowl from before my eyes.

"The glare of light to which my eyes opened, rendered me for a while incapable of distinguishing objects. After a time I perceived that I was in an elegant apartment, brilliantly lighted with wax tapers, in massy silver branches; the curtains and sofas by which the room was surrounded were of embroidered silk, and the ceiling and cornices of a light fretwork in white and gold. From marble jars placed on tripod stands, every flower that could regale the sense, or please the admiring eye, sent forth its spicy perfume; and the walls were enriched with paintings of the most exquisite workmanship.

"The friar requested me to be seated, and with a gentle inclination of his head, retired. In the course of a few minutes the door was again opened, and my venerable acquaintance of the preceding evening appeared before me; and closely nipping together the folds of her veil with one hand, and extending the other towards me as a sign of welcome to her presence, she ejaculated—'Well, signor, I give joy that your resolution has stood your friend, and tempted you hither. Well-a-day! what strange things some of you men are! I warrant now you could sooner face the mouth of a cannon than a beautiful signora. Ah, ha! in my days I have seen many a one who, after a short acquaintance with Cupid's calendar, has been loath enough to quit his mistress and face his enemy's cannon. Excuse my laughing, signor; I am an old woman, and can't help it.'

"I was beginning to reply, when I was interrupted by the gentle tinkling of a bell on the outside of the door. At the sound the old woman retreated from my side, and exclaiming—'Now, signor, prepare yourself with your best address, for my lady comes,' she darted out of the room.

"A few seconds only elapsed ere the door was once more thrown open, and three females entered the apartment. The one who appeared evidently the superior advanced towards me, whilst the other two retired to a music-desk, by the side of which stood a harp. The dress of her who approached me, and whom I naturally concluded to be the signora from whom I had received my invitation, was not less elegant than it was simply beautiful; it was composed of a robe of the whitest silk, which fell in playful folds to her feet, and artfully displayed the exquisite symmetry of her limbs beneath; a zone of emeralds bound her waist, and corresponding bracelets encircled her wrists; a diamond comb confined her luxuriant auburn ringlets, and a veil of the thinnest texture was thrown over her head.

"Continuing to advance towards me, with a step of equal grace and dignity, which added fresh charms to the elegance of her form, she invited me to place myself on a sofa, near to which she had found me standing, and after I had done so, she seated herself by my side.—'I know not, signor,' she said, 'in what words to express my gratitude to you for your kindness and condescension, in dedicating a part of your time to an isolated being like myself, when the world, in which you are at liberty to rove freely, must be hourly presenting you with so much more agreeable pursuits.'—'But with none of a more recompensing nature,' I replied, 'than that of believing myself capable of contributing to the happiness of a superior being like yourself.'—'You are doing so at the present moment,' she answered; 'your society gives me happiness, and if you really wish to act towards the promotion of my felicity, as you have just said you do—but you men are all flatterers, and I know not how to believe you—you will very frequently repeat your visit hither.'

"I bowed in reply to her invitation, and she returned me a smile eloquently expressive of thanks and pleasure; for whilst speaking, she had partially removed her veil, and discovered to me enough of her countenance for me to ascertain that it was of extreme loveliness, although she had evidently passed the glowing days of youth. 'Give me your hand along with your promise,' she said. I obeyed, and a gentle pressure of friendship having been reciprocally communicated, she continued—'I believe you, signor, for I have long since predicted that the smile upon your lips was the prototype of a heart incapable of a disobliging action.'—'I understand, signora,' I replied, 'that you have seen me before, but I cannot imagine where.'—'Like all other riddles,' she said, 'this one is very easy of solution, if you only chance to guess aright, and when it is once explained to you, you will only wonder that you did not find it out before.'—'My perceptions,' I replied, 'are very dull; have the goodness to solve it to me?'—'Not now,' she replied.—'Why not now?' I asked.—'What impatient creatures are you men!' she ejaculated. 'How long have I wished for this interview, and been compelled to check my inclinations! I am resolved, therefore, to enjoy the innocent retaliation of keeping you a while in suspense.'—'But how long is my penance to endure?' I exclaimed.—'Till you visit me again,' she replied.—'When shall I be permitted to do so?' I asked.—'Oh, we will speak of that by and by,' she answered. 'To talk of our next meeting appears as if we were this moment going to separate, and I do not intend to part with you for three or four hours at least,' Turning to her companions at the other end of the apartment, she said— 'Come, my dear friends, do me the favour of indulging the signor with one of my favourite strains?' Then addressing me, she added, 'I am certain you love music.'—'Indeed I am passionately fond of it,' I answered.—'Your eyes bespeak you so,' she replied; 'they are the index of a soul attuned to harmony, and——'

"A half-smothered sigh rendered the remaining syllable which she uttered inaudible, and instantly raising her voice to a higher tone than that in which she had pronounced the last sentence, she desired her friends to begin.

The females, who were both young and handsome, but greatly inferior in personal charms to my entertainer, returned her request with smiles of pleasure; and whilst one of them struck the chords of the harp, with a finger of exquisite skill, the other, with a voice of equal sweetness, sung the following

BALLAD.

The snow to the ground was in large flakes descending,
   The hoar-frost was nipping each bud on the spray;
On a wild barren heath I found a poor baby,
   All shiv'ring and crying in tatter'd array;
     Poor little baby boy! ah, well-a-day!

I took the child home, and I warm'd him and drest him;
    He quickly reviv'd, and smil'd me a reward;
Ah, would that some words too the urchin had spoken,
    Had kindly put my silly heart on its guard,
        For the baby was Cupid! sly little Cupid!
           Yes, he was the baby boy! ah, well-a-day!

The winter pass'd off; he talk'd not of departing,
    But still by my side, where I went he would go;
I tried to run from him, but he was too crafty;
    I ask'd him to leave me, he answer'd no, no;
        Sly little baby boy! ah, well-a-day!

To bid me adieu then he crept to my bosom,
    Said 'Press me, dear maid, in my arms, ere we part.'
Suspecting no mischief, I fondly embrac'd him,
    And one of his arrows he left in my heart;
        For the baby was Cupid! sly little Cupid!
           Yes, he was the baby boy! ah, well-a-day!

"When they had concluded their melody, and I had expressed my admiration of their skill, my entertainer said—'You perceive, signor, that though immured in a solitary prison, we have some enjoyment to cheer our hearts.'—'A prison!' I echoed, looking round upon the apartment as I spoke.—'Ah, signor,' she returned, 'volumes could not so eloquently have explained your unacquaintance with the irksomeness of restraint as these two simple words. It is a happiness for you, that you have yet to learn that a few days of privation from those scenes in which it would give us happiness to mix, render it indifferent to the enthralled captive, whether he contemplates the gaudy splendour of a decorated apartment, or the uniform gloom of a dungeon's sable walls. It is not recreation for the eye, but the mind, for which the soul of feeling pants;' and as she uttered these words, she moved a few paces apart from me, struggling, as it appeared, to subdue some unpleasant emotion which she experienced difficulty in repressing.

"During the few moments of silence which succeeded, I was engaged in endeavouring to analyse her character. Had intrigue been the object of her invitation to me, it appeared much more than probable that she would have received me alone; the presence of her friends seemed to vouch for the purity of her intentions; still the expression of her eye, and the accidental confusion of her manner, stood forth as weighty opponents against this opinion, whilst the decided difference of our ages appeared to render it unlikely that she should propose herself to me as a wife. That she should declare herself a prisoner, shut from the world, and debarred the pleasures of society at the very moment when I beheld her in the enjoyment of all the luxuries of life, and mistress, as it appeared, of a sumptuous establishment, was so irreconcilable a contradiction, that it bade defiance even to the powers of surmise. That one of her emissaries had appeared as a monk, was a trifling consideration: the habit might have been assumed, to obviate equally a knowledge of his accustomary garb and his countenance. Returning towards me, with reassumed composure, she said—'As you have promised to visit me frequently, the less formality we practise at our meetings, the greater portion of happiness we may expect to derive from each other's society; I shall therefore only address you by the simple appellation of Julio; have I your permission to use this freedom with you?'—'I believe I should find it very difficult,' I replied, 'to return a negative to any request of yours; much more so to any one which appears to increase our intimacy.'—'You are, I perceive,' she answered, 'what I already told you all men are, a flatterer; but I must allow you the merit of being a pleasing one: well then you shall be my Julio, and I will, if you please, be your Antonia.'

"This arrangement was followed by some playful rejoinders on either side, and having resumed our seats upon the sofa,

Antonia said—'I am aware that all intimacies are considerably strengthened by our acquiring some little insight into the history of those with whom our friendships are formed; and although I am not at this moment at liberty to tell you either who I am, what I am, or where I am, if you think that my tale will not weary you, I will recount to you some of the principal circumstances of my life, which has indeed been an eventful one.'

"Declaring that nothing could give me greater satisfaction than to listen to the detail which she offered, I besought her to begin her relation.

'Julio,' she emphatically pronounced, 'you will learn from my narrative that all my joys and all my griefs have sprung from that fatal passion which ensnares every sex and every age.' She had placed her hand upon my shoulder whilst speaking, and after a short pause she added—'But I am sure that you possess a heart sufficiently compassionate to look with mildness on the weakness of a frail woman; have you not, Julio?' and as she uttered these words, she bent forward her head towards me, as it appeared desirous of concealing the blushes with which her cheeks were suffused upon my breast, when her eye suddenly rested on the brooch which confined the neck of my shirt. She gazed upon it for a few seconds in speechless astonishment; her lips quivered; the blood flew from her cheeks; she uttered a convulsive shriek, and sunk fainting on the floor.

"The females hastened to her assistance, and at their call the old woman and the friar entered the apartment. Restoratives being applied, Antonia in a short time began to revive; she gazed wildly around her; and her eyes ultimately fixing upon me, she uttered a second shriek, which was followed by the exclamation of—'Take him from my sight, tear him, drag him hence, I command you!' and having thus spoken, she relapsed into insensibility.

"My senses were floating in a chaos of doubts, apprehensions, and conjectures; my utterance was chained, and almost as insensible as the mysterious being who occupied my thoughts, I was hurried out of the apartment by the old woman and the friar.

"The room into which they conducted me was handsome, but by no means so elegantly furnished as that which I had just quitted; they requested me to sit down and compose myself, and promised to return to me in the course of a few minutes. Scarcely conscious of my own actions, I suffered myself to sink into a chair, and they hastily retired from my presence. The confusion of my thoughts rendered me incapable of reflection, and almost of action; and at the return of the friar, the period of whose absence was short, I started as from a dream. He presented me with a silver cup, which, he said, contained a cordial that would be efficacious in reviving my spirits from the shock which they had sustained—'Taste it, I beseech you,' he said, 'and you shall shortly have explained to you what now astonishes and affects you.' I complied with his request, for my limbs trembled, and a faint sickness oppressed my heart. I returned the cup into his hands, and in the course of a few minutes a lethargic sensation, similar to the heaviest encroachments of sleep, and against which I struggled in vain, oppressed me; and quickly after, all sense of recollection fled from me.

CHAPTER III

Ah, me! for ought that ever I could read,
Could ever hear, by tale or history,
The course of true love never did run smooth;
But either it was different in blood,
Or else misgrafted, in respect of years;
Or else it stood upon the choice of friends:
Or, if there were a sympathy in choice,
War, death, or sickness, did lay siege to it,
Making it momentary as a sound,
Swift as a shadow, short as any dream.
If then true lovers have been ever cross'd,
It stands as an edict in destiny:
Then let us teach our trial patience,
Because it is a customary cross;
As due to love as thoughts, and dreams, and sighs,
Wishes, and tears, poor Fancy's followers.
A Midsummer Night's Dream.

"ON awaking from the trance into which I had fallen, I found myself extended on a straw couch in a pavilion at the foot of my own garden, where during the summer, which was at that time the season of the year, I was accustomed to retire in an afternoon from the heat of the day. It was already morning, the beams of the rising sun were beginning to gild the earth, and the birds were carolling their hymns to the opening day. For a few minutes the past appeared to me like a vision; but as my senses regained their wonted powers, I became convinced that the recollections registered in my mind had been produced by facts; and my astonishment increased with every moment that I continued to revolve them in my mind.

"When I became in some measure able to abstract my ideas, my attention was arrested by a gold chain which I found suspended round my neck, and to which hung a heavy substance, folded in an envelope of paper. I hastily tore open the object of my curiosity, and beheld a most striking miniature resemblance of the mysterious female to whom I had on the preceding evening been introduced, richly set in brilliants. In removing the envelope, some words of writing, traced upon the paper, had caught my eye, and after a few moments' gaze at the portrait, I eagerly perused the lines in which it had been encased. They were these:—"Signor Julio, the female to whose society you were yesterday evening admitted has discovered in you *her son:* it is your mother who addresses you, through the medium of those words which you are at this moment perusing. For the first and last time you have beheld her. Every endeavour which you can make to discover her abode, or her situation in life, must prove fruitless; she is concealed from the knowledge of the world by an impenetrable veil; bound to her seclusion by a spell which mortal means can neither penetrate nor dissolve. Knowing the independence with which you are blest, she offers you only one gift at her hands, the resemblance of her who gave you birth; she believes and trusts that you will receive it with the same satisfaction and love with which it is consigned to your possession. Wear it next your heart; and oh! may that heart sometimes heave a sigh of tenderness for her who gave its vital powers the spark of life!'

"I was lost in wonder, and as my astonishment increased, my desire augmented to solve the mystery in which my parent was enfolded. Days, weeks, and months, were passed by me in unavailing plans, fruitless stratagems, and unsuccessful attempts of every description, to gain the knowledge for which my heart so eagerly panted—a period which, although it could not fail to weary the peruser by a minute detail of all the circumstances attendant on its progress, was to me of a highly-interesting nature, as every new effort which I projected or pursued for the accomplishment of my wish, kept alive within me the sustaining essence of hope, without which my powers, enervated by disappointment, must have sunk into the torpitude of despair.

"Nearly a year had elapsed, and not a single ray of light had beamed upon my ignorance of my mother's fate, when I was prevailed on by two of my friends, natives of Padua, who were now students of St. Peter's at Rome, but who had been fellow-disciples with me in the seminary where I had completed my education, to accompany them to the carnival of Venice; and it was not so much from the expectation of deriving that excess of pleasure which my companions anticipated from their visit to that celebrated scene of mirth, as from a desire of pursuing some plan which might partially wean my mind from that subject on which it had, both for the strength of my health and spirits, been of late too forcibly bent, that I consented to accompany them. Heaven was propitious to my wish; it vouchsafed to me the boon for which I had prayed—the relief from incessant inquietude of thought for which I had panted. It was there, at the carnival of Venice, that the benignant hand of Providence led me to behold the matchless, the fascinating, the amiable Valeria di Cavetti; I saw her, I gained her acquaintance, and found in her smiles the blessing for which I had prayed. Her conversation was a magic antidote to the pangs of an unsettled mind; the elegance of her graceful form challenged the admiration which her silver voice had claimed, and her smiles communicated an electric touch of joy to the senses, which left the heart without a wish ungratified.

"Should fate ever permit the enchanting Valeria to peruse the lines which this trembling hand is now employed in tracing, she cannot fail to remember her last interview with Julio. It was at that moment, when Julio was on the point of confessing to her who was the female represented by the miniature suspended round his neck, and at that critical moment, by the confusion created in the ball-room, at the alarm of fire, they were separated from each other, and met no more. And should Valeria peruse the lines here written, will she not naturally inquire, why during the lapse of so many months, Julio has neither written to her, sent to her, nor visited her? For her reply to this question let her revert to the early part of Julio's narrative of his life, and she will recollect, that in the letter which accompanied him in his introduction into the monastery at Padua, was contained the information that he possessed a sister, whom it was not likely that he could ever know to be such, and was consequently enjoined by his unknown parent not to marry any woman of whose birth he was not positively assured. Of the origin of Valeria di Cavetti there could be no doubt in the mind of Julio; but Julio had made a promise on his deathbed to his friend, his protector, and his parent, Antonio, who had in many instances witnessed the ill effects of marriage contracted in too great precipitancy of passion, and at too thoughtless an age of life, not to become a husband, till he had attained his twenty-fifth year; and even then, not to enter into wedlock with any woman whom he had not known for the space of twice twelve months.

"To break through a line of conduct to which he had solemnly and voluntarily bound himself to his dying friend to adhere, Julio was convinced to be a step to which he could never conform with honour or happiness to his own mind.

"At the period of his introduction to Valeria, he had, according to the computation made of his age by Antonio, when he was first cast upon the benevolence of the abbate of the monastery, just attained his twenty-third year; accordingly, in the course of two revolving seasons, he would have attained his twenty-fifth year, and have known the mistress of his soul twice twelve months; and for this period accordingly he resolved to quit the presence of his idolized Valeria, distrusting, whilst he sunned himself beneath her dazzling charms, how far the lures of present joy might tempt him to disregard that sacred bond, which, by the force of principle and truth, man's two most holy ties on earth, whispered him not to break his engagement with the dead.

"Oh Valeria! Valeria! sainted maid! celestial being, submitted to the earth, a rare example of the race beyond the skies! sweet practiser of virtue's harmonizing code! possessor of each charm that lulls the soul to heavenly repose! blessed with all joys, all attributes, and all felicities, save only one, ill-fated maid! thy knowledge of the wretched, wretched Julio!"

Here followed a chasm in the manuscript, where several sentences had been blotted out by the pen, and subsequent to these appeared some lines through which the marks of erasure had been faintly drawn; and from those lines which remained legible, Valeria could gather that they had contained the description of a struggle between love and honour in the breast of Julio; and concluded by his invoking Heaven, with almost frantic earnestness, to prove his innocence; but of what act there appeared no elucidation.

The narrative was continued thus:—"At the expiration of the carnival, at the entreaty of my friends, I returned with them to Rome, where I passed a month in a round of pleasures of which my mind partook not; my heart, my senses, my soul, were with Valeria in Venice. But I must not omit to state, that in the course of my journey back to Padua, when my visit to my friends at Rome was completed, an extraordinary circumstance occurred to me, which, for a while, left an impression on my mind, which divided my thoughts with the image of my adored mistress.

"I had been about a couple of hours in the inn where I had resolved to pass the night, at the end of my second day's travelling, when my servant, to whom a long and faithful service had accorded some degree of familiarity in addressing me, entered the apartment where I was sitting.—'Pray, signor,' he said, 'did you observe a stranger, when you were taking a stroll just now round the garden, by the side of the house, leaning against the palisades which divide it from the road, and eyeing you very attentively?'—'No; why so?' I inquired.—'Because, signor,' replied my servant, 'I observed what I have been mentioning to you. The person I speak of is well drest and well mounted, for I saw him ride into the inn-yard about half an hour after we arrived here:'—'There is nothing very uncommon,' I said, 'in one stranger looking with some degree of curiosity at another.'—'But indeed, signor,' rejoined my servant, 'there was something very pointed in his manner of doing so; and when you had retired into the house, he came up to me, and asked if you were my master? To which question, when I had replied in the affirmative, he rejoined—"Your master resides in the neighbourhood of Padua; does he not?"—"He does," I said.—"I know his person well," replied the stranger, "but cannot immediately recollect his name. I have often heard it too. Oh! now I remember," he added, after a momentary pause, "it is signor Julio; ay, ay, I recollect Julio;"—and so saying he walked away from me into the house. 'This stranger,' I remarked, 'is most probably some one who, like myself, is without company on the road, and wishes for a companion to pass the evening with. As you say he appears a man of respectability, go, and present signor Julio's compliments to him, and invite him to sup with me.'

"My servant departed with my message, and in a short time returned with information that the stranger was gone to bed. 'If he had received my invitation a few minutes sooner,' I said, 'I have no doubt that he would have been happy to have deferred retiring to his chamber for two or three hours longer.'

'I inquired of the people of the house,' resumed my servant, 'whether they knew his name; but they informed me that they did not recollect ever to have seen him before.'

"Having taken my supper, and finding the hours hang heavy on my hands, as I conjectured that the stranger had done, unprovided as I was with books or any resource for passing my time, I retired to rest, and somewhat fatigued with my day's journey, I soon fell asleep.

"How long I had slept I am unconscious, but I was awakened by the pressure of a hand upon one of mine, which was extended on the outside of the bed. On opening my eyes they were dazzled by a glaring light, which I imagined had issued from a dark lantern; for on my looking up, I heard a faint creaking sound which proceeded from the same spot from whence the flame had gleamed, and the light instantly disappeared. By the momentary flash of light which had been presented to me, I had caught a glimpse of a human figure, standing by the side of the bed, and I instantly exclaimed—'Who are you? and what is your business with me?'—'*Who* I am,' replied a manly voice, composed of firm but sweet tones, 'cannot at this time be answered you; *what* I am, I may candidly confess, your most sincere friend.'—'I repeat, what is your business with me?' I replied; 'and why, if you are a friend, have you chosen this suspicious hour, and this mysterious manner of disclosing yourself to me?'—'For your sake, for my own,' answered the unknown; 'were we seen to converse together, destruction would overtake us both.'—'Perhaps it is at this moment meditating against me from your hand,' I exclaimed; 'I shall therefore call for assistance, and——' whilst pronouncing the last words, I had raised my voice, and made an effort to quit my bed. The unknown placed his hands upon my arm to retain me in my situation, and interrupted me.—'In the name of God,' he said, 'forbear; what I entreat of you is for your own peace, your own happiness, your own honour!'

"The accents in which he expressed these words were mild, and persuasive in the extreme, and he followed them with a sigh which appeared to proceed from a broken heart.

"Ere I could resolve how to act, or what to reply, he spoke again.—'I have but one question to ask,' he said, 'and one admonition to give, and we part, probably to meet no more on earth. Are you not, Julio, a foundling, reared by the benevolence of the abbate of the monastery of San Stefano, in Padua?'—'I am,' was my reply.—'Then,' emphatically rejoined the unknown, 'avoid the marchese di Valdetti!'—'Who is the marchese di Valdetti?' I asked.—'Your mortal foe,' he answered.—'I know him not,' I rejoined.—'Heaven grant you never may know him!' pronounced the unknown.—'What have I to fear from him?' I exclaimed.—'Every thing,' replied the stranger; 'persecution! dishonour! death! Farewell!' he added, pressing my hand in his as he spoke, 'oh! farewell! One anxious purpose of my heart is accomplished, and I am happier, at least less miserable than I was.'—'If you are truly thus interested in my fate,' I said, 'oh, explain to me——' 'Not one other word,' he interrupted me by solemnly pronouncing, 'nor, when I quit this chamber, offer to follow me a single step, or breathe a sound that may be overheard, unless you wish to draw down instant ruin on us both. Once more, let me behold your countenance, and then yield myself up again to grief and solitude."

"He opened his lantern, gazed upon me for a few seconds, and then again smothering the light in scarcely articulate accents he stammered forth—'Farewell! a long farewell! Heaven guard and bless thee! farewell!' Then raising his voice, he added—'Remember my injunctions; not one step or word, as you value my existence or your own;' and darted out of the chamber, closing after him the door with the utmost caution.

"The state of my mind may be easily divined, but its torments were increased by a perplexing recollection which I could not analyse. During the momentary view which the stranger had been taking of my countenance, my eyes had been fixed upon his, and I felt convinced that his features were familiar to my sight, though I could not recall to my memory when or where I had before beheld them: at length, after a considerable time passed in the torture of reflection, recollection burst suddenly upon my brain; the being who had that night addressed himself to me was the very pilgrim who, when a boy at school, had, as I had since received cause to suppose, examined the neck of my shirt, in order to ascertain whether it were clasped by the brooch which I had now for many years constantly worn, and which had disclosed me to her who professed herself to be my mother. What were my thoughts during the remainder of the night cannot require explanation; I slept no more, and rising early in the morning, and inquiring of my servant for the stranger, learnt that he had left the inn at daybreak; I asked the road he had taken, and was informed that no one had observed the direction in which he had set out.

"That every additional circumstance of a mysterious nature which occurred to me, heightened my desire to obtain the means of undrawing the veil which obscured from my view the ambiguous fates of myself and those with whom I was connected, can scarcely require to be mentioned. I have here only to remark, that even to the name of the marchese di Valdetti, against whom my unknown friend had cautioned me as my deadliest foe, I was an utter stranger.

"On my return to Padua, I became thoughtful and melancholy; my acquaintance perceived the change in my disposition, and rallied me on the score of my being in love—a charge, of which as I felt fully conscious, I candidly admitted myself guilty, in order to avoid a closer scrutiny into my feelings. After a time I endeavoured to argue with my own mind, to call the powers of reason to my aid, and to convince myself that the despondency of soul to which I had too long been yielding myself; so far from assisting me in producing the end which I was desirous of accomplishing, would only tend to enervate my faculties, and render them less competent to take an active share in any circumstances which might arise to demand my personal exertions. To this end I applied myself with vigour to the several arts of painting, music, and botany, of which I had before possessed no mean knowledge, and with which, for the sole purpose of employing my thoughts, I now resolved to court a more intimate acquaintance. I also accepted the invitations of my friends, and suffered myself to be led back to that society from which I had for a time withdrawn myself; and I found that if I experienced no other relief to my feelings from associating occasionally with my fellow-beings, a few hours passed in a crowded assembly gave a double charm to solitude on my return home.

"The period now arrived which was productive of a circumstance upon which my mind must ever look back with the keenest sensations of horror—a circumstance which has blotted out my name for ever from the book of earthly bliss—a circumstance which has rendered the world a blank to Julio, and Julio a cipher and an outcast amongst men!

"Being one day about this time invited to dine with a friend in Padua, I found the party composed of my intimate acquaintance, with the exception of one young man, whom I had frequently before observed in mixed societies, and to whom my friend now for the first time introduced me, informing me that he was a young man of good family, who had been studying the art of surgery at Pisa, and was now residing in Padua, for the purpose of perfecting himself in anatomy, under a celebrated professor of the science in that city. In the course of the varied and broken conversation which occurred during our repast, I observed the young stranger to be well-informed, but opinionated, and eager to bring his own remarks upon every subject into notice. About the usual time of separating in the evening, the guests departed, with the exception of the young stranger and myself, who being engaged in a conversation of some interest with our host, did not rise to follow their example. When we were left alone with my friend, he said—'I am very glad you did not retire so precipitately as the rest of my visitors have done; we seem so well entertained with one another, that if you have no other engagement, I hope you will pass the remainder of the evening with me.'

"We both readily complied with his proposal; fresh wine was placed upon the table, and the laugh and joke relieved the gravity with which we occasionally discussed the various subjects which were by turns started in the field of argument. At length the profession of the young surgeon was the topic introduced upon the carpet, and my friend, who was a man of an extremely-nervous habit, said—that he had reason to be thankful that the independence which had devolved to him from his father had never reduced him to the perplexity of selecting a profession; but, that had his circumstances compelled him to the exercise of one, that of a surgeon would have been the last he would have adopted, as he was certain that he never could have sufficiently divested himself of feeling, for the performance of the necessary duties of the situation.

"The young stranger strenuously defended his profession, declaring, that what was frequently placed to the score of inhumanity in the exercisers of that science, was only a commendable stifling of their own feelings, in order the more ably and more speedily to contribute to the relief of those whose sufferings it was their aim to heal.

"I strongly coincided with him in opinion, and then addressing my friend, said—'If all the world were of your sentiments, where would the sufferer obtain alleviation of his pangs? he must inevitably either linger through a life of imbecility and decrepitude, or be reduced by the anguish of his wounds to a hasty grave, when the operations of science, skilfully administered, will in few instances fail to restore him to strength and convalescence.'—'There is truth in what you advance,' replied my friend, 'but dispositions vary; and had I been fated to the exercise of a profession ignobly as that of a tailor is usually rated, I am positive that I could sooner have submitted to become a repairer of the tattered arms and legs of a doublet, or of a pair of trunks, than of the fractured ones appertaining to a human form.'

"The young stranger laughed heartily at my friend's assertion, and then said—'I am surprised, as you express yourself to be so great a victim to your nerves, how you can be sufficiently bold to receive a shock of electricity, of which I have seen you take many, apparently unmoved.'—'I confess that it is an experiment which I extremely dislike,' replied my friend; 'but as I know it to be for the good of my system, I endeavour to subdue my feelings, and assume courage to endure it.'—'And we surgeons,' answered the young stranger, 'subdue our feelings for the good of others, which you must allow is at least as praiseworthy a motive as his who stifles them for his own peculiar benefit only.'—'You have not yet practised yourself,' resumed my friend, 'or at least only to a limited extent, and cannot therefore inform me how a novice assumes fortitude to carry him through the first operation which he attempts.'—'The ardour of his zeal to excel in his profession, added to his desire of contributing to the relief of the sufferer under his hands, nerve equally his heart and arm,' replied the young stranger; 'but you are to recollect,' he continued, 'that every student of surgery has practised his art upon the bodies of the dead before he proceeds to exercise his skill on living subjects. I am surprised that, as a mere matter of curiosity, you have never procured an introduction into the anatomy chamber in the college of the Holy Cross in this city; it is easily obtained; I shall attend there to-morrow, and if you please, will take you with me.'— 'Excuse me,' returned my friend, 'it must be compulsion indeed that leads me to witness a spectacle of the kind; I deem it only suited to the observance of those who may derive professional benefit from their attendance upon it, and, moreover, regard it as a scene which should be kept strictly concealed from the eye of uninterested curiosity.'

"The conversation now took another turn, and shortly after, the young stranger and myself bade our entertainer good night. When we were in the street, I addressed the young stranger by saying—'I am of an entirely different opinion to our friend relative to the points which we were discussing, connected with your profession; I am inclined to think that no one can see or know too much of whatever relates to the acquisition of knowledge in any point of science; and if I did not deem myself to be taking too great a liberty with you upon our first acquaintance, I should be tempted to ask if you would oblige me by transferring to me your invitation to accompany you tomorrow morning to the anatomy chamber, which our friend declined.'

"The young stranger not only readily granted my request, but appeared highly gratified that I had advanced it; and the splendour of a full moon illuminating a warm autumnal evening, he proposed a short stroll about the city before we retired to our respective habitations. I agreed to his proposal, and the excellent wine, and animated conversation of the afternoon, having exhilarated his spirits, he began to address me with all the familiarity of an old acquaintance.—'There is certainly little pleasure,' said he, 'in contemplating the dead, but the subject which you will to-morrow behold in the anatomy chamber was once one of the most lovely women in Italy. I think I shall almost feel some compunction in performing the task of practice, which I apprehend will be allotted to me, upon her now-insensible form; for I believe that few have shared more of her favour than I have done.'—'Was she then a female of a publicly-unprincipled life?' I asked.—'No, not exactly so,' replied the young stranger; 'her transactions were denominated private; but so many possessed the key to the enigma, that her secret was what may be called a secret *pro bono publico*.'—'And I suppose the contempt in which her memory is held,' I rejoined, 'causes her remains to be yielded an easy purchase to the dissecting knife?'—'Oh, by no means!' answered my companion; 'she supported a style of infinite elegance during her life, and has doubtless left a fortune capable of interring her with the magnificence of an empress; indeed, I understand her funeral to have been a sumptuous one; she was buried to-day in the chapel of San Tomaso.'—'And by what means then will the college obtain the corpse?' I inquired.—'Oh, my dear signor,' replied the young stranger, 'every corpse is attainable in this city; and conscious that the remains of her of whom I have been speaking will form an admirable study, our professor has pursued infalli-ble steps for obtaining the body; and in less than two hours from this time, it will be safe in the anatomy chamber.'— 'Strangers feel nothing on these occasions,' I remarked; 'but relatives could not fail to suffer severely, were they acquainted with the remains of their kindred being thus exposed to the gaze of unfeeling scrutinizers.'—'Probably they would,' re-turned my companion; 'but especial care is taken that relatives are kept in the dark as to these matters.'

"After some farther conversation we parted, and I agreed to meet the young stranger at eleven o'clock on the following morning, in the square of San Lucco.

"The young stranger was true to his appointment, and after the usual salutations of the morning, he said—'It is somewhat earlier than the hour at which the professor generally com-mences his lecture; but if you please, we will walk on to the college; there will as yet be scarcely any one arrived in the anatomy chamber, and I shall have an opportunity of giving you a sight of this *rara avis*, as I once thought her, which you would likely not else have an opportunity of obtaining, as her countenance will probably be concealed from view whilst the professor delivers his lecture.'

"I consented, and we proceeded to the college of the Holy Cross. Arrived there, we ascended the grand staircase leading from the hall to the second range of apartments, and were admitted by a porter, to whom my companion was known, into the anatomy chamber. It was a lofty and spacious apartment, around which seats were amphitheatrically raised above each other, for the accommodation of the students; and in the centre stood a table, over which was thrown a white cloth, which, clinging to the substance it concealed, plainly discovered the outline of a human form beneath.

"As the young stranger had augured, there were as yet not more than half a dozen persons in the room, two of whom appeared servants in waiting, and the others students, who were sitting remote from each other, and appeared deeply engaged with the volumes which they held in their hands.

'The opportunity I anticipated is granted us,' said my companion; and motioning to me to follow him, he approached the table, and drew aside that part of the covering which concealed the face of the subject. I stepped forward to view the features on which his encomiums had been so lavishly bestowed, and beheld—guess, if you can, the horror, the astonishment, the convulsive pang which rent my heart, when, in the countenance of the deceased, I beheld that of my mother!

"Darting a look expressive of the fury of my soul upon my introducer to this awful scene, 'liar and villain!' inarticulately escaped my trembling lips, and clasping my hand before my eyes, as if apprehensive of being pursued by the appalling spectacle which I had just witnessed, I rushed out into the street. My brain was burning, and my heart sunk cold as ice within my bosom. In the course of the last twelve hours, I had heard my mother accused of lascivious criminality, had seen her insensible remains exposed to the most humiliating and ignominious situation to which mortal clay could be subjected! and could a son, who possessed a heart of manhood, the feelings of a human being, witness this double degradation to the character and form of her who bore him, and not seek retribution on the asperser of her fame? forbid it, every virtuous principle! forbid it, Heaven!

"I rushed into the first tavern, and calling for pen and paper, wrote a note to the following effect to the young student.

'SIGNOR,

'The female whose character you have so
falsely and so vilely calumniated is my mother! As you are
yourself a son, you may readily imagine the feelings aroused
in the bosom by an indignity offered to the name of her
who bore us; you must, therefore, either publicly retract
what you have uttered to the discredit of my parent, or decide your quarrel with me by the sword. I shall expect your
immediate apology by letter, or await you at three this afternoon, behind the ruins of the monastery on the east side
of the city.

JULIO.'

"My letter was instantly dispatched, but no answer returned. Accordingly, at the time specified I repaired to the
ruins of the monastery—a spot marked by the decision of many
a point of honour; and had arrived there only a few moments,
when I perceived my adversary advancing. I have already mentioned that I had observed this young man to possess a self-
sufficient and decided temper; my own disposition was as in-
flexible as his, when goaded to the pitch to which it was now
wound; and the expressions uttered by each at our meeting,
instantly proved that our swords must be the arbiters of our
quarrel. We immediately took our ground; our weapons were
drawn, and at the close of the second encounter, my sword
pierced my antagonist through the breast; the blood gushed
from his heart, and he fell to the earth to rise no more! Conscious that my own life was now in danger, I flew with all the
precipitancy of dread to my villa, and having provided myself
with a purse of gold, and taken the swiftest horse from my
stable, I set off at full speed from the city of Padua, almost
unconscious whither I directed my steps."

Here ended the manuscript. Attached to it was a slip of
paper, which contained these words:—"Thus far, adored Valeria, I had proceeded in the narrative of my life, ere I formed the

determination of submitting it to your inspection; and I should long since have concluded it (for little more remains to be said of the unfortunate Julio), but that I desired my tongue to impart the climax of my fate to her who governs my destiny, and for whom alone I wish to live. Come then, beloved Valeria! return to the hut of the recluse, and even beneath the pressure of disappointment, the sting of privation, let us deduce happiness from the charm of friendship and congeniality of soul! come! oh, come! and relieve my pangs by the influence of thy reviving presence! thine, and thine only, Julio."

Valeria sat lost in a trance of thought, of amazement, and of unsatisfied conjecture, as the portrait suspended round the neck of Julio, the only point on which she had ever rested an apprehension of his fidelity, was now fully proved to her to have been the resemblance of his mother; she could select no instance from those which composed the sum of his life, which could militate against that union which his words at her interview with him that morning, and now again the expressions with which he had closed his narrative, seemed so palpably to declare that he himself considered incompatible with some circumstance, arising from the events of his life, which it still remained for him to develop to her: what that circumstance was, she could not form the remotest idea; and the only relief which she could promise herself for her present doubts and anxieties, was to seize the first favourable opportunity for again repairing to his secluded dwelling by the side of the brook.

Having deposited the manuscript in a place of security, and endeavoured to dress her features in that serenity which was foreign to her heart, she hastened to join the family, conceiving that she had already been too long absent from them.

CHAPTER IV

One woe doth tread upon another's heels.

Hamlet.

ON approaching the apartment where the family of Di Borges usually assembled, Valeria heard Averilla and her niece Francisca in earnest conversation together, and on her appearing before them, the former said—"I think that is the footstep of my dear Valeria?"

Valeria replied in the affirmative, and Averilla resumed—"Is your headache removed, my dear child? have you slept?"

"I have not slept," replied Valeria; "but I think that I am somewhat better than when I retired to my chamber."

"I hoped you might be asleep," replied Averilla, "and therefore would not disturb you, although I have long been wishing to speak to you. We are all under an alarm concerning your cousin Paulina, though I hope our fears are groundless."

Valeria eagerly requested an explanation of her words.

"Give me leave, signora, to inform you what has happened," ejaculated Francisca; "I am the only person that know directly and properly, as I may say, how matters are. You must know, signora, that after you had retired to your chamber this afternoon, the signora Paulina asked me to take a walk with her, which the politeness due from one like me to a lady of her superior rank in life, caused me, of course, to consider an honour conferred on myself; for, as you have heard me say before, signora, I have lived in the service of some of the first ladies in the land, and therefore know how to demean myself to my betters, and I immediately prepared to attend her commands. Well, signora, blind chance, as the proverb says, led the way to us, and we strolled into the little wood by the side of the cornfields, of which you well know the situation; so we wandered about, sometimes talking and sometimes not, till the signora

Paulina happened to spy a most beautiful field-flower, that she felt an inclination to transplant into our garden; so she desired me to run home for a spade, saying, she would take it up, root and all. Well, home I ran, and at the door of the house, whom should I meet but Mr. Terence! 'Oh, Mr. Terence,' said I, 'the signora Paulina is going to dig up a curious root in the wood yonder; perhaps she may not be very well acquainted with the business of transplanting it herself; so, as you profess yourself to be a bit of a gardener, suppose you go back with me, and assist her in the operation; two heads, you know, are better than one, as the proverb says.—'Oh yes,' says he—you know his queer sneering way, signora; 'to be sure two heads are better than one, if the other's only a calf's head, because if you are hungry, you can eat it; but I can't be a babe in the wood with you just now; I have other fish to fry;' and away he walked: oh, how provoked I was at his impudence! 'If you are come of a bull, Mr. Terence,' said I, 'of which I understand there are abundance in Ireland, I was not born of a cow, I can tell you that, if you meant your calf's head at me.' But what he said to me I don't value a straw; all that I regard is, that if he had but gone with me to the wood, as I desired him, the dear signora Paulina might have been here safe amongst us all just now."

"For Heaven's sake proceed to what relates to my cousin," said Valeria.

"Well, signora," resumed Francisca, "when I returned back with the spade to where the plant was, and where I naturally expected to find the signora Paulina, she was not there. I looked around me in all directions, as far as ever my eyes could penetrate, but nowhere could I perceive her; so imagining she might be behind some of the bushes that are scattered about the little wood, I called out as loud as ever I was able, 'signora! signora Paulina! dear signora Paulina! for the love of the Virgin, pray answer me, dear, dear signora Paulina!' I screamed and bawled till I was as hoarse as a raven, as the proverb says, but all to no purpose; no answer could I get; upon which, signora, I became so much alarmed, that I ran home to communicate the dreadful intelligence."

"How extraordinary!" exclaimed Valeria; "and is my dear Paulina not yet found?"

"I hope she may," said Averilla; "your worthy father, my husband, and all our servants, are gone in pursuit of her; and I trust they cannot fail to discover her, whithersoever she has wandered."

"Yes, every body is gone to look for her, signora," rejoined Francisca, "Mr. Terence and all; he happened to be here at the time, just come from the Castello, on a message to his master, and he went willingly enough with them, though he would not stir at my invitation—a sulky fellow! It is very true, as the proverb says, 'that one can't turn brass into gold with whistling;' but I'll go and look if any of them are returning." And with these words she left the room.

"I never heard a more unaccountable occurrence," said Valeria; "it is impossible that she can have strayed out of her road and lost her way, she is too well acquainted with every path in this neighbourhood."

"And we have no neighbours, but the honest and innocent peasantry," remarked Averilla, "whose upright hearts would revolt at injuring any human being, and who would die in the protection of an individual respected by my husband."

"It is most extraordinary indeed," said Valeria; "how long is it since Francisca saw her last?"

"Full three hours, my love," replied Averilla.

"And why did you not summon me to assist in the search after my dear Paulina?" asked Valeria.

"You could have effected no more than has already been attempted," replied Averilla; "and knowing you to be unwell, I was apprehensive of the sudden alarm increasing your malady."

"The maladies of the body are trivial, compared with those of the mind," returned Valeria.

"They are indeed, my child! they are indeed!" pronounced Averilla, emphatically, with a sigh, which appeared to be drawn from some concealed feeling labouring in her heart.

A short and anxious silence ensued; it was broken by the return of Francisca. "I see some of them coming," she said; "but it is growing so dusk that I can't distinguish which of them they are that I see."

Valeria ran to the door, and in a few seconds was met by her father and the farmer. Urbino took her hand, and led her back into the house. "Paulina is not with you," she said; "merciful God, protect her!"

"I trust he will," replied Urbino; "she is pure of heart, and the innocent ever experience him their shield."

"This new, this unexpected calamity to follow so closely upon those we have already suffered," falteringly pronounced Valeria, through her tears.

"Such, lady," said Terence, "has ever been the wayward fate of human beings; at least, it was so in the days of our immortal bard, or he would not have declared that—

> "When sorrows come, they come not single spies,
> But in battalions."

"But how," rejoined Valeria, "are frail beings to support such an accumulation of woe?"

"By hope, my honoured lady," answered Terence O'Donnovan; "recollect what *ould* Willy says again—

> "Hope is the lover's walking staff;
> Walk hence with that."

"And why should not it be the friend's and the parent's staff too? Depend upon it, my lady, Willy took it in a general sense, for the comfort of man, woman, and beast of every description, that form a part of animal society. I remember giving that exposition of the sentence once to father O'Rourke at Ballyporeen, and he said it was worth a place in the big bishop of Ferrar's Easter-Sunday's discourse."

"Come, come," said Di Borges, "a truce to this conversation; if Paulina has had the misfortune to fall into the hands of an enemy, neither tears nor quotations will effect her rescue."

"True!" exclaimed Terence—

> "You may as well go stand upon the beach,
> And bid the——"

He was silenced by a look from the farmer, who proceeded thus—"As it is impossible to form the slightest idea of the cause of Paulina's present absence, unless it can be supposed to bear a relation to the unexplained events which have lately taken place at the Castello della Torvida, I think that the only clue we can hope to obtain to the mystery is for us to proceed thither, and pass the night as usual within its walls. Old Jeronymo, who will doubtless not have left the spot all day, may possibly be able to throw some light upon this ambiguous matter: so, signor," addressing himself to Urbino, "gird on a couple of my pistols; I shall stick another brace in my own belt to guard us on our way, as after these unparalleled events, there is no knowing whom we may encounter; and let us set out without delay."

In mournful silence Urbino prepared to follow Sancho's directions; and having bade an affectionate farewell to Valeria and Averilla, they departed, leaving behind them two of the servants belonging to the farm, for the safeguard of the females at home.

It was now within an hour of midnight, and the shades of night enveloped the earth. When the receding footsteps of their departing friends were no longer audible—"Are you inclined to retire to rest, my dear Valeria?" asked Averilla.

"No, no," replied Valeria, "I am certain I could not sleep; nor do I desire to repose, if even I believed myself able to do so."

"I cannot myself go to bed with any degree of satisfaction to-night," rejoined Averilla; "I will therefore retire to my chamber, and you shall, if you please, come and sit there with me; if we remain below stairs, we shall be unceasingly tormented with Francisca's prattle, which I am sure you must just now wish to be spared."

This arrangement was accordingly made, and Francisca was sent to bed; whilst the two male-servants were directed to remain sitting up in the kitchen. Valeria and her venerable friend sat for some time in silence, for real sorrow does not vent itself in words; at length Averilla said—"Oh, my dear Valeria, this unaccountable disappearance of your cousin brings to my recollection a circumstance, which I have for many years past endeavoured to banish from my thoughts, but which to-night will force itself upon my feelings, in spite of all my efforts to combat the impression. It was the will of God," she added, bursting into tears; "his ways are inscrutable, but always just. I may weep, but I will never murmur."

Valeria had never heard her express herself thus before, and uttered some words, indicating the surprise with which her friend's emotion affected her.

"I have experienced a calamity in life," said Averilla, "of which few have known the misery of a privation equally cruel."

"Do you refer to the loss of your sight?" asked Valeria.

"Oh! no, no," answered Averilla; "that is a misfortune incidental to the frailness of our constitutions, and one which many others have to lament besides myself; no, no, the evil to which I refer is almost unparalleled. I have often thought that I would one day tell you what I had suffered; for your heart is so gentle and so compassionate, that it is fitted for the resting-place of a melancholy tale like mine: an opportunity now occurs, and you shall know the secret that preys upon my mind." She wiped the tears from her eyes, and after a short pause continued speaking thus:—"I had been three years united to my husband, to whom

I had been betrothed from a very early age, ere it pleased Heaven to give me the promise of becoming a mother; at length I was blest with the birth of a female infant, the only babe to which I ever gave existence. My child was healthy and lovely, and grew to be the idolized object of mine and my husband's affections. I find that I cannot dwell upon the circumstance of which I am about to inform you; my feelings will not permit it; I can only in few words relate to you the heart-rending fact. My child had just completed her ninth month, when I was one day walking with her in my arms in the little garden in the front of our habitation; suddenly a person with whom I had business called me to the house; I seated my infant on a plot of grass near the door, and having placed some toys by her side, went to answer the summons which I had received from the house. I am certain that I was not absent five minutes from my child; and on returning to the spot where I had left her, oh! conceive my surprise, my anguish—my infant was nowhere to be found."

The tears burst afresh from the eyes of Averilla—"Oh, my sweet babe!" she exclaimed, "methinks I see thee now. But I shall never behold thee more—never more gaze on thy lovely smiles, thy rosy dimpled cheeks. Oh, Valeria! from that moment I never heard of her again; all inquiries, all rewards to discover her fate, proved ineffectual; and yet—yet I survive her loss, and still retain my senses. Surely I cannot have loved her as a mother, or I should have sunk to the grave ere this."

Her bursts of sorrow now became so violent, that Valeria felt it necessary to assume the task of admonitress, and to beseech her to subdue her anguish, by the remembrance of that resignation which she owed to the will of a First Cause.

"I have bowed submissively to the ordinations of Providence," said Averilla, "and I will do so again. Only grant me one indulgence, and you shall see me weep no more."

She placed in the hand of Valeria a key, and directing her to a certain drawer in the chamber, which she requested her to open, informed her that she would there find a coral set in gold, which she requested her to bring to her.

Valeria obeyed; and on clasping the trinket in her hand, Averilla exclaimed—"This coral lay by the side of my child when she was stolen from me; it is a proof that those who deprived me of her did not do so for the lucre of gain, or this had not been overlooked by them—no, no, no; and what could be their motive I shall never know. This coral has been pressed by the lips of my child; oh! let me press it to my own." She kissed it ardently, then said—"Now, my dear Valeria, replace this where you found it, and let me struggle to regain my fortitude of mind."

Valeria followed her instructions, and had scarcely returned the key into her hands, ere they were startled by the clattering of a horse's feet, which was followed by a loud knocking at the outer door. Anxious to ascertain who was the claimant for admission, Valeria opened the chamber-door; her action was heard by one of the servants, who had been summoned from the kitchen by the noise, and he inquired of Valeria whether or not he should open the door? Having received her reply in the affirmative, he undrew the bolts, and found without a man on horseback, who, putting into his hand a folded paper, said— "Deliver that to the signor Urbino di Cavetti;" and having thus said, rode off again at full speed.

The letter being brought to Valeria, she found it closely sealed, and superscribed with her father's name.

A consultation now ensued between Valeria and her friend, whether the letter should be sent without delay to Urbino, or await his return in the morning? and their ultimate decision was, that, as it might contain matter of immediate importance, one of the servants should be directed to take horse, and convey it instantly to the Castello della Torvida.

On quitting the farmhouse that evening, and arriving at the Castello, Urbino and his party found old Jeronymo, with a countenance of doleful despair, leaning against one of the pilasters which supported the flight of steps leading to the main entrance into the building. His hours, passed in solitude, had been dull and miserable, and, probably weary of empty walls, he stood contemplating the starry heavens, with a set of features which, as Terence truly observed, bespoke

> "Patience on a monument,
>   Smiling at grief;"

and to the inquiries which were made of him he replied, that no occurrence of any kind had taken place at the Castello, and that he had not seen an individual since the departure of Terence, on his walk to the farm in the afternoon.

Sancho di Borges and Urbino had agreed not to retire to rest that night, and accordingly seated themselves in an apartment, where they experienced no interruption, till Terence came to announce to them the arrival of the servant whom Valeria had dispatched from the farmhouse.

Urbino hastily tore open the letter, and found it to contain these words:—"*Fear nothing from the disappearance of your niece, Paulina; it is for her happiness and eventual good that she is for a short time removed from your presence.*"

Whilst Di Borges was descanting on the extraordinary information contained in the note, Urbino appeared to be struck by some sudden idea, and drawing his letter-case from his pocket, he took from it a written paper, which he opened, and having compared it with the one he had just received—"By Heavens!" he exclaimed, "they are the same—the handwriting of the letter just delivered to me corresponds in every point with that of the note which I received from a horseman, at the *albergo* where I slept with my family on the first night after my quitting Venice. You will recollect that the note to which I refer contained intelligence from the unknown, in consequence of whose threats I had departed from Venice, that, whilst I prosecuted the plan which I was now pursuing, I had nothing to fear from him."

"It is an enigma," said Sancho di Borges, "which exceeds comprehension."

"And requires the utmost caution and deliberation, as I apprehend," replied Urbino, "in acting towards its solution."

The friends now entered into a serious and elaborate conversation, in which we must for a while leave them engaged, and pursue the steps of the lamented Paulina.

CHAPTER V

What may this mean?

SHAKESPEARE.

WHILST Paulina was awaiting the return of Francisca with the spade, happening to turn her eye towards a knot of bushes near which she was standing, she perceived amidst the scattered branches the visage of a man, who was attentively eyeing her. Ere time was given her for farther observation, he blew a shrill whistle, at the sound of which two other men, the one on foot, the other on horseback, the latter of whom was enveloped in a loosely-flowing cloak, appeared from a clump of underwood at a short distance from their companion, and all three immediately approached Paulina. The two on foot seized her by the arms, and requesting her not to be alarmed, for that no harm was intended her, lifted her upon the horse before their companion, who instantly covering her with the long skirts of his cloak, set off at full speed.

It was in vain that Paulina shrieked aloud for help, and alternately implored and commanded to be restored to liberty: equally fruitless were her inquiries why this unwarrantable restraint was placed upon her, and whither she was about to be conveyed; the only answer which she could obtain from her conductor, was a repetition of the assurance already made her, that no evil was intended her. Still she raved for liberty, and supplicated for compassion; but her cries and prayers were unattended to; and at length overpowered by the conflicts of her mind, she sunk into a state of insensibility.

On awaking from the temporary oblivion into which she had fallen, Paulina found herself extended on a velvet couch, and the glare of wax-lights which met her eye, displayed to her an apartment furnished with the utmost magnificence. By her side stood a female in the vale of years, habited in a suit of vestments which, from their antique fashion, bore the appearance of having been at least fifty years in the possession of their owner, and which were now valuable only for the richness of the materials of which they were composed. The features of the female were plain and harsh, and appeared to partake more of the masculine than of the softness of that sex of which her dress bespoke her to be a member.

On perceiving Paulina open her eyes—"How fare you now, signora?" she asked. Her voice was as coarse as her person, but she endeavoured, as it appeared, to assume a mildness of tone, and smiling with affected benignity as she spoke, she continued thus:—"Ah, no wonder you were exhausted with galloping along upon that jolting horse, before that giant of a fellow, Philippo, who has no more feeling than the beast he sits on! Riding on horseback never agreed with me, and I dare say it is the same with you; probably too you have never been accustomed to the exercise, and that makes it worse to bear. Take a glass of wine," she proceeded, filling one, as she spoke, from a crystal vase on the table—"it cures me of most complaints;" and as she presented it to Paulina with one hand, with the other she raised a full glass to her lips, drinking to the health of her guest, and their better acquaintance.

Rising from the couch, and placing the wine, which the old woman had forced into her hand, on the table, Paulina besought her to inform her where she was, and why she had been borne away from the protection of her friends, in the extraordinary manner in which she had been torn from them.

"It is very silly of you, signora, not to drink the wine," said the old woman, regardless of her questions; "I am sure it will do you good—it always does me good. Come, taste it; you'd better be advised."

Paulina again refused her offer; and the old woman raising the second glass to her own lips, said—"Well then, I must drink it for you, that's all; for it would be a sin to let it be wasted, now it's poured out."

Paulina still more earnestly repeated the questions which she had before advanced.

"Well then, sit down here by me on the sofa," rejoined her companion, seating herself as she spoke, "and compose yourself, and I'll tell you all I know of the matter, and then you'll be convinced that you have nothing to *fear*, at all events;" and taking her by the arm, she drew her down forcibly by her side. "Now then," she proceeded by saying—"now then, signora—— I forget your name, I'm sure, although I have heard it more than once."

"Paulina," was the reply.

"Ay—Paulina, Paulina," rejoined the old woman—"and a very pretty name it is too. Well then, signora Paulina, with a bewitching face and a captivating form like yours, what motive can there be, think you, for catching a little flutterer like yourself, and shutting her up in a golden cage, but the old ruling principle, love?"

"What!" exclaimed Paulina, starting frantically from her seat; "am I then brought hither to be made the victim of a villain's passion? Sooner shall my forfeit life——"

"Pshaw! nonsense! abate your ecstasies," replied the old woman—"there's nothing amiss intended you, I promise you that. Marriage, honourable marriage, awaits your acceptance, with one of the first men, and one of the greatest men, and one of the proudest men, and one of the richest men in all Italy."

"And was it necessary to bring me hither clandestinely to receive his proposal?" asked Paulina.

"That is his business," answered her companion—"you must ask him that himself to-morrow, for you'll not see him till then. He gives you this night to repose in, and to regain your wonted tone of spirits."

Paulina sunk for a few moments into silent reflection; she recollected the conversation which had passed concerning her, between Francisca and a young cavalier who had professed himself her admirer, and doubting whether he might not be the present arbiter of her fate, turning to the old woman, she said— "What is he, whose unjust prisoner I at this hour consider myself?"

"Why I've told you already," was the answer—"great and affluent."

"Is he young?" demanded Paulina.

"No, not very—not very young," returned her companion, "nor yet very old; a good enough age, and a good-enough-looking man. But follow me, and you shall see his picture; it hangs in the room where you are to sleep." The old woman took up a candle, opening a door at the extremity of the apartment, ushered Paulina into an elegant bed-chamber, and raised her light to the countenance of a half-length portrait of a cavalier, richly habited in the Venetian costume— "There, there it is," she said; "and so like, you might almost think he was speaking to you."

Paulina directed her eyes to the picture, and an involuntary start followed her observation of the countenance pourtrayed; for in the features of the portrait she beheld the resemblance of the tall pilgrim with the dark hair, who had haunted her during the carnival at Venice.

"What do you start at?" asked her companion. "Do you know the person whom it represents? Have you ever seen him?"

"I believe—I think—I hardly know—I——" stammered out the confused and trembling Paulina.

"Well, well," returned the old woman, "you'll be convinced to-morrow morning after breakfast whether you are right or not, for at that hour the marchese will no doubt visit you."

"What is his name?" asked Paulina.

"Why, I'm not certain whether I am at liberty to disclose that to you," replied the old woman; "so you must be content to defer gaining information on that head till you see him himself. There is your bed," proceeded her companion, after a pause— "the best in the Castle, I assure you; I have known a princess sleep in it before now; but the marchese thinks nothing too good for you. And there," she added, throwing open another door, which led into a spacious closet—"there is a harp for your amusement, and sheets of music for you to play by, and materials for drawing, and books without end, and, in short, every thing your heart can desire."

"But my liberty," replied Paulina.

"Ah! many a one would joyfully give a finger to be such a prisoner," simpered out the old woman.

The chamber door was now opened, and a plainly-dressed man entered the apartment.—"Wife," he said, addressing Paulina's companion, "you are wanted below stairs."

"Well, I'm only doing what I was ordered," replied the old woman, "in attending upon the signora."

"Do as you are ordered now then, and go down stairs," returned the man.

"You are the biggest bear in all the country, Lipardo," rejoined the old woman, "that you are, and always behave to me as if I was a brute;" and with a half-curtsey to Paulina, muttering and grumbling, she left the chamber. During this conversation, a few moments had been given Paulina for observing the man. He appeared about the age of his wife; his features were stern, but the sternness seemed blended with a mixture of honesty that almost inspired confidence. Slightly as the feeling was apparent, it penetrated to the heart of Paulina, and casting herself upon her knees before him, she implored his compassion.

"I can answer no questions to-night," replied Lipardo, emphasizing the two last words of his sentence.

"When then may I hope——" Paulina was proceeding to say.

Lipardo interrupted her by loudly pronouncing—"Will you please to taste any refreshment, signora, before you retire to rest?"

Paulina replied slightly in the negative.

"My wife, Ricarda," continued Lipardo, "will visit you early in the morning. Should you require any attendance during the night, this bell," pointing to a silken cord as he spoke, "communicates with my chamber, signora; I sleep on the opposite side of the gallery;" and having uttered these words, he was departing.

"Oh! when shall I behold you again?" exclaimed Paulina, eagerly pursuing his steps.

"Good-night, signora," roughly pronounced Lipardo; and hastily quitting the chamber, Paulina heard him lock the door on the outside.

The moment her attendants had retired, taking up a waxtaper, of which four had been left by Lipardo burning on a table in her chamber, she closely examined the apartments in which she was confined; and having convinced herself that no one was concealed within them, she sunk upon the couch on which she had at first opened her eyes to the hated walls of her prison, and burst into tears; she wept for the misery which her friends would experience on her account—she wept with apprehension at the trials to which the future might subject her. Where could she be? In whom could she confide? To what hope could she look for refuge?—"Wherever I am, or in the power of whomsoever I may be placed," she at length mentally pronounced, "the same Providence in which I have ever trusted beholds me now; He is still able to control the power of my oppressors; on his mercy I rely." She sunk upon her knees, and having recommended herself to the protection of her Heavenly Father, she once more threw herself upon the couch; the bed she had determined not to enter.

Universal silence prevailed around her, and the first sound which broke the stillness of the scene, was the hollow voice of a deep-toned bell proclaiming the hour of midnight. Time moved on leaden wings, and at length the first hour of morning vibrated upon the air; still Paulina durst not sleep—a shivering coldness crept over her frame, and she wished, but feared, to taste the wine which had been left in her apartment, lest it should be drugged. The second hour of the morning sounded, and shortly after, in spite of her efforts to repel the invasion of sleep, she sunk into a confused and broken slumber.

She had not slept long, ere she was awakened by a loud and dismal shriek, which appeared to issue from an apartment at no inconsiderable distance from her own; and this was immediately followed by the hasty bursting open of a door, and a voice exclaiming—"Help, Lipardo!—I say, help!" In a few moments a second door was heard to open, and a voice, which Paulina almost believed that she recollected to be that of Ricarda's husband, inquired the cause of alarm.

"Villain! slave! miscreant!" exclaimed the first speaker, "how have you dared to do this?"

"What, my lord?" was the reply.

"To suffer him to escape from his dungeon, and to confront me in my bed!" rejoined the first speaker. "'Tis well he fled, or, by my hopes of heaven, this hand had revelled in his blood, although the——"

"My lord, my lord," exclaimed the other speaker, "you have beheld no one—believe me, you have not; these are the workings of your brain. Retire into your chamber; I will accompany you, and do not hazard any one gaining a knowledge of——"

They had now entered the apartment, the door was closed, and Paulina heard no more.

"The words to which I have just listened," reflected Paulina, "must have proceeded from the lips of a guilty wretch, who is haunted by the dread of beholding some innocent victim of his cruelty."

Sleep was now effectually driven from her couch, and she wandered mournfully about her chamber, till the rising of the dawn, peeping through the saffron windows of the east, prompted her to extinguish the lights which had been burning in her apartment, and, by drawing aside the curtains from the casements, to make at least an attempt at ascertaining where she was. Shortly the wished-for light of morning became sufficiently strong to assist her investigations. From the apartment in which she had at first been restored to recollection, she could behold only battlements, surmounted by turrets and begirt by ramparts; and immediately beneath the windows lay a small garden, surrounded on all sides by the walls which intersected the squares of the building. She next proceeded to the chamber; it was lighted by a circular casement excavated in the dome, and consequently could lend no assistance to her inquiries. Lastly, she entered the closet in which the harp and books were deposited; it had only one window, and this, like those in the first apartment, looked down upon another inclosure within the ramparts, above the walls of which appeared the waving tops of a knot of gloomy cypress-trees; and beyond these, a brown and barren mountain closed in the view.

With stifled anguish (for her overburthened heart now refused her the relief of tears) she once more cast herself upon the couch, awaiting, with undefinable sensations, the events of the morning.

In the course of time, the "busy hum of men" began to resound through the Castle halls; and shortly after this, Ricarda and her husband entered Paulina's apartment, the latter of whom was attended by several domestics bearing an elegant morning repast, which they placed upon a table, and then, conducted by Lipardo, departed.

"Perhaps, signora," said Ricarda, "you are not accustomed to make your own breakfast; so, if you please, I'll pour out your tea, and keep you company."

The old woman seated herself at the table, and began the operation of which she had spoken. Paulina appeared insensible to what was passing, and Ricarda observing her mind abstracted from the scene around her, said—"I wish, from my heart, your first interview with the marchese were over; and then, when you had once come to a right understanding of each other's sentiments, your spirits would be relieved, and you would be able to enjoy a little chat with your tea. For my part, I think the best cup in the world is good for nothing, without it's flavoured with conversation."

"I shall take a cup with pleasure," replied Paulina, "for I have been very thirsty during the whole of the night;" and as she spoke she passed her hand over her cheeks, which were flushed and burning with the fever communicated to them by the distracted state of her mind.

"Thirsty!" ejaculated Ricarda, "and all that rich Franconian wine standing there untasted! It's well it wasn't so near me, signora. Why, a few glasses of that would have made you sleep as sound and as comfortable——But, blessed Virgin! what do I see?" she added, leaning forward her head and looking into the chamber. "Why, as I'm a holy sinner, you've not been in bed to-night! I wonder you are not ill with sitting up; and yet I vow you have as charming a colour as if you were only just opening your eyes after a long sleep and pleasant dreams."

The tea being prepared, and a cup placed before Paulina—"Come now," said her entertainer, "take a slice of sweet cake, or a Naples biscuit, or a queen's thumb, with a little preserve of barberries spread over it;" each of which when Paulina declined—"What will you prefer then? You have only to ask and have, within these walls," rejoined Ricarda; and on Paulina replying that she could taste nothing—"Well, I'll indulge you with some tea this time," said the old woman; "but I must make it a condition with you, that you eat with it at another. Tea is reckoned very hurtful to an empty stomach, and therefore I always take care to lay a good foundation for it to operate upon;" an assertion in which the devoirs paid by her to the preserves and confectionary with which the breakfast-table abounded, proved her to have been perfectly correct.

"I dare say, signora," continued Ricarda, between the intervals of mumbling her sugared crusts and sipping her scented hyson, "that you and I shall pass a great deal of our time together when you come to be settled, for I'm the only woman of consequence within these walls, fit for the wife of the marchese to associate with; and as he has no female relatives, and seldom receives company here in the country, why you will see no person of your own sex above a common servant, except myself. My husband, signor Lipardo, is the marchese's major-domo and steward, and withal his most intimate friend and favourite; and I am the superintendant of his household, and regulator-general of his domestic concerns."

Paulina, uninterested in all she heard, listened in silence; at which Ricarda seemed by no means offended, being upon all occasions satisfied that it was sufficient for her to speak, and for others to receive the information which she vouchsafed them.

Ricarda having concluded her meal, was just rising to command the removal of the breakfast-table, when the sounds of a shrill horn, twice or thrice repeated on the outside of the building, arrested her attention.—"Oh ho!" she said, "are you there, signor?" Then addressing Paulina, she added—"That is the horn of the marchese's nephew, whom those sounds inform me is just returned from a sporting party, on which he has been absent from home for a few days. He's a fine young man, signora, and you will like him vastly for a companion, I am sure;

he's very handsome too, I can tell you, and reckoned very much like me into the bargain. Be kind to him, signora, when you are become his aunt, and speak a good word for him to the marchese, his uncle, upon every occasion, and you will always find a staunch friend in me in return. There are wheels within wheels in all states and families, signora; and though you may imagine me to be nobody, a friend at court is always worth having, even to one who may believe herself to be wielding the very sceptre of government. You know little of Ricarda yet, signora—you will know her better by and by." These words were accompanied with many winks and grimaces; and when she had finished speaking, she rang the bell for the servants.

When the domestics had retired—"Well, signora," said Ricarda, "you will soon see the marchese now, and all will then be put upon a right footing, no doubt. You look sweetly, upon my word—enough to charm the heart of any nobleman; and I hope to be the first to wish you joy;" and so saying, she departed.

At the expiration of another half-hour Lipardo appeared, and announced the approach of the marchese. The major-domo retired, and the apartment was entered by a man of a tall and commanding figure, handsomely attired; his height and features precisely corresponded with those of the pilgrim at Venice; but although it was only two years since Paulina had beheld him, he appeared to have added as many lustres to his age.

"Signora," he said, advancing towards Paulina as he spoke, "I have only one apology to offer for a line of conduct which you may probably conceive to require an artillery of argument for its defence: excess of love, to whose resistless influence every mortal is condemned to bend, must plead my excuse, and shield me from the terror of your frowns."

"True love it could not be," replied Paulina; "for the first principle by which true love is swayed, is delicacy of action towards the individual who has inspired the sentiment."

"Say rather," returned the marchese, "that true love is that fury of the heart, that loss of self-control, which spurs us on to deeds which, if our adoration was more calm, our reason less inflamed, we should lack fire to accomplish, and buoyant spirits to rejoice in having dared to execute."

"The feeling you describe," rejoined Paulina, "is a madman's passion, and should be fettered by the same coercion that a madman's other inclinations are restrained by."

"By this hand——" exclaimed the marchese, attempting to seize her hand, and to kiss it as he spoke.

"This hand is yet my own," pronounced Paulina firmly, "and shall be, till my heart accompany the gift."

"If you disbelieve my love——" rejoined the marchese.

Again Paulina interrupted him—"I might have believed," she said, "had you proceeded like a man of honour in disclosing it. Had you sought my protector, the signor Urbino di Cavetti, confided your wishes to his friendship, made him the mediator of your suit to me, and at a distance waited my reply, this had seemed like love; and whether or not it had been accepted by me, it would have been answered with an acknowledgment due to the honour of your proposal. But when you play the thief, and steal the boon you covet, as a bravo does a purse, because he fears to be denied if he requests it as a gift, you falsify the very doctrine you profess, and prove what you misname devotion to be tyranny."

"By Heaven! I mean you honourable," returned the marchese. "'Tis true, I might have acted as you represent; but the impetuosity of my feelings——But no more of that—I will not again offend your senses by describing the excess of my adoration; only consent to become my bride, and words cannot express the joy and triumph with which I shall restore you, as my wife, to the presence of your protector Urbino."

"Never," replied Paulina. "I fear you not—I cannot fear the man who wantonly casts aside the principles of his nature, as you have done. My friends are doubtless humble, when compared with you, but they will nevertheless find the means of searching out my prison; and, in a point of justice, the worthy Urbino will not shrink from boldly opposing himself to the first potentate in the land."

"I beseech you to compose yourself and hear me," he resumed. "Did you but know how your matchless beauty fired my soul, as I, a few days since, in passing the farm of your friend Di Borges, on horseback, accompanied by my steward, for the first time beheld you——"

"For the first time!" ejaculated Paulina—"for the first time! Do you then pretend to have forgotten the constant persecution (preference, perhaps, you called it) with which you pursued me, two years ago, at the carnival?"

"The carnival! What carnival?" demanded the marchese.

"Need I repeat it was the carnival of Venice?" replied Paulina. "I am certain that, whether or not you are pleased to avow a recollection of the circumstance, it cannot but live in your memory."

"By my fondest anticipation of your enchanting smiles!" ejaculated the marchese, "I swear that I never beheld you until that day of which I have just spoken."

"Why you prevaricate upon this point," answered Paulina, "is as indifferent to me as is the cause why you preferred to snatch me, like a ruffian, from the bosom of my family, to pursuing the steps of an honourable suitor for my heart."

"You wrong me—on my soul you do," rejoined the marchese. "I solemnly repeat that I never saw you till I beheld you in that wood."

"From whence your banditti last night tore me," added Paulina, pointedly.

"Signora," resumed the marchese, after a pause, "I perceive that our conversation will not tend to the decision of that important business upon which we are met; I shall therefore, in the course of this afternoon, send you a written scroll, containing matter of serious moment, to which I most earnestly request your calm and unprejudiced reply. Meanwhile consider yourself the mistress of all that you behold, and, most of all, of him who now reluctantly quits your presence;" and, following these words with a mild and courteous inclination of his head, he quitted the apartment.

CHAPTER VI

I do love you,
Dearer than eyesight, space, and liberty—
Beyond what can be valued rich and rare—
No less than life, with grace, health, beauty, honour—
A love that makes breath poor and speech unable—
Beyond all manner of so much I love you.

Romeo and Juliet.

SOME hours now passed with Paulina uninterrupted by visitors; the first who appeared was Lipardo, but he was attended, as in the morning, by several domestics, over whom he kept a watchful eye whilst they were engaged in preparations for her midday repast. When the dinner was placed upon the table, Paulina seated herself, and pretended to eat, in the hope of either being left alone with Lipardo, or of catching some intelligence from his eye. All the inferior domestics, with the exception of one, who remained standing behind her chair, retired, and Lipardo stationed himself near the sideboard; but he continued constantly to employ himself either with the articles upon it, or by turning his eyes to the portraits suspended against the walls; and Paulina perceiving that it was in vain to attempt to engage his attention, dismissed the repast.

A considerable time was again passed by her in solitude; it was broken by the entrance of Lipardo, followed by two servants, who remained near the door of the apartment, whilst he, with a low obeisance, placed a folded paper on the table before her, and they then withdrew together.

On examining the paper, it was, as she had predicted it to be, the one which the marchese had in the morning informed her that he should send to her, containing terms for her consideration. It began with a declaration of his unalterable attachment, and the honourable motives by which he was swayed towards her; hence it proceeded to enumerate the advantages of rank and wealth, which she could not fail to enjoy in the quality of his wife, and requesting her to fill up a blank, which was left in the articles, with her signature, and any sum which she might deem sufficient for her annual expenditure. It concluded with imploring her to relieve his anxiety, by replying to his terms before the hour of noon on the following day. It was signed, Alberto di Valdetti.

The point in agitation was one on which the sentiments of Paulina could never vary, and having perused the contents of the paper, she refolded it, and referred to it no more.

In the evening she was visited by Ricarda—"So," said the old woman, "I find that I am not to wish you joy just yet: well, well, I have no doubt it will soon be the case—but you young signoras are so shy and delicate in all affairs of the heart—though, to be sure, there are many matters to settle where an engagement is forming for life; I was five or six hours myself between Lipardo's offering me his hand and my accepting it, and greater people may probably take a longer time; Rome was not built in a day. To-morrow is a new morning, and you have a long night before you for consideration;" and, after many other sapient remarks of a similar nature, she took her leave.

Lipardo next appeared, to light her tapers for the night, but, as usual, attended by inferior domestics. When in her presence, Paulina's eyes were constantly placed on his; and she could not forbear imagining that, on this evening, he appeared to regard her with a considerable degree of curiosity and interest, although he made not the slightest attempt either to engage her attention or to communicate with her eye.

When the universal stillness which prevailed throughout the Castle bespoke its inhabitants to have retired to rest, Paulina, exhausted alike by the mental and bodily fatigue under which she had been suffering, having discovered that the door of each of her apartments was provided with a bar, by means of which she could protect herself from intruders—having carefully secured herself against all access, was on the point of retiring to her bed, when a faint blow against the casement in the closet caused her to start. Actuated equally by hope and fear, she stood scarcely able to breathe, and impatiently awaiting what might follow. In the course of a few seconds, the noise was repeated. Snatching a candle from the table, she flew to the spot from whence the sound had issued, and as she approached it, the signal was a third time given.

Placing her light upon a table by her side, she gently raised the sash; and no sooner had she done so, than a substance resembling a small white ball darted through the aperture, and fell at her feet. She eagerly took it up, and found it to be a slip of paper folded round a smooth pebble. She instantly perceived that the paper was written upon, and lost not a moment in perusing its contents. They were these:—"Dear signora Paulina, be comforted in the knowledge that you have a friend within these walls, who will defend your honour at the price of his own existence. Let your heart, for the present, rest satisfied with the certainty that you are thus guarded; meanwhile let the most rigid caution be the guide of all your actions."

In a transport of thankfulness and joy Paulina pressed the paper to her lips; and in compliance with the admonition it contained, she instantly shut the casement, and retired to her chamber.

That the friend who had conveyed to her this soothing intelligence was Lipardo, she could not doubt; and by the caution which he had enjoined her to use, he had evidently meant to warn her against endeavouring to engage his attention when he entered her apartments, lest her anxiety to do so should be observed, and thus defeat any plan which he might have in agitation for her rescue. With an emotion of the purest delight she returned her thanks to Heaven for its interposition in her favour, and entering her bed, sunk to repose with some degree of composure.

On the following morning Ricarda, as on the preceding one, presided at the breakfast-table; and after the ceremonies of the hour were concluded, Paulina applied herself to reply to the letter which she had received from the marchese, which she did, by positively assuring him that no offer which he could make, no inducement which he could present to her acceptance, could prevail on her to connect her destiny with his; and concluded by requesting, that as her determination was unalterable, he would, without delay, restore her to her connexions.

Having sealed her letter, she delivered it to one of the servants, and in a short time received a reply, by Lipardo, from the marchese, requesting her to consider deliberately of the proposals which he had made to her for the space of three days, at the expiration of which time it was his intention to receive her final answer in person; and assuring her that, till that hour arrived, he could not flatter her with a hope of being restored to her friends in any other character than that of his bride.

Relying on the promises of her unknown friend, Paulina read his resolve, if not with indifference, at least without terror, and determined to await the event with all the composure of mind which she could command.

This day passed, as the former one had done, unchequered, except by the hours of refreshment and the occasional visits of old Ricarda. When the midnight bell had tolled, she eagerly repaired to the window of her closet, anxiously expecting a repetition of the signal by which the preceding night had been marked; but it was not given; and she was compelled to retire to rest without receiving any fresh communication from her unknown friend.

Not thus unsatisfactorily passed the succeeding night; somewhat earlier than she was prepared to listen for the signal, it it was sounded; she flew to the window, and descried, through the iron bars with which it was latticed, the figure of a man.

The uncertainty of the light by which she beheld him, rendered her doubtful whether or not it were Lipardo; she gently raised the sash, and beheld a young cavalier, of a most prepossessing countenance and appearance.

The stranger instantly spoke.—"Banish all apprehension, dearest signora," he said; "it is a sincere friend who addresses you."

"Who are you?" asked Paulina, scarcely conscious what she uttered.

"To you a stranger," was the reply; "but you are not so to me—I have long known and adored you!" He paused, then added—"Did your attendant never inform you of a young cavalier who had addressed some questions to her concerning you? and——" he hesitated.

"Yes, yes, she did, she did!" falteringly replied Paulina.

"I am that person," he returned; "my name is Vincentio. I am the nephew of the marchese di Valdetti, into whose power you have so unfortunately fallen."

"What can be his motive for detaining me here his prisoner," rejoined Paulina, "when I have declared to him my fixed resolution of never listening to his addresses?"

"Hope may tempt him to believe that you will in time yield to his love, as the only means of obtaining your liberty," returned Vincentio.

"But why did he by stealth bring me hither," replied Paulina, "in preference to laying his suit before my friend, my protector, Urbino?"

"Most probably he apprehended a negative to his wishes," answered Vincentio, "and therefore transported you to a spot where he possessed absolute dominion."

"Gracious Heaven!" exclaimed Paulina, "you cannot think that he will dare——to drag me to the altar by force?" she added, after a moment's hesitation.

"Means must be devised to thwart his intentions, whatever they are," said Vincentio.

"Fly then to the signor Urbino di Cavetti," returned Paulina, "whom you will find at the farmhouse of a worthy farmer, named Sancho di Borges; it is situate close to the posthouse, near to which you first saw me; inform him where I am detained, and a few hours will accomplish my rescue."

"Such a measure would be utterly ineffective," replied Vincentio; "an armed force could with difficulty gain admittance into this castle, if stoutly opposed by the vassals of the marchese; and were your friends even within the walls, there are amidst its recesses so many spots of concealment, undiscernible to the eye of strangers, that even their presence could not act towards your enlargement."

"How then am I to be rescued from the perils which surround me?" ejaculated Paulina.

"There is no hope but to work by stratagem," answered Vincentio; "I am acquainted with all that has passed between yourself and the marchese. You have still two days your own before you will be called upon to give your ultimate reply to his proposals; much may be done in the course of that time, and believe that a heart which adores you like mine will not be inactive in your cause."

"Can I confide in Lipardo?" asked Paulina.

"I know not," returned Vincentio; "I believe his real nature to be honest and even kind; but he has so long been accustomed to be the tool of the marchese's inclinations, and to fill his purse by fawning to his will, that an artificial nature has almost superseded in him that with which he was originally gifted."

"And his wife Ricarda?" rejoined Paulina.

"Is the creature of pride and avarice united," returned Vincentio; "flattery has great weight with her, but the heaviest purse is certain to secure her its advocate and instrument."

"If you desert me then," ejaculated Paulina, "what will become of me?" and she clasped her hands in agony as she spoke.

"Say but that your good opinion will be my reward," answered Vincentio, "and I swear by yourself, the most sacred oath I can propose, either to effect your liberation, or to die in your preservation."

The tear of gratitude started into the eye of Paulina, and she suffered Vincentio to draw her hand through an aperture of the lattice, and to press it to his lips.—"An eternal bond is, I trust, now sealed between us," he said; "you are henceforth my life, and in defending you I shall only protect what is most valuable to myself;" and after a few moments' pause, during which the feelings eloquently communicated by the eyes of each supplied the deficiency of words, Vincentio continued—"I dare remain with you no longer; it has been at an extreme hazard that I have ventured to approach you at all; I have bribed one of the gardeners for the use of this ladder, and must depart, lest he should follow my steps, and learn the cause for which I have employed it: good night, and good angels guard you! confide in Vincentio!"

"Good angels prosper thy endeavours!" exclaimed Paulina.

"God grant they may!" fervently pronounced Vincentio, and quickly disappeared from her sight.

Having cautiously closed the casement, she retired to her chamber, and sunk upon a chair in deep reflection. She had at length beheld the young cavalier who had so ardently professed his love for her; and at how critical a period of her fate had she been introduced to his acquaintance! She regarded the event of their meeting as the interposition of Heaven in her favour, and considering him as the deputed instrument of that benignant

Power for her salvation, she felt a reverence for his interest in her cause, compared with which a mere requital of his passion appeared an inadequate return for his nobleness of mind.

The suspense produced by expectation is sometimes even more tantalizing than that of dread; and quivering under the flattery of hope, Paulina felt it more difficult to compose her spirits for repose, than she had done when no ray of promise had beamed upon the prospect before her. She entered her bed, but slept not, and rose early, without feeling conscious that nature's balm had been a stranger to her eyes.

When her breakfast equipage was removed, Lipardo returned singly into the apartment, and presenting her with a bunch of rare and exquisite exotics, he said—"I believe, signora, that flowers are what you take peculiar pleasure in; do me the favour to accept these at my hands;" and without waiting for a reply, he again departed.

Lipardo had placed the flowers on a table by which she was sitting, and on her taking them up, the more closely to examine their beauties, Paulina perceived, concealed amongst the leaves, a sealed paper. She eagerly tore it open, and read these words:

"For your own sake, for the sake of Vincentio, do not attempt to entertain him again at the window of your closet; you have already been observed to do so, but all may yet be well, if you desist from repeating your hazardous intercourse; should it be communicated to the marchese, the greatest misery, if not death itself, might be the consequence to one or both of you."

As Lipardo had himself presented her with the flowers, there could remain no doubt of his being himself the giver of the caution which the paper contained. She now more than ever wished for an opportunity of conversing with him; but the forbidding sternness of his countenance, when he entered her apartment, forbade all advances on her part, and she was compelled to endure the pangs of uncertainty.

Time moved on with slow and heavy progress. Every luxury which could regale the sense, or delight the admiring eye, was offered to her acceptance in lavish abundance; whilst the domestics who attended upon her bent before her person, like slaves humiliating themselves in the presence of a conquering monarch. But this unceasing splendour produced no gratifying impression on the mind of Paulina; she sighed for liberty, for home, for the embraces of her beloved friends—most of all for the success of Vincentio in her cause, and his preservation beneath the trials to which his zeal might expose him.

At length arrived the hour at which the marchese had informed her that he intended to receive, in person, her final reply to his proposals. The door of her apartment was thrown open, and she expected to behold him enter; but in his stead appeared Ricarda.

The old woman's countenance beamed with pleasure and exultation; in her hands she bore an elegant casket, which placing before Paulina, she opened the lid, and displayed within a magnificent set of jewels, resting on a bed of satin, towards which, the moment Paulina's eyes were directed—"There, there, there, signora!" exclaimed Ricarda, "if those don't make you a happy bride, I don't know what can—and those the marchese sends to you by me, and begs you to accept as a wedding present. Now are not they delightful? Well, what answer shall I return to him? of course, that you are highly gratified by his munificence, and will——"

"As I understand that I am to see him shortly, I will return my reply to him myself," answered Paulina.

"Well, well, just as you please about that," rejoined Ricarda; "he bade me say he should be here directly; and I verily believe I hear his footsteps now;" and she was departing, when casting back her eye to take another gaze at the jewels, she added—"I have seen much in the course of my life, but never saw the equal of those sparklers before; they call them diamonds of the first water, signora; but to see them twinkle in the sun, as they do just now, I should be much sooner tempted to believe they were made of fire;" and the sound of footsteps now becoming audible in the gallery, away she bustled.

In the course of a few seconds the marchese appeared. After a few words of courtesy on entering the apartment, he said—"You cannot, signora, require to have repeated to you the cause which brings me hither; and I hope that I augur prophetically in predicting that I shall win my suit."

"When I return you this," replied Paulina, placing in his hand the casket, "and tell you that it is impossible I can accept its contents, I need scarcely add that my determination is the same as when we last parted."

The marchese betrayed disappointment, and appeared struggling to subdue an emotion of a passionate nature, which was with difficulty withheld from mounting to his tongue. He had considered the dazzling splendour of the jewels as an irresistless advocate in his cause, and the cold indifference with which he saw them rejected, by appearing decidedly to deprive him of every hope of prevailing with the object of his passion, touched an ireful chord in his composition, which was beginning to string him to a display of some fiercer tones in his disposition, than those which had yet been witnessed by his innocent captive.

Still he endeavoured for a while to preserve complacency of speech and conduct; and having once more recourse to the powers of persuasion, the same arguments were again rehearsed on either side, which each had futilely advanced for the conviction of the other at their last interview.

"Were I this instant to permit you to depart from hence," pronounced the marchese, tauntingly, "it would sound well in the ears of the world, that a young and lovely female, like yourself, had for some days been singly a visitor at my castle, and had quitted it without becoming my bride."

"I am willing to bear the aspersion," replied Paulina; "suffer me but to quit these walls, and the consciousness of my own innocence will be to me a sufficient shield against the unjust tongue of detraction."

"And what will men, who, like myself, are intimate with all the powers of love and beauty," was the reply, "say of the marchese di Valdetti, when they learn that after five days residence in his castle, he suffered the object of his adoration to escape from him unwon?"

He paused a few instants, then added—"Signora, the fierceness of my passion is, if possible, increased by the procrastination which it has endured."

The thunder of his voice grew deeper, and he proceeded thus—"Mark me, signora! here, by my soul, I swear! and neither gods nor demons shall divert me from my purpose, mine you shall be! remember well my words—mine you shall be! But it is at your option to become my wife!" and darting at her a look of mingled love and rage, he quitted the apartment.

Paulina's head sunk upon her clasped hands, and she stood lost in reflection. Where was now Vincentio? was it possible that he would gain acquaintance with the threat which the marchese had uttered? Without the intercession of Vincentio, the next hour might seal her doom. The apprehension almost maddened her, and she could scarcely impose sufficient command upon her feelings to forbear calling aloud upon his name. She flew towards the casement in the closet; she did not expect to behold him from it, and yet she felt disappointed that she saw him not. At one moment she traversed the apartment with hasty and uncertain steps, as if desirous of flying from herself; at another she listened near the door, dreading to hear the returning steps of her persecutor.

At the expiration of about a couple of hours, Ricarda made her appearance; her eyes evinced displeasure, her forehead was wrinkled with a frown, and her mouth pursed. Throwing herself into a chair, near to which Paulina was standing, and fixing upon her her repellent countenance—"So here's a fine piece of business," she exclaimed, "to go and provoke the marchese, as you have done, after all the marks of esteem and affection which he has shewn you since your residence in this castle; and above all, to reject a set of jewels that would almost buy a principality! what would you have forsooth?"

"My liberty," replied Paulina, "and my restoration to that tranquillity of mind which I enjoyed before I was introduced to a knowledge of the marchese."

"Ay, but how will you come at it?" returned the old woman, somewhat relaxing from the severity of tone in which she had spoken at her first entrance; "how will you come at it? I can tell you it is much easier getting within the walls of this castle than getting out of them. I am come to advise you as a friend, and I say, marry him—marry him, for the sake of St. Ursula, and the eleven thousand blessed virgins! I say, marry him, lest worse should happen; he is frantic with love, and you must know that it is impossible to take a mad bull by the horns."

"Oh, in the name of mercy, have compassion on me!" replied Paulina; "you are the only person of my own sex to whom I have here access; do not abandon me to a fate which I dread worse than death! Oh, in pity serve me if you can!"

"Why, am not I serving you all I am able, by giving you my advice?" returned Ricarda; "and I tell you, that the only honest plan you can pursue is to marry the marchese."

"Marry the marchese!" echoed Paulina; "I would sooner—"

"I know what you would sooner do as well as you do yourself," rejoined Ricarda, rising; and half-whispering in her ear, she added, "you would sooner marry his nephew, Vincentio! Ay, you may start, but you see a little bird has been singing to me; but don't be afraid of your secret—it's safe with Ricarda. I am not always so ill-tempered as I may at times appear; but I am teazed and tormented to death with many a plague that you know nothing about. So once more my advice to you directly and peremptorily is, to consent immediately to marry the marchese. Why, he cannot live long, in the common course of nature, and then when he dies, Vincentio, as his nephew, and you as his widow, will between you inherit all he is worth; and you may then marry one another, and be the happiest couple in all Italy!"

"And do you suppose, that if I were willing to submit myself to this humiliation," rejoined Paulina, "that Vincentio would tamely consent to behold the woman whom he loved subjected to such a degradation?"

"Ah, Heaven help him! Vincentio durst not take any thing the marchese does otherwise than tamely," replied Ricarda. "And why I advise you to lose no time in the business is, because, as the widow of the marchese di Valdetti, you might make Vincentio an honourable wife; but if any thing worse were to befal you, which Heaven forbid! I am sure I have warned you sufficiently against it! Why, he could not think of uniting himself with you after that, you know."

"Could I not for a few moments see Vincentio himself?" asked Paulina.

"See Vincentio!" repeated the old woman; "I durst as soon give you leave to take out my right eye as to attempt it! See Vincentio indeed! there would be blood and murder truly, if you two were caught together!" She rose from her seat, then added—"I have done more for you now than I ought; but, as I told you the other day, there are wheels within wheels in all families, and this is one of them. So now, if you will take the advice of one who knows what is, and what is not, do as I have recommended to you; it is your only chance. Take till the evening to reflect upon it; Lipardo shall keep the marchese from interrupting you till that time. But if you don't follow my advice, I am no woman, and the marchese is no man, if you don't live to repent it! Marry him first, and I'll engage that Vincentio shall wait for you till he dies. Follow my advice! follow my advice!" and with these words she again retired.

CHAPTER VII

'Twas strange, they said, a wonderful discovery!
HOME.

THAT Vincentio should have imparted his affection for her to old Ricarda, appeared to Paulina a circumstance so unaccountable, that nothing but the testimony of Ricarda's own lips could have gained it her credit. Could it be possible that Vincentio was privy to the indelicate advice which the old woman had given her to become the wife of the marchese di Valdetti, for the purpose of inheriting from him, as his widow, and thus ultimately swelling the wealth of his nephew, by forming a second alliance with him? Her brain swam in undefined and undigested ideas, and her mind was involved in a chaos of doubt, apprehension, and despair.

Lipardo, attended by the domestics of the castle, as usual, entered her apartment with refreshments, and as usual departed again in silence.

About the hour of eight in the evening, when the shades of twilight were beginning to descend to the earth, the opening of the door of Paulina's apartment presented to her view Ricarda and her husband, each bearing a light.

"I am sorry to inform you, signora," said the former, speaking loudly and imperiously, "that the marchese does not any longer permit you the use of these apartments. I am commissioned to conduct you to a chamber in a distant part of the castle."

"Anywhere," exclaimed Paulina, "where the marchese will not——"

"The marchese is ill, and retired to bed some time ago," rejoined Ricarda; "your obstinacy has provoked him till he is perfectly unwell. And no wonder, such ingratitude to be returned for such favours, such condescensions, and such magnificent offers as you received from him; but some people don't know what they would have!"

"This way, if you please; follow me," said Lipardo.

The major-domo led the way; Paulina followed his steps, and Ricarda hobbled behind.

"You are not going to such a lodging as you have left, I can tell you," cried the old woman, as they proceeded along; "but those who are wilful must take their own way of things. You would not follow my advice, and I am sure I spared no pains in trying to persuade you to make yourself happy, when happiness was in your power."

After tracing several vaulted passages, they ascended a flight of steps, at the head of which Lipardo paused; and having drawn from his pocket a key, he opened a door, and they entered a square apartment, of moderate dimensions, the walls of which were composed of stone, intermingled with occasional pannels of a dark wainscot, and in which the furniture was a wooden stool, a small table, a lamp, and a straw bed.

"There, what do you think of that for your bedchamber?" ejaculated Ricarda; "if you had taken my advice, you might have been sleeping still in the best bed, and have been kept as warm in it too as your heart could have desired; it is cold comfort here, I can assure you. The sun does not penetrate through that grated window once in a year—the stone walls and roof make it constantly damp—and chimney you see it has none; so the benefit of a fire, if even it were allowed you, is impossible."

Paulina sunk down upon the stool, and with difficulty repressed her tears.

"The cause of your being removed hither, signora," said Lipardo, "is, that the marchese believes that in this comfortless solitude, removed from the enjoyment of every luxury, you will reflect on the advantages which you have hitherto refused to accept, and be tempted to revoke your determination of rejecting his liberal offers; and he delegates me to inform you, that you will be allowed one week to deliberate on your fate, but that you may at any time put a period to your imprisonment by acceding to his proposals."

"Oh, for the love of God, have pity on me!" ejaculated Paulina.

A stern look from Lipardo awed her into silence.—"Lipardo knows his duty to his employer, signora," he loudly pronounced; "it is in vain to tamper with an honest man! Come, wife," he added, and having lighted the lamp which stood upon the table, they were departing.

"When shall I behold you again?" inquired the weeping Paulina.

"We will bring you some bread and milk in the morning," replied Lipardo.

"Ay, you will get no Franconian wine here," ejaculated the old woman; "this all comes of not taking my advice!" and they went out, Lipardo locking the door after them.

Shivering with cold, agonized in heart, and with an almost distracted brain, Paulina sat, lost in a stupor of thought, and appeared sensible only of existence by the excess of the misery which she was enduring.

How long she had remained in this sorrowing state she was uncertain; but she was suddenly aroused from the trance of reflection into which she had fallen, by the sound of "signora!" faintly pronounced.

She hastily turned round her head in the direction from which the voice had proceeded, and beheld the countenance and arm of Lipardo issuing from a chasm in the wall. He beckoned to her to approach him, and when she had done so, he took her hand, and having drawn her through the aperture, said—"This moving pannel is known only to myself; and if you have not before suspected it, you will now find that I am your friend; though I confess that I am unacquainted how to serve you in any more material point than that of providing you with

207

such comforts as the disappointed passion of the marchese would deny you."

On casting round her eyes, which now beamed with gratitude and hope, Paulina perceived herself to be in a small apartment, where an inviting fire was burning on the hearth, by the side of which stood a table covered with refreshments.

Lipardo again spoke.—"In that corner," he said, "in that corner you will find fuel to keep your fire alive with during the night; and there," pointing to the opposite side of the chamber, "is a clean bed for you to repose on; and now I must leave you, for I always sleep in an apartment adjoining to the chamber of the marchese; and should he wake and miss me, I should find some difficulty in accounting for my absence."

Having instructed her how to move the spring of the pannel, he said—"No one will approach you during the night, and without me no one can enter your prison, even by day, for I keep the only key which procures admission into it. If at any time you hear footsteps approaching, or the wards of a key turning in the lock of the door, instantly quit the inner apartment, and close the pannel after you; I will take care always to give you sufficient time for the operation."

"Oh, how can I reward your unexampled goodness!" exclaimed Paulina.

"I have motives for my conduct which amply reward me," replied Lipardo—"motives of which you can have no idea, and of which you cannot at present be informed. Good-night—Heaven bless you!"

"It must—it will bless you for the friendship which you have extended towards my defenceless state," pronounced Paulina.

"I am, I confess, not utterly uninterested in what I am doing," answered Lipardo; "but there are worse men in the world than myself. Once more, good-night! Remember my instructions;" and taking up a small lantern from the floor, he departed through another pannel in the wall, similar to the one by which he had admitted Paulina to the comforts with which he had provided her.

Paulina seated herself by the fire, which proved a most welcome renovator of her almost-fainting frame, and the warmth of the glowing embers inviting the approach of sleep, she sunk gradually into a temporary oblivion of her unhappy situation.

Early in the morning, Lipardo was true to his appointment in bringing her the bread and milk of which he had spoken; he cast at her a glance which informed her that he was satisfied with the manner in which she had pursued his directions for her conduct, and without uttering a word, he again departed.

In the course of the afternoon the major-domo brought her a fresh supply of the same provisions with which he had furnished her in the morning; and although he entered her apartment alone, and she heard no footsteps accompanying him even to the door, so far from addressing to her a single sentence, he did not even vouchsafe her a look; a circumstance which induced her to believe that he entertained a suspicion of spies being placed upon his conduct.

The distant clock, for it appeared by the faintness of its sound to be far removed from her in her present situation, had just sounded the midnight hour, when Lipardo entered through the pannel by which he had quitted her on the preceding night, laden with such articles as he conceived might conduce to the furtherance of her comfort; and having deposited his burthen, and pleaded his former excuse of being compelled to be in attendance upon the chamber of the marchese, he left her, informing her that his wife intended to pay her a visit on the succeeding night, if circumstances favoured her putting her design into execution.

The satisfaction communicated to the heart of Paulina, by the interest displayed in her cause by the major-domo and his wife, was materially abated by the assertion which the former had made on the preceding evening, that he was unacquainted how to serve her in any more material point than that of providing her with such comforts as the disappointed passion of the marchese would deny her. Thus, at the end of the week of deliberation which was granted her, what might not still be her fate? and she shuddered with horror at the idea which her bewildered brain had conjured up to her view.

Every circumstance around her, but the ferocious passion of the marchese, appeared to her a mystery. Why did the major-domo and his wife seem unconcerned about the preservation of her honour, or her peace of mind, and yet interest themselves so warmly in administering to the minor comforts of her existence? Vincentio had represented them alike the favourites and the tools of the marchese. If they had power and inclination to serve her in the instances in which they had already displayed zeal in her cause, why not act towards her rescue from the fate which threatened her? And if Vincentio were indeed inspired with the sentiment of affection which he had professed himself to feel for her, why did he not, at this momentous crisis, boldly stand forward her protector, and avow himself the honourable rival of his uncle? But perhaps, she considered, the promised hour for acknowledging himself in that character was not yet arrived, and she might be prematurely blaming him, when in reality he merited her warmest encomiums and thanks. It was also an impenetrable enigma to her, why he had confessed his love for her to those of whom he had himself spoken as the creatures of his uncle, when his own words had convinced her that he was not ignorant of possessing a rival in the marchese. The more she reflected, the more intricate appeared to her the involvements in which she was entangled: time alone could raise the misty veil which now obscured her future prospects.

At the silent hour of midnight Lipardo appeared, bearing articles for the replenishment of Paulina's secret store, and followed by Ricarda, muffled in a long black cloak, which defended her from the chill of the night, and would have served equally to screen her from observation, had she been met on her way by any individual whom chance might have raised from his bed, unlikely as that chance was, the passages by which Lipardo had conducted her lying through a part of the castle which was scarcely ever resorted to by any of its inhabitants, and indeed utterly unknown to most of them.

"Here I am," said the old woman, as soon as the moving pannel had been closed by her husband; "you see I don't forsake you, though you would not take my advice. I have brought you a suit of my own apparel," she continued, throwing down a bundle upon the bed as she spoke, "for I am sure you must need the comfort of a change of clothes by this time. I am always very particular about my linen myself, and I dare say you have been accustomed to be the same."

Paulina was beginning to return Ricarda her thanks, in which she was interrupted by Lipardo—"You will have time enough to talk when I am gone," he said; "so let me speak a word or two to my wife, and then I'll leave you together. Well, then, Ricarda," he added, addressing the old woman, "in about two hours, or between two and three, I'll slip out of bed, if I think the marchese is asleep, and bring you my lantern."

"Do so, do so," replied Ricarda; "I seldom feel the want of sleep; a few hours are sufficient for me, and I have a great deal to say to the signora, who, I dare say, must feel the want of company all day long severely enough, and will be all the better for a little chat with me. The mind must be desponding indeed that I can't raise and enliven by my conversation."

"Farewell, signora!" said Lipardo, and disappeared.

Ricarda seated herself on the side of the bed, and motioning to Paulina to place herself by her, she said—"I am sure you must be much obliged to Lipardo for what he's done for you.

What would have become of you in that cold place, next door, without a spark of fire, and nothing to lie upon but straw?"

"I am more indebted to him, and to you also," replied Paulina, "than I have words to express; not so much even the comforts which you have afforded me, as for the consoling sensation which the knowledge of your friendship has communicated to my heart."

"And do you know," rejoined Ricarda, archly, "to whom it is that you are obliged for all that we have done for you? For I will not pretend to say that, stranger as you are to us, we should have done quite as much for you, if it had not been in compliance with the entreaties of a certain person whom you know. What think you," she added, after a pause, "of the signor Vincentio?"

"If it is the signor Vincentio," replied Paulina, "to whom I owe——"

"It is to him, you may depend upon it," said the old woman, interrupting her; "and now we have time for a little conversation, I'll tell you all about it. It is almost impossible that we should be interrupted by the marchese, for I doubt if he even knows there is such a place as the one we are sitting in, in the walls of his castle; he passed a good deal of his time here on his estate in his youth, but at that time he wasn't lord and master of the territories, as he is now, and so did not possess the clue to all the mysteries which are to be found within this building; and since he came into possession, I don't think he ever spent three days at a time here yet, till within the last five weeks; and if even he should pop upon us, which I repeat to be an impossibility, I should tell him boldly at once, that women had private affairs to arrange, in which no man, even a husband, had a right to interfere; and that in doing my duty to you, by assisting you in some little particulars where you required my helping hand, I considered myself at the same time to be doing my duty equally towards him."

Paulina listened in silence, anxious for that part of the narrative in which Vincentio was concerned.

"Could you take a little drop of Nantz brandy," rejoined the old woman, "mixed with a little water, to keep the damps of the night from giving you cold? I have brought a drop in my pocket," she added, pulling out a small bottle as she spoke; "it is a liquor I'm not fond of, but I am forced to take a spoonful when I am out of bed after my usual hour, to keep the cramp out of my stomach."

Paulina declined her offer; the old woman took her draught, and proceeded thus—"You must know, signora, that on account of a family business, which it is not material to lose time in explaining to you just now, Vincentio has not been acknowledged by his own parents since he was about a year old: ever since that time he has been brought up under the authority, and entirely at the expence, of the marchese his uncle. Many a week, many a month, and many a year, has he been left here in his younger days, under the care of my husband and myself; and by constantly living with us, we gained such a liking for him, and he became so fond of us, that he considered us as his real parents, and we looked upon him with the affection of a child. The kindness which we shewed him, contrasted with the morose and haughty disposition of the marchese, for I must own that his disposition is not at all times the most conciliating in the world; to be sure beauty, like yours, may soften and mould any heart; but I mean with regard to his intercourse with the world in general. Stay, what was I saying? Oh, ay! our kindness made such an impression on his heart, that from a boy upwards, he has all his life long entrusted us with his secrets, and never conceived himself happy but in our advice on every occasion."

"He appears a most amiable young man," said Paulina.

"No doubt you think him so," answered Ricarda, smiling; "but in sober truth, he is what you describe him to be. He was a temper of ten thousand from his cradle: I remember that he didn't even cry above ten minutes when the breast was taken from him."

"You knew his mother then?" said Paulina.

"His mother!" repeated Ricarda. "Oh, I understand what you mean. I was his wet nurse myself, signora."

"That must double your affection for him," said Paulina.

"I don't know how it is, or what it is," replied the old woman, "but he can melt my heart to any thing, as he has done towards you. But to go on with my story—about three weeks ago, Vincentio informed my husband and myself that he had seen a young lady who had inspired him with a passion which he was certain he should never be able to conquer; and then proceeded to acquaint us that you were the niece of the signor Urbino di Cavetti, who was lately come to reside with his family at the ancient Castello of——I forget the name."

"Della Torvida," said Paulina.

"Ay, that's it," returned Ricarda: "I forget names strangely of late; but forget what I may, signora, I shall not forget yours when it's Di Valdetti. I have been accustomed to that name from the day I opened my eyes: I shall never forget that, I am sure."

Paulina anxiously awaited the sequel of her harangue, eager to learn whether it was by the uncle or the nephew that Ricarda anticipated the name to be transferred to her.

"Well," continued Ricarda, "when Vincentio had informed us of his passion, he followed his account by imploring my husband to communicate the affair to the marchese, and endeavour to obtain him his consent to lay his suit before your uncle, the signor Urbino, and make you an immediate offer of his hand: but as Lipardo was aware that the marchese had lately sustained some considerable losses at play, and that Vincentio's marriage could not be concluded without a heavy draught upon his uncle's purse, he besought him to defer insisting on his making the communication to the marchese till his recent losses were in some measure obliterated from his memory, and promising to take the first favourable opportunity which presented itself to him for engaging his uncle in the promotion of his happiness. Well, all went on quietly till I was commanded to prepare the apartments which you occupied on your first arrival at the castle for the reception of a lady, whom my husband at the same time received orders to send out Philippo on horseback to escort hither; and you may easily imagine our astonishment, when on your arrival we found you to be the signora Paulina to whom Vincentio had lost his heart. Bless me! there's two o'clock! if I don't make haste with my story, I shall have Lipardo coming for me before all our business is transacted."

"How did Vincentio discover that I was here?" inquired Paulina.

"From the account given of you by some of the domestics who accompanied you hither, he suspected it to be you," rejoined Ricarda, "and bribed the truth from Philippo; and oh, if you had but seen him throw himself at my husband's feet, and implore him to lend his assistance to rescue you from his uncle!"

"And will not Lipardo consent," weepingly pronounced Paulina, "in compliance with the happiness of a youth whom he so much esteems?"

"Why, what could he do, even if he were willing?" exclaimed Ricarda: "if we were to fly in the face of the marchese on your account, it would do you no good; he has plenty about him who are willing to do any thing he would pay them for. If we were only to venture to remonstrate, he might perhaps imprison us in a dungeon for life, or poison us, or starve us to death. The blessed saints only know what he might do, especially to me; for I am sure he would think no more of killing an old woman than he would of riding over a tom-cat. No, no; we both promised Vincentio to grant you all the indulgence we

215

could, and to take all the care of you we could, unknown to the marchese; and more we cannot do, and dare not do."

"Could I not behold Vincentio here to-morrow night through the same means by which you have visited me to-night?" asked Paulina.

"No, no, no!" ejaculated Ricarda; "there can be no good purpose answered in your having a young man to visit you in the night, and in the daytime, you know, it is impossible he should approach this place. If he has any thing particular to say to you, Lipardo shall inform you of it to-morrow night."

"Will you tell him that I besought you to inquire whether he had any message to convey to me?" ardently demanded Paulina.

"I will—I will indeed," answered Ricarda; "you may depend upon me. And now be as quick as you can in changing your clothes, that I may carry your soiled ones away with me, and get them refreshed for you. These of mine, which I have brought you, are much thicker and warmer than yours, and consequently much better adapted than your own to your present lodging."

Paulina proceeded to comply with her request, and Ricarda rose from her seat to assist her in the operation.

The exchange was nearly made, when Ricarda, letting fall from her hand a garment which formed a part of Paulina's new equipment, snatched a candle from the table, and holding it close to Paulina's shoulder, upon which she steadily and inqui-sitively fixed her eyes—"What scar is that upon your arm? How did you come by it?" she exclaimed.

"Indeed I know not," replied Paulina; "but I can recollect seeing it when I was quite a child."

"It is very strange—very strange indeed!" rejoined Ricarda. "Immediately below the turn of the shoulder! And did you never hear any body mention it?—none of your friends say what had occasioned it?"

"Never," answered Paulina.

"Well, I never was so surprised by the sight of any thing in my life!" continued the old woman. "Tell me, have you one like it, that is, another scar on your back, at the bottom of your neck?"

"Yes, I have," returned Paulina, "and somewhat longer and deeper than this on my arm."

"Let me see it," eagerly ejaculated Ricarda, pulling off the drapery, as she spoke, from the part where she expected to find the object of her inquiry—"Ah! there it is indeed!" she continued, in a voice of emotion undefinable to her auditor—"there it is indeed! Great God! was there ever any thing like this? Wonders will never cease! Holy Virgin, have mercy upon me!"

"Why are you thus agitated?" inquired Paulina, who was becoming herself unnerved, she knew not why, in proportion as she observed her companion moved.

"Don't ask me; I cannot tell you now," rejoined Ricarda; "but answer me—are you sure the signor Urbino di——I can't think of his name now."

"Di Cavetti," said Paulina,

"Di Cavetti!" echoed Ricarda: "are you sure he is your uncle?"

"I have always called him so," answered Paulina, "and been taught to consider him such."

"He is no more your uncle than I am your uncle!" ejaculated the old woman. "Merciful God! oh, how my head turns round!"

"You astonish me!" replied Paulina.

"Not half so much as I am astonished myself," interrupted the old woman. "A scar just below the turn of the arm, and another on the back at the bottom of the neck! Angels of heaven! was there ever the like!"

The pannel was at this moment drawn back, and Lipardo appeared within—"Come," he said, "I havn't a moment to lose; I am never sure of the marchese for five minutes together. Come, wife, come."

"Oh, Lipardo!" she exclaimed, "I have such a thing to tell you! but I musn't begin talking here, for fear of the consequences. I scarcely know whether I stand on my head or my heels. I am sure you will not believe me, but another night shall convince you. God bless you, signora! I'll see you to-morrow night, if possible. Well, I never knew the like before in all my life!" and whilst uttering these words, she had joined Lipardo, who stood anxiously awaiting her, and closed the pannel the moment she had passed through it.

If the brain of Paulina had before been bewildered by dwelling on the extraordinary situation in which fate had placed her, what were the reflections which now harassed her mind, in consequence of the remarks made by Ricarda upon the scars on her arm and neck! Would the disclosure which appeared to have been just made to Ricarda be instrumental in developing to her some secret relative to her birth, which, believing herself the orphan relative of Urbino, she had hitherto considered unconnected with mystery? Her own mind could furnish her with no reply to the questions which tortured her imagination; and with an anxiety almost amounting to frenzy, she awaited the return of the midnight hour, which she hoped would once more bring Ricarda into her presence.

CHAPTER VIII

The tale wrapt up in your amazing words
Deign to unfold.
— — — — — — — — — —
Then, thus abjur'd, I'll speak to thee as just
As if you were the minister of Heaven,
Sent down to seek the secret sins of men.

HOME.

WE must now return for a while to the signor Urbino di Cavetti and his disconsolate family. Nine days had now elapsed since the disappearance of Paulina, and every inquiry concerning her destiny, as well as the spot of her seclusion, having proved fruitless, notwithstanding the anonymous assurance which had been received of her safety, and her eventual happiness being connected with her present mysterious absence, her friends were affected with the deepest concern at her unexplained fate, and their thoughts dwelt sorrowfully and unremittingly upon her.

On the tenth day, the morning proving damp and uncomfortable, and Urbino feeling himself neither well in health nor spirits, resolved not to quit the Castello that day, and sent Terence to the farmhouse, to acquaint Valeria, and the family of Di Borges, with his intention of not visiting them till the morrow; and Jeronymo, who seldom wandered from home, and who disliked proceeding to an distance without a companion, professing an inclination to accompany him, they set out together.

At their departure Urbino accompanied them into the castle hall, in order to close the door after them; and as they were descending the steps, he perceived old Bianca, who had been one of his regular pensioners since his abode at the Castello, hobbling along the sycamore-walk as quickly as she was able, and making the most earnest supplications to him to await her approach.

"When she had arrived near enough to be heard by Urbino—"Oh, beneficent signor!" she exclaimed, pardon me, *per l'amor Dio!* I beseech you to excuse me for entreating your charity, when I have already experienced so much of your goodness; but I never was so greatly distressed as I am at this moment. I have lost my poor boy!—lost my Calvino!"

"Lost him!" replied Urbino. "Do you mean that he is dead?"

"I don't know, signor—I don't know!" she returned, half weeping. "I hope not; the saints send he may be alive! and that when he is taken from me, I may live to see him die in a bed, like other Christians! He often leaves me, and strolls about the country for a day or two together; but he has now been absent nearly twelve days, and I am almost starved for want of his assistance, in helping me to gather firewood, and cutting pegs for the cobbler, by which we make a trifle; and pulling nuts in the woods, which we sell to the children in the autumn. Oh, poor Calvino! I am ill off without him!"

Urbino endeavoured to administer comfort to her, by telling her that her son would probably soon return to her; and giving her a few pieces of coin, he dismissed her, and retired to his study.

He had not been long engaged with a book which he had taken up to beguile his thoughts, when he was surprised by the unusual sound of a claimant for admission at the outer door of the Castello. He laid aside his book, and proceeded to answer the summons.

On opening the door, he perceived before him a man of a healthy and robust frame and countenance, somewhat beyond the middle age of life, plainly habited, but bearing an appearance which denoted him superior to the ordinary ranks of life—an opinion which his tone of voice and language instantly confirmed.

To his inquiry, whether the signor Urbino could be seen by him? having received in reply, that Urbino was the person to whom he was then addressing himself, he said—"I shall esteem it a most particular favour, signor, if I can be indulged by passing half-an-hour in conversation with you."

Urbino requested him to enter; and having conducted him to an apartment, the stranger was requested to be seated, and Urbino drew himself a chair by his side.

"A stranger," Urbino's visitor began by saying, "feels himself most awkwardly situate, when he is under the necessity of introducing himself to the person on whose time he is trespassing, without being permitted, by the circumstances which occasion his intrusion, to mention his name as a prelude to conversation." He paused an instant, then proceeded thus— "But rely on this, signor Urbino, that my heart, my soul, are devoted to one with whom you are connected; and that the lively interest which I take in her fate has brought me hither."

"Can it be my Paulina to whom you refer?" eagerly inquired Urbino.

"Paulina," rejoined the stranger, "is the name of her who is the object of my present visit."

"If you know her," ejaculated Urbino, "you are doubtless acquainted where she is at this moment concealed; I beseech you to inform me if she be well—if——"

"Is she not residing with you?" the stranger interrupted him by demanding; "living under your immediate protection?"

Di Cavetti, in few words, related the sudden disappearance of Paulina, and the fruitless inquiries which he had since made after her.

"Carried off by force!" exclaimed the stranger. "But no matter; wherever she be, I engage to bring her forth; the first man in the empire shall not screen her from my penetrating researches: that is, if she be the female whom I suppose her to be." And after another pause, he added—"Signor Urbino, I think I am right in supposing her not to be your daughter?"

"My niece," falteringly pronounced Urbino.

"No, nor your niece, signor," emphatically returned the stranger.

Urbino made many efforts to speak, but the words died away upon his tongue.

"Do not equivocate with me," rejoined the stranger. "You love her—of course you must desire her happiness; most of all, her peace of mind, and the preservation of her honour. They rest upon your conscientious reply to this simple question—are you acquainted who were her parents?"

Still Urbino hesitated to reply. The stranger repeated the assertion which he had already made, and confirmed its truth with an oath, which Urbino could not doubt to proceed from the lips of an honest man.

"If my confession of the past can produce her the advantages of which you speak," said Urbino, "it would be both contrary to my nature, and the principles of justice, to withhold from you the information which you seek. I will therefore confide to your honourable keeping the narrative of the events by which she was introduced to my knowledge, and became the niece of my adoption."

"I have no leisure at this time to listen to a detail of facts," returned the stranger; "a summary reply is all that I require; you know not who her parents were?"

"On my sacred word, I do not know them," replied Urbino.

"Enough!" ejaculated the stranger; "then Paulina is safe and happy, and you shall be most amply rewarded for the protection which you have afforded her."

"There is no return I will accept," replied Urbino, "unless, for the quiet of my agonized feelings, you will tell me whether or not you are acquainted where she now is, and when I may expect to see her? and name that the reward of which you spoke."

"It cannot be; do not urge me," returned the stranger. "You are always to be found at the Castello, I imagine?"

"Or at the farmhouse of Sancho di Borges, about a league from hence," answered Urbino.

"You will soon see me again, signor," returned the stranger; he took the hand of Di Cavetti, shook it cordially in his, and having done so, he darted out of the apartment, hastily crossed the castle hall, and issuing through the portal, moved with a hasty step along the sycamore-walk, and quickly gaining the road, he in a few minutes disappeared from the sight of Urbino.

By the visit, inquiries, and predictions of the stranger, the mystery of Paulina's absence was increased to the good physician. He knew not whether to believe the stranger acquainted with the spot of her present seclusion, and was equally at a loss whom to conceive that man to be, who had declared that he possessed the means of discovering her retreat, if even it were situate under the protection of the greatest potentate in the empire. No questions, till the present hour, had ever been asked of him concerning Paulina, except by the pilgrim at the carnival of Venice; and between the stature, the features, and the voice of the pilgrim and those of the stranger, there was so decided a contrast, that he could not for a moment suppose them to be the same individual. At all events, under the circumstances represented by the stranger, he believed himself to have exercised his duty towards Paulina, in having confessed himself ignorant of her origin; and upon the promise of the stranger, that he should see her soon again, he rested those hopes which alone enabled him to support his composure of mind, as he reflected on the obscure fate of her whom he loved with all the tenderness of a real father.

Since the disappearance of Paulina, Valeria had been constantly employed by day in attending on her father, and endeavouring to soothe by her presence the sorrows with which his mind was oppressed; consequently no opportunity had presented itself to her for repairing to the solitary abode of Julio, for the purpose of returning his manuscript, and listening to the conclusion of his narrative from his own lips. On receiving the intelligence brought by Terence, that Urbino did not intend on that day to quit the Castello, she resolved to avail herself of the occasion with which a fortunate chance had provided her, and to repair that afternoon to the cell of the recluse.

At the time which she had appointed for setting out, a lowering sky dimmed the lustre of nature's face, and a drizzly rain was falling to the earth; but the weather was a consideration which she could not admit as an obstacle to her ardent desire of beholding Julio; and easily apologizing for her absence to Averilla, who was alone in the farmhouse at the period of her departure, and who was ignorant of the state of the weather, she began her walk.

The unfavourableness of the weather increased as she proceeded, but Valeria heeded it not; and she arrived in safety, and unobserved, at the spot of her destination. She found Julio within his hut, and the joy which he expressed at beholding her, could not conceal from her observation the anxiety which he had endured on account of her long absence; she briefly explained to him the cause, which he cordially joined with her in lamenting; and after some time passed in conversation, he turned his words to the subject on which they were met.—"Has then my beloved Valeria," he said, "perused the eventful narrative of her Julio's life?"

Valeria replied in the affirmative, and Julio continued thus—"From his own lips, she now awaits a relation of the dreadful, the awful climax of his fate, and Julio is prepared to unfold it to her; for it must be known by her, and therefore cannot be too soon divulged. Oh, Valeria! Heaven grant that thou mayest receive the disclosure which I am about to make to thee with fortitude of mind; for thou, Valeria, thou art intimately connected with the sequel of my melancholy tale!"

The agitation of Valeria's mind beamed through her eyes, and she almost trembled at the solemnity of the tones in which Julio had addressed to her his last words.

"Oh, my Valeria!" he proceeded by saying; "my adored, my idolized sister!"

"Sister!" repeated Valeria, falteringly.

"Not by the ties of blood," replied Julio; "but in love, in friendship, and in soul."

Valeria besought him to speak without reserve, and to relieve her from that anxiety of mind with which his mysterious expressions affected her.

Julio consented, and spoke thus—"My manuscript, as you will recollect, broke off at the period of my flying from Padua, immediately after my antagonist had fallen by my hand. I continued to follow an uncertain course, in the hope of arriving at a spot of security; but I had left the city only a few hours, when I gained intelligence that the officers of justice were already in pursuit of me.

"For several days I hid myself during the light of day in forests, and by night stole forth to purchase necessary refreshment for the support of my existence, at various cottages, which nothing but my state of abject need could at that time have tempted me to enter. At length, after pursuing a circuitous and uncertain course, I found myself on the margin of the Gulf; immediately opposite to the city of Venice; and thither I resolved to transport myself, hoping to pass unknown and unnoticed amidst its extensive population."

The inclemency of the weather had been gradually increasing ever since Valeria had entered the hut; the rain was now descending in heavy showers—the lightning flashed vividly across the narrow casement which gave light to the abode of

the recluse, and the thunder rolled awfully through the sky.
Valeria heard the storm with sensations the opposite of satisfaction; but her desire to learn the conclusion of Julio's narrative
superseded every other feeling, and she endeavoured to bend
her whole attention towards him.

"Having crossed the Gulf, and arrived in Venice," continued
Julio, "I entered a tavern, where I had no sooner seated myself,
than I heard one of the guests informing his companions that
the officers of justice from Padua were arrived in the city, in
pursuit of a signor who had killed his antagonist in a duel, and
describing the very dress and marks by which I was identified.
I folded my cloak closely round me, and again rushed out into
the street, more than ever at a loss whither to bend my steps for
refuge.

"In this distracted state of mind I was wandering along,
when I beheld, on the point of entering a handsome mansion, a
signor of a venerable appearance, the mildness and humanity of
whose countenance immediately inspired me with the desper-
ate idea of briefly relating to him my unhappy situation, and
imploring his assistance in protecting me.

"During the few moments in which I was occupied in relating to him my case, in the most hurried accents of alarm, I
perceived him to change colour, and an almost-indefinable
expression, which I afterwards found to have been produced by
the struggle of contending feelings in his mind, took possession
of his countenance; and when I concluded speaking, he said—
'You bore your adversary then no rooted hatred—no malignant
antipathy? The cause from which you have erred, originated in
a point of what the world falsely names honour?'

"I replied in the affirmative to his inquiry.

'Cursed infatuation!' he answered; 'how many owe to thee
the subversion of their early bliss! Stranger,' he proceeded by
saying, whilst his lips trembled with the pangs of ill concealed
agony, 'the youth who owes to your hand his untimely death is

my son! Not two hours have elapsed since he was brought a corpse to his distracted father's house. You are at this minute in my power; but I extend mercy to others, as I hope one day to have it administered to myself at the throne of grace. To behold you expiate your crime on a scaffold could not restore to me my son—when the act of permitting you to exist for repentance cannot fail to yield a soothing balm to the reflections of my deathbed. One of my servants shall conduct you to a pass across the Gulf, whence you can be transported to an unfrequented country, about ten leagues from hence, where you may, in all probability, escape detection. Let my lenity towards you teach you to keep a guard over your passions in future. Farewell! But let me never behold you more.'

"Thunderstruck by what I had heard, I stood almost motionless, till aroused by the servant whom the generous Venetian had sent to conduct me to the pass of which he had spoken. I gained it in safety, and was landed by the gondoliers upon a soil which my foot had never before trodden."

At this moment a scorching flash of lightning darted past the casement; it was instantly followed by a tremendous clap of thunder, which burst immediately above their heads. Valeria started from her seat; her countenance betrayed the wildest alarm, and Julio clasped her, for security, to his bosom.

The roll of the thunder had not ceased, ere a voice without called loudly for shelter against the storm; and before Julio had either time to reply, or was thoroughly convinced that the sound which he indistinctly heard was that of a human voice, the door was hastily opened, and Urbino rushed in. He darted his eyes first upon Valeria, next upon Julio. A convulsive start shook his frame—he clasped his hands energetically together, and raising his eyes towards heaven.—"Powers of Mercy!" he exclaimed, "what is it I behold? Valeria! my child Valeria clasped in the arms of her brother's murderer!"

The truth flashed like an electric shock upon the senses of Valeria; a faint shriek burst from her lips—she disengaged herself from the support of Julio, and flying into her father's arms, sunk senseless upon his breast.

CHAPTER IX

To know my deed, 'twere best not know myself!
Macbeth.

——————Yes, yes, 'tis hers!
I know it by sure marks.
AARON HILL

THE first of the astonished group who regained the power of utterance was Julio.—"Signor," he said, "I beseech you not to imagine that I have voluntarily transgressed against that injunction which you delivered to me at an awful moment of my life, never to suffer you to behold me again. At your entrance here, I was in the act of informing your amiable daughter of the impossibility of our ever being united in those holy bonds, in which hope once promised to ally our assimilating hearts; and likewise describing to her, that it would be the last time we could ever converse together. To you and her, mutually, I now make one solemn declaration—it is, that after this hour you will neither of you either see me or hear of me again."

After a moment's pause, he added—"I entreat you, signor, so far to favour me, as to deign to peruse the narrative of those events which led me to the fatal act for which I am now suffering."

He presented to Urbino the manuscript which had already been perused by Valeria—"Your daughter," he continued, "is already acquainted with its contents; but the record of my woes is there only deduced to that period at which you preserved the life of him who had aimed the deadliest blow at your existence. This paper," he added, drawing one from the folds of his garment whilst he spoke, "contains a recital of the adventures which have befallen me subsequent to that hour; it will explain to you the motive by which I was actuated in desiring once more to commune with your daughter, before I quitted her presence for ever. But the imperious mandate of honour forbids me any longer to intrude on the feelings of those whom I have already too much wronged. This moment separates us for ever—this gaze is the last which we shall ever interchange with each other!" and with a countenance of mingled horror and despair, he then rushed out of the hut.

The bleeding image of his son was recalled to the memory of Urbino by the sight of his destroyer. The tears trickled down his furrowed cheeks, and he turned towards his daughter for that support which he had a few moments before afforded her.

"Oh, my father!" exclaimed Valeria, "deem me not guilty, I conjure you—judge me not a despiser of my brother's wrongs, or a conspirer against the feelings of my parent; believe me, till the moment at which you proclaimed him so, I knew not that Julio was———" She checked her tongue, for her father's sighs pierced her heart, and her own tears almost stifled her utterance.

Struggling to regain her composure of mind, and endeavouring to repel her tears as she spoke, she, in few words, recounted to her father her first acquaintance with Julio; and in confessing her former meeting with him on the spot where Urbino had just beheld them together, she did not omit pointedly to detail to her father the many hints which Julio had so emphatically given her, that the union of friendship must be the only bond by which their hearts could be cemented.—"My knowledge of Julio, and my love for him," she said, "are the only secrets which I ever withheld from your participation; and oh, my father! severely am I punished for having neglected to repose them in your confidence."

Absorbed in the reflections of his own mind, Urbino had not perceived the departure of Julio; and raising his eyes from the shoulder of his daughter, upon which his head had fallen, he looked around, as if in search of the being whose presence had not only caused the revival of his miseries, but had awakened in him apprehensions of the most poignant nature. Valeria repeated the words which Julio had uttered at departing.

"I heard his declaration," replied Urbino, "but was doubtful whether he had quitted the spot. Come," he added, "we will depart also—this is no place for us."

"The storm is not yet entirely abated," said Valeria.

"No matter," answered Urbino; "I will not hazard his return whilst we are here."

As Urbino was approaching the door—"These papers," said Valeria, pointing to the manuscript, and the folded sheet which laid by its side upon the rugged table—"he requested—he—" she hesitated—"You will not suffer them to remain here?"

"Do with them as you will," replied Urbino.

Valeria took them up, and put them into the pocket of her father.—"They may," she said, "throw some light upon that honourable conduct which he had resolved."

"Honourable!" echoed Urbino, with a painful smile. "Can it be possible," he proceeded by saying, after a moment's hesitation, "can it be possible that your heart still lingers after him?"

"Oh no, no! Heaven forbid it!" fervently pronounced Valeria. "I am henceforth, my dear father, thine, and thine only—a virgin in my tomb, as at my birth; if you doubt my firmness, render it impregnably secure, by enclosing me for ever within a convent's walls."

"Would you then prefer to waste your life in a monastic solitude, weeping for the past, uncheered by any future hope, to the easy task of proving yourself the active comforter of my existence?" earnestly demanded Urbino.

"Oh, my father," replied Valeria, "do not suspect me of such insensibility! Indeed, indeed, I cannot be more blessed than in my constant attempts to render you happy: render me so in return, by moulding me to your own wishes."

"Thou art still my child!" ejaculated Urbino; "oh, let me once more clasp thee to my heart, and feel thee mine!" Again the tears started in his eye, but they were now the relieving drops of returning composure and satisfaction.

On quitting the hut, Valeria could not forbear casting round her eyes, to observe if Julio were anywhere discernible near the spot, but she beheld him not. The rain had now nearly ceased, the lightning was only a shadow of its former fierceness, and the thunder had retired, in low and hollow murmurs, to the distant mountains.

Urbino drew his daughter's arm through his, and they proceeded in silence. He led her towards the farmhouse, and when they had arrived there, a few words spoken by Urbino were received as a sufficient explanation of their having met, of which he had reasons for not desiring the real cause to be at that moment known even to his friend Di Borges; and having exchanged their wet garments, Urbino declared his determination of not returning back to the Castello that night.

The motive by which Urbino had been actuated in leaving its walls at all that day, after the contrary intention which he had signified by Terence in the morning to the inhabitants of the farmhouse, was, that, rendered agitated in mind, and anxious in spirits, by the conversation which had passed between the stranger and himself concerning Paulina, he had strolled out into the woods, as a temporary relief to his thoughts, and having wandered farther than he had either intended or been conscious that he was doing, he had been overtaken by the storm near the hut of the recluse, to which he had flown for refuge from the elemental war, and entered at the important crisis of which a detail has already been given.

The temperature of the succeeding morning was mild and serene; and the face of nature, refreshed by the invigorating showers which had fallen on the foregoing evening, presented an inviting appearance, which prompted Urbino to request his daughter to walk with him to the Castello. She readily consented, and they set out. Abroad all was cheerfulness; the whistling hind joining his song with the wild notes of the feathered warblers of the air, seemed both equally to be rejoicing in the exhilarating beams of the sun; the verdure of the grove appeared more vivid to the eye; and the flowers of the field sent forth a perfume delightful to the senses.

Valeria endeavoured, by every means in her power, to compel herself to appear cheerful also, and to communicate the feeling to the heart of her father; she gradually succeeded in leading him into conversation, but their remarks were only on general subjects, and she felt gratified that he had not reverted to the occurrences of the preceding day. Whether or not he had perused the manuscript, and the folded paper which had been given him by Julio, she was unable to form any opinion, and she resolved not to mention the subject to him.

On arriving at the Castello, they were met by Terence, who said that he had been rather uneasy at his master not returning home on the preceding evening, but that he had judged that he had walked to the farm, and that the inclemency of the weather had detained him there.

"I hope you met with no alarm during the night?" said Valeria, addressing Terence, with whom she was left alone, by the retiring of Urbino to his private apartment.

"Not I, my lady," replied Terence; "you have often heard me express my opinion about ghosts; and all other intruders I *belave* to be robbers, and I dare say the best of them are wise enough to know that I am only a poor *sarvant*, and that he

'Who steals my purse, steals trash.' "

"It is a happiness to possess a courageous spirit, such as you are blessed with," returned Valeria; "but I believe courage is one of the characteristics of your countrymen."

"Faith, my lady, in my humble judgment," replied O'Donnovan, "it's the characteristic of every honest heart. 'The man who has done no ill, dreads no injury,' I have heard my poor *ould* mother say; and though she never read Shakespeare, by *rason* she hadn't the art of reading, at all at all, it was exactly the sentiment of that same great poet. Don't you remember, my lady, where he says—

> 'Thrice is he arm'd that has his quarrel just;
> And he but naked, though lock'd up in steel,
> Whose conscience with injustice is corrupted.'

Ay, ay, king Dickon found that to be true enough at the battle of Bosworth Field. By-the-bye, my lady, that same hump-backed Richard saw some ghosts, according as master Willy has drawn the story: but I fancy, like many another *crater* of his forming, they were only the visions of his own imagination." And moving away from Valeria as he spoke, he concluded his sentence with exclaiming—

> "A horse! a horse! my kingdom for a horse!"

Valeria smiled; Terence perceived it, and said—"Upon my soul, my lady, I *mane* what I say; for I am going to the mill for flour, and I can promise you, I shouldn't have the least objection, this warm morning, if I had a groom to answer to the call of—

> 'Saddle white Surrey for the field to-morrow!' "

And with an humble obeisance of his head, he then retired from her presence.

Valeria next paid a visit to old Jeronymo, who was employed in distilling rose-water in a closet, which he had amused himself with fitting up as a laboratory, and who, pointing to a quantity of leaves, which were unprepared for the still, and then to the door of Paulina's chamber, which was within sight of his workshop, signified, by a silent shrug of his shoulders, that since her disappearance he had lost all spirit for pursuing his physical labours.

234

Valeria, during their walk that morning, had been entrusted by her father with the visit which he had received the preceding day from the stranger, and the hopes which had been raised in his breast of the speedy restoration of Paulina, and she addressed Jeronymo by saying—"I hope and trust that we shall soon behold her again; you must not, therefore, relax in preparing your scents, as I am sure some of your preparing will be an acceptable present to her at her return."

Jeronymo seemed delighted with the idea, shook Valeria cordially by the hand for having inspired him with it, and immediately proceeded to put his still in order.

After some time passed at the Castello, Urbino and his daughter began to retrace their steps towards the farmhouse; they had not proceeded far on their road, when hearing the sound of some one, who appeared to be running after them, they turned round their heads, and perceived, close at their heels, Bianca's son, Calvino.

"So, you are returned?" said Urbino, addressing him.

"Oh yes! I am come back safe enough," answered Calvino. "I have only been in the woods gathering nuts; mother need not have been afraid about me—nobody would run away with a fool like myself, I am sure." He uttered a vacant laugh, then added—"You have been so good to my mother, she says, since I have been away, that I am come to bring the young signora a present of something nice to eat;" and so saying, he drew from the pocket of his vest the remnant of a handkerchief, in which was wrapt a woman's slipper filled with nuts—"There," he continued, presenting them to Valeria, "there are some of the nuts which I gathered whilst I was away, and see what a handsome thing I have got to put them in."

"Merciful Powers!" exclaimed Valeria, snatching it out of his hand, and carefully examining it, "this is one of the slippers which Paulina wore on the day of her mysterious disappearance."

"Where did you find it?" eagerly inquired Urbino.

"On a green place," returned the lad—"all green with grass, I mean; where there are trees and brambles, but no nut-bushes."

"Where is it? Can you describe it to me?" rejoined Urbino.

"Oh, it's a long way off," answered the boy.

"Is it near any habitation?" asked Urbino.

"Habitation! what's that?" said the boy.

"Does any body live near the place of which you speak?" demanded Urbino.

"There is a great house close by it," returned Calvino; "a great, great house, bigger far than that," he added, pointing to the Castello della Torvida.

"Then somebody lives in it, I suppose?" rejoined Di Cavetti.

"I suppose so too," replied Calvino; "but I cannot be sure neither."

"Why so?" asked Urbino.

"Why, I saw smoke coming out of the chimneys," replied the boy; "but that is no sure sign, for, you know, whilst no body lived in the Castello, the chimneys used to smoke."

"You cannot guess then who lives in the house of which you have been speaking?" returned Urbino.

"How should I?" exclaimed the boy. "It is such a great house, it must be a great man that lives in it, and a poor boy like me cannot be supposed to have any acquaintance with such folks. I know the name of the cobbler, Steppo, and the baker, Memmo, and all such people, but I don't know the name of great signors."

"Did you never ask charity at this great house?" inquired Valeria.

"No, signora, I know better than that," answered Calvino; "the servants would likely be so proud as to set the dog upon me for disturbing them; poor folks are better friends to the needy than the rich."

"What this lad has told us must be reflected upon," said Urbino apart to Valeria: "I will induce him to accompany us to the farmhouse, and proceed according to the advice of Di Borges, who may perhaps have some knowledge of the spot he speaks of, and who, at all events, knows better how to manage him than I do.——If you will go with us to the farmhouse of Sancho di Borges," continued Urbino, turning towards Calvino as he spoke, "my daughter, who is much obliged to you for your present of nuts, has taken so great a liking to the slipper they are in, that she will buy it of you."

"He he he!" grinned out Calvino; "she will have to get another made, if she wants to wear it."

"Certainly," answered Urbino, "it cannot be worn singly."

"Except old Bappa, the blind fiddler's sister, who has but one leg, had happened to have had the good luck to have found it instead of me," returned Calvino, again laughing.

"Come, follow us, and you shall be handsomely paid for your slipper," said Urbino; and Calvino, chuckling and smiling at the idea of the promised reward, continued close at their heels till their arrival at the house, when Urbino, learning that Di Borges was from home, and being desirous of not letting the present opportunity slip, of drawing from Calvino all the information which he was able to give concerning the spot where he had found the slipper, invited him into the kitchen, where he ordered him to be well entertained, and upon no account suffered to depart—terms upon which Calvino, although partly a fool, was not so great a one as to have refused keeping his present station for life.

CHAPTER X

If it were done,
When 'tis done, then it were well 'twere done quickly.
Macbeth.

THE hours meanwhile crept on heavily and painfully with Paulina, especially as two days and nights had passed since the mysterious astonishment evinced by Ricarda at the discovery of the scars upon her person; since which period she had not entered her prison, and Lipardo, at his nightly visits to her with fuel and other necessaries, with which he still assiduously provided her, had addressed to her only one single sentence, which was—"My wife will visit you soon—keep up your spirits with the knowledge that you are surrounded by true friends;" and these words he had uttered with rapidity, and an evident anxiety to quit the place.

On the third night after her former visit, to the inconceivable joy of Paulina, Ricarda appeared, accompanying her husband; she spoke not till Lipardo had retired, and closed upon them the pannel, and then seating herself, as before, upon the side of the bed, she said—"Well, here I am at last, and upon the most important business I ever set about in my life: no doubt but you have been anxious enough to see me, but my not coming to you before could not be prevented: all is for the best; I have always said so, and see fresh reasons every day to maintain my argument—And how do you find yourself, my sweet signora?"

"Anxious indeed, as you may naturally suppose, for some explanation of the surprise with which I beheld you affected the other evening," answered Paulina.

"All in good time," replied Ricarda; "all in good time; we shall come to that by-and-by; in the meanwhile, be satisfied that it is all to your pride, and your happiness, and your honour,

238

that I have made the discovery I have done: have patience, and let me proceed my own way—I can do nothing without I do it my own way."

After a short pause, she continued thus—"Now, my dear signora, I have a great deal to say to you, and a great many questions to ask of you; and I trust that you will hear me patiently, and answer me candidly, for I am your sincere friend, and am earnestly endeavouring to promote your happiness and welfare."

"Only shield me from the marchese," Paulina was beginning to say.

"Such a marchese!" cried the old woman, interrupting her; "but we will speak of him by-and-by; and if his face burns, it will not be without being talked of behind his back. Now listen to me attentively: you tell me that you love Vincentio; your love for him is very young—you have seen him only once—are you sure you love him well enough to become his wife?"

"It is true, I have seen him but once," replied Paulina; "but he had frequently seen me before I had an opportunity of beholding him, and professed a predilection for me; and the warmth with which he promised to defend me against his uncle, at our only interview, proves his affection to be sincere—a conviction which challenges my gratitude, and thence powerfully awakens a reciprocal feeling in my heart to his own."

"Well, well, it is all very possible, and very probable too," returned Ricarda. "I have frequently known love at first sight turn out as happily in the end as a three years courtship; it is all a chance, and in a great measure depends upon the temper of the parties united. But now listen to me, signora, and excuse my familiarity; I have my motives, ay, and good motives too, for all I am saying and doing. Should you incline as favourably as you do now towards Vincentio, if you did not believe him to be nephew of the great Di Valdetti, and heir to his marquisate?"

"I do not comprehend you," replied Paulina.

"Why," returned the old woman, "suppose he were only a cavalier of fortune—a soldier, for instance, we will say, with the prospect of no inheritance but his sword; would you profess yourself as willing to share your fate with him then as you are now?"

"I am surprised that you should have thought it necessary to have proposed that question to me," answered Paulina; "such points in my conduct as you have already observed, must have convinced you of the independence of my heart. Had I coveted wealth, was it not offered to me, in its most extensive limits, in the person of the marchese?"

"Why that is true, very true—I might have thought of that," rejoined the old woman, "but I have been so hurried and flurried, that I scarcely know what I have been doing or saying. Well, then, you positively mean that you would prefer Vincentio to every other man, and accept him as your husband, if, as the saying is, he carried his fortune on his back?"

"I should prefer him to all the men I have ever known," answered Paulina.

"Well then," replied the old woman, with a smile of inward exultation playing on her countenance, "you have led yourself into a fine scrape by your confession; for be it known to you that Vincentio is no more the nephew of the marchese than I am his nephew, but my son."

"Your son!" ejaculated Paulina.

"Ay, my son!" replied Ricarda; "you won't be ashamed of me for your mother-in-law, will you? To be sure, I am not your equal in any respect, signora; but I will be as kind and as good to you, in return for the love you bear Vincentio, as the greatest and grandest mother-in-law in all the world could be."

Paulina besought her companion to give her a solution of the new enigma which she had presented to her view.

"I cannot explain it to you just now," replied Ricarda, "for it is a long story, and we have other matter of the highest importance to occupy our time, which must be short together to-night, for various reasons. Now then," she added, assuming a solemnity of voice which denoted her deeply interested in the matter which she was revolving in her thoughts, "hear me, and mark me. You wish to escape the snares of the marchese, and you are willing to become the wife of Vincentio; there is then only one expedient by which you can ever hope to avoid the former, or to have it in your power to unite yourself with the latter—you must give Vincentio your hand to-morrow night. What say you?"

"The measure is so hasty——" Paulina was beginning to reply.

"Hasty!" exclaimed the old woman, "and is it not better to marry the man whom you can love hastily, than by pursuing deliberate measures, to fall into the net spread for you by him whom you loath and detest? Reflect on that."

"I have still no hesitation in resting my choice on Vincentio," replied Paulina; "but it would add greatly to my happiness to be blessed with the sanction of my revered protector, Urbino, to my union with the man of my election."

"But it cannot be," returned Ricarda; "as things stand, it is an utter impossibility. Believe me, on the word of a Christian, that it will be joyful news to him that your marriage is concluded; it will place you in possession of the means of requiting him tenfold for all the kindness which I understand he has shown you, and he will be doubly happy in seeing you blessed with prosperity, joy, and exaltation, as you infallibly will be, if you follow my advice. And how, on the contrary, could you ever meet him again, if, after my offer of salvation, the marchese were to obtain a triumph over you?"

"Too true," sighed forth Paulina.

"All your future days, and his also, from the interest which he feels in your welfare, and the love which he bears you, would be turned to sorrow, whilst, if you act according to my admonitions, you will have the ability of becoming the distributor of joy to all who know you."

"Still you speak in riddles," returned Paulina.

"I may do so," rejoined the old woman; "but you must, I think, be convinced that it is the most earnest desire of my heart to serve you."

Lipardo at this moment entered—"Well," he said, addressing Ricarda, "is all arranged?"

"Ask the question there," rejoined Ricarda, smiling, and pointing to Paulina.

Lipardo approached her, and repeated the arguments already advanced by his wife, with increased force and energy.

Paulina trembled, and almost wept.

"It is the only measure which can save you from the brutality of the marchese," emphatically pronounced Lipardo.

Still Paulina did not reply.

"For your own sake, I supplicate you to consent," proceeded Lipardo.

Paulina heaved a deep sigh.

"You, a few days ago," continued Lipardo, "desired Vincentio to be asked, if he had any particular message to you? he requests you to be informed, that he beseeches you, by the love and adoration which he bears you, to consent to the proposal which has been made to you by my wife; and moreover desires you to be made acquainted, that he will visit you on this spot to-morrow night, accompanied by a priest."

Paulina hung down her head.

"The day after to-morrow the marchese will come to receive your final answer," proceeded Lipardo, "and this step can alone save you from his toils. You can then declare yourself a wife, and thus defy his hated passion," added Lipardo; "you will have no occasion to acknowledge how long you have been so."

"And if he suspects how shortly I am become such," re-joined Paulina, "his rage will know no bounds, and I may sink beneath the vengeance of his disappointment."

"At your interview with him," returned Lipardo, "Vincentio and myself will be within call, and protect you in case of need; this I most solemnly promise and assure you."

A slow consent was at length wrung from Paulina, that Vincentio should visit her, with the priest, on the following night; and Ricarda and her husband, with many cordial assurances of their love and respect, then quitted her.

The day was passed by Paulina, like the former ones, in reflection on the mysteries by which she was surrounded; but the agitation of her mind was still more increased, as she dwelt on the awful ceremony, to the performance of which she had tacitly consented.

At length the shades of night enveloped the face of nature, and with slow and heavy toll, the bell proclaimed the midnight hour. It had not long ceased to vibrate, ere Paulina believed that she distinguished the sound of footsteps, on the outside of the door by which she had entered her prison. She hastily closed the pannel and listened, but the sounds, if any there had been, had died away, and unbroken silence now prevailed. She again drew back the pannel, and re-entered the second apartment; she had not long done so ere the second pannel was withdrawn, and Lipardo appeared, bearing a lanthorn, and followed by two persons wrapt in long black cloaks.

The pannel being closed, one of Lipardo's companions darted forward, and Paulina felt herself clasped in the arms of Vincentio, who, in the hurried accents of mingled joy and agitation, expressed to her in whispers his gratitude for the happiness which she had vouchsafed him.

"We have no time to lose," said Lipardo. He made a signal to the second personage, who was the priest, a venerable man, the casting back of whose cowl displayed his grey and reverend locks beneath. At his direction, Vincentio and Paulina stood forth. Their hands were clasped in each other, and a few moments rendered their fates indissoluble.

Vincentio saluted his bride with a glowing kiss of exultation, and the priest was on the point of closing his volume, when a crash like thunder echoed through the prison, the secret pannel was burst, and the marchese, followed by two of his domestics, stood before them.

The sword of the marchese was drawn in his hand, and darting towards Vincentio, at whose breast he aimed his weapon—"Villain!" he exclaimed, "take the reward of thy perfidy!"

With all the fury of an ardent lover, turned into vengeance against the being who seeks to interrupt his joys, Vincentio sprang upon the marchese, and in a few moments disarmed him.

Uttering the most dreadful imprecations, the marchese called upon one of his attendants to give him a sword.

Lipardo darted between them—"If you are bent on murder, my lord," he exclaimed, "here is a mark will teach you where to point your weapon!" Whilst speaking, he had, with one hand, snatched the lamp from the table, and with his other drawn down Paulina's dress beneath her shoulder; he approached towards it the light, and added—"Here, my lord, this scar will lead you right!"

The whole was the transaction of a moment. A deep groan burst from the lips of the marchese, and he sunk senseless into the arms of his attendants.

END OF VOLUME TWO

CHAPTER I

There cannot be a pinch in death
More sharp than this is.
....
————I beseech you, sir,
Harm not yourself with your vexation; I
Am senseless of your wrath—a touch more rare
Subdues all pangs—all fears.   *Cymbeline.*

WE must now once more change our scene for a while to the
farmhouse of Sancho di Borges. Urbino continued anxiously to
await the farmer's return, and he was ultimately disappointed
by a neighbour stopping at the house, with intelligence that he
had met the farmer in the course of his rides about the country,
and that he had requested him to give information to his family,
that some business which he had to transact at a distant vineyard would detain him from home till the following day. Urbino consequently deemed it futile any longer to entertain
Calvino; and having purchased of him the slipper, dismissed
him from the farmhouse, and compelled himself to endeavour
to lull his apprehensions for the fate of Paulina, by dwelling on
the assurance of her safety, which had been given him by his
unknown visitor.

Valeria struggled to call the assistance of duty to her aid, in
her attempts to drive from her recollection the event by which
that day had been marked, and applied herself with more than
usual earnestness to administer to the comforts of the blind
Averilla.

Urbino retired at an early hour to his chamber—not to
sleep, but in the hope of soothing his ruffled feelings by the
joint aid of solitude and reflection. Upon his table lay the papers which had been delivered to him by Julio; and without an
intention of perusing their contents, he took them up, designing

to deposit them in his writing-desk, in order to screen them from the perusal of others, when these words caught his eye:— *"As they will fully elucidate the mysteries of the Castello della Torvida, and remove all apprehension of entering its walls from the minds of those who may have imbibed such a terror."* This sentence was a most forcible appeal to his curiosity; and considering that in this part of Julio's narrative there would not, in all probability, be contained any matter connected with the fate of his lamented son, he could not forbear satisfying himself on a point which had, for some time past, so greatly perplexed him. Searching, therefore, for that period in the confessions of Julio which was subsequent to his departure from Venice in the gondola, to which the tender but broken-hearted Di Cavetti had guided him, as his only means of escape from the retributive hand of justice; and which our readers will recollect to be the exact moment to which he had deduced the portion of his manuscript confided by him to the perusal of Valeria, Urbino proceeded to read the following words:—

"On being landed, as I have already said, upon a part of the country to which I was an utter stranger, but still apprehensive that the description which had been circulated of me by the officers of justice might cause me to be identified, even by those to whom I had before been unknown, my first care was to change my dress, which having, not without some difficulty, accomplished, in such a manner as to evade the suspicion of those before whom the alteration was made—simply and rustically clad in my new attire, I took up my abode at a small country inn, from whence I wrote to my confidential servant, whom I had left in Padua, directing him in what manner to supply me with money, and at the same time strictly cautioning him not to let our correspondence be known.

"For the few first days after my becoming acquainted that Valeria was the sister of the man who had fallen by my hand, and consequently perceiving the barrier which now intervened between my ardent desires, and the probability of their ever being realized, I sunk into a stupor of faculty, which scarcely permitted me the power of reflection, or even the consciousness of my own being. When I did become capable of consideration, I earnestly desired to die, reluctant as I was to meet my fate, either from the axe of the executioner, or from my own hand; and I implored Heaven to terminate my existence, resolutely determining to spend the remainder of my days in seclusion from all society.

"My restless mind sought relief in wandering about the country, and in my rambles I was led to the Castello della Torvida; and having learnt that it had long been uninhabited, and was expected to remain so, I resolved to penetrate within its walls, and, if I found my idea practicable, to remain their inhabitant. I entered by means of a window on the ground-floor, and visited its various parts, in order to convince myself that it was as void of inmates as it had been represented to me. I found the account I had received to be true, and my resolution of becoming its tenant was immediately fixed. Little did I that moment imagine whom the progress of time was destined to lead thither, similarly determined as myself.

"In the course of my investigation of the Castello, I observed a small door opening from one of the chambers, situated in an angle of the building, which opened into a small apartment, from which branched off a narrow passage, that ran nearly round the edifice, and from which two different flights of steps conducted into a dark and vaulted way, terminating in a low arch beneath the garden-wall, the mouth of which was choked up with weeds and briars; and as the trench which ran beneath the wall was filled with fragments of stone, the withered boughs of trees, and clods of earth thrown heedlessly upon each other, this outlet was utterly undiscernible to those who had never gained the secret of its existence from within.

"On reascending and closing the door which intervened between the chamber in the angle and the small apartment with which the obscure passage communicated, I found that the door closed with a spring; and after some time and labour passed in examination, I discovered that the spring was moved by the pressure of the finger on the head of one of the apparent nails with which it was thickly studded; and it was constructed with such masterly neatness, that not a crease was visible which could betray it to be any other than a part of the wainscot with which the chamber was surrounded.

"Accordingly, in the small apartment, and the chamber between which the secret door was situated, I decided upon fixing my residence, considering that it would be infinitely preferable for me to go out and come in by the vaulted passage, which there was every reason for me to suppose I might do unobserved, than by either passing through the window by which I had gained my first admittance into the Castello, or by forcing open any one of its doors for my egress and ingress, subject myself to be seen, and if not commanded to quit my asylum, perhaps be questioned upon my motive for having selected it, in a manner which I might find it equally unpleasant as unsafe to answer.

"By degrees I transported to my new abode the few requisites of which I stood in need; and having contrived to place a couple of wooden bars across the door of the chamber which communicated with the main body of the Castello, in order to prevent the possibility of my being surprised by any visitors to the spot, my days passed on, for a considerable time, uninterrupted, till one morning, as I was sitting in the little apartment beyond the chamber, I heard voices in conversation, followed by an attempt to burst open the door; and from some words which passed between the speakers on the outside of the door, I learned that it was the design of one or more persons to fix their residence, like myself, within the Castello, and that it was the intention of one or both of those now conversing to return thither on the morrow. I had become attached to the spot of my seclusion; and desiring to remain uninterrupted in the negative comfort which it afforded me, I determined to have recourse to some expedient for endeavouring to deter the strangers from fulfilling their purpose. This, I conceived, might easily be effected, as I was led to believe that any warning of a mysterious nature must terrify strangers from becoming inhabitants of a place, of which the deserted, gloomy, and decayed state, could not fail to inspire minds, of a common nature, with sensations already prepared to encounter some event tending to the enigmatical or the miraculous. I accordingly conveyed from the chamber into the small adjoining apartment, every article which could betray the spot to have sheltered a human inhabitant; and having removed the bars from the door, I inscribed upon it this sentence—'AVOID THESE WALLS;' which, when I had done, I confined myself to the small apartment, anxiously awaiting the event of my plan.

"About the hour of noon, on the following day, I heard the approach of footsteps; and listening attentively to catch the words spoken by the unknown persons, I, to my disappointment, discovered, that, although considerably surprised by what they beheld, they were not shaken from their purpose of making the Castello their residence; and determined as I was not to hold intercourse with any human beings, and considering it impossible that if I remained in my present asylum, some chance should not lead me to an encounter with the strangers, however cautiously I might guard my conduct, my instant resolution was to seek a new abode.

"In my wanderings about the country, I had observed the deserted hut of a hermit, named Anselmo, some time dead; and this I determined to make my future abode. Thus decided, I repaired to a village at some distance; and having provided myself with the disguise of an aged beggar, and affixed a label to

my breast, signifying my loss of speech, in order to avoid replying to the questions which might be addressed to me, when, in
support of my assumed character, I occasionally appeared
abroad as a mendicant, I by night conveyed my little store of
earthly wealth to the hut by the side of the brook, and once
more hoped to be permitted to vegetate uninterrupted and
unknown.

"Once more I applied myself to the transmitting of my
eventful life to paper, with which self-imposed task I had hitherto occupied most of my time, since joint inclination and
necessity had withdrawn me from my fellow-beings; and it
caused me no inconsiderable anxiety that I could not decide on
any one individual in whose hands I could feel satisfied in
placing the transcript of my misfortunes and my sufferings.

"I accustomed myself frequently to wander about in my
disguise in the vicinity of my dwelling, for the mutual benefit
of air and exercise; and in one of my rambles, chancing to pass
the Castello della Torvida, the reader may easily appreciate the
astonishment, the powerful and combined feelings which assailed my heart, when I espied from a distance, in the garden
attached to the building, my adored Valeria, her cousin Paulina,
and her inestimable father, who had so generously preserved to
me my existence."

Urbino could read no longer; he threw down the manuscript, and starting from his chair, he began to pace the chamber with disordered steps. In the adjoining apartment slept
Averilla, whom Valeria having attended in retiring to bed, fully
aware of the unsettled and painful state of her father's mind,
from the uneven pace at which she distinguished him to be
wandering about his chamber, ventured to rap at the door; and
on his opening it, inquired whether, as he had retired so early
from society, and still did not appear disposed to rest, she could
read, or converse with him, to amuse him?

He desired her to enter, and when she had done so, he closed the door, and in a brief manner communicated to her what he had been reading, and the reason by which he had been led to the perusal, adding, that he felt it impossible to dwell with composure on characters traced by the hand which had bereft him of a name, and requesting her to cast her eyes over the continuation of the narrative, and to impart to him the heads of such matter as it contained, connected with the enigmatical cloud which had for some time past lowered upon the Castello della Torvida.

Valeria had already resolved to pursue the path which duty and religion commanded her to tread; and assuming a composure, and even firmness of countenance and voice, she proceeded to obey her father's injunction.

The subsequent pages of the manuscript stated, that being once become acquainted with the proximity of his residence to that of Valeria, he had immediately conceived an unconquerable wish of being once more able to behold her, and converse with her, for the purpose of unfolding to her the event which had for ever separated their hands, if not their hearts, and of which he had a presentiment, and a just one, as it had subsequently been proved to him, that she was ignorant. Accordingly, he had formed the plan of restoring to her the ribband which he had taken from her shoulder at the carnival at Venice, and which had ever since that moment been worn by him next his heart—a token which he judged she could not mistake to be an unequivocal proof of his being near her, if even she doubted the lines which accompanied it to be his, as it was possible she might do, having never before beheld any characters traced by his pen; and which plan he had effected on the anniversary of the wedding-day of Sancho di Borges.

There followed a few sentences, of which the sum was, that as he had not a single thought which he wished to conceal, after his death, from that world to which he was desirous of vindicating his actions from intended criminality, he could not but confess that a part of the motive by which he had been actuated in desiring once more to behold Valeria, had been the hope of obtaining a promise from her lips, that the heart which she had bestowed on him should never be transferred to another—a promise which, he declared, could alone render the residue of his earthly pilgrimage endurable.

These lines Valeria hastily read, and withheld from her father.

Next in place succeeded a brief account of his having attired himself as a cavalier, and bribed one of Sancho's domestics to deliver to her the letter in which he warned her to expect to see him at some moment when she was least prepared to expect his presence. To this were added a few words of digression, explaining, that having gained the secret of one door in the Castello which was governed by a concealed spring, this knowledge had led him to discover several others of a similar nature, opening from the narrow passage into the various chambers of the building—that by one of these, believing all the inhabitants of the place from home, he had entered, when Francisca had beheld him writing to Valeria in her closet; and that having once ascertained which was her chamber, and utterly unconscious that the alarm excited by his appearance in it had induced her father to remove thither himself, he had ventured through one of the spring pannels on that night on which he had been seen by Urbino, and fired at by him.

Here Valeria paused, for the remainder of the narrative had already been explained to her by Julio's own words, and to her father, by their unexpected meeting at the hut by the side of the brook. She replaced the manuscript on the table, and Di Cavetti, perceiving by her action that it contained no farther matter of interest for him, said—"How easily are our nerves affected!—by what slender causes are our apprehensions awakened! and when we solve the most difficult enigma which human means can present to the senses of frail man, how are we surprised that from causes so simple have proceeded effects to disturb and perplex the brains of rationality! And yet," he added, after a short pause, "there is one point connected with the events at the Castello which still remains in obscurity, and which the key that I have received to the remainder does not enable me to unlock—by what means could Julio escape being wounded by the balls emitted from the pistols which I discharged at him? Or if, as it now appears, he did escape them, to what cause could it be owing that no fractures were discernible in the wainscot through which they must inevitably have passed?"

"Oh, my dear father!" exclaimed Valeria, clasping his hand in hers as she spoke, "from me receive that explanation, and I am certain that you will not deem me culpable, for having been the means of preserving you from spilling that blood which you had once so nobly spared. From the evidence of concomitant circumstances, I ever believed the supposed apparition to be Julio; but in compliance with the injunctions to secrecy contained in his letters, I durst not confess my belief. You cannot but recollect the earnestness with which I supplicated to remain in my own chamber, nor can you have forgotten that when you positively refused to comply with my request, I excused myself, early in the evening, for retiring from your society, alleging my wish to remove some articles from my own chamber into the one I was that night to inhabit. Paulina retired to rest. Terence remained in conversation with you. I seized upon the adventitious moment, and extracted the bullets from the tubes which contained them."

As Valeria ceased speaking, she pressed the hand of her father to her lips, and burst into tears.

"Press it to thy heart, and be that heart for ever its sanctuary!" exclaimed Urbino. "Thou hast withheld it from the commission of an innocent crime, under the impression of which, I think my tired existence would have withered and decayed!"

He clasped her to his breast; their cheeks were pressed to each other, and tears of mingled gratitude and admiration flowed unrestrained from their eyes.

Equally to the father and sister of the man whom his weapon had consigned to an untimely grave, did Julio owe the preservation of his own existence! And oh! may the comparison between the feelings of the preserver and the destroyer restrain the hand of passion, and thunder with the voice of destiny into the ear of rashness, that it is better to suffer than to sin!

A considerable time was passed by Urbino and his daughter in reflective silence; it was broken by Valeria, who pressed her father to retire to rest.—"Not yet, my child," he replied; "I feel that I am unprepared for sleep; when my mind is disturbed, I am always restless on my pillow." He spoke of Paulina, and, more particularly than he had yet done, detailed to his daughter the conversation which had passed concerning her between himself and his unknown visitor; and after a few moments given to thought, he proceeded by saying—"From what passed between the stranger and myself, it appears highly probable that I shall be very shortly called upon to relate what little is known to me of Paulina's history; in which case I do not deem it just that you should be the last made acquainted with what concerns one whom you have ever loved as a near relative."

"And is not Paulina such to me?" earnestly inquired Valeria.

"She does not stand in any nearer connexion to you," rejoined Urbino, "than as the beloved companion of your childhood, the esteemed friend of your increasing years, and as a being, who, although by birth an utter stranger to your father, has received from him a parent's protection, and has planted for herself a daughter's interest in his heart. I have already said that I was not disposed to retire to rest; are you too weary to remain for an hour or two longer my companion?"

"Not weary, in truth," answered Valeria, "but never less so than when I consider my society to give you pleasure."

"I will then embrace this opportunity of acquainting you with what little is known to me of our dear Paulina's story." He drew a chair to the side of that on which Valeria was sitting, and spoke thus:—"You, my dear child, were somewhat more than two years old, when I was one day summoned to attend a lady, in my medical capacity, at the hotel of San Marco, in the square of that name in Venice. I found her to be a female, apparently of at most twenty-two years of age, of a more than usually-beautiful person, and of an extraordinary elegant form. Her manners were by no means inferior to the graces with which she was exteriorly adorned; and the affability of her conversation irresistibly won upon my senses with such fascinating strength, that I almost appeared to feel in her an old acquaintance, before I had passed an hour in her society.

"At my first visit to her, she complained of extreme ill health, which both her blooming countenance, and the state of her pulse, appeared to deny her to be suffering under; and conceiving her to be more nervous than ill, I prescribed a slight medicine, and promised, at her particular request, to call upon her again on the following day.

"At my second visit, I found her reclined upon a sofa, and in her arms lay a lovely female infant, of about ten months old. On my entrance into her apartment—'I am very glad you are come, signor,' she said; 'I am very ill indeed today—much worse than I was yesterday.' She extended her hand towards me whilst speaking; and on taking her wrist, I discovered her to be affected with a considerable degree of fever. I confessed to her the state in which I had found her, and she answered—'It is not to be wondered at, considering the extreme pain which I am enduring.'—'In your head?' I asked.—'No, no, no!' she

255

ejaculated. She paused a few minutes, during which her countenance underwent several changes; then said—'I have been acting very foolishly—I am sure I have; but under certain impressions of distress and anxiety of mind, what is it that we are not sometimes tempted to do! If I persist in the concealment of my disorder, I am more fully convinced that it will destroy me. I sent for you yesterday, with a full determination to confide to you the cause of my malady, but my resolution forsook me when we met: I can now no longer forbear seeking alleviation for my sufferings.—Here, here,' she added, tearing open her dress as she spoke, 'is the cause of my anguish!' And she followed her words by disclosing to my view a deep wound beneath her left breast, the bleeding of which had been staunched by an application of lint, containing some styptic, which, for want of being renewed, was now adhering to the part affected.

"That it must have occasioned her pain to remove it, I am certain; but she bore my operations with silent firmness, only saying—'I hope, I dare believe, signor, that men of your profession never reveal the maladies of their patients.'—'I trust that it is a general rule with men of my profession,' I returned; 'with me, at least, it is an infallible one.'—'I am satisfied,' she answered. 'Can you promise to relieve and cure me soon?'—'I think I can,' was my reply. 'But you have been ill-treated in the first instance.'—'Things hastily done are seldom well done,' she returned, attempting to smile as she spoke.—'Your wound was inflicted by the point of a poniard, or a sword?' I said.—'In God's name recall not to my mind the dreadful recollection—I beseech you do not!' she eagerly pronounced.

"In the course of about three weeks, I informed her that her cure was certain, and would now, I trusted, be very speedy. She thanked me for the attentions I had paid her, and the concern I had shown for her unhappy situation, in words and actions, both far exceeding my desires or expectations.—'You have been the saviour of my existence,' she one day addressed me by saying, 'and I must always value you as such; but alas! perhaps it has only now been preserved, that at a future period it may again become the victim of a wretch.' She paused.—'Thank Heaven, my child lives too!' she presently proceeded by saying; 'and oh! may a gracious Providence shield her innocence from the fury of her enemy! Oh! methinks I now behold his tall commanding form—his pallid, but impressive countenance, illumined by his dark and piercing eyes, and shaded by the raven locks that fall around it!—behold his sinewy arm raised with that dagger which——' She placed her hand before her eyes, as if believing herself actually to behold the form which she was describing, uttered a faint shriek, and sunk back upon the couch on which she was reclining.

"I maintained a strict silence, not only because I concluded that any questions advanced by me might add to her distress of mind, but also that I conceived I had no authority to propose any inquiries to her.

"When she again turned her eyes towards me—'I scarcely know, signor,' she said, 'what expressions my hurried imagination just now tempted me to utter. Whatever they were, I hope they are buried in the silence of your bosom. One unheeded word spoken abroad might tend to destroy the life of this inno-cent, in whose preservation I rejoice much more than in my own.'

"I assured her, that what she had uttered had not furnished me with any explanation of her private concerns, and that if it even had done so, under the circumstances which had intro-duced us to each other's acquaintance, she might have relied on my inviolable secrecy.

"Her wound continued hourly to approach towards perfect convalescence, and I thought I could perceive that her feelings became likewise more tranquillized.

"The days passed on, our knowledge of each other being now about a month old, when a note was one morning brought to me by a waiter of the hotel where she resided, requesting that I would call upon her immediately. I obeyed her summons, and on entering the apartment in which I had always been received by her on my former visits, I found no one within it but her child, who was sleeping upon the sofa. I amused myself for about a quarter of an hour with a book which lay upon the table, every minute expecting her appearance; and as she did not come, I was on the point of ringing the bell, to inquire whether she were informed that I was arrived, when the waiter entered, and presented me with a second note, of which I found the contents to be, as nearly as I can recollect, these words:

'SIGNOR URBINO,

'Farewell, for ever! I have discovered your heart to be tender and humane, and Heaven whispers to mine, that you will not desert the helpless infant before you, who has at this moment no other protector but yourself. Stern necessity ordains that she should for ever be separated from those who gave her birth; in the benevolence of your soul, supply to my poor Paulina the absence of her natural cherishers—let her name you her parent, and live in ignorance that she ever possessed any other. Do this, and your reward will be in heaven. Once more, farewell!'

"When I had somewhat recovered from the surprise into which this strange and unexpected appeal to my feelings had thrown me, I summoned the waiter into my presence, and inquired where the signora was who had commissioned him to deliver me the note which I had just received from him? and he replied, that on having put it into his hand, she had quitted the hotel. Did he know whither she had gone? was my subsequent demand. His answer was in the negative. Did she go away alone? I next inquired. He replied, that she did, and that he had never seen any person in her society, except myself, since she had resided in the house. 'She had paid liberally,' he added, 'for her entertainment, and had appeared to be supplied with a rich purse;' an observation which several points of her conduct towards myself had convinced me that she possessed. I asked if he were acquainted from whence she had originally come, on her first arrival at the hotel? and his reply was, that she had entered the house one evening, about the hour of twilight, wrapt in a travelling cloak, with her child in her arms, and had, on the following morning, asked for a recommendation to an eminent physician, in consequence of which my address had been given to her, and she had immediately dispatched a messenger to summon me into her presence."

Urbino paused an instant, and Valeria, profiting by his silence, said—"And from that moment, I conjecture, our dear Paulina became your adopted niece?"

"All endeavours to trace out her mysterious parent," returned Urbino, "proved ineffectual, and tempted by no other reward for my humanity than that which, in the words of her mother, might be laid up for me in heaven, I immediately conveyed her to the care of my lamented wife; and between us it was agreed, that in order to silence the tongue of curiosity, she should be spoken of as the orphan child of a deceased sister of mine, whom I had taken under my protection."

"And thus, I imagine, concludes the short tale of my beloved friend," said Valeria.

"Not entirely," replied Urbino; "when your mother undressed her new charge, for the purpose of changing her habiliments, she was surprised by finding a wound at the bottom of her neck, and another on her left shoulder, which, it was evident, had been healed by a part of the preparation which I had applied to that of her unfortunate parent. Why that parent had not communicated to me the state of her child, was not more strange than why an innocent babe should have suffered thus undeservedly from the brutal attempts of some unfeeling hand. There existed, however, no clue to the mystery, and the extraordinary, the piteous, the impressive situation of the hapless babe, attached me as strongly to her as if she had indeed been my own.

"Years rolled on, and no circumstance occurred which appeared connected with the fate of Paulina, till one evening in the month of that carnival at which you first beheld the illstarred Julio! It was at a masked ball, to which I had accompanied you, that I was accosted by a man in the dress of a pilgrim, who entered into conversation with me, by praising your figure and dancing, and thence proceeded to inquire if Paulina were my daughter? and to propose to me many other questions concerning her, which would alone have awakened my suspicion that he had some private motives for his inquiries; but, on observing his countenance, which was of a peculiar cast, I felt convinced that his face and person exactly tallied with the account of that being whom the mother of Paulina had once, in the horror of a nervous recollection, described to me as the dreaded enemy of herself and her child. His form was tall and commanding; his countenance pallid, but impressive, illumined by a dark and piercing eye, and shaded by the raven locks that fell around it. From the moment that I had received this instinctive feeling, I avoided him; and the carnival over, I beheld him no more. But my suspicions that he had some knowledge of the countenance of Paulina, or of the mode of her introduction into my family, were considerably heightened, when, one evening, whilst you were preparing to visit the opera, I heard Paulina describing to you the close attendance which had been paid her during the carnival, by a tall figure in the garb of a pilgrim, and which she had mistaken for the attention of a lover. At first this apparent conviction of my apprehensions alarmed me, but the impression faded under the hand of time; and till the moment of her disappearance, my fears concerning her had never again been awakened."

Here ended such particulars as Di Cavetti was acquainted with concerning the child of his bounty; and after several comments on her former fate, and prayers for the happiness of her future days, had passed the lips of Valeria and her father, the former retired to her own chamber.

CHAPTER II

But what are these,
So withered, and so wild in their attire,
That look not like th' inhabitants o' the earth,
And yet are on it?   *Macbeth.*

IT has often been remarked, that whilst the minds of the great are perplexed with the revolutions of states and politics, the souls of their inferiors in station are frequently as greatly disturbed by events which do not weigh the tithe part of a feather in the general scale of human occurrences, as if the destiny of millions, and the fate of empires, depended upon the favourable issue of their wishes. In a comparative degree, a parallel of this nature was at this time existing in the members of the hospitable mansion of Sancho Di Borges; the breast of the worthy farmer's niece, Francisca, without a real care to disturb her tranquillity of mind, was agitated by feelings which caused her to experience anxiety and torment little inferior to those with which the weightier hand of actual grief assailed the hearts of Di Cavetti and his daughter Valeria.

Francisca's misfortunes were those which the world is but too apt to deride, but which, to weak and ignorant minds, furnish serious subject for misery and dissatisfaction; they arose from envy, disappointment, and an evil temper—the most inveterate tormentors by which the breast of humanity can be inhabited.

Francisca was now in her fortieth year, and unmarried; she had been a pretty girl in her day, but, from motives of vanity, had outstood her market, and now, to her uncontrollable chagrin, perceived that the market had returned her upon her own hands as unsaleable. Upon Terence O'Donnovan's handsome face and manly person, she had cast an eye of admiration, ever since the first moment of her beholding him; but her beauty, if any she now possessed, and which consisted at best of a meagre countenance, enlivened, by the application of artificial colour, into that animation which a corpse may be supposed capable of receiving, and so diametrically in opposition to the plump cheeks, florid with the rosy hue of nature and of health, which had alone possessed charms for Terence in his native country, that she had perceived herself utterly neglected by him, and in return for his neglect, as not indifference, but hate, is too usually the consequence of a disappointed passion, had grown into despising him. By her aunt, to whose necessities she could not with any degree of temper accommodate herself, she still thought herself ill used, by the preference which Averilla displayed for the kind offices of Valeria, over her ungraciously-performed services; and in short, although she might have made every one around her her friend, she persuaded herself into believing them all her enemies; and by indulging in the chimeras of her brain, rendered her existence as unpleasant as it could have been, if her self-created miseries had been founded in reason or in truth.

On the following morning, when Valeria entered the breakfast apartment, she beheld Francisca, with her elbow rested on the mantlepiece, and her head reposing on her hand, whilst the expression of her countenance was thoughtful, and consequential.—"Ah, signora," she said, with a half-suppressed sigh, on perceiving Valeria, "Heaven and the Virgin only know where I may be this day month!"

"How so?" inquired Valeria.

"'Needs must when the devil drives,' signora, as the proverb says," replied Francisca; "I would sooner beg my bread than live here moping any longer with my stupid old uncle and my blind aunt. I dare say, signora, because you see me a single young woman, you may think that I have never been invited to change my situation. Oh dear! oh dear! the offers I have had! but we can neither count the grains of sand on the seashore, or recall the moments that are past! Well, well, I now perceive that I have wasted enough of my prime, and am resolved once more to return to the great world; as I have told you before, signora, I have waited on some of the first ladies in the land, and why shouldn't I do so again?"

"I think," returned Valeria, "that you might live very comfortably here with your relatives."

"Quiet comfort is my detestation," answered Francisca; "I had rather lodge in a trunkmaker's shop than live in a perpetual round of dulness, as I do here. Many and many a time have I repented that I did not join the army, which I might have done, a few years ago, upon the most advantageous terms."

"You join the army!" ejaculated Valeria.

"Yes, me, signora," rejoined Francisca; "a cousin of my father's, who served in our lemonade-shop in Florence, enlisted into a brigade of Florentine volunteers, and he was dying for me at the time his duty compelled him to quit our city. I have never heard of him since, but I hope he committed no rash action on account of my cruelty. He has sworn to me a million times over, that he had rather have me for his wife, if I had not a pair of shoes to stand in, than any other woman, if she were studded, from head to foot, with pearls and diamonds."

"These are the ordinary expressions of men," said Valeria.

"I don't think they are ordinary expressions at all, signora," returned Francisca: "begging your pardon for differing with you in opinion, I think they are very handsome ones, and a very handsome fellow, I must say he was, who pronounced them; but perhaps, signora, you will say with the proverb, 'handsome he who handsome does,' and handsomely he did offer to do by me, I assure you; for he would willingly have sold his silver watch out of his pocket, to buy me a pair of rose-diamond hoops for my ears, if I would but have followed the camp with him. Perhaps I shall never see him again, but I cannot help remembering what he was ten years ago; never man in Italy stood upon a finer pair of legs; one might almost have supposed them carved out of wood, they were so well proportioned—such a sharp eye in his head—such a beautiful head of curling auburn hair, and as strait as a dart even before he was drilled, signora, that what must he be now, after ten years hard service! I almost wish myself by his side again, there is something so noble in an experienced soldier!"

She was interrupted by the sound of a horse's feet approaching towards the house, and in a few seconds Valeria observed Di Borges alighting at the door. She immediately proceeded to inform her father of his return; and as soon as Urbino had descended from his chamber, he retired with the farmer to a private apartment, into which breakfast was sent to them from the family-table.

Although the friends had been separated only for a short period of time, Urbino had much to communicate. With the greatest pleasure Sancho heard that every objection was removed to the family of Di Cavetti once more taking possession of the Castello. With regard to what had occurred during his absence concerning Paulina, he deemed it advisable, that, notwithstanding the declarations made by the stranger to Urbino, for whose performance of his promise they had no security but his own word, he should see Calvino, and endeavour to gather from him the exact spot where the slipper had been dropped; and accordingly he resolved, without delay, to proceed to the cottage of his mother Bianca, in the hope of either finding him within it, or learning where he might be seen.

As he was quitting the house for this purpose, suddenly turning back, and addressing himself to Urbino, he said—"Lend me your purse, for I parted with mine yesterday on the road, and have not a coin upon me: if I had not been well known where I slept last night, I might have gone supperless to bed. Without a bribe, nothing can be done with Calvino."

Having received the required purse from the hand of Urbino, he continued speaking thus—"You well know that I am not fond of encouraging common beggars; but you are as well acquainted that my heart always melts at the sight of real misery, and I never yet saw any objects more strongly calculated to call forth my compassion, than a set of unfortunate beings whom I yesterday encountered travelling from the mountains, as they informed me, towards Venice, and who, according to their forlorn and debilitated appearance, seemed scarcely capable, as I should imagine, of crawling half a league in the course of a day. They consisted of a wounded soldier, carrying at his back a small wallet, which, I suppose, contained their all, accompanied by a delicate and sickly-looking female, whom I concluded to be his wife, bearing in one of her arms an infant, and dragging along with her other hand another child, who seemed hardly old enough to walk. I gave them my address, with permission to call here, and refresh themselves on their way. I think they can hardly have yet performed the distance between this spot and the one where I saw them; but should they arrive in my absence, I leave you in possession of my directions to see them well entertained."

"I believe you know that they are entrusted to one who will not discredit any exertion in the cause of humanity," replied Urbino; and, with a reciprocal smile, the friends then parted.

When Di Borges was gone, the morning being unusually fine for the season of the year, which was that of the decline of autumn, Urbino conceived an inclination to walk to the Castello, and relieve the minds of his humble friends, Jeronymo and Terence, by acquainting them that they had in future no visits to apprehend from the supposed spectre which had lately haunted the building; and leaving in charge, with a confidential servant, Sancho's commission to have the poor travellers well entertained, and detained until his return, if they should arrive during the period of his absence, he went in quest of his daughter, whom he was desirous of engaging as his companion in his walk.

He found her in the apartment of Averilla, in which was also Francisca, who had been repeating to her aunt the sentiments which she had already that morning delivered to Valeria, and who, as he entered the chamber, was just declaring that she was more than half resolved to proceed to Florence, where she felt almost certain that she must fall in with her dear Bernardo, as she called him, who, there could be no doubt, was now settled in that city, as she had understood that the Florentine brigade in which he had served had been disbanded, in consequence of the late peace, and he would, in all probability, be settled in business with his brother, who had succeeded to the lemonade-shop on the death of her uncle.

Averilla represented to her, that setting aside the gross indelicacy of a female going in pursuit of a once-rejected admirer, the many chances there existed of his having fallen in battle, or, if he had survived the perils of steel and powder, the probability of his having never returned to the spot where she had known him; and if even he had done so, the possibility of his passion, which must undoubtedly have been cooled in the first instance by the rebuffs with which she had treated him, having been so far smothered by the progress of time, that it might be hopeless to expect again to rekindle the suffocated embers.

"Oh, no!" Francisca replied; she had never really loved any man but him, though she had concealed her affection from him, and she was sure that he would love her alone till the day of his death; and to set out for Florence she was determined, be the event of her journey what it might; chance what would, she could easily provide for herself—she had lived by her own endeavours before. The best of places she had had the good fortune to procure; and as the proverb wisely observed; "there was as good fish in the sea as ever came out of it."

Urbino readily perceived, that not so much her affection for her dear Bernardo, as that fretfulness of disposition which not unfrequently assails the unmarried of the softer sex, at the age to which Francisca had advanced, was the enemy of her peace, and sorry likewise to observe the anxiety with which Averilla heard her strange declaration, and the earnestness with which she endeavoured to dissuade her from her purpose. Ill as his own spirits were at that moment adapted to becoming the consoler of another, he endeavoured first to rally her upon the romance of her intentions; and perceiving his attempts to promise little success, he next sought to divert her thoughts from the subject on which they were bent, by informing her that he had discovered the cause from whence her alarm at the Castello had proceeded, and inviting her to walk thither that morning with himself and Valeria, promising to point out to her, on their arrival there, the hitherto-concealed means by which the supposed apparition had gained access into the building.

Valeria, perceiving the motive by which her father was guided, warmly seconded his invitation, which Francisca, with little reluctance, accepted, saying—"Oh, I don't intend to set off to-day, nor perhaps for a week, or it may be a month to come; and I am sure I am always proud of the honour of being in the company of a real signora, like yourself, as you have often heard me say before, and nobody knows better who is who than I do. Living where I have lived, if I did not, who should? But, ah! dear signora!" she whispered, as they quitted the apartment together, "you don't know what it is to have lost the man of your heart."

Valeria did not reply, but hastened to her chamber, to prepare for her walk.

On arriving at the Castello, it so chanced that Urbino's attention being attracted by some stones which had fallen from the top of the building, and which he was detained by reflecting on the necessity of engaging a workman immediately to replace,

Valeria and Francisca had preceded him a considerable number of paces, and entering the edifice by the principal door, which in the daytime was not unfrequently set open for the admission of air, and advancing towards an apartment which, during the residence of Francisca at the Castello, had been appropriated to the use of Terence and herself, when they retired from the labours of the kitchen, their ears were greeted with the voice of Terence singing the following words to a national tune, which he was particularly attached to chanting in his moments of mirth and recreation—

> "Then kiss me again, my own little life!
> I like you so well, I could take you to wife:
> I never lov'd any so dearly as you,
> Your cheeks are so red, and your eyes are so blue.
> Sing tillalew, tillalew, tidalalew!"

And these words were followed by a cordial smacking of lips, accompanied by a titter of satisfaction.

At the sound of the singing, Valeria and Francisca had both stopped, as they had frequently done before, to listen to the unadorned notes of Terence; but on the sound of the accompaniment—"Blessed Virgin! hear that!" exclaimed Francisca. "Why, signora, did you ever know the like? 'As sure as eggs are eggs,' as the proverb says, that impudent Irish fellow has had the audacity to introduce some vile woman into the Castello."

The flush of jealousy and disappointment started into the countenance of Francisca, and she appeared half prepared to dart forward and satisfy her curiosity, whilst Valeria, moving to an opposite side of the hall, expressed her wish that her father would appear.

At the same moment the door of the apartment, from whence the singing had proceeded, opened, and from it slowly issued old Jeronymo, bearing in his arms an infant, to whose cheek his own was pressed, whilst from his lips proceeded a scarcely-audible murmur, intended to lull his charge to repose.

"Jeronymo!" pronounced Valeria, on beholding him—"whose child is that, Jeronymo?"

The countenance of Jeronymo, on perceiving Valeria, assumed a cast which plainly manifested that he was placed in a situation which compelled him to dissent from his taciturn habit—"Mine—mine—mine, signora!" he exclaimed; and as he spoke, the tears streamed down his furrowed cheeks.

"Yours, Jeronymo!" replied Valeria.

"Yours!" echoed Francisca—"and at your years too! You may well shed tears of repentance; I never heard the like in all my life!"

"It's devilish little, in my opinion, that you ever heard or saw either, notwithstanding all your braggery," cried Terence, proceeding as he spoke from the apartment; "but, be that as it may, I think you are come to an age that might teach you compassion for a fellow-*crater's* misfortunes."

"Now, unmuzzle your wisdom."

"Misfortunes!" rejoined Francisca; "such misfortunes indeed! But let me get out of the house, for I expect the roof to fall in, and crush us all;" and thus saying, she darted towards the outer door, at which she was met by Urbino; and when he had entered, she glided into a spot of concealment, desirous of being thought to have left the place, but still more anxious for the development of what she had seen and heard.

"*Plase* your honour," said Terence, advancing to meet his master, "we have got a strange family in the Castello. I hope I have not done amiss; but I think I have acted just as you would have done yourself, and as I am never so proud as when I expect your commendations, I hope, for the sake of the poor souls that I have made *bould* to harbour, that myself will not be disappointed of *recaving* them now."

Jeronymo burst into a fresh flood of tears, advanced towards Di Cavetti, and extended forward to his notice the child in his arms, with a mingled look of sorrow, entreaty, and compassion.

Urbino requested an explanation of the scene before him, and it was given him by Terence to the following effect.

It appeared that about the hour of twilight on the preceding evening, Terence had discovered a female lying in a state of apparent insensibility at the foot of a tree near the entrance to the sycamore walk. By her side slept an infant, and bending over her in an attitude of the deepest concern, stood the meagre and disabled figure of a man, at whose feet sat a second infant, weeping bitterly.

Terence advanced towards them, and addressed the man, who, in reply to his inquiries, informed him that they were travelling towards Venice, but that his companion, who had long been labouring under ill health, had become suddenly so much exhausted as to be unable to proceed, and in despite of his remonstrances, had thrown herself down upon the ground, where he beheld her, and where he believed her to have fallen asleep, as some minutes had passed since he had been able to make her speak. The man added, that they were not so much in want of money as of a place to repose in, as a kind signor, whom they had that day had the good fortune to meet upon the road, had made them a handsome present, and, moreover, given them his permission to call and refresh themselves at his house, which they were to pass in the course of their journey.

Terence immediately guessed their benefactor to be Di Borges, and having inquired if such were the name of the signor whom they had encountered, and learned that it had been the worthy farmer, he no longer hesitated to give them that shelter which their necessities required within the Castello, until the female were sufficiently recovered to proceed on her way.

Accordingly, with the joint assistance of Terence and Jeronymo, the sufferer was conveyed into the Castello; and having been provided with a bed, Jeronymo undertook to furnish her with such nourishment and medicine as he judged would best suit her weak and delicate state; and her younger infant, at her particular request, having been placed beside her, Terence took upon himself to provide for the wants of the man and the other child, who was a beautiful and engaging little girl, of about three years and a half old, who at this moment appearing, ran up to Terence, clung to his leg, and explained the mystery of the caresses in which he had been overheard to indulge himself, by begging him to sing her another song, and promising him, if he did so, to kiss him again for his reward.

Terence took her up in his arms, and giving her a silencing nod, which she, with a smile, obeyed, proceeded in his narrative. The man, he said, though not much beyond the prime of life, was one of the greatest cripples he had ever beheld. He had been a soldier, and so greatly wounded in battle, that it was almost a miracle his life had been preserved to him.

"Oh, holy apostles!—poor boy! *lasso! lasso!*" ejaculated Jeronymo; and again the tears gushed from his eyes.

The repeated tears and increasing agitation of the old man excited the concern of Urbino; and turning aside from Terence, he compassionately inquired the cause of his unusual emotion.

Though now willing to speak, the tumult of Jeronymo's feelings tied his tongue; and Terence perceiving his efforts to articulate vain, spoke for him, by saying—"It has been a strange affair that has happened, your honour; I was just coming to that part of the story, if you had listened to me a little longer: it seems this poor *ould jontlemon* was once the father of a brace of sons, and this wounded soldier, now in the house here, turns out to be the one of them."

Jeronymo seized the hand of Urbino, and dragged him into the apartment, where he placed him opposite to a figure which was indeed an object of commiseration; what remained of his emaciated form was supported on two wooden legs; his right hand was rendered nearly useless by a wound which he had received in his wrist; and one of his eyes was covered with a black patch.

"Are you Fernando di Zubica?" asked Urbino, when recovered from the momentary surprise into which the uncouth appearance of the unfortunate being whom he was addressing had thrown him.

"No, signor; I am his younger brother," replied the soldier: "Fernando is dead."

At these words a deep sigh accompanied the tears of old Jeronymo.

"Both you and your brother," rejoined Di Cavetti, "deserted your father in a cruel and unnatural manner; and it appears that *you* have met the punishment due to the neglect of filial duty."

"I was only eighteen when I ran away from Venice," answered the soldier; "my elder brother prompted me to the action. I have many a time since reflected on the impropriety of my conduct: if I had been as wise then as I am now——But there is a vast difference, signor, between the ideas of eighteen and forty-four."

"When you did repent, why did you never inquire after your father?" demanded Urbino.

"Indeed, signor," replied the soldier, "I felt ashamed of my past conduct, and reluctant to meet the parent to whom I had been unfeeling; and nothing but the unceasing entreaties of my sister-in-law could ever have prevailed on me to visit this part of the country again; though indeed I have often wished to know if my father were still alive, and how he fared, equally regretting that it was not in my power to add any comforts to his declining years, and blaming myself for having abridged his means of procuring them, by my dissolute conduct in my youth."

"Well, well," pronounced Urbino, after a short pause of reflection, "repentance, in any shape, deserves a welcome; and I trust that your presence may still add a gleam of sunshine to the closing years of your parent's life."

Jeronymo clasped his arms round the neck of his son, and pressed him to his heart—"I forgive you all," he ejaculated; "and I would willingly have forgiven Fernando too, for all his cruelty, from the very bottom of my heart, if I could but once more have held him thus."

It was the longest sentence which the old man had perhaps ever uttered in the course of his life; and overpowered by the effort, he sunk, with his eyes half-closed, into a chair, by the side of which his son was standing.

At the expiration of a few seconds, Urbino proceeded to inquire of Jeronymo's son, in what circumstances, and in what situation of life, his brother had died? But Jeronymo prevented his reply, by explaining, partly in words and partly by signs, that his feelings, were so much overcome by the occurrences of the few last hours, that he, at least, could not, for the present, be an auditor of any farther detail relative to the ill-fated beings to whom he had given birth; and with his hand pressed to his temple, indicative of the disturbed state of his brain, he retired, to compose his mind in the solitude of his private apartment.

Valeria having heard the conclusion of Terence's account, had immediately proceeded to the chamber of the female, whom Jeronymo's son had represented as the widow of his deceased brother, and in whom she found an interesting young woman, of speech and manners superior to the common orders of society, and who wept tears of gratitude at the kind expressions with which Valeria endeavoured to sooth her feelings, and to assure her of the protection and friendly services of those to whose acquaintance her fate had conducted her.

At the departure of Jeronymo, his son began to reply to Urbino's inquiries, by saying, that after his brother and himself had quitted Venice, being as careless of the preservation of the little property which they possessed, as they had been indifferent about the means which had made it theirs, they had for many years struggled with various turns of fortune, and often desired to revisit a home, to which pride and shame had jointly withheld them from returning; that at length he had enlisted, and his brother, by the death of a friend to whom he had been servant, had been enabled to settle in a small business.

For some years they were then separated. On his regiment being disbanded, he had proceeded to seek his brother, and had found him upon his deathbed. He was married, and the father of two children—"Those two babes whom you behold here, signor," he continued—"he strongly recommended them to my protection; and little, as I was conscious, that in my disabled state it could be in my power to do to serve them, I promised never to desert them; and I never will, to the day of my death, signor, while they require my presence.

"In the course of a few days Fernando died; and his interment being passed, his widow, reminding me of the promise by which I had bound myself to my deceased brother, entreated me to accede to a proposal which she was going to make to me. I desired her to explain herself; and she said, that the trade of their shop had of late been so very small, as scarcely to afford them a maintenance; that the business was not worth retaining; and that she had resolved to convert the little she possessed into money, and to set out for Venice, the neighbourhood of which city she had a most unconquerable desire to visit. I inquired her reason; she unfolded it to me; and finding it impossible to overrule her inclination, or to withstand her entreaties, her little property was disposed of to the best advantage, and we began our journey."

"And what could be the urgent motive which induced her to this step?" inquired Urbino.

"You must pardon me, signor, for refusing to be your informer on that head," replied the soldier; "I have given her my solemn promise never to divulge it without her permission; and I love and respect her so much, that nothing could induce me to break my word with her, or to give her pain."

The sentiments expressed by Jeronymo's son began to redeem his character in the opinion of Urbino, who having declared his approbation of his conduct, the soldier continued thus:—"Unable to afford the expence of any conveyance, you may imagine, signor, how slowly our journey was performed; at last our little stock of money began to be nearly exhausted, and I perceived, with an anxiety which I endeavoured to repress within my own breast, that my companions were becoming hourly more unfit for the task which they had undertaken. Ours was a group to excite compassion; and as there are always some charitable hearts scattered over the face of the earth, we were always tolerably well supplied with the necessaries of life. It is needless for me, signor, to dwell on the particulars of our progress; you have heard already how fatigue and weakness had overpowered my poor sister, when we last night reached this spot; and it must be alike needless for me to repeat with what joy I recognized, in the person of one of those who humanely came forward to administer to our necessities, my long-lost and lamented father."

"It is a merciful Providence, I think, which has conducted you hither," rejoined Urbino; "I cannot pretend to say how promising your sister's prospects may be on arriving at the spot of your destination; but the most flattering of human expectations are liable to disappointment, and in that case what could have been your resource?—whence was the maintenance of you all to be derived?"

"I have a small pension, signor," replied the soldier; "but it would scarcely have supplied us with dry bread. It is a miracle, signor—it is the hand of Heaven itself which has guided us hither."

"The age of miracles is past," returned Urbino; "that is, the age of those open interpositions of Providence in the affairs of man which once procured that title. But it is my fixed opinion, that the finger of Omnipotence still often in mercy points out that way to the earthly pilgrim, to which short-sighted man but too frequently believes that a blind chance has led him."

Their conversation was here interrupted by the appearance of Valeria, who came to inform her father, that she had left the female in so alarming a state of debility and fever, that she deemed it necessary he should immediately see her and prescribe for her relief.

Urbino, without delay, proceeded to accompany his daughter to the chamber of the stranger; and the disabled soldier and Terence were thus left together. After a silence of a few moments—"Ah!" ejaculated the former, with a half-suppressed sigh, "it may well be said, 'what has mortal man to be proud of?' I remember the time when I was foolish enough myself to be vain of my person; and what am I now? These," he added, pointing to his wooden legs as he spoke; "these afford an excellent lesson for the coxcomb."

> "Get thee to my lady's chamber, and tell her to paint
> an inch thick—to this complexion she must come at last!"

solemnly pronounced Terence.

The soldier well understood the meaning of the sentence, although he was ignorant whence the words were deduced, and proceeded speaking thus—"What fools the women often make of the men, and of themselves too at the same time! When they admire a man solely for his person, must he not be a fool to be gratified by their admiration? and must not they be equally fools themselves, to give all their consideration to his outside, and not to investigate what he is made of within?"

"By the powers, and you may say that!" replied Terence; "in my judgement, a woman that looks only for beauty in a husband, can never make a wife

> 'As chaste as ice, as pure as snow,'

as *ould* Willy expresses it; for if beauty was all she married for, *divil* a bit myself would wonder if her husband chanced to fall in *wid* any little sort of an accident, like yourself, but she might continue to look out for beauty still, and be after forgetting her husband altogether."

"And what could be said to her then?" ejaculated the soldier.

"It is not what could be said to her then," replied Terence, "but it is what should have been said to her before she got *hould* of the chance of making any thing worse of an honest man than Heaven intended that he should be.

"Get thee to a nunnery—to a nunnery go!"

"I was once myself so silly as to be in love with beauty," rejoined the soldier, "and when I went to the wars, leaving the girl of my heart behind me, was the only part of the business that gave me pain; though I have often thought, upon consideration, that I was most likely quite as well without her; for she was a great coquette, and, perhaps, when she had seen me with these wooden supporters, might, as you say, have forgotten the husband, and only continued to look out for beauty. Her temper was not one of the best either, and that is a bad ingredient in the compound of matrimony. I can't say but I should like to see her once again, though I dare say she would scarcely recollect me, if she saw me thus."

"If she could think the worse of you for bearing the marks of your bravery about *wid* you," replied Terence,

'Let her beauty
Look through a casement to allure false hearts,
And be false with them;'

her love never was worth the dregs of an empty *poteen*, take my word for it. Talking of that," continued Terence, "I am after thinking yourself would not be the worse to wet your one eye *wid* a drop of wine, this morning, to keep your heart up after your journey, and myself has a flask in this closet that is not for sneezing at."

Terence rose to fetch his flask, and at the same instant, Francisca, who had been loitering about the hall, anxious to learn every particular relative to the strangers, without having any one to whom she durst apply for information, and who had for some time past been listening, at the door of the apartment, to the conversation of the soldier and Terence, but who, on the rising of the latter, feared to be detected on her post of curiosity, darted into the room, and placed herself upon the first vacant chair.

Having poured out a draught of wine for the soldier, and drank another himself, Terence turned to Francisca, and bidding her good morning, inquired if she would take a sip of the water?

"No, indeed," replied Francisca, with an affected toss of her head, "I never drink any thing but lemonade."

"It was in a lemonade-shop," said the soldier, addressing Terence, "where I became acquainted with my beauty; she was, as I have already told you, too much of a coquette to confess her love for me to myself; but she used to speak freely enough about me to my neighbours—a way that many young women have of conveying their sentiments to the men of their choice; she used to say, that I had a piercing eye, and that my legs were so well proportioned that she could almost believe they were carved out of wood. I wonder what she would say, if she could behold me, now I have only one eye, and my legs are indeed carved out of wood? I wager it would not be—'Oh, my beautiful Bernardo!' and 'Oh, my dear Bernardo di Zubica!' with her, as it used to be."

At these words Francisca made a violent start, and sunk, with an hysteric shriek, upon the floor.

The soldier and Terence both proceeded to raise her up, and place her again in her seat; and when they had done so—"What can be the matter with this poor woman?" said the soldier.

"Likely a little touch of the wind cholic," answered Terence; "if she had sucked a drop of the wine I offered her, it might have kept the complaint under; but I'll take out the flask again, and try her now."

"Wind cholic!" ejaculated Francisca, whose momentary insensibility had been affected; then addressing the soldier, who was supporting her, she added—"Keep your hands off me, and don't annihilate me with your touch."

"What have I done to offend you?" asked the soldier.

"Oh, you wretch! to go to the wars, and make that fright of yourself!" exclaimed Francisca, pretending to burst into tears, and hiding her face in her hands.

"I cannot perceive how my misfortunes can have excited your displeasure," was the soldier's reply.

"Why, don't you know Francisca?" roared out the disconsolate damsel, starting upon her feet as she spoke, and clenching her hands in the violence of her mortified feelings.

"Francisca!" exclaimed Bernardo, for Bernardo was indeed the person speaking, "why, you cannot mean that you are that Francisca who was niece to old Lupo, who kept the lemonade-shop in Florence, to whom my brother Fernando was first shopman, and then succeeded him in business? why, that Francisca had plump cheeks and a natural colour, sparkling chesnut eyes, with the whites as clear and as bright as——"

"But," ejaculated Terence, interrupting his harangue, "when nature hath made a fair creature, may she not by fortune fall into the fire?"

"Hold your tongue, you impertinent Irish monkey!" cried Francisca, "and 'speak when you are spoken to,' as the proverb says: it is no such thing—I have not fallen into the fire, and I am Francisca, the niece of old Lupo who kept the lemonade-shop in Florence, and you must know me, if you are indeed Bernardo: what can have changed me?"

"Why, the hand of Time," answered Bernardo; "why may not you be grown old, as well as I be grown ugly?"

"Oh mercy! oh Holy Virgin! what have I done that I should live to be called old, and by one too who once professed to adore me? I would rather be called anything than old—what have I done to be thus mortified and despised?"

"Done!" replied Terence; "why, you have lived so long an *ould* maid, that amongst your other losses, you have lost your temper, and view men and things through a wrong *madium;* there was a time you would not marry him for love, though it seems the biggest disappointment, after all, fell upon yourself in that same case; now, then, marry him for tenderness and compassion, that would once have married you for love, and apply the remainder of your days to make him a good nurse—the best office a woman of your years can undertake!"

"What!" exclaimed Francisca, "marry a man with wooden legs! it would be a standing joke against me as long as I live; my very children would cast it at me, as a reflection upon my choice of their father!"

"No fear of that," replied Terence; "poor Bernardo's is an infirmity that I never heard of its descending to the next generation."

The presence of Urbino, who informed Bernardo that his sister-in-law requested his presence in her chamber, put a stop to the conversation, and the soldier accordingly accompanied the worthy physician to the bedside of the suffering female, where a detail of some past circumstances was confided to the knowledge of Di Cavetti and his daughter, which will hereafter be laid before the reader.

CHAPTER III

My circumstances
Being so near the truth as I will make them,
Must first induce you to believe; whose strength
I will confirm with oath; which I doubt not,
You'll give me leave to spare, when you shall find
You need it not.   *Cymbeline.*

ON arriving at the cottage of Bianca, which consisted of one apartment of the meanest description, Di Borges found Calvino and his mother within, the former of whom, as he entered, was looking with ecstacy into the hand of the latter, in which were contained some pieces of silver coin, which the old woman appeared to be counting.—"I fear I interrupt you," said Sancho, smiling.—"I am glad, however, to find you so well employed."

"Ah, signor," returned Bianca, "Heaven knows it is very seldom I have money to count; the most of it I finger comes from your charitable hand; this was given to me by a poor creature who is reposing on my bed yonder."

Sancho directed his eyes to the spot at which she pointed, and through the ragged and flimsy curtains with which the bed was inclosed, he could perceive the outline of a human form in male attire.—"That is," continued Bianca, "when I say, 'poor creature,' I don't mean poor in purse or in person, but to be pitied is what I mean; for I verily believe the signor's brains are disturbed."

"Do you know him?" inquired Di Borges.

"No, signor," replied the old woman; "this morning, when Calvino was returning from the spring with water, this young signor darted across his path, and asked leave to drink out of his pitcher, which Calvino, poor boy, of course permitted."

"And he drank, and he drank, and he drank," cried Calvino, laughing vacantly at the recollection, "as much water as I could have swallowed, if there had been wine in the pitcher."

"The poor soul is burnt up by an inward fever," said Bianca; "I went out at the moment, for it was close by my door they met, and I was so struck by the signor's melancholy appearance, for it had rained hard all night, signor, and his clothes were wet through and through, and his hair was drenched; for he had no hat on his head and his face was as pale as a shroud; and seeing him so distressed, I made bold to ask him if he would condescend to walk into my cottage, and dry himself? He didn't say a word in answer, but suffered me to take his hand, and lead him in; and, oh dear! signor Sancho, his hand burnt like a living fire."

"He's asleep," said Calvino, who had been peeping into the bed through a rent in the curtain, "or at least his eyes are shut; but I have often been wide awake with mine closed before now."

"When I had led him in," continued Bianca, "I asked him if he would take a little refreshment, such as I could give him, or suffer me to dry his clothes? and he replied, in a still slow voice—'Suffer me to sleep a while, if it be possible that I can sleep—I need no other nourishment.' I showed him what my bed was, and told him he was heartily welcome to make use of it, if he could deign to repose upon it. He did not turn his head to observe it; but drawing from his pocket the pieces of silver now in my hand, he threw them upon the table, and then cast himself upon the bed. It is now some hours since he arrived, and he has not spoken, nor attempted to undraw the curtains which I closed around him. Peep at him, signor, and see if he is known to you."

Sancho complied with her request, and discerned sufficient of the countenance to have recognized an acquaintance by; but the person of him whom he beheld was unknown to him.

After some farther comments had passed between them on Bianca's guest, and Sancho had declared his intention of remaining a while at the cottage, in the expectation of the stranger waking, that he might offer him his services, or afford him that protection which Bianca seemed to apprehend that his apparently-disturbed state of mind required, he proceeded to the business which had brought him to the old woman's dwelling, and began to question Calvino relative to the spot where he had found the slipper of Paulina?

After many ambiguous answers and descriptions, which his mother, who was his usual interpreter, managed to explain with tolerable perspicuity, it was ascertained that the place where he had discovered the slipper was an acclivity of green sward, leading to the drawbridge of a stupendous Castello, situate at the distance of about a league and a half from the spot where they were standing.

"It must be the Castello Alfonta that he means," observed Sancho.

"It can be no other, signor," replied Bianca.

"Though at so short a distance from my own abode," replied Sancho, "that is a part of the country I seldom visit, and know less about, as the whole territory belongs to the proprietor of the Castello, and, consequently, presents no invitation to the speculator or the farmer; but if I recollect rightly, it has for many years past been deserted by its owner, and inhabited only by the steward and his family."

"You are right, signor," answered Bianca; "the steward's name is Lipardo di Moralta; but the name of the marchese, for he is a marchese to whom the Castello Alfonta belongs, I cannot recollect."

"Nor I," rejoined Sancho, "though it must be impossible but what I have heard it."

"The signor Lipardo, as he is called, has a fine place of it, by all accounts," resumed Bianca; "I can remember when his wife was only a servant in the Castello, and now she dresses in her silks and satins, Sundays and working-days, and all alike. I warrant me, the steward, or major domo, or whatever he may be, for some call him one, and some the other, hasn't his good fortune for nothing; he has done his work for his money, I'll be bound to say. He brought up his master's nephew from his infancy, just as if he had been his own child; that's one thing he has done—but there's more than that, I dare say."

Sancho did not immediately reply, and Bianca, with a look of infinite sagacity, added in a half-whisper—"I suppose you have heard, signor, that there was once a murder said to have happened in that family?"

"Come, come, Bianca," replied Di Borges, smiling, "none of the marvellous; you know I don't relish it."

At this moment a deep sigh proceeded from the bed, which was followed by other sounds, which bespoke the stranger to be awake, and Sancho was on the point of proceeding to address the unfortunate person, in whom he felt no inconsiderable interest, from the account which had been given of him by Bianca, when the old woman, suddenly clapping the palms of her hands together, exclaimed—"I have it, signor—I have it—the name of the great marchese to whom the Castello Alfonta belongs is Di Valdetti."

"So it is," answered the farmer, "and I now remember hearing one of my neighbours mention, the other day, that the marchese Di Valdetti was come on a visit to his Castello; but it had escaped my recollection."

"The marchese Di Valdetti so near at hand!" exclaimed the stranger, starting up from the bed as he spoke: "direct me instantly," he added, addressing Calvino, "where to find this Castello Alfonta." Then apparently sinking into an abstraction of thought, he muttered between his lips—"'Avoid the marchese Di Valdetti,' pronounced the mysterious pilgrim; 'you have every thing to fear from him—persecution, dishonour, death!' No matter, Heaven grant us but to meet! then, if he possesses the secret of my birth, let me either tear it from his heart, or, failing in the only wish now left me, let him free the wretched Julio from an insupportable existence! Come, where is this Castello Alfonta?" he repeated, and, with a piercing and bewildered eye, he darted out of the cottage.

"There, signor Sancho," said Bianca, "I told you how it was with the poor creature; he is quite distracted, quite mad!"

Calvino, who was at other times prone to be too forward in giving his services, appeared half-terrified by the wild aspect and solemn tones of his mother's guest; and instead of presenting himself to point out the way to the spot required, had retired to the most distant part of the dwelling.

On hearing the name of Julio, Di Borges had been instantly convinced who the speaker was, and he stood for some moments irresolute how it became him to act, or in what point of view to consider the words which he had heard. He at length stepped out of the cottage, to observe what direction the unfortunate being had taken; but Julio was nowhere to be seen.

It will be recollected that such pages of Julio's manuscript as contained an account of the visit which he had received from the mysterious pilgrim by night, at an inn upon the road between Rome and Padua, had not been read by Urbino, and, consequently, their contents were unknown to Sancho di Borges, who had received the information of whatever he was acquainted with concerning Julio from his friend Di Cavetti; hence the agitation evinced by Julio at the sound of Di Valdetti's name was to him incomprehensible, and he could only resolve to refer the question to the solution of Urbino.

Julio himself, on rushing out of the hut by the side of the brook on the preceding evening, had darted into the midst of the forest, and had wandered there through the night unsheltered, but senseless of the fury of the storm to which he was exposed. He had believed that he had armed himself with fortitude to bid Valeria farewell for ever, without a tear, but the moment of trial unmanned his most firm resolves; the power of nature triumphed over that of reason; and the task was rendered more severe than he had apprehended to find it, by the unexpected entrance of Urbino into the hut, and especially by his presence having withheld him from receiving, at the lips of Valeria, that promise of fidelity, possessed of which, he had nursed himself into the belief that he could endure with resignation an eternal exile from the idol of his soul.

In the course of a few hours, the agitation of his mind produced a violent fever in his blood, which, contrasted with the damp earth upon which he was extended, created a painful shivering in his frame, which was only equalled by the scorching thirst which he was enduring. At this moment, chancing to raise his eyes, he beheld Calvino bearing his pitcher, and flew towards him. Almost insensibly, as the old woman had described it, he had suffered her to lead him into her dwelling, and in that state of mind which has no choice of situation or pursuit, had cast himself upon the bed, and professed a desire to sleep, in order to avoid being compelled to speak. Here, as he lay, once more he fervently wished and prayed to die; but still he revolted, as he had before done, at the thought of meeting his fate from the hand of an executioner, or staining his memory with the crime of suicide. The name of Di Valdetti, pronounced by Bianca, conjured up a host of new ideas to his imagination. The pilgrim's injunction to him respecting the marchese of that name had always led him to conclude that being, whoever he was, acquainted with the secret of his birth; no event could render his existence more miserable than it was at the present moment, and he considered it a satisfaction to be enabled to rush upon his fate; and thus impressed, as his own words have already acquainted us, he quitted the cottage of old Bianca.

Unconscious of the chord which had been touched in the heart of Julio by the name of Di Valdetti, Di Borges conceived the exclamation which he had uttered, and his subsequent conduct, to be the effects of a wandering brain; and uncertain how Urbino might wish him to act, either in his case, or that of Paulina, he resolved to lose no time in returning home, and advising with him upon the subject.

On reaching the farmhouse, and learning that Di Cavetti was gone to the Castello della Torvida, the impatience of mind which he felt to commune with him determined him to follow him thither. He had not proceeded far on his way, ere he was met by the friend of whom he was in pursuit; and placing themselves upon a bank by the side of the road, a considerable time was past in recapitulating to each other the adventures which each had encountered during the short period of their separation, all of which have already been circumstantially laid before our readers, with the exception of what had passed in the chamber of Bernardo's sister-in-law, after he had entered it, in compliance with the summons to that effect delivered to him by Urbino.

"On entering the chamber of the unknown female with Bernardo," said Di Cavetti, "she beckoned him to her bed-side, and spoke thus—'From the proof which I have already received of the tenderness of heart of this excellent signor, and his daughter, and also from observing the kind esteem with which they honour your father, I judge that I cannot ask advice of any persons who will more condescendingly bestow it on me, relative to the object of my journey to this part of the country, than themselves.'

"Bernardo warmly coincided with her in opinion, and she rejoined—'I must intrude upon you to listen to a short account of my past life; it is necessary to the introduction of the point upon which I wish to obtain your counsel.'

"We begged of her to proceed as best suited her story; and as she appeared almost too weak to enter into conversation, at least upon any subject in which she was deeply interested, we proposed to her to delay her disclosure till she was restored to better health; but as she replied that her mind would be easier when her secret was committed to the confidence of those whom she regarded as friends, we consented to hear her, only begging that she would proceed slowly, and not agitate herself in her present weak state.

'The first years of my life,' the female began her account by saying, 'were passed in travelling about the country, with a woman named Leonora Velinos, who sold French lace, and other trivial articles, for the embellishment of dress, to such signoras as she could prevail on to become her customers. Whilst an infant, I was carried in one of her arms, and her box of wares in the other. As I advanced in age, I ran by her side, and was provided with a little basket of toys, for which I was instructed by her to solicit purchasers amongst the younger branches of those families in which she courted the favours of the adult.

'When I was between ten and twelve years of age, Leonora settled herself as a milliner in a small shop in Florence. Besides the shop and a contiguous apartment which we inhabited, the house contained a chamber and a closet, which Leonora let as a lodging. Various were the tenants which, in the course of four years, possessed it; and at the expiration of that time it was hired by Fernando di Zubica, who served in a lemonade-shop, situate in the street in which we resided.

'It is needless to dwell upon circumstances irrelevant to that point to which I am desirous of directing your attention; suffice it therefore to say, that from my first knowledge of Fernando, he paid me the most marked attentions, and ultimately sought me for his wife. I was at that time just turned of seventeen, and Fernando more than double my age. I liked him as an acquaintance, but as a husband I could not view him with the same favourable eye. Thus passed on another year, Fernando nothing diminishing in his assiduities, and Leonora backing his suit by every means in her power. At this time Leonora was taken extremely ill, and her life despaired of. She now represented to me, that at her death, which she foresaw must shortly be expected, I should stand alone in the world, without a natural or an allied protector, unless I consented to accept the hand of Fernando. She repeated to me, that the age of the parties united in wedlock was not of so much consequence as the amicable sentiments which they felt for each other; said she was sure that Fernando loved me, and that with him I was certain of enjoying a comfortable independence, as his master, who was so old that he could not, in the course of nature, live very long, had promised that he should succeed him in trade. Her arguments prevailed, and I became Fernando's wife.

'The last moments of Leonora continued to be very rapidly approaching; and one day calling me to her bedside, she said— "Come to me alone to-morrow evening—I have something of consequence to unfold to you before I die." I obeyed her injunction, and after a few sentences, intended to prepare me for the disclosure which she was about to make, she informed me that I was not her child. I was beginning eagerly to interrogate her who my parents were, and why my birth had been thus long concealed from me, when we were interrupted by the arrival of a priest, who daily attended her, and his office was scarcely ended ere her physician appeared. After a few moments passed by her bedside, the physician quitted the chamber, and beckoned to me to follow him.—"It is my duty," he said, "to inform you that you must not flatter yourself with the expectation of your mother's existence being prolonged; she has now but a very short time to live."

'He departed, and I hurried back to Leonora, and hastily repeated my question, who are my parents? I perceived that a considerable change had taken place in her countenance since I had last conversed with her, before the entrance of the priest, and that it now cost her a severe struggle to articulate. At length—'Venice——' she, with difficulty, pronounced, 'Venice——The marchese di Valdetti——'—'Is he my father?' I hastily asked. With still greater difficulty she whispered forth—'He can inform you—he knows your story——he——' Again she paused, exhausted, and almost speechless—'Oh! for Heaven's sake,' I exclaimed, 'leave me not in this suspense! in the name of mercy unfold this riddle!' Moved by my earnestness, she made an effort to collect her fleeting strength—'There is a woman near Venice,' she said, 'who knows all that——' Once more she paused, and once more she spoke—'Her name is——' The words were her last, and she sunk back lifeless on her pillow.

'Some time after the decease of Leonora, I imparted to my husband what had passed between us previously to her death, and besought him to take me to Venice, and endeavour to prove the truth of her confession. He derided my idea, said, that probably the senses of the old woman had been wandering in her last moments, and that, at all events, we must be regarded as distracted beings, if we were to set out upon so blind a business. If there is a marchese di Valdetti in Venice, he said, how could we expect to gain his attention to such a vague account as we have to offer? We should only put ourselves to expence and trouble, and be laughed at for our pains. To the day of his death he persisted in not listening to my entreaties on the subject, whilst the inclination which had seized upon my heart from the moment of my receiving Leonora's confession, continued hourly to gain strength.'

"And here," said Urbino, "concluded her simple narrative, with the exception of her having repeated to us the difficulty with which she had prevailed upon Bernardo to consent to her pilgrimage, and to attend her on it.—'I dare say,' she added, 'that I almost appear in your eyes, as my deceased husband foretold, that I must be regarded in the opinion of any strangers to whom I should ever confess the object of which I had suffered myself to be led in pursuit. I know not how deceptive my feelings may be; but they urge me forward, with a degree of warmth, which appears to me as if it were imparted by the breath of destiny.'

"It does indeed appear a most infatuated idea upon which this poor being is acting," said Di Borges; "and it is not a little extraordinary that the name of this marchese di Valdetti should thrice, within so short a space of time, have occurred to us in connexion with different objects who excite our interest, the unfortunate Julio, our dear Paulina, and the unknown sufferer at the Castello. Are you acquainted with the marchese di Valdetti, or his history?"

"Not in the least," replied Urbino. "When I was informed by my servant Terence a few weeks ago, that such a nobleman was come to reside in the neighbourhood, was, I believe, the first time I ever heard the name, and I conclude from your question, that you know as little of him as I do."

"I know no more of him," replied Sancho, "than that the family, of which he bears the name, are reputed to be very rich and powerful, and that many years have passed away since any of them have resided at the Castello Alfonta; but where their residence has been held, I am ignorant. I do not perceive," continued the farmer, after a pause, "that we are authorized to display ourselves as interferers in the cause of any one of those persons, between whom and the marchese there appears to be an obscure chain of connexion; but our dear signora Paulina, and indeed the finding of a slipper, which she once wore, in the front of a man's dwelling, appears in itself a very slender reason for accusing him of being the thief who stole her."

"The point requires consideration," returned Urbino.

"And it must have it," rejoined Di Borges; "we must strictly guard against drawing down upon ourselves the vengeance of a powerful man like the marchese, by a false accusation against his honour."

"The promise which I have received in writing of her safety would, in such a case, operate against us," remarked Urbino.

"Materially," answered the farmer; and expressing a wish to see the female at the Castello, they turned their steps towards its walls, both deeply buried in reflection.

CHAPTER IV

There stand—for you are spell-stopp'd!
SHAKESPEARE.

WE must now return to the long-neglected Paulina. At the sight of the marchese di Valdetti, a breathless trepidation seized upon the heart of Paulina; fears, not inferior to those which she entertained for her own safety, assailed her breast for that being to whom the most solemn ties had just united her, and she sunk senseless into the supporting arms of Lipardo.

On recovering from the stupor of faculty into which she had fallen, she found herself extended upon a bed, and by the flame of a lamp, which was burning in a distant part of the apartment, she could discern the figure of a man standing by her side—"Where am I?" she hastily exclaimed.

"In safety, signora," replied the man: "let that assurance satisfy you."

The voice of the speaker was unknown to her; and after a moment's pause—"Where are Vincentio and Lipardo? Why are they not with me?" she demanded.

"Hush!" answered the man, "name them not; hush!" and with this injunction, whisperingly conveyed, he glided out of the apartment.

She started from the bed, and examined the apartment: she had no recollection of having seen it before. It was meanly furnished, and received its light from a circular window in the roof. She listened; not a sound broke the stillness of the hour. She knew not where to conclude herself, and trembled with agony, as she reflected to what fate her friend Lipardo, her husband Vincentio, and herself, might not be doomed. She knew not whether to consider the voice and words of the man who had just left her, as friendly to her interests, or the reverse; his countenance, the dimness of the light which the lamp afforded, had not given her an opportunity of beholding; and the ambiguity of the admonition with which he had left her, might equally construe him into an adherent of either party.

In the course of about an hour, the lamp faded and died away; and its extinction enabled her to behold the first tints of the rising dawn appearing through the casement. In a state of mind which ignorance of the truth, and apprehensions founded on conjecture, rendered almost insupportable, she continued to watch the increasing light, but when it had reached the brightness of perfect day, no sounds which announced the operations of life to be passing near her met her ear, and she knew not whether to believe herself in a retired part of that building which she had for the few last days been constrained to inhabit, or removed to some other spot.

After a time, the door, which she now found to have been bolted on the outside, was opened, and a man entered.—"How fare you, signora?" he said, and she was immediately convinced that it was the voice of him who had addressed her that morning, when she had first been restored to recollection. "Here is some breakfast," he continued, placing some articles which he took from a basket in his hand upon the table as he spoke; "they are not of the most delicate kind, signora, but the best which your friends are at the present time able to send you."

"My friends! What friends?" ejaculated Paulina.

"Do you know this ring, signora?" rejoined the man, extending towards her his hand.—"But you cannot fail to remember it."

Paulina perceived it to be a topaz, set in a circle of emeralds, which she remembered to have observed on the finger of Lipardo.—"Yes, I think—I—yes, I am certain I have seen it before," she replied.

"Then you must know who it is that employs me," rejoined the man, with a significant motion of his head, which drew the regards of Paulina to his countenance, and subsequently to examine his features and person. He was tall and muscular, but the contour of his face presented no remarkable impression— "Keep it, if you please, signora," he continued, and restore it to the owner when you see him; it has done its duty, in convincing you that I come to you commissioned from him."

"But may I not behold him," rejoined Paulina, "or be made acquainted why he does not visit me himself?"

"Before this time to-morrow, signora," rejoined the man, "you will know all; but the utmost caution is necessary in the proceedings of those around you; for myself, I dare remain with you no longer: but observe this one admonition which I give you; for upon your observance of my words depends the event of a stratagem now working. When you see me again, do not fail to follow my directions for your conduct, which I may point out to you by signs, as it may perhaps be unsafe for me to address you. About the hour of twilight you will, at all events, behold me: till then, farewell, signora!" and so saying, he departed.

It was equally impossible for Paulina to divine what events had taken place since she had last beheld Vincentio and Lipardo, as for her to attempt to explain the concealed meaning contained in the ambiguous address of the man who had just left her; and she could only await the development of her situation with anxious impatience.

The hours passed on leaden wings; at last the shades of twilight began to veil the lustre of day, and these had been some time succeeded by the raven tints of night, ere the door of her apartment was again opened. The same man once more appeared; and placing a lamp upon the table, he laid down a bundle of clothes by its side, and whisperingly addressing Paulina, said—"Make all the haste you are able in exchanging your own garments for those I have brought you. You must assist me to relieve the guard at the foot of the drawbridge." The last sentence he particularly emphasized, and again quickly retired.

Paulina examined the bundle, and found it to contain a suit of regimentals, such as the armed vassal of an Italian nobleman might he supposed to wear. The man who had brought them to her was habited in a similar suit; and from the words which he had addressed to her concerning the drawbridge, she concluded herself to be still in the Castello of the marchese di Valdetti, and that her escape from it was to be effected by means of the disguise with which she had just been provided. At any other moment, her feelings would have revolted at the idea of exchanging her own habit, for that of a sex whose manners she knew so ill how to assimilate; but her situation was such as silenced the fainter voice of delicacy, and she proceeded to equip herself in her new habiliments, which she found accompanied by a military cap, with a deep verge in its front, well calculated for the concealment of her countenance.

In less than an hour the man returned. He expressed his satisfaction at her equipment by a silent nod of approbation; then again addressing her in a whisper, he said—"Take my arm, and speak not, on your life!" and with these words he led her out of the chamber.

They passed on in silence, and without meeting a single individual, through many long and intricate passages, faintly lighted by occasional lamps placed against the walls, and at length entered an enclosed square, where the first person whom they had encountered hailed them, in the voice of a sentinel, with the demand of—"Who goes there?"

"Honour!" replied Paulina's companion, and they were suffered to pass on.

Having crossed the square, and passed through an enclosed archway, they found themselves at the portcullis leading upon the drawbridge. The same question was again advanced, and the same reply given; which ceremony being passed, Paulina's conductor stopped before an open door, through which, perceiving some men habited in suits similar to her own, sitting round a wood fire, she conjectured to be a guardhouse.

"Come, Giraldo, are you here?" said her companion.

"No, he's not here," replied a voice from within; "you will find him waiting for you at the foot of the drawbridge."

"Very well," answered Paulina's companion, and was moving away, when one of the men who had been sitting before the fire, starting from his seat, and darting forward, seized him by the arm, and in a voice rendered scarcely articulate by intoxication, exclaimed—"You shall drink with me before you go—by all the saints, you shall, Philippo! not one step do you stir till you have put my flask to your mouth."

"For shame! for shame, Paulo!" replied Paulina's companion, whose name she had thus discovered to be Philippo; "you are drunk. Lie down upon the bench yonder, and take a sleep to sober you."

"It's not your fault, Philippo," exclaimed the sentry, "that any of us are sober; you have plied us often enough with French brandy to-day to have turned all our brains for us; but we are much obliged to you for your kindness, I am sure, comrade."

"Whenever I have any good luck, I like to share it amongst you," answered Philippo. "My nephew here, who has just received the marchese's sanction to become one of us, procured me the treat of which you have partaken."

"The devil he did!" cried the intoxicated Paulo; "and do you think I will not make him drink my health in his own liquor?" and, as he spoke, he endeavoured to put the mouth of his flask to the lips of Paulina.

"Be quiet, I tell you!" returned Philippo, protecting Paulina from his intrusion. "The lad does not like liquor; besides, he is bashful amongst strangers; he'll know you all better when he comes back; I have the marchese's permission to go with him to-night to his mother's, who resides at a short distance from hence, and acquaint her with his new occupation; and to-morrow I shall bring him back, and commence drill-serjeant over him."

"Well, that is all very well, very well, indeed," stammered out Paulo, still placing himself in their road; "but if your nephew cannot drink with me, why cannot you? By St. Agnes, you shan't stir a step till you have taken a pull!"

"Well, well," replied Philippo, "if that will content you, I will not refuse to oblige you;" and having taken a momentary draught, he returned the flask into the hand of its owner.

"Now that is like an honest man and a soldier," returned Paulo; "and now you and your nephew both shake hands with me, and wish me good-night, and I will go and take a sleep as you desired me."

This was directly agreed to; and Paulina, on receiving the hand of the soldier in hers, felt him place a slip of paper in her palm, to which he endeavoured to arrest her attention by the emphatic pressure of his fore-finger, with which he accompanied the action; his meaning was understood by her, and she immediately clenched her hand, equally to conceal and to secure his mysterious gift.

A general good-night now passed between the soldiers and Philippo, and he and Paulina then passed across the drawbridge. At its foot they were hailed by another sentry; and the same forms as before having been gone through, a man, who had been standing by the side of the sentinel, advanced a few paces towards Philippo, and said—"Here am I, comrade."

"Giraldo?" inquired Philippo.

"The same," was the reply.

"Now then we start," rejoined Philippo; and Giraldo placing himself by the side of Paulina, invited her to take his arm also to assist her in walking.

The night was extremely dark; a few faintly-shining stars rendered the canopy of heaven dimly visible, and the air was raw and uncomfortable. Paulina shivered as the dews of night fell upon her; which Philippo observing, said—"You are cold, signora, and no wonder, for I dare say you are not accustomed to nightly walks like this; you should therefore endeavour to fortify yourself against the necessity which circumstances impose on you; so take my advice, and drink a little of a cordial which I have here in a small flask," producing one from his pocket as he spoke.

Paulina declined his offer, and besought her companions to inform her whither they were conducting her, and when she might expect to see Vincentio and Lipardo?

"Signora," answered Philippo, "it is said, and with great truth too, that walls have ears, and windows have eyes; so why may not the trees, amongst which we are passing, conceal listeners? On this account I have already been cautioned to avoid conversation on the road, and I beg of you to subscribe to the admonition."

"Was it Lipardo who gave you this injunction?" asked Paulina, whisperingly.

"I hope you have not lost his ring, signora?" ejaculated Philippo.

"No, no," answered Paulina; "I have it very safe;" and having some time before taken an opportunity of placing the paper given her by Paulo in her breast, she pressed the finger upon which she wore Lipardo's ring against the hand of Philippo, in order to convince him that it was still in her possession, conceiving, from the earnestness with which he had inquired after its safety, that it was intended for some future service.

"I know it by the touch," replied Philippo; "thus, if we only abstain from speaking, all is well."

After about an hour and a half of leisure walking, as nearly as Paulina was able to estimate the time, a faint and twinkling light appeared in the prospective of their path, which Giraldo observing, said—"I see Bellini's house; we shall soon reach repose and refreshment now, signora."

Another quarter of an hour brought them to a house, from one of the windows of which the light, which they had lately been observing, had proceeded; and Philippo knocking at the door, it was opened by a stout and decent-looking woman, who saluted Paulina's companions by their names; and as soon as they had entered, placed seats before the fire, which she invited them to occupy. Philippo, without replying to her invitation, drew the hostess aside; and during this period Paulina stood silent, still supporting herself upon the arm of Giraldo. Her eyes wandered round the place, and she concluded it to be the common apartment in a house of public entertainment. In one corner of the chimney sat a young man, whose head was rested in a melancholy position upon his hand; and around the fire were gathered the children of the hostess.

After a few minutes had passed in conversation between the hostess and Philippo—"All shall be as you request, depend upon it," replied the former; "the youth shall have as comfortable a chamber as he can wish to repose in, and may ascend to it immediately, if he pleases."

"Follow the hostess," whispered Philippo, addressing Paulina; "this is no place for you; and if you are not satisfied with your accommodation, ask for me."

The hostess took a lamp from the table; and desiring Paulina to accompany her, led the way up a few stairs into a neat chamber; and telling her, that when she required attendance, she had only to stamp with her foot upon the floor, which was immediately over the kitchen, set down the light, and left her.

The moment she was alone, Paulina took from her bosom the paper which had been put into her hand by the intoxicated soldier. At the first glance, the characters which it contained appeared almost illegible, and were evidently traced by a hand little accustomed to the exercise of the pen. After some time she deciphered this sentence—*"Make your escape as quickly as possible from your present companions; they are the emissaries of the marchese di Valdetti."*

The paper fell from her hand, and she sunk into a chair, overpowered by contending feelings.

If she were in the power of the adherents of the marchese, what might not be the fate of Vincentio and his father? This was the only idea on which her mind for a time was capable of dwelling. Gradually the tumult of her feelings began to subside into the power of reasoning, and she endeavoured to reflect in what manner it might be possible for her to follow the advice which she had received from her unknown friend.

As there was no appearance of her conductors intending to remove her that night, she considered that her most probable chance of escape must rest upon her efforts during the hours that they were locked in sleep, and accordingly she resolved to watch for a period when universal stillness prevailed through the house, and then to make the best attempt she was able for her own preservation.

After a short interval, the hostess appeared, bearing in her hand some refreshments, which she placed before her, saying, that the signors below begged she would partake of them, and endeavour to compose herself to rest; and Paulina, in order to lull suspicion, replied, that she was so weary as to require only repose, and should very shortly cast herself upon the bed, and hoped to sleep.

When the hostess had retired, Paulina knelt down, and applying her ear to the various chinks which occurred between the boards that formed the floor of the chamber, endeavoured to gather some part of the conversation which was passing in the kitchen; but the whistling of the wind without, and the incessant strumming of an old musical instrument, with which one of the children was amusing its comrades, rendered only partial sounds audible; and these did not appear to bear any reference to herself or her situation.

From the few words which she could distinguish, and which were spoken by her guards, the hostess, and a voice of which she had no recollection, she understood that some person had been inquiring his way to the Castello Alfonta, which some subsequent sentences informed her was the name of the building inhabited by the marchese di Valdetti.

The history and character of the marchese seemed to be the next points of discussion; but almost every other sound was drowned in the active preparations now making for supper; and a knocking at the outer door put a final period to the conversation.

From what followed, it appeared that a stranger had just arrived, who had found some difficulty in obtaining accommodation, but was at length promised shelter for the night; and in the course of a few minutes, the hostess, making her appearance in Paulina's chamber, said—"There is a holy man just arrived, who requires to pass the night here, and we dare not, as Christians, refuse the protection of our roof to one of his religious order: I hope, therefore, that you will not think me impertinent or troublesome, in desiring that you will permit him to sleep in a small closet through your chamber: you can have nothing to apprehend from a man of his function."

"If he be a man worthy of the profession of which he is a member," reflected Paulina, "I may, perhaps, be able to interest him in my cause: the providential care of Heaven may have sent him to my rescue;" and she requested the hostess to use her pleasure without ceremony.

The hostess thanked her by the name of an obliging young signor; and opening a narrow door, gave to view a small closet, in which stood a bed.

"Here is a bolt," said the hostess, "with which you may, if you please, lock the father in; and there is another on the other side, with which he can, if he thinks proper, fasten the door upon himself."

The hostess now went down stairs, and in the course of a few minutes returned, lighting the way to the holy man of whom she had spoken. He was clad in a friar's habit of brown serge; the cowl was drawn down over his face, and as he passed through the chamber in which Paulina was sitting—"*Benedicite*, youth!" he mildly pronounced; and entering the closet appropriated to his use, into which he carried with him a lamp that he had received from the hand of the hostess, he closed the door, and drew the bolt.

In the course of another hour the sounds in the kitchen became less frequent and lower-toned, and Paulina cast herself upon the bed, without undressing, simply drawing over her the coverlid, in order to affect the appearance of careless repose, if any inspector visited her chamber.

By degrees all sounds died away, and she concluded every inhabitant of the place to be retired to rest; and now, as the moment of action approached, she felt more and more undecided in what manner to proceed. She crept towards the door of the closet in which the holy man was reposing, and by his heavy breathings found that he already slept.

To awaken him might inspire him with a sudden surprise, under the influence of which he might communicate his alarm to the house. Again she considered whether it might not be practicable for her to effect her escape unknown to any of the inmates of the place: with caution, she believed that it might be possible for her to accomplish her purpose. She again leant down her head to the chinks in the floor: not a sound met her ear, and from this she concluded that there were no reposers in the kitchen, as, were there any, she could not, in the present absence of other sounds, fail to hear their suspiration.

She accordingly resolved to blow out her lamp, and bearing it in her hand, in its extinguished state, to descend into the kitchen; and if met by any one in her way, to advance her wish to re-illumine it, as her excuse for having quitted her chamber.

She now blew out her lamp, and with every caution proceeded to open the door of her apartment, when, to her inconceivable disappointment, she found it fastened on the outside.

The extinction of her own lamp enabled her to perceive a faint glimmering of light which shone through a crevice in the door, and acquainted her that the holy father had not extinguished his. But if she were now to awaken him, and even found him inclined to serve her, of what use could his sympathy be under the present circumstances?

More than ever alarmed by the precaution of the bolted door, which she could not doubt to be a caution used by her guards for her security, she opened her casement, in the faint hope of descrying some means of effecting her escape from thence; but she found it raised considerably higher above the level of the earth than she had believed it to be, and the light of a rising moon enabled her to perceive that it was placed immediately above a rushing stream, on the waves of which danced the beams of the silvery planet.

Wretched beyond expression, and almost hopeless of relief—in a state of mind scarcely conscious of its actions, she cast herself upon the bed; and here, in agony of heart, she called, in smothered tones, upon Vincentio and Lipardo, to come to her rescue, unmindful how futile were her stifled shrieks and bursting sighs.

In the fervency of grief and Christian hope, she addressed herself to the Universal Distributor of events, and her address was followed by a short-lived calm, in which nature seemed to have exhausted all her powers. To this feeling gradually succeeded an absence of recollection, the joint effect of misery and fatigue, and a faint slumber stole over her senses; but it was not accompanied by the refreshing balm of undisturbed repose. She imagined herself in the Castello Alfonta—believed that she saw Vincentio bleeding under the poniard of the marchese—herself assailed by his ruffian touch, and fainting beneath his brutal menaces. In vain did she call for rescue—"Vincentio! save me, Vincentio!" burst unanswered from her quivering lips. Vincentio came not, and the tyrant of her fate caught her in his loathsome arms.

At this juncture terror burst the bands of sleep, and awaking, she started up wildly on the bed; her eyes rested upon a light which gleamed by her side, and thence wandered to a dusky figure, in whose hand the light was held. She gazed an instant on the countenance—"Shield me! protect me, Heaven, from the marchese di Valdetti! or in thy mercy snatch me hence!" burst frantically from her lips; for in the person of the figure now bending over her, she beheld the tall and commanding form—the pale and impressive visage—the piercing eye, and the raven locks which characterized the dreaded marchese.

"In the name of Heaven, why does my presence thus alarm you?" asked the object of her terror: "I intend you no harm. I am the holy man who this evening passed through your chamber to the bed provid——"

"Oh, monster of deceit and iniquity!" Paulina interrupted him by ejaculating, "I see—I perceive the infamy which you have practised towards a defenceless being! Oh, thou wretch without a heart! instantly quit me, or the only resource left me from your tyranny shall be joyfully flown to;" and whilst speaking, she darted towards the casement, and throwing open the sash, gave unequivocal proof of the wild intention which was passing in her mind.

The lamp dropped from the hand of the friar; he ran to Paulina, and clasping her forcibly in his arms—"Whoever thou art," he exclaimed, "oh, listen to me, and let not a false imagination be the cause of thy destruction! If I am the marchese di Valdetti, greatly as I am perplexed to divine how I can be known to thee——"

The struggles of Paulina to free herself from his grasp increased, and as he pressed her more strictly in his arms, in his attempts to withdraw her from the window, shrieks, long and piercing, issued from her lips, mingled with the detested name of Di Valdetti.

In the course of a few seconds, the door of the chamber was burst open, and a motley group, consisting of the various inhabitants of the house, rushed in; but foremost darted forward the young man whom Paulina had, at her entrance, observed seated in a disconsolate position by the kitchen fire—"Who names the marchese di Valdetti?" he exclaimed: "if he be here, let him stand forward—I demand to see him!"

"The marchese di Valdetti is not here," replied Philippo; "he is safe enough at his own Castello; but," stepping forward, and addressing Paulina, "what has alarmed you," he added, "that we have all been disturbed by——"

At this instant his eye fell on the figure from which the alarm of Paulina was proceeding, and after gazing a few moments on the countenance of Giraldo—"What is this?" he said.

"The marchese himself," falteringly pronounced Giraldo. "Your excellency would have done well to have forewarned us of this," he added.

"The marchese himself!" repeated the young man. "Well met, marchese; long have I sought you, and Heaven is at length propitious to my wishes. My name is Julio—a foundling, laid at the gate of a monastery in the city of Padua, and thence——"

And here, as if an electric shock had convulsed his senses, he suddenly paused, and fixing his eyes, with a look of indescribable emotion, on the features of the being whom he was addressing—"I cannot be mistaken," he solemnly pronounced; "you are—you must be the pilgrim who once, in a mysterious manner, addressed himself to me when a boy at school, and since that period visited me once by night, at an inn near Rome."

For the space of a few seconds, the apparent friar gazed, in expressive silence, on the countenance of Julio; a tear started into his eye, and in tremulous accents he said—"This is, indeed, an unexpected meeting; but this is not a place for conversation: retire with me to some private apartment."

"Why, we have been nicely deceived," ejaculated Philippo, addressing his companion. "I'll swear this priest is not the marchese, our master: the voice is not his. You are not his excellency the marchese Alberto di Valdetti—are you, father?"

"Indeed I am not Alberto di Valdetti," was the reply of the person addressed; and motioning to Julio to follow him, he was proceeding towards the door of the chamber, when Paulina, rushing forward, cast herself upon her knees between them, and exclaimed—"Oh, pity my defenceless state! rescue me from these my enemies! I am not what I appear, but a weak and suffering woman—betrayed—stolen from my friends—abused by——" Her tears choked her farther utterance.

Philippo and Giraldo both stepped forward to contradict her assertions, and to endeavour to force her from the spot.

Julio darted between the suppliant and her foes, and in a voice of hasty, but impressive feeling—"Your features are familiar to me," he said; "tell me, what is your name?"

"I am Paulina, the niece of the signor Urbino di Cavetti," was the reply.

"The friend, the cousin of Valeria?" demanded Julio.

"Oh, yes, yes!" ejaculated Paulina, "wretchedly fallen into the toils of the marchese di Valdetti."

"Heaven has now then placed it in my power," cried Julio, "to confer a service on the house of Di Cavetti, as some slight reparation of the evil which it owes to my hand. I bless the chance with which it has presented me. Fear nothing, my dear Paulina," he added; "with my life I will protect you." Then, turning to her guards, he said—"Quit this place instantly, nor dare to return into it at the peril of your existence!"

"Why, who are you," exclaimed Philippo, "who dare thus to interfere with the commands and concerns of the marchese di Valdetti?"

"Or what has persuaded you that we are such poltroons as to fear your threats?" ejaculated Giraldo. "We have a solid argument or two to offer you before we yield. Run to the chamber where we slept, Philippo, and bring hither our swords; their eloquence may be more effective than ours."

Philippo instantly prepared to follow his directions, and Julio darting forward, and placing himself before the door, in order to prevent his quitting the chamber, spoke thus—"Hold an instant, and hear me! If I were dealing with men, I should endeavour to prevail with them by the arguments of truth and reason; but as the horror which this helpless being, to whose rescue the hand of Heaven has guided me, argues you to be the hired bravoes of a villain's licentious will, I shall treat you as it becomes every man, who possesses the feelings of a human being, to deal with those who bring contempt upon their own species by their disgraceful actions. You heard me last night mention that I was desirous of procuring an interview with the marchese di Valdetti; I apprehended to find him a being of the nature which you, his adherents, have sufficiently proved him; and thus forewarned by instinct, I provided myself for encountering any reception he might give me. These," he added, drawing a pistol from each pocket, "once intended to have forced a confession from the tongue of your employer, shall now be directed to a more beneficial purpose—the preservation of an innocent female, inhumanly trampled upon by that sex which nature ordained to be the guardians of her weakness. Instead of commanding you to leave the chamber, I now direct you to remain, till I permit you to retire; I have business with you yet; and by the sacred blood of my Redeemer, I swear, that he who first attempts to leave the place dies upon the spot!"

"My pride! my glory! my Julio! my son!" exclaimed the supposed friar, flying as he spoke towards Julio, and clasping him to his breast, "I can no longer conceal myself from thee, thou reward of all my sufferings! thou balm of all my woes! oh! call me father, and overwhelm me with the bliss of that ecstatic sound!"

"My father! thou my father!" ejaculated Julio; "oh, Providence! how impenetrable to the narrow limits of human comprehension are those labyrinths through which it is thy will to produce a revelation of the truth! though what I listen to appears almost incredible to my bewildered senses, there is a pulse which beats within my heart, that throbs with joy and with conviction."

The pilgrim again cast himself into the arms of Julio, and for a few moments a silence, more affecting and expressive than the most laboured eloquence, ensued.

CHAPTER V

We know what we are, but know not what
We may be——I hope all will be well.
——We must be patient.   *Hamlet.*

DURING the time that the scene just recorded was passing between the newly-found son and father, Philippo and his companion, although not unobservant of the discovery which had been made, had been conversing together in whispers, and Giraldo, interrupting Julio, who was beginning to propose to his father such inquiries as were the natural consequence of the surprise with which he had just been affected, said—"Permit me, signor, to say a few words to you: I am sure it has been far from us to conduct ourselves unhandsomely towards the young signora; I am certain she must vouch for us, that we both behaved towards her with the greatest civility."

"To what purpose is this declaration?" demanded Julio.

"Why, signor," replied Giraldo, "after what has just happened, we dare never return to the marchese, as his vengeance would, in all probability, deprive us of our lives, for having failed in a business which he had entrusted to our execution; and though we have been for a considerable time his servants, especially myself, he has always kept us so poor, in order that when he wished to engage us in the performance of any secret transaction, his bribes might the more readily win our services, that we have not the means of flying from him."

Tempted by this confession on the part of Giraldo to address him, Paulina stepped forward, and said—"Since you cannot now apprehend an increase of the marchese's displeasure from any disclosure which you may make concerning him, I beseech you to acquaint me whether Vincentio, and his father Lipardo, have escaped his fury?"

It was a question, Giraldo replied, which he was unable to answer; his companion, he added, might perhaps be able to satisfy her, as he was sometimes in the habit of sharing a greater portion of the marchese's confidence than himself.

Philippo's features betrayed that he was in possession of the information required; his countenance underwent several changes, and at length—"No, I will not betray my trust," he said; "I am sure I didn't wish the young signora any evil, nor was any intended to her, to my knowledge; but it is cursed hard to meet with such a disappointment as I have done, and to have been foiled in the execution of my business, in the unexpected manner I have, when I was to have received a hundred pieces of gold from the marchese on my return to the Castello."

"I think," said Paulina, gazing earnestly upon Julio as she addressed him, "that I cannot be mistaken in supposing you that Julio to whom the heart of Valeria di Cavetti——"

"I am the same Julio," he interrupted her by exclaiming; "and for her sake, and those to whom she is allied, bound in faith and honour to render you every assistance which my abilities can be capable of affording you."

"I beseech you then—I implore you," returned Paulina, "use any arguments that will prevail with this man to unfold to me the fate of Vincentio; I am but young a wife, yet it is for a husband's safety that I express my anxiety."

"Hear me!" pronounced Julio, addressing the vassals of Di Valdetti; "although you behold me in this plain attire, I am perhaps as able to reward your services as the marchese. You are aware that I have at this moment absolute power over your actions; be wise then for yourselves; yield the information of which you have confessed yourselves in possession, and trust to my generosity in paying you for the communication; and let me solemnly advise you, in the temper of mind in which you just now behold me, not to provoke me to force from you the intel-

ligence which I demand, or to punish your obstinacy in with-
holding it."

"If I were sure of the hundred pieces of gold," replied
Philippo, "it's all the same to me from whose hand I receive it."

"I could satisfy you, if it were my inclination to do so,"
replied Julio; "for when I expect to meet knaves, as I predicted
would be the case, if I visited the Castello Alfonta, I always take
care to be provided with the different weapons by which they
are to be combatted; but if the gold were once in your possession, what security have I for your speaking the truth?"

"Why, signor," returned Philippo, "I should have no temp-
tation to deceive you, and it is never worth a man's while to lie
for nothing; and if even I were to attempt to play the dumb
game with you, you have pretty good security in your hands for
either keeping me dumb for ever, or making me speak out
plainly, which you choose."

Julio's heart acknowledged that there was some truth in the
arguments of Philippo; and the streaming eyes of Paulina, eagerly bent on his countenance, appeared so irresistibly to plead
for the information which she desired to gain being at any price
procured her, that he was on the point of drawing from his
pocket the bribe by which it was to be purchased, when the
attention of all was arrested by a loud knocking at the outer
door of the house, accompanied by voices which impatiently
demanded admittance.

The light of day was already in the heavens, and Paulina
flew to the casement, in the hope of descrying from it who
were the claimants for entrance; but the door was not within
her view.

Various sensations and conjectures passed in the mind of
each, whilst they listened to the opening of the door by the
hostess, and endeavoured in vain to catch the short conversation which ensued between her and the persons whom she had
admitted into the house. In the course of a few minutes the

step of the hostess was heard upon the stairs, and when she had nearly reached the top—"Here is an old woman below," she cried, "who requires instantly to see the young signor who slept in that chamber last night."

Unable to divine who it could be that sought her, but cherishing the hope of meeting a friend in the inquirer, Paulina ran down the stairs, and beheld a form standing on the opposite side of the kitchen, which, though the face was at that instant averted, immediately drew from her lips the exclamation of— "Ricarda!" for the dress of that ancient female, as has already been remarked, was too singular to be mistaken. The figure instantly turned towards her, and to her surprise and joy she beheld that the habiliments of Ricarda now enveloped the person of her husband Lipardo.

"Blessed be Heaven! my dear lady and daughter!" he exclaimed, clasping her to his breast, "that I hold you once more in my arms! Thanks be to God that I have overtaken you on this spot, or it might have been too late——"

"For what?" ejaculated Paulina.

"Oh! no matter now," answered Lipardo; "praised be the Virgin! all danger of evil is over, and before I can explain matters to you, you must give me time to recover my breath, for I have run like a roebuck from the Castello. Paulo has been my companion—there he stands," he added, pointing to him as he spoke; "didn't he do his business very well? he is an honest lad, and has bound me his friend for ever; and I hope his information was of service to you?"

"But," said Paulina, "you have not told me of Vincentio?"

"That," replied Lipardo, "is because I am quite easy that he is as safe as I can wish him; he is in the Castello, to be sure, and in the custody of the marchese, but he [would] dare as soon swallow his own poniard as touch a hair of my son's head; so let that assurance keep your heart at rest. But where are the rascals who had you in charge from the marchese? I must treat with them before I can say another word to you."

Paulina hastily explained to him the position of affairs in the chamber above, and, with an emotion of the deepest agitation taking possession of his features, he instantly proceeded thither:—whither, before we accompany him, it is necessary that we should give a detail of such circumstances as had taken place at the Castello Alfonta since the night of Paulina's marriage with Vincentio.

The marchese di Valdetti was a man whose life had been replete with schemes, devices, and nefarious transactions of every nature, which had rendered it indispensably necessary for him to employ agents, who had, of course, participated in his secrets, and thence become acquainted with the springs by which his heart could be moved. The principal of these was Lipardo di Moralta, his former major-domo, and now his steward; but his agency had only been employed in one transaction, of a nature far exceeding in its weight and importance such every-day matters as were confided by the marchese to any ready instrument in whom a temporary confidence could be placed. The secret which reposed in the breast of Lipardo was one which involved the fortune, the fame, and the life of the marchese; and the security with which he believed him to have guarded it, had raised him in his opinion far above the agents of his minor concerns; and the cause which had kept Lipardo a stranger for the last twenty years to the circumstances of the marchese's life was, that he had constantly resided at the Castello Alfonta, whilst the marchese had lived alternately in Florence and Venice, seldom visiting his estate, and when he by chance did so, remaining upon it only for a very few days together.

Amongst those who viewed the prime favourite of the marchese with the most jealous eye, was he who himself stood second in the partiality of the marchese; and this was Philippo, who had been nearly as long in his service as Lipardo, and had lived constantly about his person; and when any transaction, in the execution of which he required assistance, was entrusted to him by his employer, the objects whom he selected as the participators of his disgraceful exertions were Giraldo, and another man named Duretti, who having both been for a considerable time the servants of the marchese, necessarily shared a portion of his pretended esteem.

The marchese di Valdetti had never been married, but he had been a most fervid and universal admirer of the sex, of whom not a few had been left to bewail the witchery of his tongue, and of his purse. From the first moment of his beholding Paulina on one of his rides near the farm of Sancho di Borges, he became enamoured of her person, and resolved, if possible, to possess her. He was the supreme of the territory on which he resided, and consequently had no immediate interference of the law to dread, where he was himself the distributor of justice; the injured might indeed refer their cause to a higher tribunal; but even there his political influence, and exalted situation in life, had on similar occasions so frequently enabled him to throw almost-insurmountable delays and obstacles in the way of his opponents, that his inclination had become his sovereign rule of life, and Paulina was, without hesitation, doomed to be his victim.

He inquired who she was, and learnt her to be the niece of the signor Di Cavetti, once an eminent physician, who had retired from Venice with his family, to pass the evening of his days in seclusion from the world. Upon this information he paused; it vibrated upon a secret chord in his heart; and he changed his purpose from the dishonour of Paulina into the resolution of elevating her to the rank of his wife. He accordingly issued his commands to Philippo, and by the joint exertions of himself and his companions, Paulina was transported to the Castello Alfonta.

It was not till within an hour of the time at which she was expected to arrive, that the marchese communicated the information of what was passing to Lipardo, and commanded preparations of the handsomest nature to be made for her reception.

Lipardo, who satisfied himself with the lucrative situation of which he was already in possession, and with the place which he held in the esteem of the marchese, had always resolved not to run the hazard of diminishing the favour which now shone on him, by interfering with his actions, heard his commands without a reply, and was departing to execute them, when the marchese recalled him into his presence, and said—"Two material points I had forgotten to mention to you; the first, that the young person whose arrival I am momentarily awaiting, is not brought hither for the purpose of seduction; the other, that I wish your wife to be her occasional companion, and to treat her with all the delicacy due to a female who possesses my most honourable esteem."

The words of the marchese were frequently so ambiguous, and his actions so indescribable, that they could only be developed through the progress of time; and Lipardo, with a slight answer, proceeded to make the arrangements for which he had received instruction. But when, on the morning following the arrival of Paulina at the Castello, Ricarda was summoned by the marchese into his presence, and charged by him to use her utmost endeavours to induce his guest to the friendly acceptance of his hand in marriage, at the same moment an unexpected discovery, and a subject of perplexing consideration, were opened to the mind of Lipardo. In Paulina he found the very female to whom his son Vincentio had for some time past been declaring his heart devoted, and imploring his permission to marry; and in the intention which the marchese had declared of becoming a husband, he saw him prepared to dissolve the very tie by which he was bound to him for his past services, and a continuation of his fidelity. Whatever the secret which rested mutually in the hearts of the marchese and his steward, the terms upon which it had been maintained sacredly inviolate by the latter, were, that the marchese should lead a life of celibacy, and at his death bequeath his title and estates to Lipardo's son, Vincentio, in quality of his nephew, in which character Vincentio had from his infancy been educated and considered.

Ricarda, in surprise, imparted to her husband the injunctions which she had received from the marchese, and required his advice how to act. A short interval of reflection determined Lipardo, and he directed her to follow the instructions which she had received, and to confide the rest to him.

Lipardo soon found an opportunity of conversing privately with the marchese, and reproaching him with the breach of articles, towards which he was proceeding.

The marchese replied, that he was urged to the step which he was about to take, by a circumstance so intimately connected with his peace of mind, so entangled with an occurrence of which the constant recollection laboured painfully in his breast, that its achievement could alone procure him relief for a tortured imagination, and besought his sympathy.

The concise reply of Lipardo was, that if Vincentio were to be cut off from the inheritance which had been promised him, or at least to be subjected to the chance of an heir arising from the marriage-bed of the marchese, that he must be indemnified for his loss, by the receipt of ten thousand pieces of gold, before the union could be permitted to take place.

Extravagances of every description, and, not least, of the gaming-table, had lately so much reduced the finances of the marchese, that the curtailments in his usual state and luxuries, to which he was now compelled to submit, had driven him to his estate, where his retrenchments would not be observed by the eye of the contemptuous world. Between the two points which agitated his breast, anxiety and fear mutually assailed him on either hand; and the only determination to which he could bring himself was, at all events, not to accede to the demand of Lipardo, till he had gained the consent of Paulina to become his wife; and with his proceedings to this end we are already acquainted.

The kindness shown by Lipardo and his wife to Paulina was, as may readily be imagined, at the instigation of Vincentio, to whom it was difficult for them to refuse any request, but that of their sanction to his union with Paulina; to which they could offer no other objection, than the hope with which they had ever buoyed themselves up, of his one day forming one of the most exalted alliances in Italy, in his character of the marchese di Valdetti. But the discovery of the scars on the person of Paulina opened to them a secret, not less important than unexpected; and the sole and darling object of their wishes now was the completion of that union on which they had before frowned.

Rivals, in every station, are naturally jealous of each other, and Philippo had long looked with an evil eye upon Lipardo; he saw the steward raised to a situation of the first respectability, and living in a happy independence, when he had once known him by no means his superior in the advantages of fortune; whilst he, who considered himself to have done as much to deserve the liberal rewards of the marchese, was still in the humble trammels of an ordinary domestic, and so involved with his employer, that he could not hope readily to effect a change of situation.

A note, conveyed in a bunch of flowers to Paulina, and which she conjectured to have been written by Lipardo, had warned her not to attempt a second interview with Vincentio at the window of her closet, as they had been observed; by Lipardo it had indeed been written, and he had been urged to what he had done, by a suspicion which he entertained of Philippo having gained some knowledge of their meeting. The questions asked by Vincentio of the servants of the Castello, concerning the stranger within its walls, had given rise to some ideas in the breast of Philippo, which determined him to watch what was passing on the part of Lipardo, his wife, and son, eagerly desiring, with the natural avidity of all jealous and interested minds, to find some opportunity of aggrandizing himself upon the downfall of others.

The long, dark, and intricate passages, adapted to stratagem and concealment, leading from the inhabited parts of the Castello to the prison of Paulina, favoured the lurking curiosity of Philippo; and he descried enough to ascertain that Lipardo and his wife were friends to the prisoner, towards whom he could not doubt them to be kindly affected by sympathy in the feelings of their son, whose emotion at learning Paulina to be an inhabitant of the place, had sufficiently disclosed the sentiments which he bore her. On the arrival of the priest who had been selected for uniting the fates of Vincentio and Paulina, on a pretended visit to Lipardo, and understanding that he was to pass the night at the Castello, a conviction of the truth flashed upon his mind, and he judged it expedient immediately to place himself in the road to better fortune, by disclosing his suspicions to the marchese.

The event of his information, in leading the marchese to the prison of Paulina, at the critical moment at which he appeared before the astonished group which it contained, has already been described. A few moments recovered the marchese from the emotion into which he had fallen, at the sight of the scars upon the person of Paulina; and starting from the arms of his attendants, Giraldo and Duretti, he commanded them to seize Vincentio, and redeem from him the weapon which he had just wrested from his hand; and calling upon Philippo, who had hitherto been guarding the door, to enter, and prevent the interruption of Lipardo, he snatched the senseless Paulina in his arms, and bore her to a chamber in a distant part of the Castello.

After no inconsiderable struggle, the adherents of the marchese succeeded in so far overpowering Vincentio and his father, who possessed only the single poniard of the latter for their defence, as to inclose them within the prison, and fasten upon them the door. The aged priest, alarmed at the tumultuous contest, had fled the spot, and Giraldo, encountering him in one of the passages, conducted him to an apartment to await the decision of the marchese upon his conduct.

When Philippo rejoined the marchese, he commanded him to go and watch by the side of Paulina; and when she recovered from the state of insensibility in which he had left her, to address to her a few words, calculated to dispel her apprehensions, by leading her to believe that she had been conveyed to the spot where she now was by her friends, Lipardo and Vincentio; and when he had done so, to return to him for further orders.

Philippo obeyed, and once more returning to the marchese, found him employed in writing, which when he had concluded, he put his epistle into the hand of Duretti, who was in waiting by his side, and directed him to take one of the fleetest horses from the stables, and to use every expedition in proceeding to Venice, and delivering the letter which he had given to him, according to the superscription with which it was inscribed.

When Duretti was gone, the marchese addressed Philippo, inquiring of him if he were acquainted with any house at the distance of about a league from the Castello, where it might be possible for him to procure accommodation for Paulina, his comrade Giraldo, and himself, during the ensuing night? Philippo replied, by informing him of a house of public entertainment, little frequented, belonging to a widow named Bellini, where he conceived they might be safely lodged.

"About the hour of twilight, then, you shall depart," answered the marchese; "but as it might create suspicion, if a female were seen in your society, or even by one of those unaccountable channels through which intelligence is so often found to be conveyed, lead to a disclosure of the past to her uncle, Di Cavetti, you must persuade her to equip herself as one of the armed vassals of my Castello, whom, from many causes, it is this day my intention to assemble. To your comrades speak of her, in her disguise, as a relative of yours, whom I have admitted into the ranks of my adherents; and for this reason, more imperiously than any other, because it is impossible to decide which amongst my servants, with the exception of yourself, Giraldo, and Duretti, may remain faithful to me, and which incline to the side of Lipardo; and impossible as I conceive the escape of either himself or Vincentio to be, I do not wish them to gain any intelligence of Paulina, till I judge it expedient to release them from their present confinement."

Philippo remarked, that he believed he might, with the greatest facility, impose himself upon Paulina for an emissary from her friends, had he but any token which she would recognize to be Lipardo's, and which he might adduce to her as an evidence of his truth.

The marchese agreed with him in opinion; and a sufficient number of his domestics having been sent, under the guidance of Philippo, to the prison, to defy the efforts of the captives for liberty, Lipardo and his son were forced into separate cells, and the ring, with which Philippo subsequently presented Paulina, taken forcibly from the finger of the steward.

The day was passed in assembling those vassals who were compelled to bear arms at the call of the marchese, who appeared himself agitated with some apprehension extending beyond the boundary of present circumstances; and desirous of winning the hearts of those whose exertions he was suspicious of soon requiring in the support of his cause, the marchese distributed freely to his soldiers, by the hand of his confidant, that animating draught for which they falsely believed themselves indebted to Philippo and his supposed nephew.

Every attention, but their restoration to liberty, was paid to Lipardo and his son, for the heart of the marchese silently confessed him not so great a conqueror as he was willing outwardly to profess himself; and in the course of the afternoon, an imperious demand, on the part of Lipardo, to behold Di Valdetti, brought him to his prison. The marchese expected him to speak of Paulina and his son; but he perceived him standing against the wall, with his arms folded together, and a serene expression beaming on his countenance.—"It is not for myself; nor any one connected with me," said Lipardo, "that I have required this interview—I only beg to inquire of you, whilst you detain me a captive, what becomes of my prisoners?"

A deadly paleness overspread the countenance of the marchese, his lips quivered, and he replied—"Give me the keys of their prison, and I will assume the fortitude to——" he hesitated.

"There are no keys connected with the spot which they inhabit," replied Lipardo: "besides, you are well aware that you are not yourself acquainted where that spot is situate; and were the situation disclosed to you, the entrance could not be discovered without my instructions."

"Will you not, in such a case as this, impart to me your knowledge?" demanded the marchese.

"Never! never!" emphatically pronounced Lipardo.

"Then the prisoners must die!" falteringly pronounced the marchese.

"If it is your will, they must," rejoined Lipardo; "you know you are absolute."

"I am wretched!" ejaculated the marchese. "A combination of circumstances drives me to distraction!"

"A just dominion over your passions might once have spared you those feelings," calmly replied Lipardo.

"It is too late to comment on the past," rejoined the marchese; "the present is almost too much for patient endurance! You will not then oblige me, Lipardo?"

"I have already told you—no!" sternly answered the steward.

The marchese slapped his palm in agony against his forehead; then, after a few moments of hurried reflection—"I will see you again at midnight—perhaps in the course of a few hours," he said, and quitted the cell.

Whilst this was passing in the Castello, Philippo, who had been regaling such of his comrades in arms as had, at the command of the marchese, already mounted guard, with the treat of brandy, of which he had taken the credit to himself, and his nephew, who was supposed to have entered the Castello unnoticed, or at least unknown, amidst the bustle of military preparation, which had brought many other strangers to the same spot, had retired with Giraldo behind a low buttress, where he was communicating to him the plan in which he was to participate, as arranged between the marchese and himself.

It so chanced, that on the other side of the buttress, lay one whom his share of the liquor would soon have lulled into the forgetfulness of sleep, had not his curiosity, excited by accidental expressions which he overheard, as they fell from the lips of Philippo, kept him waking; and this was no other than Paulo, the relation of the miller of Molina, whom we have already heard warm in the praise of Vincentio, whose favourite domestic he was, and to whom many an act of kindness had strongly attached him. Acquainted with the outline of what was passing in the Castello, the broken sentences of—"Paulina in a soldier's habit—pass out unsuspected after it is dark—cottage of the widow Bellini—believes me the emissary of Lipardo, as I gave her his ring," convinced him what was practising against the idol of his beloved master's heart; and unable to convey intelligence to him, he formed the plan of acquainting Paulina with the deception of which she was the innocent dupe. Accordingly, assuming the appearance of intoxication, and awaiting the arrival of Paulina and her guide at the portcullis, he entered boldly upon his attempt; and as the success of almost every endeavour depends upon the courage with which it is undertaken, his efforts were crowned with success.

At the last interview to which Philippo was summoned with the marchese previously to his departure from the Castello, he commanded him to avoid returning direct answers to any questions advanced by Paulina, and to remain with her at the house of the widow Bellini, a particular direction to which he obtained from him, till he either saw him, or heard from him, which he intended should be on the following morning.

Paulina and her guards having crossed the drawbridge, the marchese visited the aged priest, and after a severe reprimand for the step of which he had been guilty, commanded him to quit the Castello; and this done, the order which had hitherto subsisted—that males only were to be allowed to pass the drawbridge, was revoked, and a command issued that none but females should now have the liberty of crossing it; and immediately after this mandate had been published, domestics were sent to give enlargement to Lipardo; but Vincentio was still detained a prisoner.

Lipardo smiled inwardly at the motive for which the marchese had permitted him his liberty, and immediately retired to his private apartment; at the door of which, soon after, appeared Paulo, just relieved from a duty of twelve hours, who requested to see him. He was admitted; and his communication being made, Lipardo expressed his gratitude for his kindness in the warmest terms, and directed him to call upon him again in the course of two hours. When Paulo was gone, Lipardo sent to request an audience of the marchese; it was immediately granted; and on his entering the apartment—"Have you visited your prisoner since your own enlargement?" eagerly inquired Di Valdetti.

"Being again at liberty myself," replied Lipardo, "I alone am now accountable for whatever befalls them; you are relieved from the charge. The reason of my having desired to see you, is to ask the liberty of my son, and an interview for myself with his wife."

"To-morrow any thing you please shall be complied with," answered the marchese, "but to-night——" He hesitated.

"Nothing," said Lipardo, completing the sentence. The marchese did not speak, and Lipardo resumed thus.—"I accept your silence as a negative to my request. Marchese, I have never yet spoken harshly to you, but the present moment nerves my heart, and strings my tongue; if you have the hardiness to raise but a finger of injury against my son, from that instant dread the resentment of his father's power!" and having uttered these words, he haughtily quitted the apartment.

No message recalled him into the presence of the marchese; and at the appointed time Paulo returned to his apartment.

"What is the word of the night?" asked Lipardo, on his entrance.

"Treason, signor," answered Paulo.

"It is well," replied Lipardo. "About the hour of three in the morning be near the portcullis; and when you behold a female crossing the drawbridge, which will be myself, disguised in the habiliments of my wife, for in no other shape can I hope to pass out of the Castello, after the order which has this evening been issued, prepare to follow me, for we must depart together."

"I would do any thing to serve you or the signor Vincentio," answered Paulo; "but will not my life be in danger, signor, for quitting the Castello, since I have been ranked amongst its armed force, without the permission of the marchese?—Not that I so much value existence on my own account, but I have a poor old father, whose sole dependence is on me, and who would be destitute without me."

"Fear not," replied Lipardo; "whilst under my protection you can have nothing to apprehend from the authority of any one within this place. If it were my will, and my time for action were ripe, I would crumble this proud building into fragments, and humble its haughty possessor with the dust!" Paulo was now departing, when Lipardo detained him, by saying—"You are certain that it was not before to-morrow morning that the marchese prepared his emissaries to see him, or to hear from him?" Paulo replied that he was certain; and Lipardo rejoining—"About the hour of three, then, as I before appointed, expect to meet me near the portcullis," they parted.

When left by Paulo, Lipardo proceeded to acquaint his wife with his intentions, and to instruct her in what manner to reply to any inquiries which the marchese might advance to her in his absence; and the hour of two being arrived, and it being ascertained by Ricarda that the marchese had retired to rest, Lipardo made the necessary exchange in his dress; and, under the cloak of his female attire, and his knowledge of the word of the night, he crossed the square without obstruction, and quickly reached the portcullis, where he was punctually met by Paulo, with whom he immediately set forward to the house of the widow Bellini.

On entering the chamber where Julio was guarding the humbled Philippo and his companion, and the supposed friar was watching with an eye of anxiety over the safety of his long-lost son, Lipardo, addressing himself to the father of Julio, said—"You will scarcely recognize me in this attire, but I am sure you will be glad to see me, and I never in my life was so truly happy to behold you. Had I offered up my most ardent prayers at the present crisis to Heaven, and they had been benignly accorded, this meeting had been the grant bestowed upon my wishes."

"My friend!" exclaimed the friar, "no disguise can conceal you from the penetration of my eye.—Welcome, welcome! my best friend, Lipardo!" he added, pressing the extended hand of the steward in his own.

Unmindful of the silent sneers, the muttered threats, and the uncontrollable agitation of Philippo and Giraldo, Lipardo, addressing Julio, said—"Permit me those pistols"—a request to which, as it was urged by the acknowledged friend of his father, he readily acceded; and when Lipardo had received them at his hands—"Signora Paulina," he continued, "do me the favour to direct Paulo to attend me; and do you, my friends," he added, turning to Julio and his father, "retire to another apartment, and I will immediately follow you thither."

Paulina had already descended in quest of Paulo. Julio and his father prepared to quit the chamber at the request of Lipardo; and as they retired from it, Paulo entered.

"Look you, Philippo and Giraldo," said the steward; "your lives are in my power; but I do not wish to shed your blood, unless you are refractory to my commands; and if you become so, no mercy shall be shown you. The only condition upon which you may consider yourselves in safety, is to remain patiently and quietly in this chamber, till I think proper to release you from it. I shall place Paulo with these pistols at the head of the stairs, in case you should endeavour to force your way out; and I am too well acquainted with the situation of this house, to apprehend that you should attempt to effect your escape by the window."

The culprits, not less indignant at beholding the detested Lipardo the arbiter of their fate, than aggravated at the loss of the reward which Julio had, at the time of his entrance into the house, been on the point of bestowing on them, began to solicit permission to see the young signor once more; but Lipardo did not listen to their entreaties; and having bolted upon them the door, he put Paulo in possession of the pistols, and directed him to take his station upon the stairs.

Lipardo now proceeded to the apartment to which Paulina and her companions had retired; and upon his entrance, he immediately discovered that she had been unfolding to them the relation in which he stood to her.

"Oh, Lipardo!" exclaimed the pilgrim, the moment he observed him, "how miraculous are the events of this hour! The protector of your Vincentio's bride is my son!"

"Your son!—your son!" ejaculated Lipardo, clasping his hands together in astonishment as he spoke, "can it—can it be possible that this is indeed your son? He paused a moment; then catching one of the hands of Julio, and pressing it affectionately in his—"Welcome! welcome, youth!" he added, "not less for thy father's sake than for thine own!"

A short interval of expressive silence on the part of the pilgrim and Lipardo, and of doubtful anxiety on that of Julio, followed. Paulina spoke.—"Was it not strange, Lipardo," she said, "that my bewildered senses mistook this stranger for the marchese di Valdetti? and there is a resemblance between them, which makes me still almost incline to believe him so."

"Continue to think him so, signora," pronounced Lipardo, "and you will not be deceived."

"Oh, my friend, beware!" ejaculated the pilgrim; "this disclosure——"

"Is unattended by danger," replied Lipardo; "I am prepared to attest you what you are—the marchese di Valdetti!"

"The marchese di Valdetti my father!" exclaimed Julio; "and thou——" he added, in a voice of inquiry.

"We are a family united beyond the power of fate to solve the bonds that form our coalition," answered Lipardo. "Oh, my friend," he continued, addressing the pilgrim, "you have often averred that the bands of friendship could never be drawn too strictly between us; they are at this hour cemented more strongly than it is possible that you can conceive them to be. This day, which has restored to you your long-lost son, has made you parent of a second son, who likewise claims from you the name of father."

"Explain this riddle," ejaculated the pilgrim; "I cannot penetrate your meaning!"

"My son Vincentio," replied Lipardo, "is your son also. My heart was, as you know, ever devoted to you; you now possess my heart and soul. In this lovely being, behold the chain which thus indissolubly links us to each other; she is the wife of my Vincentio, and your daughter!"

The scene which followed was acted by the feelings, and mocks the insufficiency of the pen to portray it with adequate effect.

CHAPTER VI

I, under fair pretence of friendly ends,
And well-placed words of glozing courtesy,
Bruited with reasons not unplausible,
Wind me into the easy-hearted man,
And hug him into snares.

MILTON

LEAVING for a while the parties, whom we have just seen overwhelmed by the extremes of joy and of astonishment, it may not be improper to lay before our readers a recapitulation of past events, in a less interrupted manner than the detail proceeded, for the information of Julio and Paulina, from the lips of Lipardo and the marchese; for as such we must now know the pilgrim.

The marchese Claudio di Valdetti was the father of two children, who were both sons, and twins. To the elder his own name of Claudio was given; the younger was distinguished by the appellation of Alberto. The wife of the marchese was the descendant of a family of the first distinction, who had brought him an immense dower at her marriage, upon which prerogative, added to her exalted birth, she assumed an imperial authority over the actions, and almost the thoughts, of her husband. The spirit of the marchese was benevolent, and his temper mild; he was a man who would sooner submit to an acknowledged wrong, than enter into a controversy for the support of his rights. The marchesa, on the contrary, was proud, selfish, and overbearing in her disposition—a woman who appeared to nourish a nature which triumphed in every success, according to the struggle by which the victory had been obtained.

From the hour of their birth, the persons of the two boys bore so great a resemblance, that they could scarcely be recognized from each other, when not seen together; and the likeness strengthened progressively with their years. But this similarity in form and countenance did not extend to their minds; in disposition they were as dissimilar as the extreme of feelings could render them. Their opposite characters a few words will explain. Claudio was the gentle prototype of his father's mild and unassuming temper; Alberto was a strengthened picture of his mother's imperious and unbending soul.

As they advanced in years, each naturally grew in the favour of the parent whom he resembled. With such a strong dissimilarity of temper, it was impossible that the brothers could take delight in the society of each other. Claudio, perceiving the soul of Alberto incapable of being softened by friendly argument, retired from the gusts of passion which his advice had frequently provoked from his lips, and the harsh spirit of Alberto hated Claudio for having ventured to disapprove his conduct.

In this cold and unsocial intercourse had nearly twenty-one years passed over the heads of the family Di Valdetti, when the marchese was called from his transitory existence upon earth; and from the moment of his death, Claudio became exposed to all those open insults and attacks from his remaining parent and unnatural brother, which their inability to drive him from that succession to which his primogeniture entitled him, created for him in their hearts.

Another year passed on, at the expiration of which the marchesa followed her husband to the grave. The residence of the late marchese had been alternately at the Castello Alfonta, and at a palazzo which he possessed in Florence: his death had occurred at the Castello, and the period which had intervened between his decease and that of the marchesa, had likewise been passed there by his sons and widow.

Claudio and Alberto, thus left upon the field of life, unprotected by the shield of parental authority, began, in some measure, to draw towards each other. Claudio had ever been desirous of displaying his heart, as a brother's, towards Alberto; and Alberto, for the present, seemed disposed to stifle the real feelings of his soul. Claudio was a fervid admirer of the beauties of nature, and a lover of literature and of the arts, and hence he resolved that the Castello should in future be his constant residence. Alberto, on the contrary, turbulent in disposition, and a votary of pleasure, existed only in the crowd of a city, and the animating successions of varied society; and declaring Florence to be the place in which he was most delighted, Claudio requested him, in addition to the fortune which their father had by will bequeathed to him, to accept the family palazzo in that city, for which he said, that he was certain that he should himself have very little occasion.

Alberto accepted the gift with great demonstrations of joy, and for a time conducted himself in the most friendly manner towards his brother; for the most unruly tempers, under the influence of displeasure, are not unfrequently found to be the most ostentatious in the display of their satisfaction.

Some months after the interment of the marchesa, Alberto, conceiving a sufficient time of seclusion from the world to have been given to her memory, became impatient to visit Florence, and Claudio, whose temporary presence was required in that city, for the regulation of some of his late father's concerns, agreed to accompany him.

For the first few weeks after their arrival, the affairs which had called Claudio to Florence occupied his time, whilst the hours of Alberto were constantly employed in those festivities and gallantries which make up the sum of every day's business, to a young man of an untempered spirit and a well-filled purse.

One day, when Claudio was expressing his intention of shortly returning to the Castello Alfonta, Alberto said—"You must not depart till you have given me your opinion of a beautiful girl with whom I have fallen desperately in love."

"Is she in love with you in return?" asked Claudio, smiling.

"I hope so," replied Alberto; "but my acquaintance with her is so short, that I have hardly had time to ascertain. Her name is Camilla di Zelti; she lives close by the city, with an aunt, who, with herself, are almost the sole surviving branches of a once-noble family fallen into decay; and in the hope of partially reviving their faded splendour, her aunt is unceasingly weary-ing her to give her hand to a rich old conté, named Del Faressi, a withered gallant, who pants and quivers for a decision in his favour, whilst she seems tacitly to pray that some younger adventurer in her cause may relieve her from the fear of wear-ing the conté's trammels."

Alberto, having received a general invitation to the house of Camilla's aunt, insisted upon introducing Claudio there. He found Camilla more than answerable to the description which his brother had given of her perfections, and was so much charmed with her beauty and conversation, that he frequently repeated his visits; and in the course of a short time, it was unequivocally evident that Camilla beheld him with the eye of partiality with which it was the desire of Alberto to be regarded by her, whilst the favourable sentiments which Claudio in return entertained for her, although suppressed by delicacy towards his brother's passion, were still sufficiently palpable not to escape the eye of jealousy; and with a burst of ire swelling every vein, Alberto accused him of having treacherously un-dermined him in his affections.

Claudio denied the charge of having endeavoured to sup-plant him in the heart of Camilla, but, with the truth and can-dour natural to his undissembling mind, confessed that she had given rise in his heart to feelings unknown to him before, and that as Alberto had never yet made to her an open declaration of his passion, and consequently could not consider himself as her acknowledged suitor, he considered it most satisfactory to each, that their pretensions should both be laid before her, and her decision cast the die of happiness.

Not without some reluctance, which the flattery of self-love alone enabled him to overcome, Alberto acceded to Claudio's proposal; and a petition, in writing, for her hand, was sent to her by each of the brothers.

Camilla, it has already been said, had imbibed the liveliest affection for Claudio, almost from the commencement of their acquaintance. Her aunt, who had only desired her union with the conté del Faressi as a feeble prop to their declining honours, joyfully listened to the marchese di Valdetti's proposal to lend the giant support of his alliance to their fading name; and Claudio was immediately made happy by the permission which was granted him to consider Camilla as his destined wife.

Upon gaining this intelligence, the disappointment and rage of Alberto—the joint effects of his wounded pride, not less than passion, burst out in the most violent and opprobrious epithets, against his more fortunate brother and his chosen bride. At one instant, he vowed immediate revenge against them both, for his neglected and injured love; at another, he declared them beneath either his recollection or contempt; and at length, in a paroxysm of mind, almost bordering upon frenzy, he quitted Florence, declaring that he would never suffer himself to behold either Claudio, or the object of his affections, again.

At the expiration of a limited period, Claudio led his lovely bride to the altar, and shortly after conducted her to his Castello, at which he had commanded every preparation to be made for her reception.

Two years glided on happily after their marriage, the first of which produced them a son, and the second a daughter, and during which time Alberto was not heard of by them. About the commencement of the third year, a courier one day arrived at the Castello Alfonta, with a letter for the marchese, which he was not a little surprised to find signed by the hand of his brother, and dated from Venice. The contents also were very opposite to what the peaceably-inclined disposition of Claudio had led him to expect, and almost to fear that they would prove.

The sum of his epistle was, "that he regretted the folly and ungenerous conduct of which he had been guilty at Florence, and that, wishing his brother to be convinced of his repentance, not only from his words, but by an observance of his actions, he requested his permission to visit him and his marchesa at the Castello Alfonta."

Claudio was not a little gratified by the step which his brother professed himself to have advanced towards the amendment of his temper and his morals, and sent him back a most cordial invitation to come and visit him.

At the time appointed Alberto arrived, like the tempter of Eden, dressed in a fair outside, whilst in the secret recesses of his heart rankled projects of the blackest art and treachery. All the scenes of dissipation and of gallantry, in which he had been engaged since the hour of his quitting Florence, had not been able to diminish his passion for Camilla; and by indulging in those ideas which a due obedience to the mandates of honour would have instructed him to banish from his thoughts, he wound himself into the determination of using all his arts for entangling the marchesa into a return of his caresses.

He commenced his operations by those wily insinuations which the female to whom they are addressed cannot misapprehend; and Camilla, safe in her own honour, satisfied herself with imperiously repelling his advances in private, and so conducting herself towards him in public, as not to communicate pain to the heart of her husband, by awakening his suspicions of the villany of his designing brother.

Thus passed on several weeks, during which the ambiguous Alberto conducted himself in the most specious and friendly manner towards his brother, and during which, the repulses which he daily experienced from Camilla determined him to make one final essay to gain the desired object of his soul, or upon the failure of his attempt, to involve the innocent beings with whom the frustration of his wishes rested in irretrievable misery and despair.

His plan was deeply laid, and adroitly executed. The apartments usually inhabited by the marchese Claudio and his Camilla in the Castello, were a dining-room, communicating with a library, through which was the chamber in which they reposed. On the other side of the dining-room were a sleeping apartment and closet, which had been appropriated to the use of Alberto, and beyond these a chamber occupied by his confidential grooms, who were Philippo and Duretti.

On the day appointed for the trial which he had resolved upon making, Alberto, by design, encountered the major-domo, Lipardo, on the lawn in front of the Castello; and entering into conversation with him—"So, you are still a bachelor, I perceive," he said; "I thought long ere this to have found you united to your favourite Ricarda, the superintendant of the kitchens."

Lipardo replied, that if he were able to maintain a wife, he would undoubtedly not remain long single.

"I wish, for your sake, I were the lord of these domains, instead of my brother," rejoined Alberto; "I would instantly place you in a superior situation, of which I think that your long services to our family render you highly deserving."

Lipardo bowed in silence in return to this compliment, and Alberto continued—"By-the-bye, I know you are acquainted with all my late father's secrets, and I wish you one day to shew me the concealed dungeons beneath the Castello, of the private entrance to which I understand that you alone possess the secret, since the death of my father."

"I should imagine," replied Lipardo, "that there could be but little pleasure, signor, in visiting places which damps and darkness must render it disagreeable to enter, and which are of no use in the time of peace."

"I must, however, have my curiosity gratified," answered Alberto, and the approach of Camilla put a period to the conversation.

In the evening, Alberto conducted himself at the supper-table with an assumed hilarity very foreign to the real tone of his agitated spirits; and when the marchesa, who retired early to rest, on account of her being by night, as well as by day, the nurse of her female infant, had repaired to her chamber, Alberto entered into conversation with his brother on many occurrences which had marked some of the most memorable days of their youth, and professing, in the progress of their discourse, to have forgotten the handwriting of his father, requested Claudio to fetch him a specimen from his writing-desk in the library; and when the unsuspicious dupe of his arts had retired to comply with his demand, he poured into a cup of wine, which had already been filled out by Claudio, a sleeping draught of the strongest nature which could be administered, without endangering the life of the person by whom it was swallowed.

When Claudio returned, he presented Alberto with a few papers, which exhibited the handwriting of their parent upon different occasions; and Alberto, after having professed to examine them with the utmost attention, proposed to his brother that they should, in silent reverence, drink to the memory of him to whom they mutually owed their existence; and Claudio, instantly complying with his brother's request, emptied the prepared cup to the bottom.

Alberto still continued to converse gaily, and Claudio, after gradually sinking under the influence of the drug which he had swallowed, yielded to the influence of the soundest sleep.

The time of action was now arrived for Alberto; he crept softly to the chamber of the unsuspecting marchesa, and observed her sleeping with her infant in her arms. He awakened her, and drawing, at the same moment, a dagger from his side, with the fierceness of a monster, he presented to her the alternative of death or dishonour.

On perceiving by whom she was addressed, the confused exclamations and smothered shrieks of Camilla for a while rendered him incapable of fixing her attention to his question; and when she heard his menaces, struggling to avoid the upraised steel, yet cautious not to unfold the arms which clasped her infant to her breast, the dagger of Alberto wounded, first the shoulder, and immediately afterwards the neck of the child. At the sight of her infant's blood, Camilla uttered a loud and piercing shriek.

"Wilt thou be mine?" roared out Alberto.

"I will sooner die!" replied Camilla.

Alberto heard no more, but plunged his dagger, as he hoped, into her heart.

An awful silence of some minutes ensued, during which Alberto employed himself in dragging the senseless form of his brother into the chamber; and having cast him upon the floor, and placed the dagger with which he had himself just perpetrated his crime, in his hand, he stained various parts of Claudio's person and dress with blood, and having washed the damning witness from his own hands, he opened one of the doors leading from the suite of apartments upon the gallery, and called aloud for help and rescue against murder.

In the course of a few moments the chamber was filled with various domestics, bearing lights, who found Alberto half fainting, and leaning for support against the door of communication between the apartments, and Philippo and Duretti standing near him, the first of whom said, that on hearing the cries of his master Alberto, he had rushed into the chamber, and had arrived there just in time to rescue him from the upraised dagger of Claudio, who now lay stunned by a blow which he had given him, in defeating his attempts upon his brother's life.

"He has long been jealous of me," said Alberto, "and I have known him to be so; but conscious of my own innocence, I have forborne to speak my thoughts, or to use security against his ill-placed suspicions. This night, it appears, he had destined for the immolation of his hapless wife and myself, and I can only bless Providence for having sent my faithful servants to my timely rescue."

An universal tumult now prevailed throughout the Castello, and the extraordinary intelligence, that the marchese had murdered his wife, flew from tongue to tongue.

CHAPTER VII

————————To do a great right,
Do a little wrong.
                    Merchant of Venice.

THE females flew to the assistance of Camilla, whilst the males used their endeavours to revive the insensible marchese; and a very short time only had transpired, ere Alberto directed the major-domo to be sent to him into a private apartment. Upon the entrance of Lipardo, Alberto closed the door, and spoke thus—"It cannot be requisite for me to declare to you the anguish with which my heart overflows, at beholding my brother amenable to the laws of his country, for the rash act of which he has just been guilty. I fear there can be very little hope of the marchesa's recovery, and even if she should survive, does there not exist the most incontrovertible evidence of his ruffian attempt upon my life also? He must be found culpable in the eye of justice, and be condemned, at least, to pay the penalty of attempted homicide, if not of murder. Would to Heaven that it were in my power to rescue him from the ruin and disgrace which are preparing to overwhelm him! I think—I believe that the means are in my power; with your adjunction in my wishes, I am persuaded that they might be so. I am certain that you ever respected Claudio; will you then refuse to stretch out to him your saving hand at this moment of his need?"

Lipardo begged him to proceed.

"You will recollect," he rejoined, "that no longer ago than this morning, I was speaking to you of certain concealed vaults beneath the Castello."

Lipardo did recollect; and if he had before entertained a suspicion of the foul conduct of Alberto, in the ambiguous transaction of the night, it was infinitely strengthened by the connexion which he was now drawing between his former inquiry, and the present object of his thoughts.

"You must be aware," continued Alberto, "that if he is permitted to appear before a judge, condemnation must be the issue of his trial; the evidence against him, in the persons of my servants, who by their timely interposition so happily preserved my life, is too strong for the voice of a brother singly to counteract; we can only save him, then, by conveying him to those hidden vaults, where the eye of man can never trace him out."

"It may indeed be the only way to save him," considered Lipardo, who now believed that he could clearly penetrate into the views of Alberto; and without dwelling on a part of our history which must be obvious to the reader, as must also the motives by which Alberto and the major-domo were actuated in the conduct which they severally pursued, it will suffice to state, that effective means were taken by them for conveying the still-insensible Claudio into one of the dungeons beneath the Castello, unknown to all but Lipardo, and his nefarious brother.

Enclosing himself within the library with Lipardo, Alberto professed himself to be passing the night in watching over the senseless form of the marchese, which was believed by the domestics to have been borne to a couch in that apartment; and here were arranged between them all those plans to which the future was to give birth. Such relief as the inhabitants of the Castello were capable of affording the marchesa, was carefully administered to her, and the flowing of the blood having been staunched, information was brought to Alberto, about the middle of the night, that she was reviving, and had asked for her husband. Alberto, in reply, directed that evasive answers should, for the present, be returned to her inquiries, and that they should endeavour, if possible, to compose her to sleep.

Early in the morning, taking with him Lipardo, Alberto proceeded to the chamber of Camilla. They found her not less inclined than unable to converse, but still clasping her infant to her breast; and on returning to the library, which they had only quitted for the purpose of visiting the marchesa, Alberto instantly raised an alarm that the marchese had fled during their absence; and directing the attention of the servants to a window in the library, which he had himself thrown open previously to his leaving the apartment, a pursuit after the supposed culprit was instantly set on foot, in the direction towards which the casement led, and which, of course, proved fruitless; Alberto professing to satisfy himself with the confession of Claudio's guilt having been tacitly acknowledged by him in his flight.

The astonishment of the marchese, on awaking from the lethargy into which he had fallen, may be readily imagined. The lamp, which had been placed by his side, smothered by the surrounding damps, scarcely emitted sufficient light for him to distinguish that there was one burning near him; and when Lipardo at length entered, it was only by his voice that he recognized whom he was addressing: but it was not long that Lipardo permitted him to continue in his present uncomfortable situation; Lipardo, who had been the confidential servant of his father, was, as Alberto had imagined, acquainted with many secret recesses within the walls of the Castello, of which his deceased master had given him a knowledge; and he soon found an opportunity of conveying Claudio to that very apartment in which it was afterwards his fate to ameliorate the lot of his daughter.

An explanation quickly took place between Claudio and his sincere friend the major-domo; and too well acquainted with the nature of his brother, to hope that any step, but the one which had been pursued, could preserve to him his existence— overwhelmed with gratitude to Lipardo for the interest which he had taken in his fate, and the promises which he had made to him of protecting his wife and children, till some apt opportunity should present itself for unveiling his wrongs, and proving his innocence to the world—with a religious meekness inherent in his disposition, he bent himself before that Supreme Power, under whose influence he considered that his enemies were, for some hidden cause, allowed a temporary triumph over his feelings.

Not a day had passed, after the transaction which had reversed the fortune of the brothers in the scale of human prosperity, ere Alberto preferred the major-domo to the situation of steward, and fixed upon him a handsome annual stipend, out of which he was only required to provide for the necessities of Claudio; and then hastily quitting him, lest their being seen too frequently together should breed suspicion of a concealed understanding existing between them, Alberto appointed to meet him on the ensuing night in the library, and consult with him concerning the future destination of the marchesa and her children.

Lipardo went to the library at the time appointed, and was greeted by tidings which he little expected to meet. Alberto informed him that Camilla, notwithstanding the weak state into which they had supposed her to have been thrown by the loss of blood which she had suffered, had still retained sufficient strength to fly the Castello, and to convey her infants away with her; that the time of her flight could not be ascertained, as her absence had been very lately discovered; and all the inhabitants of the Castello solemnly declared themselves unacquainted with her means of escape.

Lipardo doubted the words of Alberto; he believed him accessory to the fate of Camilla, whatever it might be, and threatened to give up all agency in his affairs, if he did not instantly confess to him the truth. The repeated oaths which Alberto swore of his innocence, did not carry with them so much weight to the heart of Lipardo, as the evident disappointment with which he saw him affected at the loss of Camilla. He at length maintained the appearance of silent belief, and Alberto seized this opportunity for thus addressing him—"The rewards which I have already conferred on you, for your kindness to my unfortunate brother, are trifling to those with which it is my intention hereafter to remunerate you; but I have also another service to require at your hands. As you have already succoured the father, do not suffer an innocently-afflicted babe to escape your pity! I told you that the marchesa had carried with her both her infants, and the inhabitants of the Castello believe her to have done so; for on the moment that I was made acquainted with her having conveyed hence the girl, I seized an opportunity, unobserved, of stealing the boy from the chamber of his nurse, and immediately promulgated the intelligence of his mother having made him also the partner of her flight. But behold him here," he added, drawing aside a cloak which was thrown over a couch in the apartment, and upon which Lipardo beheld the son of Claudio, an infant of about fourteen months old, sleeping.

After a short pause, he continued thus—"Not less to shield the unfortunate son from the contempt which he might meet from the world, in consequence of his father's crime, than to cheer the solitude of the father in his perpetual imprisonment, make him the partner of his father's seclusion, and the reward which I propose for your humanity is this:—Espouse, without delay, your favourite Ricarda; I will present her with a handsome dower. Should fortune smile upon you, in giving you the promise of an heir, remove your wife to some distance from hence during the period of her confinement; and should your child prove a son, give out, on your return, that your own offspring is dead, and that the child which accompanies you is an orphan nephew of mine, whom your wife has kindly undertaken to nurse at her own breast; and should circumstances thus turn out agreeably to our wishes, I will pledge myself, in any manner you please, to confine myself to a life of celibacy, and at my death your son will consequently inherit the title and domains, which, according to the arrangement that I have just stated, I shall from this day possess."

The agreement was accordingly entered into; Julio was conveyed to the cell of his father; Lipardo became the husband of Ricarda; and, in the course of time, the parent of a son, named Vincentio, who was published to the world as the nephew of the marchese Alberto di Valdetti.

Under the religious influence by which the mind of Claudio was swayed, he did not vent his sorrows in complaints against the cruelty of his enemies, because he considered them equally to denote a repining spirit against the decrees of Providence, by whose permission alone the actions of man could be accomplished; but the two points which created him the greatest anxiety of heart were, his ignorance of the fate of his beloved wife and female infant, and the dislike which he entertained to the idea of his boy being reared in a solitude, where his faculties could not have an opportunity of expanding themselves, or his understanding of receiving the cultivation of science.

Almost immediately after the arrangement concerning Julio had been made between Alberto and his steward, the former had quitted the place, and taken with him his own favourite domestics; and Lipardo so cautiously conducted himself in his visits to his prisoners, that not an individual in the Castello had the slightest idea of his possessing such a charge.

The friendship which subsisted between Claudio and the steward, who had ever loved the former from a boy, having been attracted towards him by those virtues which so conspicuously shone in his character, and in which Alberto was so rudely deficient, was of a nature which could not admit a doubt of its truth or constancy on either side; and Claudio having explained to Lipardo the motives by which he was actuated in ˉ to emerge from his seclusion for a certain period of ˉorld, received from him a sum of money suffi- ˌpenditure on his expedition, and, in the disguise of a pilgrim, bearing in his arms his child, he conducted him safely and secretly without the walls of his Castello.

Claudio directed his steps immediately towards Padua. He was acquainted, from report, with the excellent disposition of the abbate of the monastery, to whose protection he had resolved to commit his son; and having written the letter, which we are already acquainted was found with him in the basket in which he was conveyed to the holy mansion, he remained in Padua a sufficient length of time to understand that his petition had been complied with, and then set out upon a hopeless search for his Camilla—a search which he had now nearly for twenty years, at intervals, pursued, and again and again returned heartbroken and disappointed to his prison in the Castello Alfonta, to taste in the friendship of Lipardo the only balm which was now left him upon earth, to a visit of which nature he had been proceeding, when he accidentally stopped for refreshment and repose at the house of the widow Bellini.

Thus far had the narrative of past events, detailed for the information of Julio and Paulina, been deduced, sometimes by the lips of Claudio, sometimes by those of Lipardo, and not unfrequently by their intermingled voices, when Claudio thus addressed his son—"From that hour I have only twice beheld you—at the seminary where the good father Antonio had placed you, and at the inn where you slept on your journey from Rome to Padua, upon which occasion the brooch which you wore was my certain guide to the identification of your person; it was the first gift of your mother's love to me, and of so peculiar a form and composition, that, believing there could not be another found to resemble it, I had directed it to be constantly worn by you, that it might upon any emergency infallibly lead me to your discovery."

"And why, my dear father," asked Julio, "did you not on that night address me as your son, confide to me the secret of my birth, and admit me to the confidence of your heart?"

"In all my actions, since the hour of my brother's treachery," replied Claudio, "I have been governed by him," pointing to Lipardo, "to whom we owe obligations, which make his word a law, and never have I beheld him without his exacting from me the most solemn promise, that I would never confess myself to any individual being, till the moment of my retribution, if such a moment were ever fated to arrive, should appear to be at hand. I have this day broken my promise to him, in the acknowledgment which I made to you before his arrival; but he is himself a father, and will know how to pardon my feelings."

Paulina spoke.—"It must have been you, my father," she said, "who, in your disguise of a pilgrim, addressed such numerous questions to me, and to my protector, the signor Di Cavetti, at the carnival of Venice?"

"Yes, my child," replied Claudio, "I believed myself to behold an unequivocal likeness in your countenance to that of your lovely mother, and on that account used every endeavour, but in vain, to learn who you really were; from being too minute in my inquiries, I was restrained by the sacred promise which I had made to Lipardo. My children," he continued, "by the blessing of Heaven, I have recovered you both; but whether your beloved mother be still in existence, is a point which all my wanderings over Italy have not enabled me to ascertain."

It now became a necessary task for Julio to relate, in as few and as chosen words as the subject would permit, what had been known to him of Antonia at Padua.

"I cannot—I will not believe a syllable that sounds to her discredit, even though my son aver it!" ejaculated Claudio; "Camilla was of all earthly beings the most pure; dishonour and her heart could never meet in unison!"

Julio produced the portrait which was still suspended round his neck, and placed it in his father's hand, accompanying his action by a short account of the means by which he had become possessed of it.

Claudio gazed upon it a few moments in silence, the colour fled from his cheeks, his lips quivered—"It is, it is," he falteringly pronounced, "the very portrait with which she presented me on the day of our marriage; but yet I cannot—will not believe her to have deviated from the path of virtue!"

"Can it be possible" said Lipardo, "that your villanous brother eventually triumphed over her innocence, and——"

"Oh, name it not!" exclaimed Claudio; "the bare idea banishes my present joy, and recalls the agony of the past with tenfold strength!"

Paulina burst into tears, and the emotion of all present closed their lips in silence.

But whilst we are occupying ourselves with those characters of our drama whose misfortunes and whose virtues challenge for them our interest and our sympathy, we must not neglect to record the progress of those actions on the part of their nefarious persecutor, by which the pitying hand of Providence gradually wrought the disclosure of his villany and the catastrophe of his fate.

Immediately on his brother's infant son having become the sharer of his unfortunate father's prison, Alberto, as has already been said, taking with him his confidential servants, quitted the Castello Alfonta. He considered, that if he returned to Florence, where his family was well known, that various questions, which he might find it difficult to answer, would naturally be proposed to him concerning the fate of his brother; he therefore resolved in future to make Venice the scene of his unchecked pleasures, and accordingly repairing thither, under the newly-assumed title of the ducca della Riviera, he purchased a handsome mansion, and surrounded himself by a sumptuous establishment.

Thus passed on a considerable number of years, during which he seldom visited the Castello Alfonta; going thither occasionally solely for the purpose of consulting with Lipardo upon the means of increasing his income, for the supply of his daily augmenting extravagances; and when he did so, remaining upon his estate only for a very few days at a time, during which he exhibited, to the gratified, but silent Lipardo, all the symptoms of a mind suffering under the terrors of a guilty conscience.

At these his visits, the portraits of his brother and Camilla were taken down from their stations on the walls; the suite of apartments which they inhabited were never entered by him; and he slept regularly with fire-arms on a table by the side of his bed, dreading the appearance of his injured brother, whom he believed still a prisoner in the dungeons amidst the foundations of the Castello, and whose image, haunting him in his dreams, not unfrequently drove him in frantic wildness from his couch, as it will be recollected was the case on the first night passed by Paulina beneath his roof.

At his last visit to the Castello, not only immense losses at the gaming-table, but transactions of a dishonourable nature, in which he was whispered, amongst other suspected characters, to have been a partaker, against the state of Venice, had driven him from the city to the refuge of his own domains; and here, during the first weeks of his constrained residence, he experienced the most tormenting sensations with which a fallen mind could be assailed. Compelled to inhabit the same walls of which he believed that brother and nephew, against whom he had so grievously sinned, to be inhabitants—withheld, by the reduction which had taken place in his purse, from purchasing himself such pleasures as could steep in a temporary oblivion the stings of thought—he was reduced to a state of mind almost insupportable, when he first beheld Paulina, whose beauty, captivating with more than common force his senses, he resolved to possess her, careless, as it has already been shown, of the consequences of his actions.

The motive by which he was actuated, in desiring to make Paulina his wife, on learning her to be the supposed niece of Urbino di Cavetti, our own time for revealing is not yet arrived. The vengeance with which his soul was fired on being acquainted by Philippo that the son of Lipardo was not only his favoured rival, but on the point of becoming her husband, cannot require a comment; and on the disclosure of the relation in which they stood to each other, unfolded to him by his observance of those scars with which he had himself, in her infancy, marked her person, resolved, in revenge for his own disappointment, to defeat likewise the views of Lipardo and his son, he formed the instant determination of conveying Paulina to a nunnery, and compelling her to take the veil.

On the road to Venice, between the pass to that city across the Gulf, and the Castello Alfonta, was a foundation of this nature, for the reception of females of family, in which he possessed considerable interest, the present confessor of the house being a man whom he had materially served in the early part of his life, and who was also in some measure indebted to him for the situation which he now held. To him accordingly he wrote, explaining that he had a niece whom he wished immediately to place in the community of which he was a member; and requesting that he would, without the slightest delay in his proceedings, send proper delegates from the holy mansion, to receive her at his hands, to the spot where he wished to meet them, he concluded by saying, that his confidential servant, by whom his letter had been conveyed, would conduct them; and this was the epistle with which Philippo had supposed Duretti commissioned to Venice, and the spot of appointment the cottage oft the widow Bellini, to which Alberto had himself resolved to repair in due time to meet the envoys from the nunnery.

Having thus, with the exception of the reason by which Alberto was actuated in desiring to make Paulina his wife, in the belief of her being the niece of Di Cavetti, deduced to the same period the antecedent histories of our most prominent characters, we may once more regularly pursue the thread of our narrative.

CHAPTER VIII

My hour is almost come!   *Hamlet.*

A CONSIDERABLE time having now elapsed since Lipardo had placed Paulo sentry at the door of the chamber in which he had confined Philippo and Giraldo, having first exchanged his habiliments for those of his own sex, by procuring the loan of a coat and a hat from the landlady, in addition to such of his own vestments as had been concealed beneath his disguise, he proceeded to inquire of his centinel how his prisoners had conducted themselves in his absence, when, on reaching the foot of the stairs, he observed Paulo place his finger on his lips, as a caution to him to be silent, and at the same time beckon him to advance, and by signs invite him to listen to what was passing in the chamber. When he had approached near enough to hear the conversation of those within—"I repeat," said Giraldo, "that I feel persuaded, that friar can be no other than the marchese Claudio himself; the resemblance is so striking that I cannot be deceived."

"Well, and suppose it should?" gruffly answered Philippo.

"Why then we are in a hopeful way, depend upon it," replied Giraldo; "I always thought that major-domo was no friend in his heart to our master Alberto; he is a deep fellow, and depend upon it, that the marchese Claudio is not so near the Castello without his knowledge, and to answer some good purpose into the bargain. However, come what may, my mind is made up."

"To what?" asked Philippo.

"To act like a wise statesman," answered Giraldo, "and withdraw my countenance from those who are going out of place, and adhere to those who are coming in. All the world has witnessed great generals, who, having made war their trade, did not care what side they fought for, so their services were but well paid. And do you suppose that any transaction I have had a share in, was undertaken by me from goodwill to the party that employed me? No, no, friend Philippo, my affections were always given to the purse, and not the man; and I am sure Alberto di Valdetti has not conducted himself towards me in a manner to work a change in my habits; I have been paid sparingly enough for the dirty work I have done for him,"

"You would have been worse than sparingly paid," grumbled out Philippo, "if he had known of the bribe which you took from the marchesa Camilla."

"Likely," answered Giraldo, "but a man in business must run the risks of his trade; to further the interests of an one who hires my services, is my profession; and if I do the best I can to serve all my employers, where can be the harm of my taking a fee on both sides, like some of the lawyers?"

"Why, truly, if this be the marchese Claudio," rejoined Philippo, "our evidence can alone save Alberto."

"And setting that aside," rejoined Giraldo, "if we were to blab what we know of the marchesa Camilla, his business would be settled in a trice."

Lipardo could restrain himself no longer, and darting into the chamber, he exclaimed—"I have overheard your conversation; it is useless for you to attempt to retract one word of what you have uttered, for I have a witness of all that has been said; but from what I have heard you declare of your motives and your principles, I expect that when you understand me, you will answer me explicitly. You were, I think, to have received an hundred pieces of gold from Alberto, if you had successfully executed the business upon which he last night dispatched you from the Castello; only acquaint me what was the fate of the marchesa Camilla, and you shall receive two hundred from me."

"Philippo," said Giraldo, in a tone of voice which denoted him half-undecided how to proceed without his comrade's sanction.

"I am content, if I share the money," replied Philippo.

Greatly delighted at the prospect which now presented itself to him, of being enabled to relieve the marchese Claudio and his children from the agony of suspense with which they were affected, by their ignorance of Camilla's real fate, Lipardo repeated his promise to the iniquitous pair, and the following confession proceeded jointly from their lips.

It appeared that the marchesa, on receiving the intelligence which had been circulated by the designing Alberto, of her husband having fled from the Castello, in consequence of his having been detected in an attempt to murder her, dreading alike to encounter the passion or the menaces of Alberto, formed the resolution of quitting the spot, and besought the assistance of a female who attended upon her, and who had displayed herself upon every occasion attached to her mistress, in the execution of her design. This girl had conceived an affection for Giraldo; he had thence become the confidant of all her secrets, and the one with which she had been entrusted by the marchesa was consequently alike divulged to him.

Giraldo, who, as his own words have already informed us, was always ready to serve any liberal employer, advised the girl to accept the reward which the marchesa had offered her; promising that if she would give him half the bribe, he would find the means of accomplishing Camilla's wish. Matters were accordingly arranged to that effect; the marchesa provided herself with money and jewels from the cabinet of her lamented husband, and Giraldo conducted her and her female infant, by night, to the nearest posthouse, from whence she immediately procured a conveyance to carry her on her journey; but of the road which she had taken he was ignorant.

"From that period," continued Giraldo, "I had heard nothing more of the marchesa till about a year, or somewhere thereabouts, from the present time. It was one day about that period, that Alberto, having summoned Philippo and myself into a private apartment, informed us that he had seen Camilla in the streets of Venice, and having described to us the dress in which she had appeared, he commanded us to search for her; and when we had found her abode, to watch a proper opportunity for waylaying her, and bringing her to his palazzo.

"In the course of a few days, we discovered that her residence was in a mean little dwelling in the suburbs of the city, and that most of her time was passed in a little garden at the back of the house; we lurked constantly near the place about twilight, and after a few evenings, succeeded in carrying her off unseen; and our superior strength enabling us to stifle her cries for assistance, we conveyed her in safety to the palazzo of Alberto. Various circumstances had already convinced us that his passion for her had entirely died away, and that the only sentiment with which he was now affected towards her, was the dread of her evidence ever rising against him."

"Her evidence!" ejaculated Lipardo. "Alberto then it was, as I ever suspected, who inflicted that wound of which the innocent Claudio has so long borne the guilt!"

Giraldo hesitated, and again looked for counsel at Philippo, who said—"Nay, it matters not now; we have ventured so far into the stream, that nothing but a bold plunge through the water can serve us."

A full avowal was now made by them of the drug which had been administered by Alberto to his brother, and of the bribe which they had received of him to deliver it as their evidence, if called upon in a court of justice, that Claudio had been stunned by a blow from Philippo, in repelling the stroke which he had aimed with his dagger at the breast of his master.

"But the marchesa Camilla!" ejaculated Lipardo; "what more is it that you know of her?"

"Immediately after we had lodged her in the palazzo," said Philippo, "we were again sent out in disguise, with one of our companions named Duretti, and two others of his domestics, whom Alberto selected for the undertaking, to convey to his mansion a physician of eminence in the city, in the same obscure manner in which we had brought thither the marchesa. In the course of an hour after the departure of the physician, Alberto informed us that Camilla was dead; and a few days after she was privately interred, and her funeral spoken of as that of an inferior domestic of the family."

This strange account Lipardo considered incompatible with the description which Julio had given of his having, about two years since, beheld her a corpse in the anatomy chamber at Padua; and the contradiction of the two assertions cast him for a few moments into a reverie of reflection, from which he was aroused by Philippo adding—"The physician who attended her in her last moments was the signor Urbino di Cavetti, who is the uncle of the signora Paulina, and who immediately quitted Venice, and has ever since resided at the Castello delta Torvida."

"Could it be possible," Lipardo considered, "that the man of whom Paulina had spoken in terms of the highest commendation, both for the humanity and the honour of his heart, could have been an abettor in the murderous plans of a being like Alberto!" He returned to the apartment where he had left his friends, and submitted his doubts to Julio and Paulina, both of whom, with the greatest warmth, declared themselves incredulous of the assertions of Philippo, and indignant at the calumny with which he had aspersed so worthy a man.

Lipardo observed, that it was his opinion, that an explanation of past occurrences from the lips of Urbino himself, could alone unravel the maze of perplexities in which they were enveloped with regard to the fate of Camilla; and was proceeding to inquire in what manner they could most readily see him, when the voice of Alberto, who had just entered the house, sounded on his ear.

With a signal to his friends for maintaining silence, Lipardo descended into the kitchen. He perceived Alberto standing with his back towards him, in the act of disencumbering himself from a cloak, in which he had been muffled; and having done so, he drew from his girdle two pistols, which he placed upon a table and which Lipardo, moving cautiously behind him, eagerly secured, and was in the act of fixing in his own belt, when Alberto turned, and beheld him.

"Lipardo here!" he exclaimed, and directing his eyes towards the pistols, on the head of each of which a hand of Lipardo was rested—"What mean you by this?" he added.

"Self-preservation!" replied Lipardo; "the character of every man determines me how far it is wisdom to trust him with the instruments of life and death; I shall therefore, for the present, keep these in my own custody."

"What!" ejaculated Alberto, "am I menaced by thee, thou——" He checked the epithet which was rising to his tongue, and in a softened tone of voice continued—"Replace the pistols where you found them, and Vincentio shall immediately be liberated from his confinement."

"He shall be freed from it when I think proper to command his enlargement," answered Lipardo. The stern frown of the steward struck terror to the heart of Alberto, and he called aloud upon Philippo and Giraldo.

"They are engaged, and cannot attend you," replied Lipardo, deliberately.

"Am I then beset by villany!" exclaimed Alberto; and casting his eyes wildly around, in the hope of espying some relief at hand, for the consciousness of his crimes augmented his fears of danger, they fell upon a casement, through which he beheld Duretti advancing on horseback towards the house.—"Thank Heaven!" he added, "here is one who will not desert me!" and with these words he flew towards the door, which he had no sooner opened than he perceived a vehicle approaching, through one of the windows of which instantly descrying the figure of an ecclesiastic, he doubted not that it contained the delegates from the nunnery.

With the most feverish trepidation Alberto awaited the approach of the carriage, from which at length descended the confessor, to whom his epistle had been addressed, and two nuns, who had been commissioned to take the charge of Paulina.—"Welcome, welcome, holy father!" ejaculated Alberto, as they entered the house.

"*Benedicite*, son!" answered the confessor; "we have attended thy summons, to receive under our protection thy niece, whom thou hast so laudably devoted to the service of the church."

"I forbid the act!" solemnly pronounced Lipardo.

"Thou! who art thou?" demanded the holy man.

"Her father," replied Lipardo; "and I deny her to you."

"Duretti, will you see me thus insulted?" cried Alberto; "draw your sword against this daring man."

"Is it thus," said the confessor, "that you would recommend yourself to the servants of the church?"

Duretti, awed by the solemnity of his voice, checked the hand by which he had been preparing to draw his sword, the only weapon of defence with which he was armed.

"This man is not her father," rejoined Alberto; "he is only the father of a youth with whom, as my heiress, he would trepan her into marriage."

"I am the father of a youth to whom she is bound by the most sacred ties of religion," said Lipardo.

"But their marriage is happily not yet consummated," answered Alberto, "and she is therefore still a virgin in the eye of the law; at all events, I must possess a right to the greater authority over her, as being her relative in blood, whilst he can only claim an adventitious connexion with her, formed by the unjust device which he had planned to worm his son into my inheritance."

"Yield then those possessions, of which you display yourself so strenuous in the protection, to their just owners," pronounced Lipardo, "and I will instantly forego my son's claim."

"I — I am myself that just owner," stammered out Alberto.

"Have then an elder brother and his son no superior claim to yours?" asked Lipardo.

"But where," ejaculated Alberto—"where are those unfortunate, those lamented beings, to whom you refer, to be found?"

"Here!" emphatically pronounced Lipardo; then, in a heightened tone of voice, he added—"Claudio! Julio! appear! I am your protector!"

His mandate was obeyed; and upon the appearance of the marchese and his son, to the latter of whom clung the trembling Paulina—during the first moments of excessive astonishment which chained the senses of Alberto, the sounds of "Claudio! Claudio!" proceeding from the lips of one of the nuns, arrested the attention of all present—the veil of the speaker was instantly thrown back—"Dost thou still live to me, my Claudio?" she added, and flying into the arms of him whom she addressed, sunk fainting on his breast.

In the person of the nun, Julio believed himself to behold the countenance of that Antonia who had been known to him at Padua; Claudio, Alberto, and the steward, recognized in her the marchesa Camilla.

"My mother! can this be my mother?" ejaculated Paulina.

Her question was addressed to Lipardo; and as he turned to answer her, Alberto seized the moment in which he believed him to be thrown off his guard, and snatching one of the pistols from his girdle, pointed it at the pair whose reunion communicated a pang worse than death to his heart. With the swiftness of the lightning's flash, Lipardo flew to wrest from him the upraised weapon. In the struggle which ensued, the mouth of the tube was turned to the breast of Alberto. At the same instant the spring was touched; and the sound of its explosion was the last instant of Alberto's existence.

CHAPTER IX

I have a tale t'unfold, so full of wonder,
As cannot meet an easy faith;
But 'tis true.   *King Lear.*

IT was indeed the long-lost Camilla whom Claudio now pressed to his overjoyed and astonished heart; but as the account which she was competent to give of past occurrences was insufficient to elucidate some of the mysteries apparently connected with her fate, which have been presented to our readers, we shall here explain some circumstances, which the progress of time, aided by unceasing inquiries, alone developed to the marchese Claudio and his family.

The marchesa Camilla di Valdetti was one of three sisters, equally distinguished for their personal beauty; and there existed amongst them a family resemblance, by which they could not fail to be recognized, and which, although considered as remarkably strong when they were separately seen, lost a considerable portion of its force when they were compared to each other.

Camilla, as has already been said, on quitting the Castello Alfonta, repaired to Venice; and under the dread which she entertained of the unprincipled disposition of Alberto, considering that her infant would be safer in the protection of any other individual than herself; she formed the resolution of casting it upon the humanity of Di Cavetti, in her opinion of whose benevolent nature she believed that she could not be mistaken; and having bedewed the cheeks of her infant with the tears of separation, she had no sooner ascertained the arrival of Urbino at the hotel of San Marco, than she proceeded to seek her aunt at Florence.

On her arrival there she found her aunt dead, and her elder sister, Lucia, married to the conté del Faressi, whose hand she had herself formerly refused. The death of their aunt having bereft her sisters of their only protector, and also diminished their means of existence, as the principal part of their support had been derived from an annuity which had died with her, her slow consent to become the wife of the conté had been wrung by the force of circumstances from the lips of Lucia; and her younger sister, Antonia, she understood to have fled from Florence, with a young officer of a wild and profligate disposition, to whom it was surmised that she was not allied by any stronger bonds than those of inclination.

Had Camilla found her aunt in existence, it was her intention to have retired with her to some solitary abode, and there have awaited the intelligence of her husband's fate, with which the progress of time might furnish her; but her relative being no more, she did not explain the nature of her visit to Florence, which was consequently supposed to have been merely one of friendship to the deceased; and again quitting the city, procured a retired lodging in its vicinity, where she formed an acquaintance with a venerable ecclesiastic, who attended her as her confessor, and of whom she inquired where an asylum adapted to the exigency of her situation could be found for her, in a religious house, in her character of a wife; under which title she could not be permitted to take the veil, even if it were her inclination to do so—a step from which her hope of being one day reunited to her Claudio would at all events have withheld her.

The holy man informed her, that there was a foundation of the nature which she desired to find in the neighbourhood of Venice, and that he was intimately acquainted with the superior of the house, and could furnish her with an introduction, which would admit her an inmate of the community upon her own terms. With the most fervent thanks, Camilla accepted his proposal, and once more set out in search of a new asylum.

In the course of her journey she was one evening surprised at being informed by the servant of an inn at which she was going to repose, that there was a signora in the house, who had seen her enter, and requested to be admitted to her presence. It was equally disagreeable to her to assign any reason for not seeing visitors, as to be compelled to a conversation with those in whose society she felt no interest; and at a loss which of the evils to choose, she desired the signora to be introduced into her apartment, and was not a little astonished to behold her sister Antonia.

Camilla considered, that as Antonia had yielded her honour to the flimsy security of a lover's promise, every lesser confidence would, of course, be entrusted to his discretion; and not desiring her own immediate concerns, or those of the persons with whom she was connected, to be made the subjects of a stranger's conversation or animadversions, she resolved to withhold from her a knowledge of her circumstances, and replied evasively to all her inquiries.

The object of Antonia's passion had already, as it appeared, been three weeks absent from her, without her being acquainted whither he was gone, or what was the cause that delayed his return; but she existed on the hope of his speedy arrival, with which flattering belief her wishes fed her expectation; and with difficulty brought herself to confess to Camilla that she was already reduced to some pecuniary embarrassments by his absence.

This was an irresistible appeal to the feelings of Camilla, and she presented her with some valuable trinkets, of which she could easily procure the exchange into coin.

Antonia received them with the most gracious thanks, and said—"How have you disposed of that remarkable brooch which you inherited from our father?"

"I presented it to my husband previously to our marriage," replied Camilla; "and he promised me never to part from it, except as a bequest to one of our children. But," she continued, looking, as she spoke, into her jewel-case, which she held in her hand, "here is a likeness of myself which you must remember being painted; and as it is possible that we may never meet again, and my own portrait can be of no use to me, wear it for my sake, and give me your word that you will never part from it, unless, in your intercourse with the world, chance should throw in your way my son (for I am the mother of a son); and should accident ever lead him to your acquaintance, transfer it to him, and tell him that it is the gift of his mother."

Antonia promised obedience to her sister's injunctions; and in the morning they parted, Camilla pursuing her journey towards Venice; and on arriving at the nunnery, she found the introductory letters with which she had been furnished highly satisfactory to her wishes, and immediately became a lay-sister of the establishment, where we must for a while leave her, and follow the steps of Antonia.

The man who wins a prize too easily is generally the first to neglect its keeping, especially in the affairs of the heart; and the possessor of Antonia's, after the first dream of joy was past, fled the once-adored idol of his soul. Difficult is the task of inconstancy to the woman who has once tasted the blessings of a pure affection; but to her who at her first acquaintance with love has overstepped the barrier of feminine delicacy, a transfer of the heart naturally becomes a subject of lighter consideration. Deserted by her first love—cast upon society without a natural or an adventitious protector, Antonia sought the countenance of strangers, and submitted to win them at the price of her wounded feelings; and thus became gradually habituated to the capricious fluctuation of ever-changing favourers. But at length, becoming wise from mortification, she began to nourish the wish of defending herself against the frowns of fortune; and reversing the scale of extravagance upon which she had hitherto lived, now studied the amplification of her purse.

There is not a situation in life in which caution will not, in some measure, lead to independence; Antonia's system proved successful; and after many years past in smothered restraint, and an affectation of enjoyments which never reached her heart, she found herself in possession of a considerable sum; and well had it been for her, if she had then closed a career upon which reflection could only dwell with sickening or with horror, and endeavoured to repair the errors of the past by the virtues of the future. But daily are the proofs adduced to the eye of observation, that the mind must be cast in a mould of a more than commonly strong nature, which can reclaim itself either suddenly, or altogether, from those practices which have, from habit, almost formed a coalition with its blood.

Chance had placed Antonia in the city of Padua, at the period at which she had resolved to commence a reform of conduct; but what the vicious denominate a reform is too frequently, in the opinion of the virtuous, no more than a counterpart of the former evil; and Antonia became the possessor of a splendid mansion, where all the mysteries of dissolute pleasure were solemnized under her sovereign nod.

She had not been long in this situation, when the person of Julio, whom she often beheld from her window, for she now seldom passed through the streets, made so forcible, so unconquerable an impression upon her heart, that she conceived the desire of making him her husband. But wishing, if possible, to inveigle him into a passion for her, before she disclosed to him her wishes, those plans which have already been detailed in the course of our narrative, were pursued by her for bringing him into her presence; and this end being accomplished, she was on the point of disclosing to him her heart, at the moment when her eye rested on the well-known brooch which had been bequeathed by her father to Camilla; she recollected the words which Camilla had spoken at their last meeting, and disappointment, mingled with horror at the idea of the crime, from the commission of which she had just been rescued, deprived her, for a few seconds, of all recollection.

On reviving, she remembered the request which her sister had made of her concerning the portrait; she resolved to obey her wish; and accordingly, hastily tracing the few lines which communicated to Julio that it was sent to him by his mother, she caused the portrait and her epistle to be placed in his possession, and then gave directions for him to be conveyed to the pavilion in his own garden, in the manner with which we are already acquainted.

From the period of this occurrence the spirits and health of Antonia lost their usual flow, pleasure no longer animated her senses, nor did the temptations of varying society carry weight with them to her heart. The dreadful crime into which her devotion to self-gratification had nearly plunged her, preyed upon her mind; she did not sicken, but she drooped; that one act, upon which she could not incessantly forbear to reflect, appeared to have opened her eyes to all the atrocities of her past life; and when the world, for which she had before lived, had lost its charms, she silently withered to the grave.

The assertions consequently made by the ill-fated brother of Valeria, concerning her whom he, as well as Julio himself, believed the portrait worn by the latter to represent, were founded in truth, and the form which Julio had beheld exposed to the knife of science was that of Antonia.

Lucia, meanwhile, after experiencing various changes and misfortunes, originating in a conduct the very opposite of that which her heedless sister had pursued, after passing a life of restraint in her union with a man whose person and age were incapable of challenging her love, and whose selfish nature forbade her to supply the deficiency of affection with respect, saw him sink gradually and peevishly to the tomb, pampered with luxuries, which his fortune, already too much diminished by the gratification of every idle appetite, could ill afford, and was left to sorrow away the remainder of her life on a miserable stipend, which denied her alike the charms of society or of solitary enjoyments.

In this state she had lingered through six years, when seized by the emissaries of Alberto, on the belief of her being the marchesa Camilla, and hurried by them to his palazzo; and on being seated in an apartment of the mansion, overcome by terror, and happy to accept any relief which appeared to present itself to her insupportable feelings, she drank unhesitatingly of a cup which she received from the hand of Philippo, containing a refreshment which had been commanded for her by Alberto, and sunk into that sleep from which she was fated never to awake on earth.

Determined on her death, yet dreading himself to perform the awful act of murder, and equally unwilling to confess his crime to any of his attendants, lest he should place himself still more in their power, than he with pain reflected that he had already done, Alberto resolved to call upon the aid of the signor Di Cavetti, not doubting that the profuse bribe which he was prepared to offer him would have effect with a man who could cover his action with the cloak of his profession.

The mind of Alberto, although that of a villain, was in other respects a common mind; he did not conceive himself equally guilty in commanding the perpetration of an act of unfair death, as in executing it; and upon a similar argument, he feared not to find Urbino compliant to the performance of a deed, which might be attributed to the failure of his medical endeavours for the restoration of a patient, whose case had been misrepresented to him. But the mind of Urbino was not a common mind. We have seen the contempt with which he spurned at a participation of Alberto's villany, and can hardly require to be told that Alberto, roused to desperation by his refusal, himself accomplished the bloody act. And thus perished the innocent Lucia, unrequited for a life of patient suffering—an incontestible proof that the final account of the human race is closed beyond the limits of this earth.

And here it may not be improper to remark, that Alberto, who had ever stood in that awe of Urbino with which every criminal mind considers the being who possesses the secret of his guilt, upon learning Paulina to be his niece, immediately entertained the wish of making her his wife, in the hope of an alliance cemented between their families effectually closing the lips of the physician upon the revelation of those shades in his character with which he was but too well acquainted; and the ignorance which we have seen Urbino to profess of the name of the marchese di Valdetti, although a resident in Venice, arose from Alberto having been known in that city only as the ducca della Riviera.

To Camilla, the last, but hitherto not the most unfortunate of her race, we now return. Year after year had passed tediously on, during which the existence of Camilla had been but as a vegetation upon earth, animated solely by the offices of religion, and her unceasing prayers for her husband and her children, when the epistle of Alberto was brought by Duretti to the nunnery. The confessor read it aloud to the community, and having received the sanction of the abbess to admit the claimant for reception, the swell of joy with which the heart of Camilla was dilated, may be readily imagined, when, after having in painful silence listened to the perusal of the letter, of which neither the writer nor the female referred to in it could be mistaken by her, she heard herself named as one of the delegates commissioned to undertake the charge of the intended nun, on her journey to the holy mansion.

Further explanation must be unnecessary. On beholding her husband and her children, all that the world possessed for her of value was presented, at one view, to her acceptance—all her past sufferings overpaid. But when we consider the fate of the unfortunate Lucia, as a lesson that final retribution rests beyond the skies, let it equally prove a precept to the mind of reason, that where remuneration is made to the sufferer upon earth, tenfold will be the requisition demanded at his hands in heaven.

Upon the death of Alberto, his former attendants were immediately set at liberty by Lipardo, who, availing himself of the overpowering raptures into which Claudio and his family were thrown by their unexpected and happy meeting, caused the dead body to be removed from their sight—thus sparing them the shock of beholding a countenance which the reproaches of a guilty conscience had stamped, in the moment of its dissolution, with the most horrid expression of agony and dread.

The confessor from the nunnery insisted on remaining a while in prayer over the corpse of the man from whose hand he had once received acts of friendship, and whose present humbled situation moved his feelings to pity.

Claudio and his relatives were no sooner capable of listening to the admonitions of Lipardo, than they were hurried by him on their way towards the Castello Alfonta, attended by Giraldo, whose companions were left by him in charge of their deceased master, and who did not lose a moment in offering their services, and declaring their allegiance to his brother.

One mingled sensation of joy and gratitude flowed in the hearts of all; for, however a character like that of Alberto might, as Christians, excite their pity, it was impossible that their sorrow could be awakened for one from whom they had individually so severely suffered.

On arriving at the Castello, where Camilla and her husband found it difficult to believe themselves once more reinstated in their so-long abdicated possessions, an addition was made to their joyful party by the presence of Vincentio, whom Claudio thus addressed—"If any event can add to the happiness which I enjoy, in my reunion with my family, it is the alliance so indivisibly formed between my valued friend Lipardo and myself, of which you and my dear daughter form the connecting bond."

Vincentio returned a suitable reply to the kind address of the marchese; and Ricarda, who, for a short time after her receiving the information of the unlooked-for events which had marked the few last hours, had considered it very hard that her son, who had not only been bred to believe himself heir to a marquisate, but who had also espoused the presumptive heiress of the family, should be reduced a step in the scale of worldly dignity, at length reflecting that it was, after all, infinitely better to be mother to the husband of a marchese's daughter, than only the simple wife of a steward, complacently added the mite of her congratulations and smiles to the sum of general happiness.

CHAPTER X

Last scene of all,
That ends this strange eventful history.
As You Like It.

NOT less in compliance with his own feelings than the entreaties of Paulina, that her revered protector Urbino should immediately be made acquainted with her present happiness, Lipardo proceeded to the Castello della Torvida, and was received by the worthy physician, who instantly recognized in him the stranger by whom he had been a short time before visited, and who had so ambiguously made inquiries of him concerning the origin of Paulina, and left him with those assurances of her safety, which had alone supported him during the period of her mysterious absence.

The detail which the steward had to make could not be easily concluded; but in as concise a manner as it was possible to render the substance of past events comprehensible to the senses of his auditor, they were narrated by him to Di Cavetti, who introduced to Lipardo his daughter Valeria, and the worthy Di Borges, as participators of his joy.

After a due time had been given to those comments and reflections which naturally arose from the narrative of Lipardo, Di Borges said—"As you, signor, are doubtless well acquainted with every member of the late Alberto di Valdetti's family, you will be able to inform me whether he had a domestic in his service named Duretti?"

"I am," replied Lipardo; "the man you mention is now at the Castello Alfonta."

"You will excuse me," returned Sancho, "for interrupting the joy of yourself and your friends," pointing to Di Cavetti and his daughter as he spoke, "by requesting your attention to an extraordinary circumstance which particularly affects me, and which, if I delay to investigate, may be past the possibility of solution. You must know an old woman, who lives not far from hence, named Bianca; she has just been here to inform me that a sister of hers, whom she has not seen for many years, is just arrived at her cottage, in an apparently-dying state, who says that she has travelled hither from a considerable distance, in order to relieve her mind before her death, by the disclosure of a secret with which it is burthened, and in which I am concerned, but which she refuses to reveal to me, except in the presence of a servant of the marchese Alberto di Valdetti, named Duretti."

Lipardo perceived equally the anxiety of the farmer, and the urgency of the case, and immediately dispatched a servant, who had accompanied him to the Castello, to command Duretti to attend him.

During the absence of the messenger, Lipardo invited Urbino, Di Borges, and Valeria, to return with him to the Castello Alfonta, where he said their presence would communicate the most heartfelt satisfaction to the happy beings within its walls.

Urbino and the farmer gave a ready acquiescal. Valeria retired from the apartment, and shortly after returning with two letters, which she had written, one of which was directed to Paulina, the other to Julio, requested Lipardo to deliver them into the hands of those to whom they were addressed, and to excuse her attendance at that time.

Duretti without delay attended the summons of Lipardo, who, at the urgent request of the farmer, consented to accompany them to the cottage of Bianca.

On entering the place, Di Borges perceived, lying on the bed on which he had at his last visit beheld Julio extended, the pale and emaciated form of an aged female, who appeared upon the verge of earthly dissolution.

"This, signor," said Bianca, addressing Di Borges, "is my sister Rodovina, whom I have not seen or heard of for these twenty years past, and whom I believed dead."

The half-closed eyes of Rodovina wandered amongst the assembled group which surrounded her bed, and at last fixing them on Duretti—"Do you not know me?" she said.

"No, I do not," was the reply.

"Do you not," she rejoined, "remember a poor woman, one Rodovina, who used to gain her livelihood by telling fortunes, and whom you once employed, at the command of the marchese di Valdetti, to steal you a child?"

"Can you be she?" said Duretti.

"I am indeed," replied the woman; "and feeling that I could not die easy, without I had made all the reparation in my power to the injured parents of the babe, with infinite pain I have travelled hither, for the purpose of informing them that their infant was conveyed by you to the marchese di Valdetti, and of calling upon you to acquaint them what has been its subsequent fate."

Lipardo looked at Duretti for an explanation of what he heard; in reply to which inquiry Duretti said—"Alberto once entertained an idea of bringing up a child, to represent the infant daughter of his brother, conceiving that, as her lawful guardian, he might enjoy those possessions of which she would be considered the heiress, with greater security than by openly declaring his own; but the child had been only a few days brought to his palazzo in Venice, when, considering how easily the imposition might be detected, by the child being free from those scars with which the person of the signora Paulina was marked, he changed his purpose, and commanded her to be removed from him."

"And what became of her then?" asked Rodovina.

"By the order of Alberto," answered Duretti, "I placed her, with a considerable sum of money, in the hands of a woman who travelled the country with merchandize, and who promised to bring her up as her own; her name was Leonora Velinos."

"And that of the parents of the child whom you stole," said Sancho, eagerly, "was Di Borges!"

"Ay, ay; you are her father; I know you well—too well," ejaculated Rodovina. "Oh, forgive me, dear signor! forgive me, that I may die in peace!"

The agitation of his mind for a while imposed silence on the lips of Sancho. After a short interval—"Woman!" he said, "ask forgiveness of Heaven, for thy soul's sake; as a Christian, I cannot deny thee mine;" and quitted the cottage, followed by Urbino and the steward Moralta, whom he requested to proceed to the Castello Alfonta, and permit him to visit his daughter alone, for the purpose of disclosing to her the discovery which he had just made.

In a narrative, as in a drama, when the anticipated events are drawn to a certain point, the sooner the curtain falls upon the scene, the more impressive the effect; in conformity with which rule, a few words will now lead us to the conclusion of our tale.

The marchese di Valdetti and his Camilla enjoyed the most perfect happiness, in deriving their chief gratification from contributing to the felicity of others. Vincentio, with his Paulina, and the parents of the former, all formed a part of the establishment at the Castello Alfonta; and as Urbino had resolved upon fixing his future residence solely in the country, almost every day witnessed an exchange of social intercourse between their two families, and that of the worthy Sancho di Borges.

"Oh, my dear child!" exclaimed Averilla, on clasping her long-lost daughter in her arms, "is it possible that I once more fold to my breast that beloved infant, whose golden coral I have so often wept over! Blessed be Heaven, that has restored you to me in my present dark and helpless state!—But I have not been neglected by its goodness, even in your absence; it supplied me with an angel's kindness, when it led me to the knowledge of the dear signora Valeria."

Old Jeronymo wept aloud, and pressed the hand of Averilla to his quivering lips.

When arranging his future establishment, Urbino gave Terence his choice of being either made the superintendant of his affairs, or of being presented with a sum of money, to convey him back to his own country; of the former Terence made choice.—"I cannot be happier than I am here in your *sarvice*," he said, "and why should I be after making a change? I only desire an honest man for my master; I am sure you are that same; and if Providence kindly suffers me to outlive you, I'll end my days *wid* you, depend upon it." Urbino smiled at the national slip of the tongue into which the fervency of Terence's feelings had led him; and Terence resumed—"I am sure we shall all be as happy as sweet butter-milk; and whenever you and the signor di Borges, who is as kind and as condescending a man as your honour, do me the favour of a little chat *wid* me in the garden, to pass off the time like, when I am at work about the *Munster apples,* or any thing of the sort,

"Thou, he, and I, retir'd to some close cell,
Will gently pass our short reserves of time
In calm reflection on our fortunes past.
        Thus our remains
Shall in an even course of thoughts be past,
Enjoy the present hour, nor fear the last."

Francisca, completely weaned from the fascinations of love and beauty, was contented to live in the service of Valeria. Bernardo also continued to reside with his father in the Castello della Torvida; and continuing single by joint consent, they jogged on through life, as friends, in a much more unruffled course than they would probably have done in the characters of man and wife.

The letter which Lipardo had been requested by Valeria to present to Julio, contained her promise to live unmarried, and her request, that if any correspondence existed in future between them, it might only be by letter.

Julio had now obtained the darling wish of his heart; and having described to his parents the delicate situation in which he stood to the family of Urbino, declared his intention of becoming, for life, an inhabitant of the monastery in Padua which had sheltered his infant state—a resolution which he a few days after carried into effect. In his correspondence with Valeria, he uniformly declared himself perfectly happy, and only regretted, that her acquaintance with him, and the constancy of her affection, had rendered her less blessed upon earth than her existence might have proved had he never known her; to which assertions Valeria regularly replied—"Whatever the happiness which you conceive me to have lost, I am contented with that which I possess; and shall ever consider, that no felicity can exceed that which results from the recompensing consciousness which I feel, *of having done my duty.*"

Urbino would frequently aver, that the event of his life that he most regretted, was the loss of his son; and that the recollection which, of all others, gave him the greatest satisfaction, was that of having preserved the life of Julio.—"FORGIVENESS," he said, "IS THE UNIVERSAL DUTY OF MAN, AND THEY MUST BE EITHER COLD IN HEART, OR ARROGANT IN SPIRIT, WHO CAN HOPE TO RECEIVE THAT FORGIVENESS OF HEAVEN, WHICH THEY DENY TO THEIR FELLOW-BEINGS UPON EARTH."

THE AUTHOR'S NOTES

SINCE I wrote the preceding work I have been credibly informed, that within the space of the last ten years, there were resident in Scotland two brothers, of the first distinction in life, the prominent features of whose history form a parallel to that of Claudio and Alberto di Valdetti.

The circumstance of a physician being seized and conveyed blindfold from the opera in Venice to an elegant mansion in that city, for the purpose of being employed to bleed a female to death, is a well-known fact. It is related of an Englishman, a doctor Fisher, who treated the endeavours which were made to gain his consent to the wishes of his tempter in the same indignant manner in which those of Alberto were repulsed by Di Cavetti.

About the time of the revolution in France, there were residing in Paris and its neighbourhood three sisters, whose resemblance to each other, for several years, by turns, involved them in unmerited misfortunes, or overwhelmed them with unexpected successes, to the cause of which they were for a considerable time strangers.

It is not half a century ago since a young man, of the first respectability, was so much hurt and astonished at beholding the corpse of his mother, upon the dissecting-table in a theatre of anatomy in Edinburgh, as to have been nearly deprived of his senses, by the shock which his feelings had received.

Terence O'Donnovan, at least as far as similarity of character can render him such, is at this moment residing in Quebec; his name is Felix Nulty, and he informs me that he was once servant to the late celebrated performer, Cooke. When I inquired of him if he had any objection to my introducing him into my pages, his characteristic reply was—"By the powers! none at all at all, sir; only *wid* this one proviso—

> "Speak of me as I am,
> Nor set down aught in malice."

I believe I have honestly complied with his terms, and hope to receive his commendations on my performance when next we meet.

THE END.

NOTES

Page

3   **epigraph**: This quotation is not from Sir John Denham's *The Sophy*, but from John Dennis's *Iphigenia* (1700).

4   **"'Tis now the very witching time of night"**: *Hamlet*, III, ii.

5   **'Fast bind, fast find'**: *The Merchant of Venice*, II, v.

     "I do remember an apothecary/And hereabouts he dwells": *Romeo and Juliet*, V, i.

9   **'All who live must die/Passing through nature to eternity'**: *Hamlet*, I, ii.

     'Dispute it like a man': *Macbeth*, IV, iii.

11   **the momentary degradation of a link in the chain of humanity**: In 1819, when Lathom wrote *Italian Mysteries*, he was living in America, where slavery still thrived. In his novels, Lathom frequently showed himself to be liberal-minded with regard to such issues as women's rights and slavery. His comment here may be seen as a criticism of what he saw in America during his travels.

     "lean and slipper'd pantaloon": *As You Like It*, II, vii.

13   *lasso:* "Alas!" (Ital.)

17   **epigraph**: Nicholas Rowe, *Lady Jane Grey* (1715), I, i.

21   **Sleep, that knits up the ravelled sheave**: *Macbeth*, II, ii.

29   **epigraph**: The quote is not from Walpole's *The Mysterious Mother*, but from Dryden's *Oedipus*. The error is particularly puzzling, as the same quotation is used by Lathom as an epigraph in his *The Castle of Ollada*, with the proper attribution.

33   ***un soldo, un soldo, per l'amor di Dio:*** A soldo is an old Italian coin. The Italian means "A *soldo*, a *soldo*, for the love of God!"

40   **epigraph**: *Hamlet*, I, v.

     "The cloud-capt towers...": *The Tempest*, IV, i.

     Ballyporeen: a town in County Tipperary, Ireland.

41   **"unreal mockery, hence!"**: *Macbeth*, III, iv.

50   **epigraph**: The song is from Prince Hoare's *My Grandmother* (1794).

62 **epigraph**: John Home, *Douglas* (1757).

64 **Are not these woods/More free from peril than the envious court**: *As You Like It*, II, i.

65 **usquebaugh**: from the Irish *uisce beatha* ("water of life"), a kind of whiskey.

   "Sack, two gallons, five shillings and eightpence": *1 Henry IV* II, iv.

70 **Algerine pirates**: North African pirates from the city of Algiers, who plagued vessels throughout the 17th and 18th centuries.

74 **epigraph**: Edmund Waller, "In Answer of Sir John Suckling's Verses."

79 **I am after fancying**: A construction unique to Irish English, which uses a form of the verb "to be" with "after" and a participle ending in "-ing," to express an event which has happened very recently, as, "I'm after going to the shop"; the equivalent in American English would be "I just went to the shop." Lathom uses this construction several times in the novel to lend authenticity to Terence's character, but here, as elsewhere in the book, Lathom's rendition of Terence's Irishisms isn't particularly convincing.

85 **simple**: a medicinal plant, or the medicine derived from it.

86 **peculate**: embezzle

87 **"The oppressor's wrong, the proud man's contumely"**: *Hamlet*, III, i.

89 **epigraph**: *Julius Caesar*, IV, iii.

99 **"Come what, come may/Time and the hour runs through the roughest day"**: *Macbeth,* I, iii.

103 **epigraph**: *Julius Caesar*, II, i.

105 **La Clemenza di Tito**: Wolfgang Amadeus Mozart's penultimate opera, *La Clemenza di Tito* (1791).

110 **epigraph**: John Milton, *Paradise Lost*, Book VI.

126 **epigraph**: *Measure for Measure*, V, i.

131 **Cephalus and Procris**: Cephalus and Procris were husband and wife. Cephalus believed Procris was cheating on him, and so, to test her, he approached her disguised as a handsome youth. She fell in love with the youth he pretended to be, and he then revealed himself to her. She felt deeply

sorry, and made him a gift of a javelin. However, she eventually came to believe he was cheating on her, so she followed him on one of his hunts. Cephalus, hearing her rustle in the bushes and mistaking her for a wild animal, cast his javelin at her and killed her by mistake.

136 **First Cause:** that is, God. The phrase originates from St. Thomas Aquinas, who posited that, since all things in nature have a cause, the universe must have had a cause, and that this "first cause" is God.

137 **epigraph:** Nicholas Rowe, *Lady Jane Grey*, IV, i.

150 **epigraph:** *A Midsummer Night's Dream*, I, i.

167 **epigraph:** *Hamlet*, IV, vii.

170 **When sorrows come, they come not single spies/But in battalions:** *Hamlet*, IV, v.

Hope is the lover's walking staff: *The Two Gentlemen of Verona*, III, i.

171 **You may as well go stand upon the beach:** *The Merchant of Venice*, IV, i.

175 **"Patience on a monument/Smiling at grief":** *Twelfth Night*, II, iv.

177 **epigraph:** *Hamlet*, I, iv.

184 **"busy hum of men":** Milton, "L'Allegro"

191 **epigraph:** These lines are from Act I, Scene i, of *King Lear*, not *Romeo and Juliet*.

205 **epigraph:** John Home, *Douglas*, Act V.

219 **epigraph:** Home, *Douglas*, Acts I and III.

229 **epigraphs** *Macbeth*, II, ii., and Aaron Hill, *Zara*, II, i (slightly misquoted).

233 **"Who steals my purse, steals trash":** *Othello* III, iii.

234 **"Thrice is he arm'd that has his quarrel just":** *2 Henry VI*, III, ii.

234 **Dickon...Bosworth Field:** King Richard III was defeated at Bosworth Field in 1485.

"A horse! a horse! my kingdom for a horse!": *Richard III*, V, iv.

"Saddle white Surrey for the field to-morrow": *Richard III*, V, iii.

238 **epigraph:** *Macbeth*, I, vii.

245 epigraph: *Cymbeline*, I, i.

262 epigraph: *Hamlet*, I, iii.

270 "Now, unmuzzle your wisdom": *As You Like It*, I, ii.

277 to this complexion she must come at last: *Hamlet*, V, i. The lines are spoken whilst Hamlet is holding Yorick's skull; "complexion" thus refers to the appearance of the skull.

As chaste as ice, as pure as snow: *Hamlet*, III, i.

278 "Get thee to a nunnery!": *Hamlet*, III, i.

Let her beauty/Look through a casement to allure false hearts: *Cymbeline*, II, iv.

294 epigraph: *The Tempest*, V, i.

311 epigraph: *Hamlet*, IV, v.

331 epigraph: John Milton, "Comus"

339 "he stained various parts of Claudio's person and dress with blood": Almost the same scenario as Duncan's murder in *Macbeth*.

341 epigraph: *Merchant of Venice*, IV, i.

353 epigraph: *Hamlet*, I, v.

362 epigraph: Not from Shakespeare's *King Lear*, but from Nahum Tate's alteration of the play (1681).

372 epigraph: *As You Like It*, II, vii.

376 "Thou, he, and I, retir'd to some close cell": From Nahum Tate's version of *King Lear*. These lines do not appear in any of Shakespeare's works.

Gothic Classics

NOW AVAILABLE

THE ANIMATED SKELETON, Anonymous
128 pp. March 2005 0-9766048-0-9, $12.95

THE CAVERN OF DEATH, Anonymous (Ed. Allen Grove)
104 pp. July 2005 0-9766048-3-3, $12.95

THE CASTLE OF OLLADA by Francis Lathom
192 pp. March 2005 0-9766048-2-5, $14.95

ITALIAN MYSTERIES by Francis Lathom
350 pp. June 2005 0-9766048-6-8, $16.95

MYSTERY OF THE BLACK TOWER by John Palmer, Jun.
200 pp. July 2005 0-9766048-1-7, $14.95

THE PHANTOM OF THE CASTLE by Richard Sickelmore
128 pp. June 2005 0-9766048-9-2, $13.95

COMING SOON

WHO'S THE MURDERER? by Eleanor Sleath
700 pp. December 2005 0-9766048-8-4, $18.95

ETHELWINA by T. J. Horsley Curties
400 pp. December 2005 0-9766048-7-6, $16.95

All titles can be ordered at www.valancourtbooks.com or from
any fine local or online bookseller.

Valancourt Books, P.O. Box 220511, Chicago, IL 60622
http://www.valancourtbooks.com   gothic@valancourtbooks.com